Knight of Desire

"Mallory's debut is impressive. She breathes life into major historical characters...in a dramatic romance."

—*RT Book Reviews*

"An impressive debut...Margaret Mallory is a star in the making."

—Mary Balogh, *New York Times* bestselling author

"Spellbinding! Few writers share Margaret Mallory's talent for bringing history to vivid, pulsing life."

—Virginia Henley, *New York Times* bestselling author

"A lavish historical romance, evocative and emotionally rich. *Knight of Desire* will transport you."

—Sophie Jordan, *USA Today* bestselling author

Knight of Pleasure

"Mallory has an amazing ability for creating a riveting story, intertwining adventure and history overlaid with great depth of emotion and laced with a constantly increasing level of sensuality. Such depth and sensuality are a rare treat."

—*RT Book Reviews*

Rogue Warrior

ALL THE KING'S MEN

Knight of Passion

THE RETURN OF THE HIGHLANDERS

The Guardian
The Sinner
The Warrior
The Chieftain

Rogue Warrior

2-in-1 Edition with *Knight of Desire* and *Knight of Pleasure*

MARGARET MALLORY

FOREVER

NEW YORK BOSTON

Rogue Warrior is copyright © 2021 by Peggy L. Brown

Knight of Desire is copyright © 2009 by Peggy L. Brown
Knight of Pleasure is copyright © 2009 by Peggy L. Brown

Cover design by Daniela Medina
Cover © 2021 Hachette Book Group, Inc.

Grand Central Publishing
Hachette Book Group
1290 Avenue of the Americas, New York, NY 10104
grandcentralpublishing.com
twitter.com/grandcentralpub

Knight of Desire originally published in mass market by Hachette Book Group in July 2009
Knight of Pleasure originally published in mass market by Hachette Book Group in December 2009

First mass market compilation: March 2021

Grand Central Publishing is a division of Hachette Book Group, Inc. The Grand Central Publishing name and logo is a trademark of Hachette Book Group, Inc.

The publisher is not responsible for websites (or their content) that are not owned by the publisher.

The Hachette Speakers Bureau provides a wide range of authors for speaking events. To find out more, go to www.hachettespeakersbureau.com or call (866) 376-6591.

ISBNs: 978-1-5387-5408-5 (mass market)

Printed in the United States of America

CW

10 9 8 7 6 5 4 3 2 1

ATTENTION CORPORATIONS AND ORGANIZATIONS:

Most Hachette Book Group books are available at quantity discounts with bulk purchase for educational, business, or sales promotional use. For information, please call or write:

Special Markets Department, Hachette Book Group
1290 Avenue of the Americas, New York, NY 10104
Telephone: 1-800-222-6747 Fax: 1-800-477-5925

Contents

Knight
of Desire

*To Cathy Carter, my sister and
librarian extraordinaire, who read
my first pages and told me to go for
it, and to my husband, Bob
Cedarbaum, who supported me on
faith without ever reading a word.*

Prologue

Monmouth Castle
England, near the Welsh border
October 1400

The creak of the stable door woke him.

William's hand went to the hilt of his blade as he lifted his head from the straw to listen. Soft footfalls crossed the floor. Soundlessly, he rose to his feet. No one entering the stable at this hour could have good intent.

A hooded figure carrying a candle moved along the row of horses, causing them to snort and lift their heads. William waited while the man reached up to light a lantern hanging on a post. No matter what the intruder's purpose, fire was the greater danger. The moment the man blew out his candle, William closed the distance between them in three running strides.

As he launched himself, the intruder turned.

William saw the swirl of skirts and a girl's face, her eyes

wide with alarm. Reflexively, he threw his arms around her and turned in midair to cushion her fall just before they slammed to the ground.

"Please forgive me!" he said, untangling his limbs from hers and scrambling to his feet. "Have I hurt you?"

He would have offered his hand to help her up, but she sprang to her feet as fast as he, her hair falling free of the hood in a mass of bright waves. She stood with her weight forward on her feet, eyeing him warily.

William stared at her. How could he have mistaken this lovely and fragile-looking girl for a man? Judging by the fine silk gown showing at the gap in her cloak, this was a highborn lady he had assaulted. Her features were delicate, her full lips parted.

He squinted, trying to tell what color her eyes were in the dim light. Without thinking, he reached to pull a piece of straw from her hair. He drew back when he caught the gleam of the blade in her hand. He could take it from her easily enough, but it unsettled him to know he frightened her.

"Who are you, and what are you doing here?" she demanded. She was breathing hard and pointing the blade at his heart. "Answer me at once, or I will scream and bring the guard."

"I am a knight in the service of the Earl of Northumberland," he said in a calming voice. "I arrived late, and the hall was filled with guests, so I decided to bed here."

He was not about to tell her he was hiding in the stable. When he had delivered Northumberland's message in the hall tonight, he had glimpsed a certain widow he knew from court. Preferring to sleep alone, he had made a quick escape.

"Now that you know my purpose in being here, may I ask the same of you?" he said, cocking his head. "I believe it is you who should not be found out alone at this hour."

She did not answer him, but even in this poor light, he could see her cheeks flush.

"Surely you know it is dangerous for a young lady to be wandering about alone at this time of night—especially with the castle crowded with men and the wine flowing freely."

"I could not sleep," she said, her voice sharp with defiance. "So I decided to go for a ride."

"You cannot go out riding by yourself in the middle of the night!" Lowering his voice, he added, "Really, you cannot be that foolish."

Her eyes flashed as she pressed her lips together—and a disturbing explanation occurred to him.

"If it is a man you are meeting, he does not value you as he should to ask you to come out alone like this." He judged her to be about sixteen, half a dozen years younger than he was. Young enough, he supposed, to be that naive.

"Running to a man?" she said, rolling her eyes heavenward. "Now, that would be foolish."

She slid her knife into the sheath at her belt, apparently deciding he was not a threat after all. Before he could feel much relief at that, she turned and reached for the bridle hanging on the post next to her.

"I am going now," she announced, bridle in hand.

"I cannot let you," he said, wondering how he would stop her. It would cause considerable trouble for them both if he carried her to her rooms, kicking and screaming, at this time of night.

"Surely this can wait for the morning," he argued.

She stared at him with a grim intensity that made him wonder what trick she would try to get past him.

"If I tell you the reason I cannot wait," she said finally, "will you agree to let me go?"

He nodded, though he still had every intention of stopping her.

Margaret Mallory

She's a minor...

"Tomorrow I am to be married."

The surge of disappointment in his chest caught him by surprise. Although he was told the castle was crowded because of a wedding, it had not occurred to him that this achingly lovely girl could be the bride.

When he did not speak, she evidently concluded more explanation was required to convince him to let her go. "I do not expect this will be a happy marriage for me," she said, lifting her chin. "My betrothed is a man I can neither like nor admire."

"Then you must tell your father; perhaps he will change his mind." Even as he said it, William knew that with the wedding set for tomorrow, it was far too late for this.

"I am the only heir to an important castle," she said impatiently. "I could not expect my father or the king to take my wishes into account in deciding what man will have it."

"What is your objection to the man?" William had no right to ask, but he wanted to know. He wondered if this young innocent was being married off to some lecher old enough to be her grandfather. It was common enough.

"He has meanness in him, I have seen it." Her eyes were solemn and unblinking. "He is not a man to be trusted."

Her response surprised him once again. Yet, he did not doubt she gave him the truth as she saw it.

"Tomorrow I will do what my father and my king require of me and wed this man. From that time forward, I will have to do as my husband bids and submit to him in all things."

William, of course, thought of the man taking her to bed and wondered if she truly understood all that her words implied.

"Tonight you must let me have this last hour of freedom," she said, her voice determined. "It is not so much to ask."

William could have told her she should trust the judgment

of her father and her king, that surely they would not give her to a man so undeserving. But he did not believe it himself.

"I will ride with you," he said, "or you shall not go."

She narrowed her eyes, scrutinizing him for a long moment. With the lamp at his back, the girl could not see him nearly as well as he could see her. A double advantage, since he did not want to frighten her. He was well aware that, despite his youth, there was something about his strong features and serious countenance that intimidated even experienced warriors.

"You must let me do that for you," he said, holding out his hand for the bridle. He almost sighed aloud in relief when she finally nodded and dropped it in his hand.

As he saddled the horses, he tried to ignore the voice in the back of his head telling him this was madness. God's beard, the king himself had a hand in arranging this marriage. If he was caught taking her out alone at night on the eve of her wedding, the king would have him flailed alive.

"Keep your head down," he instructed as they rode across the outer bailey toward the gate. "Make certain your cloak covers your gown—and every strand of that fair hair."

The guards remembered he arrived carrying messages from Northumberland, "the "King-maker." They gave him no trouble.

William and the girl rode out into the cold, starlit night. Once they reached the path that ran along the river, she took the lead. She rode her horse hard, as if chased by the devil. When at last she reined her horse in, William pulled up beside her, his horse's sides heaving.

"Thank you for this," she said, giving him a smile that made his heart tighten in his chest.

His breath came quickly as he stared at her. She was stunning with her face aglow with happiness and her fair hair shining all about her in the moonlight. When she flung her arms out and threw her head back to laugh at the stars, he stopped breathing altogether.

Before he could gather his wits, she slipped off her horse and ran up the riverbank. He tied their horses and followed. Pushing aside thoughts of how dangerous it was for them to be here, he spread his cloak for her on the damp ground beneath the trees.

She sat beside him in silence, her gaze fixed on the swath of moonlight reflected on the moving surface of the dark river below. As she watched the river, he studied her profile and breathed in her scent. He thought she had long since forgotten his presence when she finally spoke.

"I will remember this night always," she said, giving his hand a quick squeeze. "I will hold it to my heart as a happy memory when I have need of one."

He took hold of her hand when she touched him and did not let it go.

She fell silent again, and he sensed that her thoughts, unlike his own, were far away again. Experienced as he was with women, he was surprised by his intense reaction to this girl. All of his senses were alive with the nearness of her— his skin almost vibrated with it. And yet, he felt a profound happiness just sitting here with her and gazing at the river on this chilly autumn night. He never wanted to leave.

When she shivered, he forced himself to break the spell. "You are cold, and we have been gone too long already. If someone notices you are missing..."

He did not finish. She knew as well as he the disaster that would follow if she were caught. Resigned, she let him help her to her feet.

They rode back at a slower pace, riding side by side this time, still saying little. William tried to fix it all in his memory: the moonlight, the dark river, the gentle snorting of their horses. The girl, he knew, he could not forget.

The guards at the gate wordlessly let them in. When they reached the stable, William helped her dismount. The feel of his hands on her slender waist as he set her down—closer to him than was proper—made his heart race and his head feel light.

Looking down at her, he felt a longing so intense it caught at his breath. His gaze dropped to her mouth. Only when she took a step back did he realize he had been about to kiss her. It was wrong for many reasons, but he wished with all his heart he had done it. With a sigh, he left her just inside the doorway and led the horses into the pitch-black of the stable.

When he returned, she whispered, "I am most grateful to you."

"Lady, I would save you from this marriage if I knew how."

He spoke in a rush, not expecting to say the foolish words that were in his heart. He was as good as any man with a sword, but he had no weapon to wield in this fight. Someday, he would be a man to be reckoned with, a man with lands and power. But as a landless knight, he could only put her at risk by interfering with the king's plans.

"I will do my duty and follow the wishes of my father and my king," she said in a strong voice. "But I thank you for wishing it could be otherwise."

He wished he could see her better. Impulsively, he reached out to trace the outline of her cheek with his fingers. Before he knew what he was doing, he had her face cupped in his hands. He felt her lean toward him. This time, he did not stop himself.

Very softly, he brushed his lips against hers. At the first touch, a shot of lust ran through him, hitting him so hard he felt light-headed and weak in the knees. He pressed his mouth hard against hers. Dimly, through his raging desire, he was aware of the innocence of her kiss. He willed himself to keep his hands where they were and not give in to the overpowering urge to reach for her body. If she had shown the slightest sign she had been down this path before, he would have had her down on the straw at their feet.

He broke the kiss and pulled her into his arms. Closing his eyes, he held her to him and waited for the thundering of his heart to subside. God have mercy! What happened to him? This girl, who trusted him blindly, had no notion of the danger.

Swallowing hard, he released her from his embrace. He could think of no words, could not speak at all. With deliberate care, he pulled her hood up and tucked her long hair inside it. Then he let his arms fall to his sides like heavy weights.

"I did not want his to be my first kiss," she said, as though she needed to explain why she had permitted it.

His gut twisted as he thought of the firsts the other man would have with her.

She took a quick step forward and, rising on her tiptoes, lightly touched her lips to his. In another moment, she was running across the yard, clutching her cloak about her.

* * *

For many years, William dreamed of that night. In his dreams, though, he held her in his arms by the river in the moonlight. In his dreams, he kissed the worry and fear from her face. In his dreams, he rescued her from her unhappy fate.

In his dreams, she was his.

Chapter One

Ross Castle
England, near the Welsh border
June 1405

*L*ady Mary Catherine Rayburn sat on the bench in her bedchamber and waited for news. If the prince received her latest message in time, the king's army should have caught her husband with the rebels by now.

She pulled up the loose sleeve of her tunic and examined her arm in the shaft of sunlight that fell from the narrow window. The bruises were fading; Rayburn had been gone a fortnight. She let the sleeve fall and rested her head against the stone wall behind her.

Not once in all this time did her husband suspect she had betrayed him. But he would know it now. She had been the only one in the hall, save for the men who went with him, when he disclosed the time and place of his meeting with the Welsh rebels.

She buried her face in trembling hands and prayed she had not made a mistake. What else could she do? Nothing short of discovering Rayburn with the rebels would convince the king of his treachery.

If Rayburn escaped unseen, he would return and kill her. What then would happen to Jamie? It was unthinkable that her son would be left alone in the world with that man.

The cold of the stone wall penetrated the heavy tapestry at her back, causing her to shiver. Her raging fever had only broken the night before. She'd been the last to fall to the illness that had swept through the castle.

Exhausted, she closed her eyes. How had she come to this? She thought back to the beginning, before Rayburn's betrayal of the king—and before her betrayal of Rayburn.

The king had been so certain of Rayburn's loyalty when he chose him as her husband. At sixteen, she had been quite the marriage prize. She possessed that most rare and appealing quality in a noblewoman: She was her ailing father's only heir. More, she was heir to one of the massive castles in the Welsh Marches, the strategic border area between England and Wales. That made her betrothal worthy of the king's personal attention.

At the age of ten, she was betrothed to a young man whose family, like her own, was closely aligned with King Richard. The match lost its luster the moment Henry Bolingbroke usurped the throne. Consequently, her father was pleased when, a short time later, the young man had the courtesy to fall from his horse and break his neck. When the new king "offered" to select a husband for her, her father was happy for the opportunity to demonstrate his new allegiance.

King Henry deliberated carefully, dangling her as a prize before powerful men he wanted in his debt. When her father fell gravely ill just as the Welsh revolted, however, the king acted swiftly. He could not afford to leave Ross Castle and the surrounding borderlands without a strong man to defend them. As her father lay on his deathbed, the king's soldiers escorted her to his castle at nearby Monmouth for her wedding.

She crossed her arms over her chest and rocked herself as the memories came back to her. She had known Rayburn to be a cold man. She did not expect tenderness from him. Still, her wedding night had been a shock. He managed, just, to take her virginity.

Perhaps it was the novelty that made it possible that first time. He ordered her to put out every candle and wait in silence on the bed. Only later did she understand that the sounds she heard in the dark were her new husband touching himself to prepare for the task.

There were no kisses, no caresses. It was, at least, mercifully quick. As soon as he was finished, he left her. She cried through the night, believing her life could not be worse.

How naive she had been.

He made weekly visits to her bedchamber, intent on getting her with child. She tried not to hear the foul things he said in her ear or to feel the rough hands rubbing over her thighs and buttocks. When he succeeded, she forced her mind far away as he pounded and grunted against her flesh.

Over time, it became increasingly difficult for him to do his duty. When he could not, he beat her. Sometimes the violence excited him, for just long enough. He took to drinking heavily before he came to her. The drink only made him more violent.

By a miracle, she conceived. Her pregnancy saved her life. Rayburn still lacked any redeeming qualities, but he ceased to terrorize her in the bedchamber.

Then, a few weeks ago, he decided he must have "an heir to spare."

She had no regrets about what she did to save herself this time. And to save the Crown for Harry. One day, Harry would be a great king, the one England deserved. Still, she was bone-weary from the strain of her deceit.

Her eyelids grew heavy as her mind drifted to the soothing childhood memories of playing with Harry at Monmouth. Those were happy times, before her mother died and before her friend became prince and heir to the throne. She curled up on the hard bench and let her eyes close.

"M'lady, what are you doing out of bed?" The maid-servant's voice roused Catherine from a troubled sleep.

"What is it?" she asked, sitting up.

"Men at arms approach the castle," the woman said, her voice pitched high with tension.

"What banner do they fly?" Catherine demanded.

"The king's, m'lady."

The surge of relief that flooded through her was so intense she had to grip the bench to steady herself.

"What does it mean, m'lady?" the maid asked, twisting her apron in her hands.

"I do not know," she said, trying to sound reassuring, "but we should have nothing to fear from the king's men."

If Rayburn was caught, why would the king send armed men here to Ross Castle? Perhaps Rayburn had escaped and they were looking for him? Would he come here to hide? Panic rose in her throat. She forced herself to be calm.

Nay, if Rayburn's treason was found out, he would hardly come here. Faced with the risk of execution or imprisonment, he would flee to the Continent. She was almost sure of it.

"M'lady, the king's soldiers are almost to the gate. The men are waiting for you to say what they must do."

"Since they fly the king's banner, we must open the gate to them," she said. "But tell the men to wait until I come."

"But, m'lady, you are too weak. You must not—"

Catherine silenced her maid's objections with the lift of her hand. "Help me dress. I must know what news they bring."

Holding the maid's arm for support, she got to her feet. Her head swam at first, but the feeling passed quickly enough. She nodded approval at the first gown the maid held out and let the woman dress her. Her mind was occupied with a single question: Why would the king send his men here after the battle?

"There is no time for that," she said when the maid brought out an elaborate headdress in blue brocade. "A jeweled net will have to do."

Ignoring the maid's protests, Catherine twisted her hair in a roll and shoved it into the net. As soon as the maid fixed a circlet over it to hold it in place, Catherine sent her running to the gate with her message.

She was relieved to find Jacob waiting outside her door. Gratefully, she took the arm the old man offered and smiled up into his weathered face.

"Let me give your apologies to the visitors," he said, his brows drawn together in concern. "I'll tell them you are too ill to greet them."

"Thank you, Jacob, but I must do this," she said. "They shall not set foot inside the castle walls until I assure myself they are truly the king's men." *And until I know what it is they want.*

After so many days in the darkness of her bedchamber, the bright sun hurt her eyes when she stepped outside the keep. She felt weak, but the fresh air cleared her head as they walked across the inner and outer bailey. Half the household waited near the gate, anxious about the armed men on the other side.

As soon as her son saw her, he broke free from Alys and flung his arms around her legs. She knelt down to kiss him.

"Jamie, stay here with Alys while I go speak with these men," she told him firmly. "Do not go out the gate." She gave a meaningful look over his head to the housekeeper, who responded with a quick nod.

When she stood up again, bright sparkles crossed her vision. She'd never fainted in her life, and she could not permit herself to do so now. She would meet her duty to protect her household.

She waved the others back and went to stand alone in front of the gate. At her nod, the men dropped the drawbridge over the dry moat with a heavy thud.

Through the iron bars of the portcullis, Catherine could see the men on horseback on the moat's other side. They had a hard look to them, as though they had seen much fighting and were prepared for more.

She turned and gave the order. "Raise the portcullis, but be prepared to drop it at my signal."

The iron chains clanked and groaned as the men turned the crank and slowly raised the portcullis.

As soon as it was high enough for her to pass under it, she stepped out onto the drawbridge. She sensed the waiting men's surprise. They stared at her, but they remained where they were, just as she intended.

* * *

As they rode toward Ross Castle, William Neville FitzAlan's thoughts kept returning to the traitor's wife. The traitor's widow now. Lady Rayburn's last message to the prince led to her husband's capture and execution. Rayburn deserved his fate. But what kind of woman could share a man's bed for years and yet betray him to his enemies?

William wondered grimly if she had been unfaithful in other ways as well. It seemed more than likely. In his experience, fidelity was rare among women of his class. The knightly ideals of loyalty and honor certainly did not guide female behavior. Perhaps it was desire for another man, then, rather than loyalty to Lancaster, that led her to expose her husband's treachery.

Regardless of her motive, both he and the king had cause to be grateful. The lady, however, now presented a political problem for the king.

With his hold on the Crown precarious, King Henry needed to give a strong message that traitors *and their families* would be severely punished. The powerful families needed this message most of all. As the wife of an English Marcher lord who turned against the king, Lady Rayburn should be sent to the Tower—a place where "accidental" death was a common hazard.

On the other hand, Prince Harry insisted it was Lady Rayburn who had sent him the anonymous messages about rebel forces. However, few of the king's men believed it, and the man who delivered the messages was nowhere to be found.

The king was keeping his own counsel as to what he believed. The truth, in any case, was irrelevant. In the midst of rebellion, the king could not leave a border castle in the hands of a woman. The Marcher lords who were supposedly loyal were nearly as worrisome as the rebels. If one of them took Ross Castle—whether by force or by marriage—the king would be hard-pressed to take it back. The king wanted it in the hands of a man of his own choosing.

William was the man the king chose. His loyalty had been

proven through the severest of tests. Even more, the king understood that William's hunger for lands of his own was so deep that, once he had them, no one would ever take them from him. Ross Castle would be safe in his hands.

William led the attack that morning, catching the enemy unprepared. At the king's command, his guard executed Rayburn on the field. The traitor's head barely left his shoulders before the king declared his lands and title forfeit and granted them to William.

William rode straight out from the battlefield to secure his property, the blood of the enemy still wet on his surcoat. But there was one last price he had to pay for it.

The king put the fate of the traitor's widow in his hands.

The choice was his. He could send the lady to London to be imprisoned in the Tower for her husband's treason. Or, he could save her—by making her his wife. The king sent the bishop along to grant special dispensation of the posting of banns in the event William chose to wed. The king knew his man.

The prince would be enraged if Lady Rayburn was imprisoned. While the king could disregard the prince's feelings, William could not. Young Harry would be his king one day. William would have wed the widow regardless. It was not in him to let harm come to a woman or a child if it was in his power to prevent it.

His thoughts were diverted from the problem of the woman when he crested the next hill. Pulling his horse up, he stopped to take in the sight of his new lands for the first time. Lush green hills gave way to fields of new crops surrounding the castle, which stood on a natural rise beside a winding river. The castle was an imposing fortification with two rings of concentric walls built around an older square keep.

Edmund Forrester, his second in command, drew up

beside him. "On the river, easy to defend," Edmund said approvingly.

William nodded without taking his eyes off the castle. All his life, he'd wanted this. In his father's household, he was provided for, but he had no right, no claim. His position was always precarious, uncertain. Now, at long last, he had lands of his own and a title that declared his place in the world.

If only John could be with him on this day of all days! Four years since his brother's death, and he still felt the loss keenly. John was the only one with whom he shared a true bond. Still, he was glad to have Edmund along. They had fought long years together in the North. There were few men he trusted, but he trusted Edmund.

William spurred his horse and led his men in a gallop down the path to the castle, his heart beating fast with anticipation. Although the lookouts should have seen the king's banner as they rode up, the occupants of the castle took their blessed time opening the gates. He was fuming long before the drawbridge finally dropped.

As the portcullis was raised, a slender woman ducked under it and walked out alone onto the drawbridge.

William squinted against the sun, trying to see her better. Something about the way the young woman stood, staring them down with such self-possession, caused his men to shift uneasily in their saddles.

Her move was so daring that William smiled in appreciation. Clearly she intended to give the guards opportunity to drop the portcullis behind her, should he and his men prove to be enemies. There was one flaw in her scheme, however: The castle might be saved, but the lady most surely would not.

Chapter Two

Catherine scanned the soldiers on the other side of the dry moat as she waited for one of them to come forward. They wore armor and chain mail, and their horses looked as if they had been ridden hard. A lone churchman rode with them, his white robes bright in a sea of burnished metal.

She watched as the churchman dismounted and walked onto the drawbridge.

"Father Whitefield!" Fortunately, her father's old friend did not hear her exclamation. Recalling his quick rise in the church since Henry took the throne, she dropped to a low curtsy.

"'Tis good to see you again, child," the bishop said, holding out his hands to her.

"What is this about, m'lord Bishop?" she whispered. "Why does the king send armed men here?"

"I bring you a message from the king," the bishop said in a voice that echoed off the castle walls.

What sort of message required a bishop and armed men?

"I am sorry to tell you this, my dear," he said, patting her hand, "but your husband was killed today."

"Praise be to God!" Catherine cried out and fell to her knees. Squeezing her eyes shut, she clasped her hands before her face. "Praise be to God! Praise be to God!"

"Lady Catherine!" the bishop roared above her. "You must beg God's forgiveness for such sinfulness."

Catherine knew it was a sin to wish her husband dead. But God, in his infinite wisdom, had answered her prayers and removed Rayburn from this world.

Praise God, praise God, praise God.

"...shameful behavior...unwomanly..."

She was dimly aware the bishop was still speaking. She ignored him and continued praying.

"Mary Catherine!"

When he shouted her name, she opened her eyes.

"Get up, get up," the bishop said, jerking her up by the arm. "There is more I have to tell you."

He pulled a parchment from inside his robe, broke the seal, and unrolled it. Holding it out at arm's length, he gave her a solemn look over the top. Then, he began to read. "All lands...forfeit to the Crown...grant these same...for faithful service..."

Catherine could not take in the words. Her head spun as the bishop droned on and on.

"In plain terms," he said as he rolled up the parchment, "the king declares Rayburn's title and all his property, including Ross Castle, forfeit. He grants them to the man who defeated your traitorous husband in battle today."

The breath went out of her as if she had been punched in the stomach.

"Why would the king do this to me?" she asked in a whisper. "After all I have done for him? After the risks I took?"

The bishop leaned forward and narrowed his eyes at her. "You should have foreseen this from the moment your husband raised his hand against the king."

"But *I* did not raise my hand against the king!" she protested. "It was the king's decision, not mine, that I should marry Rayburn. You know that very well."

"Mind your tongue," the bishop warned, his face red with anger. "'Tis not wise to criticize your sovereign."

"Does the king say what I am to do?" she asked, panic welling up in her. "Where Jamie and I shall live?"

The bishop cleared his throat. "All is not lost, my dear." He paused to give significance to what he was about to say. "With the king's blessing, the new lord of Ross Castle has agreed to take you as his wife."

"The king wishes me to marry again?" Her voice was rising, but she could not help it.

The bishop's steady gaze told her she had not misunderstood him.

"Nay, he cannot!" She backed away from him, shaking her head from side to side. "He cannot ask this of me again!"

The bishop grabbed her arm and whispered ferociously in her ear, "This is the only way the king has of saving you."

She covered her face. "I will not do it! I will not!"

"Catherine!" the bishop shouted. "Stop this at once!"

"You must ask the king to spare me this," she pleaded, clutching his sleeve. "Please, Your Grace, you must ask him!"

"Come to your senses, woman," the bishop said, taking her by the shoulders. "You have no choice."

"What if I refuse?" She felt the anger rising in her chest.

"That would not be at all wise," the bishop said, his voice quavering.

"You must tell me, Your Grace," she pressed.

"The king will have you imprisoned."

The blood drained from her head as she finally understood. Why did she not see it before? Henry was fighting rebellions on both borders. His hold on the throne was weak. If he did not move quickly to put her estates into the hands of one of his own men, one of the Marcher barons would take it.

"You should be grateful this FitzAlan will have you," the bishop spat out. "The king did not require it of him."

Through clenched teeth, she said, "Perhaps the Tower would be a better choice for me."

"Think of your son. What will happen to him if you are imprisoned?"

The bishop hit his mark squarely. There was nothing she would not suffer to save her son.

"How long do I have," she asked weakly, "before I must make my choice of prisons?"

When her head was clearer, when she did not feel so ill, perhaps she could find a way out of this.

The bishop's nostrils flared. "The marriage is to take place at once."

"At once?" she asked, stunned. "Am I to go from one hell to another with no reprieve!"

Her burst of anger left her feeling drained and light-headed.

"When?" she asked, fixing her gaze on the wooden planks of the drawbridge beneath her feet. "When will he come?"

Please, God, let it be weeks and not days.

"He is here now."

She looked up to find the bishop peering over his shoulder. In her distress, she had forgotten about the others.

The soldiers at the front moved aside to allow a single rider on an enormous black warhorse to come forward. Unable to move, Catherine watched in horror as the huge animal bore down on her. Its hot breath was on her face before the man reined it in.

She swallowed and forced her gaze slowly upward to take in the man. Her eyes rested first on his hand, grasping the hilt of his sword as though he sensed danger and was prepared to meet it. She followed the line up his arm. When she reached his chest, her stomach tightened. His surcoat was streaked with blood. Blood of his enemies, blood of the vanquished.

Her eyes were drawn inextricably upward toward his face. She saw grime and blood and matted hair. Then her gaze met the raging fury in the beast's eyes, and she fainted dead away.

* * *

When the bishop greeted the bold young woman on the drawbridge, William realized this was Lady Rayburn herself. Since he knew what the bishop had to tell her, he shut out the bishop's words and lost himself in contemplation of the woman.

Of course he hoped she would be attractive, though it made no difference to his decision. Luck was with him. While she may have the soul of a snake, Lady Rayburn appeared—at least from this distance—to be young and exceedingly pretty, with a lithe, shapely form.

He was jolted to attention when she dropped to her knees, crying out, "Praise be to God!" It took him a long moment to comprehend she was thanking God for her husband's death. How could the woman weep on her knees with joy at the news of her husband's death? Even his mother was not as heartless as that.

When he heard her liken her prospective marriage to him to a prison, his shock turned to outrage. She should be grateful to him for saving her. Instead, she was ridiculing him!

Edmund grabbed his arm, but William threw him off and spurred his horse onto the drawbridge.

As he rode toward them, the bishop took several steps backward. But the woman did not move, even when his horse was snorting above her. Haltingly, she raised her eyes, as if taking in every inch of horse and man. When her gaze finally reached his face, their eyes locked.

His heart stopped.

It was her. He was almost sure of it.

Her eyes lost focus, and she swayed on her feet. With a quickness learned in battle, he swung down from his horse and bent to catch her before her head hit the ground. Her fair hair fell free of the mesh net and spread in silken waves over his arm and the rough wooden boards of the drawbridge.

Chaos swirled around him. But William saw nothing but the young woman in his arms. It was her. The girl he dreamed of.

Before he could lift her, a weight slammed onto his back. Small fists beat him as a high-pitched voice wailed in his ear, "Let go of my mother! Let go of her!"

"Get the boy off me!" William called to the nearest man.

The man pulled the boy off and held him with out-stretched arms as the boy kicked furiously at the air. He was a dark-haired boy who looked to be only three or four.

William held the boy's eyes. "I will not harm her. I promise you."

The boy nearly succeeded in kicking him in the head.

No sooner was the boy lifted away than a face as round and pink as a fat friar's was before him, shouting, "My lady has been in bed with a fever these last five days!"

William leaned back to see who was chastising him so harshly. It was an older woman, clearly a servant of some kind.

The woman put her hand to the pale cheek of the lady in his arms. "What have you done to her?" she wailed. "My poor mistress! God save us!"

William stifled a curse. Through clenched teeth, he said, "I have come to save the lady, not harm her."

The edge in his voice should have sent the woman running. It did not, but at least she ceased her yowling.

"Show me where I should take her," he said, making an effort to speak calmly. "We cannot leave her here in the middle of the drawbridge."

The woman blinked at him and then hoisted herself up with astonishing speed. She picked up her skirts and bustled past him, calling, "This way, this way!"

William got to his feet with the lady in his arms and walked through the gates of his castle. He followed the plump servant, who glanced over her shoulder every two or three steps and waved her hands about. He heard the murmurs and knew the servants dipped their heads and stepped back as he passed.

But he did not truly see any of them.

All his attention was on the warmth of her body against him, the feel of slippery silk fluttering against his hand. She weighed almost nothing. When a breeze caught her hair, the scent of wildflowers filled his nose, sending him back to a moonlit night by a river.

Before he knew it, he was climbing the steps to the keep. Just then, the boy broke free of his captor and wrapped himself around William's leg.

"Do you want him to drop your mother, you foolish boy?" Before any of his men could move, the plump servant charged back and grabbed the boy by the scruff of the neck.

"I shall see to your mother, child," she said as she thrust the squirming boy into the arms of another servant. "Be a good boy and Mary will take you to the kitchen for a sweet bun."

William signaled for his men to remain behind in the hall and followed the woman up the circular stair to the family's private rooms above.

"I am Alys, the housekeeper," the woman informed him as she puffed up the steps before him. "I've known Lady Catherine since she was a babe."

The woman in his arms stirred. Forgetting himself, he bent down to shush her and almost kissed her forehead. He gave his head a sharp shake to remind himself that this woman, who seemed so fragile in his arms, argued with bishops. And worse.

At the entrance to the solar, he paused to survey the elegantly appointed room, with its dark wood furniture, rich tapestries, and lovely window seat overlooking the river. This was his. No more having a home at the pleasure of another man. His children would grow up knowing where they belonged.

With a start, he realized the woman he carried was the one who would bear those children.

He looked down at her. Though her eyes were closed, he saw the pinch between her brows. Just how long had she been awake?

"In here, m'lord," the housekeeper called from one of the bedchambers that adjoined the solar.

He carried the lady into the chamber and carefully laid her down on the high bed. As he stepped back, he caught sight of his blood-smeared surcoat. What he must look like to her, coming straight from the battlefield. No wonder she fainted.

He took Alys by the arm. "I need to wash," he said as he walked her out of the bedchamber, "and my men need food and drink."

"I'll see to it at once, m'lord." Alys turned to leave, but he kept his hand firmly on her arm.

"I know you care for your mistress." He could tell by the spark in her eyes that she was pleased he saw this. "So you must help her understand."

Alys looked up at him, her expression serious. "Understand what, m'lord?"

"It is the king's wish that she and I marry this very day." He ignored Alys's sharp intake of breath and continued. "It will not be safe for her if we do not. That is what you must make her understand."

Alys pressed her lips into a firm line and nodded.

"I will return within the hour to tell her how it will be done," he said. "Now, where can I have my bath?"

Chapter Three

*W*illiam recovered his senses as he scrubbed himself clean of battle grime. Over and over, he reminded himself of what he knew about the woman he was about to wed. She spied on her husband, delivered him to his death. Without a shred of regret or pity, she betrayed the father of her child, the man she shared a bed with for five years.

These were truths. What were dreams to these?

Either she had changed since she was that girl in the stable or he was mistaken about her then. How long were they together that night? An hour? Two? What could a man know in that time? Especially a young man driven to distraction by the nearness of a beautiful girl in the moonlight.

He learned about the nature of women at his mother's knee. The only time he forgot the lesson was with the girl in the stable.

She was as beautiful as ever, so he'd have to be cautious.

He felt ready to take charge when he returned to the solar, dressed in his finest. Thank God the bishop had insisted he retrieve his best clothes from his packhorse before they rode off. He lifted his hand to knock, then stopped himself. He needed no one's permission to enter here.

When he pushed it open, he found Lady Catherine and Alys sitting at a small table near the window. Alys toppled her stool leaping to her feet. Lady Catherine, however, watched him steadily through the steam rising from the cup she held to her lips. She did not flinch a muscle.

Without taking her gaze from his, she set the cup down and said in a clear voice, "Alys, go ask the bishop to join us."

William wondered what she was up to but figured he would find out soon enough.

Alys gave her mistress a look that said she did not think it wise to leave her alone with him. But when Lady Catherine nodded, Alys did as she was told.

Alone for the first time, he and his soon-to-be wife assessed each other for a long moment. He did not see even a flicker of recognition in those vivid blue eyes. Wisps of memory whipped through his head. He could not reconcile those brief, intense memories of the girl with what he knew of the woman before him. But then, she was so very lovely, he was finding it difficult to think at all.

Her smooth porcelain skin held a faint touch of color now. "I am glad to see you are not so pale as before," he said.

"I do not usually faint," she was quick to assure him, "but I have been ill."

"I hope you are feeling better, for we must settle matters between us now."

Something about the set of her jaw told him she had used the last hour to assess her situation and make a plan. It made him glad for the negotiation skills he had learned in the service of Northumberland.

"It was kind of you to agree to marry me," she began.

So, her opening gambit was a blatant attempt to appease him.

"You did not seem to think so upon first hearing it." He meant to convey amusement, but a trace of anger showed in his voice.

Ignoring his remark, she continued. "I understand the king gave you a choice."

Her slight emphasis on the word *you* was not lost on him.

"In sooth, he did not," he said with a shrug. "I could not have it on my conscience that a lady might be unjustly imprisoned when I could prevent it."

"Many men in your position would not make the same choice."

Only if they had not laid eyes upon her. Any man who looked upon that face would not find the choice a difficult one. Desire burned in him, hot and demanding, at the thought that he would have her in his bed this very night. The knowledge that she betrayed her first husband and loathed the idea of marrying him did not dampen his ardor at all.

Desiring her was one thing. Trusting her, quite another.

"Will you flatter me by saying you prefer marriage to me over imprisonment, or do you yet see the two as equal?" Again, he was unable to keep the edge from his tone.

She had the grace to blush. "My objection was to another marriage and so soon," she murmured, dropping her eyes. "Not marriage to you, in particular."

"Well, it is about me, is it not?" he snapped.

His instinct for masking his feelings had been honed at an early age. Why did it fail him now? Exasperated with himself, he got up from the table and stood with his back to her, looking out the window. Hell, he would have married her, regardless of his own desires. But now he wanted her. Badly. Very badly. He hoped she had not seen it.

Her next words brought him sharply back to the conversation.

"I will agree to marry you on one condition."

He turned and raised an eyebrow at her. "You believe you are in a position to bargain?"

"I do."

The firmness in her tone told him she had seen the naked desire in his eyes and realized the power it gave her.

"Your safety, your home, your position—these are not sufficient reasons for you?" he asked.

"If you cannot also promise me this," she said, unmoved, "I will choose exile or prison, rather than wed you."

He could not believe his ears. She *preferred* prison to marrying him. "What is it, then, that you must have from me?"

She took a shaky breath, giving away how tense she was beneath her outward calm. Still, she looked directly into his eyes as she made her demand.

"I must have assurances about my son. You must promise me that you will not harm him. More, that you will protect him and his interests." She cleared her throat. "That is my price."

He told himself she did not know him, could not know how much her words affronted him. Taking a deep breath, he sat down beside her and placed his hand on top of hers on the table. She flinched but did not attempt to remove it.

"I will do these things," he said, holding her gaze, "and I would have done them without your asking."

She hesitated, then gave him a faint smile.

At that moment, the subject of their discussion burst into the room. Lady Catherine did not chastise the child for interrupting. Instead, she enveloped the boy in her arms, kissing the top of his dark curls. The love between mother and son was so palpable that William felt warmed by his nearness to it. His throat felt tight, and he knew he wanted this also for his own children.

The bishop entered the room at a slower pace.

"I asked you to come, Your Grace," Lady Catherine said, "because there are certain promises that must be included in the marriage contract."

So that was her purpose in calling for the bishop. His oral assurances made in private were not sufficient.

William was not offended. On the contrary, he admired the lady's determination—and her cleverness—in finding a means of binding him to his pledge. He hoped she would be as fierce in protecting the children they would have together as she was her firstborn.

"The contract is already drawn." The bishop touched his fingertips together and shifted his eyes to William as he spoke. "I assure you, all matters of importance are covered."

William held his hand up. "I will give your clerk the necessary changes. We've no more time to waste, so let's be done with it."

The bishop made a sour face. "As you wish."

The door banged behind him.

"Come, Jamie," Lady Catherine said, sounding exhausted now. "Mother must rest now."

Her son kissed the cheek she offered and scampered out of the room. As soon as he was gone, she slumped against the back of her chair.

"I cannot give you more time," William said, looking at her pale face and feeling guilty. "The wedding must take place today."

She gave him no response but merely turned those startlingly blue eyes on him.

"I am known as a strong fighter and commander. Once

you have the protection of my name, you will be safe," he explained. "Even the king will not threaten you as he does now."

He fixed her with unwavering eyes. "And no one will dare touch you once you carry my child," he said, the words coming out hard, fierce, "for they know I would follow them to hell and back to take my vengeance."

* * *

Catherine felt clearheaded as she sat in the steaming tub of water, sipping another cup of the hot broth Mary forced upon her. Remarkably, she'd fallen into a deep sleep after FitzAlan had left her. She felt much better for it.

She carefully reviewed her meeting with FitzAlan. His short bronze hair had been damp, and he looked freshly shaved. Without the blood and grime, he was a handsome man. He had a strong face, with broad cheekbones, a wide mouth, and hard amber eyes. He was tall and well built, with a commanding presence that made him seem much older than he probably was.

Aye, he was a handsome man. A very handsome man, indeed.

He wore a tunic of rich forest green that reached to his knees, with a dark gold cotehardie underneath. A jeweled belt rode low on his hips. The fine clothing did not disguise the warrior beneath. As he said, he was a soldier and commander other men feared.

Her mind went to his bald statement that she would be safe once she was known to carry his child. She quickly pushed aside the thought. She would marry this stranger to protect her son, but she could not think now about sharing his bed.

She recalled how he looked looming above her on the drawbridge. Despite the warmth of the water that enveloped her, she shuddered. In dealing with him, she would do well to remember the raging lion splattered with blood.

Alys burst into the room, bringing a rush of cold air with her.

"Are ye not dressed yet?" Alys said, wide-eyed. "Mary, what is wrong with you? FitzAlan's pacing the hall like a caged bear."

"Two hours to prepare for a wedding," Mary grumbled as she held Catherine's robe out for her.

Two hours to prepare for a marriage. Water streamed down Catherine's legs as she stepped out of the tub.

"I laid out your best gowns on the bed," Mary said as she wrung water from Catherine's hair.

"This one is still your finest," Alys said, wistfully running her hand over the finely stitched beading of the gown Catherine had worn to her first wedding.

"There's no time to alter it," Catherine said. While she was still slender, she had been slight to the point of frailty at sixteen. "The blue will do."

"Ah, this one is lovely on you," Mary said, picking up the gown and matching headdress made of intense blue silk with gold trim. "Your eyes look bright as bluebells in it."

The two women worked fast, braiding, pinning, lacing, and prodding. When they finished, they cooed over the gown. It fit snugly from the bodice to the decorative belt low on her hips, then fell in soft folds to the floor.

Her hair was still damp and itched under the heavy headdress. When she looked in the polished steel mirror Mary held for her, she was glad she wore the sapphire earrings and necklace. They had been her mother's favorites.

The rumble of men's voices rose to meet her as she

descended the stairs. Catherine touched the necklace at her throat. She could do this. She must.

As she entered the hall, FitzAlan's men seemed to turn to her as one. The cavernous room grew quiet.

From across the room, FitzAlan's amber eyes fixed on her, freezing her in place. Her heart thundered as he strode toward her, his expression intense, determined. She felt a surge of sympathy for the men who faced him in battle. If she could have moved, she would have fled back up the stairs.

She tried to get her breath back as he bowed and took her arm.

Before she knew it, they had signed the marriage contract, said their vows, and followed the bishop across the bailey to the chapel in the East Tower. The bishop must have said the blessing and the Mass, though she heard not a word of either.

Numbly, she placed her fingers on her new husband's arm and stepped out of the chapel. She shivered at the unexpected coolness and looked up to see that the sun had sunk below the line of the castle walls.

It was done. In a single day, she'd gone from being wife to widow to wife again. Her heart seized as she realized she had not even told her son.

She was unsure what would happen next. She stole a glance at FitzAlan but could read nothing from his stern expression.

As they reentered the hall, Alys appeared at her side. "The wedding feast is ready to be served." With a roll of her eyes, she added, "Such as it is."

"And Jamie?" Catherine whispered, her throat tight.

"Don't you fret about him, m'lady. His nursemaid's taken him off to an early bed."

Thank God for that. Jamie had grown used to having free

rein of the castle in Rayburn's absences. It would not be easy to keep him out of FitzAlan's way.

Catherine mustered a smile for Alys and let FitzAlan lead her to the table. Cook and the other kitchen servants had worked a minor miracle to provide them with an impromptu wedding feast. She knew they did it for her. She appreciated their kindness, but she was far too tense to eat a bite.

She took a piece of bread and looked down at the table, barren of adornment. She could not help thinking of her wedding at Monmouth Castle. Despite the servants' efforts, this one could not be more different from the first.

Monmouth was where her friend Harry—*Prince* Harry now—had spent most of his childhood, so she'd been there many times before her wedding. Still, she had never seen it so crowded with guests, all dressed in expensive silks and velvets. The Mass was long, the wedding feast elaborate, the entertainment endless.

She had been so anxious to perform her part with dignity, she scarcely gave a thought to what awaited her in the bed-chamber. Perhaps it would have been different if she'd had a mother to warn her.

She thought fleetingly of the wild midnight ride she took the night before her marriage. If she had known what her life with Rayburn would be like, would she have kept riding?

She thought of the young man who accompanied her that night. 'Twas a shame she had no face to go with the memory of him. When he knocked her to the ground, she was so terrified she noticed nothing beyond the sheer size of him. Later, she saw the outline of his shoulder-length hair, but his features above the full beard were always in shadow.

In sooth, he'd seemed all hair and beard to her.

Her thoughts were so tumultuous that night, and they had been followed by her first harrowing night with Rayburn. It was surprising her recollection of the young man had not been lost altogether beneath the layers of terrible memories since.

But she did remember him. The warmth of his large hand holding hers as they sat watching the river. The tickle of his beard against her skin in that brief kiss. The unexpected comfort of his arms when he held her at the end.

What she remembered most clearly and held to her heart, though, was the young man's kindness and gallantry. When her life was at its lowest ebb, it was this memory that saved her.

* * *

William stole glances at his new wife as they ate, though she was so lovely it made him ache to look at her. When she entered the hall, he thought his heart would stop. The gown she wore hugged and flowed, showing every feminine curve and line. And how could eyes be that blue? He had no notion how long he stood gaping before he went to greet her.

She was tearing her bread to bits now. It wounded his pride to see how wretched and tense the woman was. God knew, she was not a virgin bride, with reason to fear the unknown. She had shared a man's bed for years and borne him a child. Admittedly, he was a stranger to her. He would expect her to feel some unease. Yet, her reaction was so extreme he could not help feeling it as a personal slight.

What did the woman think? That he would throw her on the floor and force himself upon her the moment the bedchamber door closed?

Lord above, he did want her enough to take her like that. He could think of little else except having her naked beneath him. Still, it was disturbing that what he looked forward to with such lust, she so obviously dreaded. Once he had her alone, he was confident he could change that. When a man has no wealth of his own and no real status, he knows why women come to his bed. And why they return.

It was not good for a man to want his wife this much. Surely, once he bedded her a few times, he would be over his obsession. Perhaps it would take a few dozen times. His palms were sweaty and his breath came fast just thinking of it.

He was a fool to be disappointed she did not recognize him from that night long ago. True, he had filled out since then, and he no longer wore a beard. He should thank his lucky stars she did not know him as the bedazzled young man who lost his judgment and gave in to her whims.

He turned to look at her again. She was gazing off at nothing, her lips curved up in a slight smile. A wave of longing came over him. God help him, but he hoped a time would come when she would think of him and smile that same dreamy smile. Aye, she already had too much power over him without reminding her of that night.

He would make sure, however, she did not forget their wedding night.

He touched her arm.

She jolted upright and turned wide eyes on him.

"Everyone is waiting," he said in a low voice. "'Tis time for us to go up to the bedchamber."

From the look of horror on her face, he might have said he was going to take her there on the table, with all the guests watching. He took her arm and helped her to her feet. The castle household clapped and shouted as they followed them across the hall toward the stairs.

God's beard, the lady was shaking! Where was the bold woman who met him at the gate a few hours ago?

They had made short shrift of many of the usual traditions with this hasty marriage, so he felt no compunction about turning the crowd back before they reached the bridal bed-chamber. After barring the solar door behind them, he turned to face his bride.

She looked like a goddess, with her head held high and her chin out. But her eyes gave her away. He would have done anything to wipe away the fear he saw there.

He was at a loss as to how he should approach her. Glancing about, he was relieved to see that someone had had the foresight to leave them wine and bread and cheese. Though the refreshments were meant to revive the newly-weds after their efforts in the bedchamber, he could use the diversion now.

"Come sit with me and share some wine," he said, gesturing to the small table.

Catherine's shoulders seemed to relax just a bit. "Thank you, Lord FitzAlan."

"Now that we are husband and wife, you must call me William," he said as he watched her slide gracefully into one of the two chairs at the table. "And I shall call you Catherine."

He remained standing behind her, wanting to put his hands on her shoulders and run his thumb along the curve of her neck. He had been longing to do it all evening. She gave him a furtive look over her shoulder, uncomfortable having him where she could not keep watch on his movements.

"Why don't you pour?" he suggested.

She did as he asked, then took a long drink.

"Let me help you take off your headdress." He leaned down and whispered, "I want to see your hair, Catherine."

"My maid can do that." She reached up quickly, as though to prevent him from touching it. "I will call her."

"Don't."

She began to unfasten the headdress, but her hands were shaking so violently that William took over the task. When all the pins were out, he lifted the headdress off and set it on a nearby stool. He uncoiled the thick braid from around her head then loosened it with his fingers.

Her hair was still damp in places. He sank his fingers deep into the waves and shook her hair free, releasing the scent of wildflowers. Closing his eyes, he put his face into her hair and breathed in until he was dizzy with the smell of it.

He pushed the hair aside to kiss the delicate curve of her neck. At last. Another woman would have sighed and leaned back into him, or turned and pulled him into a deep kiss. But his new wife remained rigid.

So much for his resolve to calm her with conversation before touching her. He sighed, knowing he should not have lost himself like that. Sinking into the seat beside her, he took her hand. He was glad for some physical connection, however tenuous.

Catherine covered her eyes with her other hand. To his bewilderment, her shoulders were shaking. She was weeping! After what seemed like an eternity to him, she seemed to recover herself somewhat.

"I am sorry," she said in a tremulous voice. "I do not mean to annoy you."

What was he to do with her? He patted her hand, which seemed so small in his, and waited. He felt desperate, but he could think of nothing else to do. At last, her breathing steadied and she dropped her hand from her face. She looked at him cautiously from red-rimmed eyes and attempted a smile.

Even this small sign caused hope to spring up in his heart.

"I wish I did not frighten you," he said.

"You are not to blame." She spoke so softly he had to lean forward to hear her. "My husband...Lord Rayburn..." She cleared her throat and tried again. "He was not a kind man. I had cause to fear him."

"If you truly feared him, how could you risk betraying him as you did?" He knew he was being blunt, but he found it hard to believe her.

"I had to." From the way she pressed her lips together, he could tell this was all the answer she intended to give him.

"In what way was he unkind to you?" William asked.

"It would distress me to speak of it."

He did not want to upset her just to satisfy his curiosity. "You need not speak of it. But I would have you know, you need not be afraid of me."

He patted her hand again, since that seemed to be the only thing he could do to soothe her.

What now? It did not look too promising a wedding night, with her so pale and miserable beside him. He'd never forced a woman. He was not going to start now with his wife. In his youth, he'd seen soldiers rape peasant women. As a commander, he prohibited such vile behavior in his men. It violated everything a knight should be.

He rubbed his hands over his face and gave a long sigh. "Perhaps you are too soon from your sickbed to make a marriage bed," he said, pushing a stray strand of hair behind her ear. He paused to give her time to contradict him before giving her his final dispensation. "God willing, we have many years of married life ahead. Tonight, you must sleep."

The relief in her eyes hurt his pride.

"Thank you. I am so very tired," she said, rising from the table.

He grabbed her wrist. "Catherine, it is important that

everyone believe we consummated our marriage this night. No one must think we are not fully bound."

"Yes, of course," she said, pulling away from him.

Good Lord, she looked as if she intended to run before he changed his mind. He stood and rested his hands firmly on her shoulders.

"I *will* have my rights as a husband." He held her eyes with a look that was meant to sear through her. "I want children, and I will have them only with my wife."

After a moment, she said in a soft voice, "I would like more children as well."

Her words set off such an intense surge of longing that he had to struggle to keep from pulling her hard against him. She must have sensed his weakening resolve. When she tried to step back, he tightened his grip on her shoulders.

"I want you in my bed," he said. "And I will not wait long."

He kissed her lightly, holding back the passion that threatened to overtake his will. She held herself very still, as if she knew that if she responded in the slightest, she would find him pressed against her, every inch touching, and there would be no turning back.

But she gave no quarter. He broke the kiss, his heart pounding in his chest. Without another word, he led her to her bedchamber door. She closed it swiftly behind her.

He told himself he had waited years for her; he could wait one more night. But sleep would not come easy. Not with Catherine so near and his body aching for her.

Chapter Four

*C*atherine paused at the entrance to survey the room. The hall was empty, save for a few of FitzAlan's men, who sat near the hearth cleaning their weapons. FitzAlan, praise God, was not among them.

The rest of the household must have broken their fast hours ago. How did she sleep so late? It was a wonder she was able to sleep at all with FitzAlan so near. She awoke feeling almost in full health again. However, after days of eating almost nothing, she was famished.

Nodding to the men, she hurried to the table to take her breakfast. She was so hungry she could think of nothing but the food in front of her for some time.

After putting away an unseemly amount of food, she looked up and caught the men exchanging amused winks and nods. Apparently, they had set aside their work to watch her eat.

Did these Northerners have no manners? She gave them a severe look. She was gratified to see them go back to cleaning their weapons, albeit with a snort or two of stifled laughter.

Alys bustled into the hall, calling, "Good morning, m'lady!"

Heavens, why was everyone full of cheer this morning? First those men acting like boys, and now Alys smiling as if she'd found a bag of gold coins.

"Where's Jamie this morning?" Catherine asked her.

"Jamie? Why, he's gone with Lord FitzAlan."

Catherine jumped to her feet. "What? He has taken Jamie?" Her throat was closing in panic. "Where, Alys? Where has he taken him?"

"Pray, do not fret, m'lady. He only took the boy to the stables to look at that huge animal of his. Jamie begged him." Touching Catherine's arm, she added, "I would have come for you if there was anything amiss."

Catherine closed her eyes and tried to calm herself. Jamie was all right. He had to be.

At the sound of a loud commotion coming from the entrance, she opened her eyes just as FitzAlan strode into the hall. Jamie was on his shoulders, grinning from ear to ear. The relief that flooded through her made her knees feel weak. She took a half-step back and put a steadying hand on the table behind her.

Jamie waved wildly at her, shouting, "Mother! Mother!"

He gave a high-pitched giggle as FitzAlan swung him down. As soon as her son's feet touched the floor, he ran to her, excitement radiating from his face. She dropped to one knee to catch him and clutched him fiercely to her chest. Praise God, he was all right. Forcing herself to release him, she leaned back and gave him what she hoped was a cheerful smile.

"He says I may ride on his horse with him," Jamie told her, his eyes dancing. "Can I, *pleeaaase*?"

"Of course." Looking up at FitzAlan, she added, "I hope I may come along when you do."

She was not about to let FitzAlan take her son outside the castle without her. Anything could happen.

"You could show me the lands near the castle, if you feel well enough to ride." FitzAlan examined her so closely she felt her face flush. With a slight lift of his eyebrow, he said, "You do look in fine health today. Very fine."

Her blush deepened; she could not mistake his meaning.

"The rest of my men just arrived, and I need to arrange an escort to travel to London with Bishop Whitefield," he said. "Can you be ready in an hour?"

* * *

Glancing at her son, Catherine was amazed by how at ease the boy was. He rested one small hand on FitzAlan's arm while pointing at one thing after another.

Jamie's excited chatter gave an unexpected sense of normalcy to the ride. As they rode across the green fields, she found she was almost enjoying herself. She leaned back and closed her eyes. The warm summer sun felt good on her face after so many days indoors.

"I understand from Alys and Jacob that you managed the estates for your father when he was absent."

She snapped her eyes open. So, FitzAlan already knew to go to Alys and Jacob for information rather than the useless man Rayburn had appointed steward. She must keep her wits about her. This was not a man she should underestimate.

The muscles in his jaw tightened, and then he said, "Of course, you did the same for Rayburn."

"I have been the mistress of Ross Castle since I was twelve, when my mother died," she answered him. "I only did as other women do when their lords go off to fight, though perhaps I took on the duties younger than some."

"Then you can tell me what I need to know."

He proceeded to pepper her with questions about the tenants and about what most needed his attention on the estates. At first, she believed he was merely making conversation. But when he pressed her for her opinions and listened closely to what she said, his interest seemed genuine. Never once had Rayburn—or her father—sought her advice.

"May I go?" Jamie interrupted. He was pointing toward a small group of men and boys working in a nearby field.

FitzAlan raised his eyebrows at her in a silent question. Pleased that he would defer to her, she nodded. Jamie ran off to greet the tenants as soon as FitzAlan set him on the ground.

Before she could dismount, he was at her side. He lifted her down as though she weighed nothing at all—and did not release her. With his large hands holding her waist, she felt like a trapped hare. It did not help that he was looking at her as if he'd like to gnaw her bones.

She twisted away from him and hurried after Jamie through the field. In an instant, FitzAlan was beside her. He walked so close the heat from his body seemed to pass through their clothing to her skin. Each time his arm brushed hers, it sent tingles through her body.

"Those are two of our tenants, Smith and Jennings, and some of their children. Smith is always willing to take on extra work."

Good heavens, she was blabbering, but the way his gaze swept her from head to foot made her nervous.

"Why is Smith so willing to do extra work?"

"Smith?" She looked at him blankly before she recalled what she had just said. Without stopping to think, she blurted out the truth. "His wife is such a shrew that he is glad for any excuse to be away from his cottage."

FitzAlan responded with a smile that reached his eyes. The saints be praised, the man had a sense of humor. What next?

"What of the other man, Jennings?"

"If you want something delivered far from home," she said, "Jennings is your best man."

"He is the most responsible?"

"In sooth, he is not, though he serves well enough," she admitted. "But none of the other men like to leave if Jennings stays behind. They fear if they leave their wives alone, their next child may have Jennings's green eyes."

God help her, had she truly said that?

FitzAlan's deep laugh rang out over the fields. The sound startled her; it seemed so at odds with his serious nature. He looked younger and less formidable when he laughed. And even more handsome. More trouble, that was. All the maids would be atwitter over him.

FitzAlan nodded toward a third man, working apart from the others. "Who is that?"

"Tyler. The only one to give me cause for complaint," she said as she watched the man in the field with narrowed eyes. "Tyler is not blessed with an honest nature."

When they reached the tenants, FitzAlan spoke with them about the crops and the weather. As they took their leave, Jamie begged to stay and "help" Jennings's children with their work.

"I'll look after the lad, m'lady," Jennings assured her, "and return him to the castle before supper."

She thanked the man. Too late, she realized this would leave her alone with FitzAlan.

It was a perfect day, so clear she could see the Black

Mountains across the border in Wales as they rode. The warmth of the sun and the gentle breeze touching her face soothed her. As FitzAlan asked her questions about various noble families of the area, the ease she felt earlier returned.

After a time, she ventured a question of her own. "I hear you come from the North. Did you know Northumberland and his son 'Hotspur' Percy?"

"It is not possible to live in the North without knowing something of the Percys." Giving her a sharp look, he asked, "Why do you wish to know about them?"

Clearly, it was a mistake to ask about the powerful family that had twice conspired to remove the king. Why could she not be quiet?

"I am curious, that is all," she murmured. "There are so many stories about them, especially Hotspur."

"Hotspur was as brave and reckless as they say," he said in a flat tone. He paused so long she thought he meant to close the subject. Before she could think of something to say to fill the awkward silence, he spoke again.

"When Hotspur was sixteen, he was in such a rage after a skirmish with the MacDonald clan that he chased after them alone into the hills." His tone held a note of disapproval. "Northumberland and King Richard had to pay a fortune in ransom for his return. Hotspur was always rash and hot-headed; he did not change as he grew older."

Encouraged by this lengthy response, she risked asking another question, one that had long plagued her. "Why do you suppose the Percys turned against King Henry?"

It was well known that Henry Bolingbroke would not have been crowned in the first place without Northumberland's support. Catherine had never understood why the Percys later became so intent on removing him.

"The Percys resented Henry for not rewarding them more

for their support," FitzAlan explained. "King Henry, on the other hand, believed they already held too much power and wealth."

He glanced at her, as if checking to be sure she was truly interested, before continuing.

"Relations went from bad to worse when they argued over who should collect the ransom for some Scots Hotspur captured in battle. The king insisted the ransom go to the Crown."

"Was that the usual custom?" she asked before realizing the awkwardness of her question.

"'Twas customary for the man who made the capture to collect the ransom, but the king had the right," he answered carefully. "I will tell you, Hotspur had strong feelings about making these particular hostages pay him. They were men from the MacDonald clan—the ones who took him hostage as a youth."

Catherine leaned forward in her saddle. "Hotspur must have waited years to make them pay for that humiliation."

He nodded. "Eventually, Hotspur joined forces with Glyndwr in open rebellion and called on his father, North umberland, to do the same."

Fascinated, she asked more questions. He answered, though somewhat reluctantly. When she pressed for details about battles he fought in, he pulled his horse up and turned to look at her.

"*Was* it you who sent the messages to Prince Harry?" His voice held surprise and a touch of uncertainty. "You truly did serve as the prince's spy?"

"Did you think a woman not capable of seeing what was under her nose?" she asked, narrowing her eyes at him. "Or did you think that, though seeing it, a woman would lack the courage to do what ought to be done?" She knew she should not be belligerent with him but could not seem to help herself.

"I had not made up my mind what you did." Oddly enough, he was smiling. It did nothing to dampen her temper.

An even more insulting possibility occurred to her.

"Did you believe I was a traitor?" Her voice was high-pitched, even to her own ears. When he did not deny it, she demanded, "You could marry me believing I might have supported Rayburn in his treason against the king?"

What made her dare speak with such insolence to FitzAlan? Rayburn would have pulled her from her horse and beat her to within an inch of her life for less.

"I should apologize for upsetting you," he said, though he did not look sorry.

Behind the laughter in his eyes, there was a fire that burned right through her and made her throat go dry. She heard his words from the night before in her head: *I will not wait long*.

She kicked her horse and rode ahead.

After a time, he eased his horse beside hers. In a mild tone, he asked, "How did you obtain your information for the prince?"

She took a deep breath. He had answered her questions; in fairness, she should do the same.

"Whenever my husband discussed rebel plans with his men, he would send the servants away and have me wait on them."

She refrained from telling FitzAlan of her other sources of information.

"Your husband trusted you."

She shook her head. "'Twas more that he never considered I would act against him."

"How soon after your marriage did you begin spying for the prince?"

"I did not think of it as spying, not at first," she said as she guided her horse around a rabbit hole in the path. "I would tell him bits of news I happened to hear. I gave him nothing truly useful until just before the Battle of Shrewsbury."

"What was that?"

"I learned Glyndwr was leading a Welsh army in the direction of Shrewsbury, to join Hotspur's forces," she said. "So I sent an urgent message to the prince to warn him."

Hotspur, in his usual headlong fashion, had moved his army so quickly that neither his father nor the Welsh could get to Shrewsbury before the king engaged his army there. Hotspur's death in the Battle of Shrewsbury ended the first Percy conspiracy.

Thinking of that now, she asked, "Why do you think the king did not take more retribution against Northumberland after Shrewsbury?" She and Prince Harry had discussed this many times, but a Northerner might have a different perspective.

She was letting her curiosity get the better of her again. FitzAlan, however, did not chastise her.

"Northumberland was too powerful," he said. "Since he had not taken up arms with Hotspur at Shrewsbury, the king could wait. Northumberland was growing old. Hotspur's death should have put an end to his ambitions."

It had not. Only this spring, Northumberland was involved in a second conspiracy to remove Henry from the throne. This time, he barely escaped into Scotland with his life.

"They said the messages the prince received were anonymous," FitzAlan said, turning the subject back to her.

"The prince knows my script, so I never took the risk of signing or using my seal."

"When did Rayburn cross over to the rebels?" he asked.

"'Tis difficult to say," she said, looking off at the horizon as she thought. "For a long time, he played both sides. He provided funds and information to the rebels but would not risk meeting with them."

"Until yesterday," FitzAlan said in a flat tone. "When, thanks to you, we captured him."

Just yesterday! A single day since she waited in her bed-chamber for news of Rayburn. She shook her head. So much had happened since. For a time this afternoon, she'd forgotten how her life was tied to the stranger riding beside her.

She thought she could like this William FitzAlan, if she did not have to be married to him. Already, he had shown her more kindness and respect than Rayburn ever had.

She would put off her marital duty for as long as she could. For once he took her to his bed, she might not like him nearly so well.

Chapter Five

Catherine's tight-lipped expression made William want to pound his fists on the table in frustration. No matter how congenial their conversations during the day, each evening she grew withdrawn. Four days—and four long nights—he had waited to consummate this marriage.

And yet, she remained as skittish as ever.

He went riding with her each afternoon, though he had no time for it. While it was good for the tenants to see their new lord riding his lands, his first priority was the castle. He did not know when he would be called to fight again, so he was working feverishly to shore up its defenses.

Ross Castle would be safe before he left it.

He was equally determined to consummate this marriage. With luck, Catherine might conceive a child before the king sent him off chasing rebels through Wales for weeks on end.

And so he went riding. He hoped the ease that was growing between them during their afternoon sojourns would lead her to accept him as her husband at night.

So far, it had not.

At first, he brought Jamie along on their rides to please her. To his surprise, he found he enjoyed the child's company.

A smile tugged at the corners of his mouth as he recalled how Jamie had leapt on his back and pounded at him when he first arrived. After the violence of their initial meeting, Jamie took to him quickly. In sooth, William liked the way the boy pulled at his sleeve and chattered away at him.

Aye, he and young Jamie got along just fine. If only the boy's pretty mother took to him half so well.

Busy as he was, all he could think of was bedding her. He imagined her delicate fingers running down his belly, her warm breath in his ear, her soft skin under his hands. Four days wed, and he had not even seen his wife's breasts! Lord, how he wanted to. He swallowed hard and looked at her again.

Seeing how she clutched her goblet for dear life, he had no reason to hope tonight would be different. And yet, he did.

He stood and held out his arm to her. He was not amused by the looks his men exchanged. It was early to retire, but he did not care. He was done with waiting.

As soon as they reached the solar, she fled into her bedchamber with her maid.

"Come sit with me when you have finished preparing for bed," he called after her as the door closed in his face.

His irritation rising, he stalked into his own bedchamber to undress.

"Good evening, m'lord." His manservant's voice startled him from his thoughts. It had slipped his mind that Thomas had arrived today and would be waiting to help him undress.

"I hope you did not look at your new bride like that," Thomas remarked as he knelt to remove William's boots.

William gave him a quelling look. "Just because you

have served me since I was twelve does not mean you can say what you will," he said, though they both knew Thomas could speak his mind with impunity.

William pulled his tunic over his head and threw it in Thomas's direction. Unperturbed, Thomas snatched it from the air and waited for the shirt to follow. Showing his usual good sense, Thomas helped William into his robe and left the room without another word.

William washed his face and hands in the basin of water Thomas left for him. Frustrated, he ran wet fingers through his hair.

Surely Catherine must be ready by now.

The solar was empty, so he called her name outside her chamber door. Getting no reply, he eased the door open. God grant him patience. His wife was sitting on the trunk at the foot of her bed, wringing her hands as if waiting to be taken to her execution.

As he stepped into the room, she gave a startled yelp and jumped to her feet. He might have laughed if his heart did not feel so heavy. When he noticed the maid cowering in the corner, he jerked his head toward the door. It gave him some small satisfaction to see her scamper out like a frightened mouse.

"M'lady wife, I have told you I will not harm you," he said in a quiet voice. He held his hand out to her. "Come, let us sit and talk."

Hesitantly, she came to him and took it; her fingers were icy cold. He led her to the window seat in their solar. After handing her a cup of warm spiced wine, he sat beside her. To calm her, he talked about what he accomplished that day. Then he asked her advice about the stores that would be needed to withstand a long siege.

When he felt her tension subside, he risked resting his

hand on her thigh. She started, but he did not remove his hand. The warmth of her skin through the thin summer shift filled him with such lust. He wanted to lift her by her hips onto his lap and have his way with her right here.

It took all his concentration not to rub his hand up her thigh. He would force himself to go slowly, but he was determined to move things forward tonight.

"Catherine." He lifted her chin with his finger so she would have to look at him. "Surely you know this cannot go on."

He dropped his gaze to the swell of her breasts beneath the thin cloth. His throat was dry, his erection painful.

He brushed his lips against her cheek. "How can I make you forget your fears?" he breathed into her ear. "What can I do?"

He pushed her heavy hair back and moved his mouth along her jaw. "Does this help?"

As he made his journey down her neck to her delicate collarbone, he asked his questions against her skin. "What of this? And this? And this?"

He was lost in the smell of her skin, the feel of its softness against his lips. And the anticipation of having her naked beneath him. To be inside her at last. For surely it would happen this time. He ran his tongue over the swell of her breast above the edge of her tunic.

"Perhaps you could tell me something of your family?"

Her voice, high-pitched and sudden, startled him. He bolted upright.

"Catherine, when I asked what I could do, I was not asking you to suggest new topics of conversation, and you know it."

She was pressed against the wall behind her. But he would not be deterred so easily this time. He eased the shift off her shoulder with his finger and kissed the exposed skin.

"Mmm, lavender," he said, nuzzling her neck.

She remained as stiff and unyielding as ever.

Since his efforts at seduction were failing so miserably, he would try goading her.

"You are being a coward, Catherine."

Looking straight into her eyes, he put his hand again on her thigh. This time, he did rub it firmly from knee to hip. Lord in heaven, it felt good. So good, he almost could not hear her speak over the rush of blood in his ears.

"Truly, I do wish to know more about you. Do you have brothers? Sisters? What of your parents?" She spoke in an insistent, frenetic rush. "I know you come from somewhere in the North, but where precisely is your home?"

Exasperated, he cut her off. "I have no home in the North."

Perhaps if she had asked him to speak of something else, his patience would not have snapped. But he had his own secrets, and he saw no reason to share them with his wife. He pulled her roughly to her feet.

"I have waited longer than any other bridegroom would," he said, so frustrated he wanted to shake her. "You made vows to me before God. As your husband, I could order you to my bed. I could drag you there kicking and screaming. It is my right."

"I know it," she whispered, her eyes cast down.

His anger seeped from him. God in heaven, she was still frightened of him.

"I don't want to force you," he said, and heard the pleading in his voice. "I am asking that you come to me, Catherine. And that you do it soon."

He wanted her warm and willing in his arms. He wanted her clinging to him as he carried her to his bed. He wanted to see her weak and spent from their lovemaking. He wanted her to reach for him in the morning and do it all again.

He wanted, he wanted, he wanted.

She held herself rigid, waiting for him to release her. Unhappily, he let her go. He went to his bedchamber alone, hoping it would be the last night. Without bothering to remove his robe, he fell facedown across his bed.

He must have dozed, for he woke with a start to the sound of her screams. Heart pounding, he grabbed his sword from where it hung on the bedpost and ran to her bedchamber. In the darkness, he nearly collided with her maid.

"Lady Catherine is having one of her nightmares, m'lord," the maid said breathlessly. "I will fetch Alys. She knows what to do."

"Go quickly," he urged her, and went to Catherine.

She was thrashing on the bed and moaning, "No, please, no!" When he tried to quiet her by taking her in his arms, her movements became more violent. He stood back, feeling helpless.

Alys came rushing in, her voluminous night robe billowing behind her. By now, Catherine had awakened. She sat up in the bed, her hands over her face, shaking violently. And still, she could not bear to have him touch her.

The housekeeper put a steadying arm around his wife and held a small vial to her lips. She drank it down and rested her head on Alys's shoulder.

"That devil Rayburn is gone, thanks be to God," Alys murmured as she held Catherine and smoothed back her hair. "He cannot harm you now."

After a time, Alys eased Catherine onto the pillows and gingerly backed down the steps from the high bed.

"The draught will bring her a peaceful sleep, m'lord," Alys whispered as they left Catherine's bedchamber. "You've no cause to worry now."

Alys would have continued out the solar, but he put his hand on her arm to stop her.

"But I do have cause to worry." He nodded to a chair, and Alys sat down obediently. "Tell me what Rayburn did to her. All of it. Now."

Alys looked away and said, "Lord Rayburn beat her viciously. We could hear her screams." There was a note of pleading in Alys's voice. "There was nothing I could do, save tend to her after."

She grabbed a handful of her robes and wiped her nose and eyes. "May that man burn in hell for all eternity!"

"You would have protected her if you could," William said. "He was a powerful lord and her husband."

"I told Lady Catherine it would be a simple matter for me to slip poison in his soup, but she forbade it." Alys shook her head in obvious regret. "She would not have me blacken my soul by committing a mortal sin."

She stopped to blow her nose again. "The beatings stopped once she was with child."

"That was the end of it?" He hoped she would tell him it was, but he did not think so.

"That's what we thought. But then Jamie caught a fever and nearly died, poor lamb."

William was confused. "Are you saying Jamie's illness led Rayburn to mistreat her·again?"

"I know it did," Alys said, nodding her head vigorously. "I heard him shouting at her about one son not being enough, that there was nothing for it, but he must get her with child again. She cried and pleaded with him, promising nothing would happen to the boy."

"I heard her screaming as he dragged her up the stairs." Alys bit her lip and sniffed. "Next morning, I took care of her, as I always did."

William did not know what to do with his rage. It pulsed through him, blurring his vision. He wished Rayburn were still alive so he could kill him. No matter how Catherine deceived Rayburn, she did not deserve such treatment. No woman did.

Could she not see he was different from Rayburn? He would never lay a hand on her. He was a man of honor; it was his duty to protect her. He renewed his determination to be patient. In time, she would see he would not harm her. She would come to him.

* * *

Three more days of waiting, and William's patience had worn thin to breaking. He could not sleep and was so short-tempered that his men had taken to avoiding him. Edmund— the only man who dared—finally confronted him.

"What is it with you, man?" Edmund demanded as William stomped past him in the bailey yard. "I had supposed bride-grooms to be a cheerful lot, but the men are ready to join the Welsh just to get away from you."

When William only growled at him in response, Edmund said, "What complaint can you have? You have a woman in your bed every man here would sell his soul to the devil to have."

A glint came into Edmund's eyes. "Oh no, William, tell me you did not do something foolish to upset that pretty wife of yours?" Grinning now, Edmund shook his head in mock disbelief. "Did you let her catch you with that serving maid? The one who flounces her wares at you every chance she gets?"

"Don't insult me," William said sharply. "I am wed but a week, and you think I've already committed adultery?" William turned on his heel and resumed his march across the yard.

"If married life suits you so poorly," Edmund said, catching up to him, "you can send her away."

When William ignored him, Edmund took hold of his arm, forcing William to turn and face him.

"If it is your new wife who is making you such a miserable horse's arse, 'tis an easy matter to be rid of her. All you need do is tell the king she was party to Rayburn's treachery."

"Never speak against my wife again." The deathly calm of his voice made Edmund step back. "'Tis only because of the bond we share from many years of fighting that they will not be scraping your bloody carcass from the bailey ground today."

His body vibrated with anger as he stepped close to Edmund. "It will not save you a second time."

Chapter Six

*W*illiam strode toward the stables, hoping a long, hard ride would improve his mood. Before he reached them, he heard a trumpet blast.

"Who comes?" he called up to one of the men on the wall.

"They carry the king's banner, m'lord."

There was no time to change into something more suitable for greeting a royal visitor, so he headed straight for the gate. It could not be the king. Henry was in the North finishing off the last remnants of the rebellion there.

William recognized the young man who rode through the gate at the front of the men-at-arms as Prince Harry. As the prince dismounted, William dropped to his knee. At the prince's signal, he rose to receive his future king.

"FitzAlan, I am glad to find you here. The king wishes me to report—" The prince stopped midsentence, his attention caught by something behind William.

"Kate!" the prince called out, his face transformed by a boyish grin.

In another moment, Catherine was beside William making a low curtsy. Prince Harry pulled her to her feet. After bestowing enthusiastic kisses on both her cheeks, he lifted her off the ground and spun her in his arms.

If the prince's behavior was not surprising enough, Catherine's was astonishing. She threw her head back and laughed. Then she pounded on the prince's shoulders, shouting, "Harry! Harry, put me down at once!"

The prince did as she commanded. "I am always happy to do the fair Catherine's bidding," he declared, giving her a dramatic bow.

The prince turned and gave William a grin and a wink. "Truth be told," he said in a loud whisper she was meant to hear, "your lady wife was a tyrant as a child."

The prince put his hand to his heart and gave an exaggerated sigh. "I was in love with her when I was a lad of seven. But, alas, she was an older woman of ten and would not have me."

The men crowded around them laughed. William did not.

Catherine stood too close to the prince, squeezing his hand, chatting at her ease. William would have given a good deal to have her smile at him in precisely that way. Seeing her grace another man with it hit him like a blow to the chest.

He ceased to follow the words of their conversation, seeing only the affection and delight the two found in each other. Before he knew it, the three of them were walking to the keep. Focused as he was on how tightly she held the prince's arm, he almost failed to notice that Prince Harry was speaking to him.

"If you would be so gracious as to put me and my men up for the night," the prince was saying.

"It would be an honor." William was surprised by how normal his voice sounded.

"Only one night?" Catherine asked.

"I am sorry, my dear Kate," Prince Harry said, patting her hand on his arm, "but you know my time is not my own."

My dear Kate? The prince was talking to him again, but William could barely take in the words. *My dear Kate?*

"The king wishes to know whether there have been rebel attacks in the area since your arrival at Ross Castle."

He must have mumbled something appropriate, for the prince seemed satisfied.

William narrowed his eyes at Catherine. She was looking radiant in a close-fitting, rose-colored silk gown that flowed gracefully as she walked. Had she dressed with particular care today? The prince had given no advance warning of his visit. At least not to William.

Once inside the keep, Catherine sent servants scurrying in every direction to prepare rooms and refreshments. As soon as the prince excused himself to change, William took his wife by the arm. He marched her into a passage just outside the hall, where he could speak with her in private.

"You appear to know the prince quite well," he said in a harsh whisper.

"We have known each other all our lives," Catherine said, surprise in her voice. "You must know he spent his early years close by, at Monmouth Castle. Our mothers were close friends."

"Yes, of course," he said, feeling foolish.

"William, I must speak with the cook now," she said, clearly anxious to get back to her duties.

He could think of nothing else to say, so he let her go. At least she had called him "William" for once.

At supper, the prince chose to sit between William and his wife. And William chose to refrain from pushing his royal arse onto the floor. It annoyed him further to see what the kitchen, under his wife's direction, had produced on such short notice for their royal guest.

William was heaping pheasant onto his trencher when he became aware that the eyes of everyone at the table were on him.

"What is your opinion?" the prince asked, leaning forward and looking at him expectantly. "Will they come this summer?"

Fortunately, it was easy to guess what the prince was asking. The question was on everyone's lips: Would the French send an army to support the Welsh?

"I cannot say," William said, shrugging a shoulder, "but we must be prepared for it."

"Aye, we must!" Without pausing, the prince began to speculate as to where the French might land their forces. Then he launched into a discussion of how the English could then drive them out of Wales.

William should be glad for the opportunity to discuss military strategy with Prince Harry. After all, the prince was in command of all English forces fighting the Welsh. The young man showed such remarkable talent for military command that Parliament had given him the responsibility two years ago, at the age of sixteen.

Tonight, however, William did not care about a French invasion. To hell with the damned French.

As soon as the nursemaid took Jamie up to bed, William began to calculate how many hours before he could follow with Catherine. When the prince rose to his feet, he felt hopeful.

"May I take your wife for a walk in the garden?" The prince was already holding his arm out to Catherine as he asked the question.

William could not very well tell the heir to the throne

he would rather have a dagger twisted in his gut. If he gave his consent without much grace, the prince did not seem to notice.

* * *

Catherine took great solace in having even a short visit with her friend. Though Harry had an air of authority about him now, she could still see in him the boy who pulled her hair and slipped beetles down her back. Despite his annoying pranks, they had always been close.

She was glad Harry had those early years running wild at Monmouth, before his father usurped the throne. Being heir to the throne, especially in such troubled times, was a heavy burden.

"You make a fine prince, dear Harry," she said, squeezing his arm as they left the hall. "One day, you will make an even finer king."

"God grant my father many years," Harry murmured.

They sat on a bench in the garden to talk.

"You should not have taken the risks you did," he said, shaking his head.

They had had this argument many times before.

"It is over now, and I am safe," she reminded him with a smile.

"It was a close thing. My father—" Harry stopped and seemed to struggle to rephrase his words. "The king was so angry with Rayburn that he was inclined to send you to the Tower, despite my arguments."

The tension between the king and his heir was no secret. After criticizing Harry for being too weak when he was young, the king now appeared at times to consider him a threat. The king resented all the praise of Harry's military successes and his popularity among the common folk. For Harry's part, his innate sense of honor was violated time and again by actions his father took to retain power.

"'Tis a good thing FitzAlan chose to wed you." Harry looked off into the distance, his face grave. "If the king had imprisoned you or permitted an 'accident' to befall you..." He sighed and squeezed her hand. "I have forgiven my father many things, but I could not have forgiven him that."

They sat in silence for a time.

"FitzAlan seems to be a good man," Harry said in a soft voice. "Can you be happy with him, Kate?"

"Happy?" she said, surprised at the question. She paused to consider it. "You would not want to stand in William's way. But, beneath his fierceness, there is kindness in him."

In sooth, there was much to like and respect about her new husband. She felt more at ease with him each day. Soon, she would trust him enough to go to his bedchamber, as he asked.

* * *

Luckily, William could follow the men's conversation at the table with only half an ear. They talked, as they always did, of the Welsh rebels and their leader, Owain Glyndwr. For the hundredth time, he heard them complain of the rebels' uncanny ability to strike and disappear into the woods. They made the usual uneasy jests about the claim that Merlyn, Arthur's mythical magician, had returned to aid Glyndwr. William had heard it all before.

He flicked his eyes to the doorway again. Catherine and the prince had been gone for the better part of an hour.

At the sound of a woman's laughter, he leapt to his feet. Prince Harry and Catherine entered the room, arm in arm and smiling into each other's eyes. Someone tugged at William's arm. Without taking his eyes off the pair, he shrugged the man off.

"William!"

"What is it?" he hissed, turning to find Edmund beside him.

"Do you want to find yourself in chains in your own dungeon, man?" Edmund said out the side of his mouth.

William turned his attention back to the couple. His blood pounded through his veins as it did on the verge of battle. Feeling a hard jab in his ribs, he turned and glared at Edmund.

"You are looking at the Prince of Wales with murder in your eyes," Edmund persisted in a low, urgent voice. "Some of his men have taken notice."

This time, William took heed of the warning. Glancing about, he saw the two knights watching him, their hands touching the hilts of their swords. He relaxed his stance and smoothed his features, and the two knights did likewise.

He did not slip again. He maintained an easy, bored expression—even when Prince Harry drew his wife to a small table against the far wall for a game of chess.

From the corner of his eye, he watched the two laughing and talking. Just when he was sure he could not feel more wretched, their laughter died. They leaned across the table and spoke in low voices, their game forgotten.

Frustrated that he could not hear their words, he moved closer. His heart missed several beats as Catherine reached out to touch the scar under the prince's eye, where he had taken an arrow at the Battle of Shrewsbury. Despite the wound, he led the attack on Hotspur's flank.

The prince made a face and leaned back from her touch. "Please, Kate, I know it is hideous to look at."

"Nay, it is not. That mark is a sign you are special to God, that he protects you," Catherine said earnestly. "If it were otherwise, that arrow surely would have killed you."

Their exchange ended when William took position behind his wife and put a possessive hand on her shoulder. Feeling her body tense at his touch, he clenched his jaw so tightly it began to ache.

The prince showed no sign of discomfort at being caught in the midst of an intimate conversation with another man's wife.

"Becoming a prince must have made me a better chess player," he said in a voice heavy with irony. "Lady Catherine is the only one who has retained the ability to beat me."

William had not bothered to observe the chess pieces before. Dropping his gaze to the table now, he saw that the prince's king was caught in the cross paths of Catherine's bishop and queen.

"You win this time." With a flick of his finger, the prince knocked his king on its side. Then he stretched his arms and added, "But once is luck."

"'Twas much too easy," Catherine said, looking off to the side as though exceedingly bored. "Soon I shall find it too dull to play with you at all."

William was startled to hear her openly insult the prince. Before he could gather himself to say something to soften her words, the prince guffawed and slapped the table.

"You shall regret those words, sweet Catherine," Prince Harry said, his eyes gleaming. He began putting the pieces back into place for another game. "This time, I shall humiliate you. Nay, I shall make you weep with remorse!"

The prince's loud challenge drew the other men, and wagers were made. Observing the game, William could see that the two players were well matched. Catherine fought hard, but this time it was her king that was toppled.

William pulled out his leather purse and paid coins all around. None, save him, had dared bet against the prince.

Catherine excused herself then, and the men settled into talk of war and rebels again. Without the distraction of his wife, William's usual interest in military matters returned. As they talked into the wee hours, he found he could not help liking Prince Harry. He was so young and earnest. Yet, there was power in him, too. He was a man other men would follow.

William chastised himself for overreacting. Harry was an honorable man. He and Catherine were friends. William was slow to see it, since he never had a woman friend. Even his lovers were not friends. Especially his lovers.

These finer thoughts left him as he came into the hall the next morning. Prince Harry and Catherine were already at table, engrossed in conversation. When Catherine saw him, she murmured a greeting and went silent.

The prince, however, enthusiastically resumed their conversation of the night before.

"The Welsh rebels have only succeeded in taking control of most of Wales, because English forces have been divided," the prince said. "Now that the rebellion in the North is crushed, we shall turn all our attention to Wales."

Prince Harry expounded at length upon his strategy for laying siege to the castles the rebels had taken in Wales. All William wished to know, however, was what the prince and his wife had been talking about before he sat down.

It was not, he was certain, strategies for laying siege.

To his surprise—and growing annoyance—the prince did not take his leave after breakfast. He stayed for the midday meal, which had even more courses than last night's supper. Then, he suggested taking a ride around the lands surrounding Ross Castle.

God's blood, would the man never leave?

William's mood darkened further when Prince Harry dropped back to ride beside Catherine. He could hear their light chatter and Catherine's occasional laughter behind him. When he could take no more, he turned his horse and led the way back to the castle.

He made a point of riding just in front of the pair. "Such a wicked girl you were," he heard the prince say. "You were older and bigger, yet you never once let me win."

"It was skill, not size, that decided it," she replied.

What on earth are they talking about? William pulled his horse up and turned around to look at them.

"Then let us have a race now," the prince said.

"Harry, I cannot!" Catherine protested. "I am a grown woman. You know I cannot."

They were even with William now. Prince Harry turned away from Catherine to address him. "She—"

The moment the prince's back was turned, Catherine spurred her horse and took off.

William could not believe it. Too stunned to move, he watched her ride so recklessly that he feared she would fall. She was several lengths ahead when the prince took off after her. Soon, he streaked past her.

When William caught up to them at the gate, Catherine was shouting at her opponent. "If I did not have to ride in this cumbersome gown, I would have won!" It was an outrageous lie, and the gleam in her eyes made it clear she knew it.

Prince Harry called out to William, "You are a fortunate man to have such a wife!"

Before William could get to Catherine, the prince had his hands on her and was lifting her to the ground. William came up behind them in time to hear Prince Harry say in a low voice, "Will I ever find a woman like you, dear Kate?"

The good-byes were tedious. William was anxious for them to be done. At long last, the prince was mounted and headed out the gate. And still, the man turned one last time to wave at Catherine. William ground his teeth as he watched her wave back. When she wiped away a tear, he turned on his heel and strode off with no destination other than to be away from her.

A true knight did not murder his wife.

* * *

Catherine felt William's eyes burning holes into her as she waved good-bye to Harry. When she turned, he was stomping off as if headed for a fight. She had sensed his anger building since the chess games the night before. Fearful of aggravating him further, she did her best to speak to him as little as possible.

What happened to the kindness she thought she saw in him? Just when she began to trust in it, the man turned back into the furious warrior on the drawbridge.

To think she'd nearly convinced herself to go to his bed!

Chapter Seven

*A*pparently, his lady wife was too despondent over the prince's departure to show her face at supper. She sent word down that she was not well and would not join them in the hall. The surreptitious looks his men exchanged when they thought he was not looking only confirmed his fears.

William began to drink in earnest.

Irritated by the sight of the empty seat beside him, he grabbed a full pitcher of wine from the table and stomped out of the hall. He was well into his cups when Edmund found him on the outer curtain wall, perched on the lower ledge of the crenellated parapet.

He gazed out at the countryside in the fading light of the summer evening. "I have my own land now, Edmund," he said, swinging his arm in a wide arc. "And by God, isn't it fair!"

Edmund grabbed William's other arm. "This may not be the best choice of seats for serious drinking."

"'Tis a fine spot," William countered. "I've never seen

better." He tilted his head back and took another long drink from the pitcher, ignoring how it spilt down his chin and neck.

Edmund leaned against the parapet. "Are you sharing?"

William turned the empty pitcher upside down. "We shall have to get more. I, for one, have not drunk nearly enough."

Edmund let out a long sigh and shook his head. "William, William, William. You are not looking at how the situation is to your advantage. If you consider it properly, you will see you have much to gain here."

Even drunk as he was, William understood the direction of Edmund's remarks.

Edmund held up his hands. "Do not get angry with me. I am just looking out for your interests."

He should stop Edmund now. Instead, he waited to hear Edmund confirm the ugly suspicions that had been playing in his head since the prince's arrival.

"Young Harry is not the first royal to find himself desperate to have another man's wife in his bed," Edmund said. "Kings have been known to provide titles and riches to a husband who will turn his head and forgo his rights for a time."

Edmund took his lack of response as permission to go on.

"From the hungry way he looks at her, I don't believe he's had her yet," Edmund said in a thoughtful tone. "The arrangement will be worth a good deal more to you when he is king. Rumor has it the king is ill, and Harry may be on the throne before the year is out. It would be best to make him wait, if she can manage it, but I would not count on it."

He should encourage his wife to manage the prince's "interest" to his own advantage? The rage that roared through him was so great he could not speak. He feared he might lose his reason and murder Edmund on the spot.

"You cannot expect the prince's interest to last long once he has had her, especially with all the great families thrusting their daughters under his nose," Edmund continued, oblivious to the danger he was in. "When he is done with her, you can take her back...or not."

Blithely, he gave William his final word of advice. "If you want to be sure your heir is your own blood, you'd better get her with child now, before the prince takes her to his bed."

In one motion, William surged up, lifted Edmund off his feet by the front of his tunic, and threw him hard against the parapet. The man was lucky William did not toss him over it. Without looking back, he stormed down the walkway and took the steps down the side of the wall two at a time.

He would see this wife of his, and he would see her now.

She played her first husband false. Why did he think she would not do the same with him? What had made him so ready to believe the tale of Rayburn's violence against her? She had played him for a fool, all the while saving herself for her lover.

She acted like a frightened, untouched virgin with him. But she'd shown no fear with Harry. Even through the haze of drink, he knew what bothered him most was her obvious affection for the prince. He thought of how she stood so close to the prince, smiled at him, touched his face. It tore him apart.

He would show her what a man could give her, and she would never want that boy again.

As he made his way up the stairs to their rooms, the steps seemed to shift under him several times. He found the solar dark and empty, but there was a dim light under her bedchamber door. When he pushed it open, it made a very satisfying bang against the stone wall.

Catherine and her maid sat up straight in their beds,

staring at him. With the single word "Out!" he sent the maid scurrying from her pallet. He barred the door behind her.

When he turned to face his wife again, she was standing beside the bed. Her hair fell in a tumble of golden waves over her shoulders. With the candlelight behind her, he could see the outline of her body through the thin night shift.

God, but she was beautiful. And she was his.

* * *

Catherine jumped from the bed but got no farther. The drunken madman towered over her, huge and menacing. She struggled to breathe against the rising hysteria closing her throat. Covering her face with her arms, she turned and cowered against the bed.

Suddenly, he was behind her, his heavy weight pinning her against the bed. The hot breath on her neck, the smell of sour wine, sent memories of Rayburn flashing through her head. She closed her ears to the man's drunken mutterings so she would not hear the vile things he said.

His hands were everywhere, rubbing up and down her sides and moving over her breasts. When he lifted her shift and moved his hands over her bare buttocks and thighs, panic nearly paralyzed her. Desperation gave her the strength to pull herself along the side of the bed to reach for the blade under her pillow. When she moved, he fell against the bed. Then he slowly slid to the floor.

She stood over him, breathing hard and holding her knife in front of her. When he started to push himself up, she made ready to stab him. His attempt was a feeble one, though, and he collapsed back onto the floor. Except for making occasional piglike snorts, he lay still after that.

Her only thought was to get away before he awoke.

She found her maid hovering outside the solar door. "Go fetch Alys and Jacob at once," she said, shaking the woman's arm. "And take care not to wake anyone else."

She stepped cautiously around the large form sprawled on the floor. She stayed in her chamber only long enough to slip a gown over her head and grab her riding boots and cloak.

Alys and Jacob were waiting for her on the stairs.

"Fetch Jamie and meet me at the stables," she whispered to Jacob.

As soon as Jacob had gone, she turned her back to Alys and held her hair up.

"What has happened, m'lady?" Alys whispered as she fastened the gown. "Where are you going?"

"Come, I must hurry." Catherine took Alys by the hand and pulled her down the stairs.

She did not speak again until they were crossing the bailey in the pitch dark. "I am going to the abbey. I will ask Abbess Talcott to let me take vows and remain there."

"But you cannot, m'lady," Alys protested. "You have a husband."

"I will seek an annulment."

Jacob arrived at the stables just behind them with the sleepy boy in his arms.

"Let me take Jamie on my horse, m'lady," Jacob said. "I can manage him better, if it's a fast gallop you have in mind."

Fortunately, the guards at the gate tonight were men who had long been in her family's service. They asked only if she wanted more men for protection. When she refused, they followed her order to open the gate.

* * *

William lay very still, eyes closed, knowing any movement would worsen his already throbbing head. The carpet beneath his face was uncomfortably damp from his drooling. His mouth was gaping like a fish, so he closed it. It was as dry as dust. Still, he would have resisted the driving need to quench his thirst a while longer if he did not need to piss so badly.

He eased himself to his hands and knees, intent on making his way to the garderobe.

Looking around the room from his position on the floor, he tried to place where he was. In front of him was an open chest with gowns hanging over the sides in a jumble. He stared at the bed and the tapestry on the wall.

Catherine's bedchamber. He was in Catherine's bedchamber.

Bits of memory from the previous night came to him. He sat back on his heels and tried to recall the whole of it. He remembered drinking on the wall. And Edmund talking. A surge of anger made his head pound as he recalled Edmund advising him to turn a blind eye while the prince bedded his wife.

The anger was replaced by mortification as he recalled the sound of the chamber door banging against the wall and the sight of the two women cowering in their beds. Had he really come to her so drunk he could barely walk?

A feeling of longing swept over him as he remembered the feel of Catherine's soft skin, warm from her bed. Then he recalled how roughly he had handled her. When she was finally ready, he had meant to be gentle with her. Instead, he had rubbed his hands over her as if she were a whore, unceremoniously pulled up her shift, and pushed her against the bed, ready to take her standing then and there.

He covered his face. God help him, he could not have behaved worse if he set his mind to it.

When he stumbled into his own chamber, he found Thomas had thoughtfully left a large cup of ale and bread slathered in salty pork grease. He poured water into the basin and washed the grime from his face and neck. He took his time, trying to think how to make his apology. No matter what she had done, it did not excuse his behavior. And, in the clear light of day, he had to admit she may not have done anything inappropriate with Prince Harry.

He looked down at himself. Well, at least he could attempt to look like a lord rather than a disheveled drunkard. Clairvoyant as usual, his manservant appeared at his door at that moment. Thomas, however, refused to meet his eye. Damnation, he did not need his manservant condemning him as well.

Without a word, Thomas brought him a rich dark brown cotehardie and matching hose to wear. He then helped William into a rust-colored houppelande that fell to the knee. Its wide sleeves were slit from below the elbow to the shoulder to show the cotehardie beneath.

"Is this not a bit dull, Thomas?" Noblemen were typically outfitted in more colorful attire.

"I thought dullness might be an advantage today, m'lord."

"Thomas—" he began to shout, but winced when it gave him a blinding flash of pain.

"You want to give the *appearance* of quiet dignity." Thomas pursed his lips and nodded. "Aye, the penitent look of a pilgrim would be best."

"Enough, Thomas."

He did not think Thomas would show such disapproval over mere drunkenness, but he could not fathom how the man could know of his other behavior. Then he remembered the maid he had sent scurrying from Catherine's bedchamber.

He raised his arms as Thomas fastened the rich jeweled

belt Northumberland had given him low on his hips. So, he was to have a touch of finery after all.

"Where is she?" It hurt his dignity to ask Thomas, but the sooner he found Catherine and tried to make amends, the better.

"Who, m'lord?"

"You know very well who." William ground his teeth, which only aggravated his pounding headache. "My lady wife. Where is she?"

"I do not know, sir," Thomas replied with annoying calm. "She certainly would not have informed me."

"Get my boots so I may go find her," William said, wanting to throttle the man.

"You will need these," Thomas said, bringing him his tall leather riding boots.

"What? She has left the castle?" William asked. "I thought you did not know where she was."

"I don't," Thomas replied as he helped William into the tight boots. "But I did hear she left on horseback late in the night."

"What?" William shouted. "When was this?"

"I understand she left not long· after you went to bed, m'lord." Thomas's voice was rich with unstated meaning.

William pulled the man up by his tunic until they were nose to nose. "Where has she gone?"

Thomas remained unruffled. "I suggest you ask the housekeeper." As though it was an afterthought, he added, "I heard old Jacob accompanied your lady."

"What other escort did she take?" William asked.

"None but Jamie."

God help him, she rode out into the night with only an old man as escort. It was madness.

He stormed down the stairs to find Alys. Was it his

obscene behavior that drove Catherine to go, or had she planned to sneak away to join her lover all along?

He would find her and bring her back, prince or no prince.

He found Alys in the kitchen, consulting with the cook. "Now," he ordered, pointing toward the open door.

After exchanging glances with the cook, Alys followed him out.

"Alys, if you value your life, you will tell me where she was meeting Prince Harry."

"Prince Harry?" Alys pinched her brows together. "What are you asking, m'lord?"

"I know she has gone to meet him." He was so angry he could have shaken the woman, if it would have done any good. "Where are they?"

"She would not trouble the prince, what with the rebellion and all." She made it sound as if he was accusing Catherine of rudeness rather than adultery. "Nay, she sought refuge elsewhere."

Refuge.

He threatened and cajoled. It was only when he gave Alys his solemn promise he would not harm Catherine that she finally told him where his wife had gone. When he heard it, the blood drained from his head.

Good God, he had driven his wife to a nunnery.

Chapter Eight

When they pounded on the abbey gates in the middle of the night, Abbess Talcott asked no questions and calmly ordered a guest room to be made ready. This morning, she sat patiently while the three ate their breakfast. As soon as they finished, however, she sent Jamie off with a young novice to feed the animals. One look from the abbess and Jacob made his own exit.

Catherine sat across from the abbess now in her personal parlor. It was clear the older woman would be put off no longer. The abbess poured sweetened wine and let the silence between them grow as she waited for Catherine's explanation.

Abbess Talcott had been a close friend of Catherine's mother. Like her mother, the abbess had come from one wealthy family and married into another. When her husband died leaving her with no children, she announced her intention to take vows and lead the quiet life of a nun. She backed up her intention with the gift of a substantial portion of her lands to the church. That gift was how she came to be the head of this fine abbey straddling the Welsh-English border.

After recounting the events of the past two weeks, Catherine told her of FitzAlan's drunken attack on her the night before.

"So you see," Catherine finished, tilting her chin up, "I had no choice but to flee."

If she expected words of sympathy from the abbess, she was to be disappointed.

"Let me review what you've told me, Mary Catherine," the abbess said, fixing Catherine with direct eyes. "This Fitz-Alan agreed to marry you to save you from imprisonment—or worse. He did this knowing little about you, except that you spied on your first husband and helped bring about his death."

The abbess pursed her lips and tapped a forefinger against her cheek. "He is either a brave man or a foolish one.

"The king granted your lands to FitzAlan, whether or not he married you," the abbess continued. "As I see it, the man gained nothing from this marriage, save for the honor of rescuing an innocent woman—or rather, a possibly innocent woman—from the Tower."

The abbess took a sip of her wine. "A chivalrous gesture, I must say. And all he expected from you was that you share his bed and provide him an heir—what any wife is expected to give her husband."

As the abbess put it, her behavior did not seem as justified as she knew it to be.

"But, m'lady Abbess—" she began, but stopped when Abbess Talcott put her hand up, commanding silence.

"You entered into the marriage contract and yet you have refused the man your bed. You are not an underage girl, my dear. When you did not willingly submit, he would have been within his rights to force you. Instead, he was kind and patient with you, beyond all reasonable expectation."

This time, Catherine could not help interrupting to defend herself. "But he was senseless with drink when he came to me last night!"

The abbess arched one eyebrow. "Few new husbands would wait so long without turning to drink."

Catherine looked down at her hands, twisted in the skirt of her gown. "When he came to me like that, I could only think of Rayburn."

She stilled her hands and lifted her head to meet the abbess's eyes. "I cannot live like that again. I will not. I've come to ask your permission to take vows and remain here at the abbey."

The abbess patted Catherine's knee. In a kinder tone, she asked, "Did FitzAlan harm you, my dear?"

Catherine shook her head. "But I feared he would."

The abbess sighed. "Mary Catherine, you cannot punish FitzAlan for the sins of your first husband." Under her breath, she added, "May God punish him throughout eternity.

"Do you understand what FitzAlan has done for you?" the abbess pressed. "What would happen to your son if you went to the Tower?"

"Must you remind me?" Catherine asked.

"Jamie would be taken from you. As you have no close male relative, he would be placed under the guardianship of someone unknown to him—someone likely to feel burdened by the care of a traitor's son."

Catherine did not want to hear this.

"FitzAlan could have sent your son away. Instead, you say he is kind and affectionate to the boy." The abbess's tone had a sharp edge of exasperation now. "You are foolish if you do not recognize this for the great gift it is.

"You know what you must do," the abbess concluded. It was not a question. "Return to your husband, ask his forgiveness, and fulfill the vows you made before God."

The abbess poured them both more wine and gave Catherine time to mull over what she had said. When the chapel bell rang to call the nuns for Terce, Catherine expected to be dismissed. But the abbess was not finished with her yet.

"Since your good mother is not here to advise you..." The abbess hesitated, as if unsure how to put her thoughts into words. "I will tell you, most men are not like Rayburn."

The abbess cleared her throat and began again. "It may be hard for you to believe now, but many women find happiness in the marriage bed. It can be...joyful." Her eyes were moist as she patted Catherine's hand. "You must let yourself be open to it."

The quiet of the abbey was suddenly broken by the clatter of horses' hooves and the discordant sound of men's voices. The two women rushed to the window overlooking the courtyard to see what was causing the commotion below.

Catherine drew in a sharp breath. "It is Lord FitzAlan."

A half-dozen men on horses accompanied FitzAlan, but Catherine could look at none but him. The courtyard seemed to reverberate with his presence as he circled, his horse prancing and tossing its head. He was hatless. The late morning sun showed the hard planes of his face and glinted on the sun-lightened streaks of his bronze hair.

William must have sensed them watching, for he looked up then with an expression so fierce Catherine gripped the abbess's arm for support. He kept his eyes fixed on her as he dismounted, threw his reins at one of his men, and strode purposefully toward the entry below.

A high-pitched sound came from the back of her throat. Frantically, she looked about the room for a means of escape.

"This way." The abbess stepped briskly to the opposite wall and opened a narrow door hidden by the paneling. "Wait in the chapel until I send for you," she said, motioning for Catherine to hurry. "Pray that God grants you the strength to do your duty—and the wisdom to be thankful for his blessings."

As soon as Catherine had made her escape, FitzAlan burst in through the other door. He looked sharply around the room before bringing his gaze to rest on the abbess.

A nun stepped around him, giving him wide berth. "My Lady Abbess, I tried to stop him and ask his business here, but—"

"It is all right, Sister Matilde," the abbess said, staring down the tall, well-muscled man filling her doorway. "If this is Lord FitzAlan, I have been expecting his visit."

Belatedly recalling his manners, FitzAlan made a low bow. "M'lady Abbess, I am Lord William Neville FitzAlan. I hope you will forgive me for interrupting you."

Ignoring him for the moment, the abbess sent a second trembling nun for honey cakes and more sweet wine. Since propriety did not permit her to be left alone with a man, she directed Sister Matilde to take a seat at the far end of the room, where the nun could not easily overhear their conversation.

Only then did she gesture to FitzAlan to sit in one of the ornately carved chairs she had brought to the abbey from her home. She permitted herself some minor comforts here in her private parlor, where she received guests from the outside world.

The abbess took more than a little satisfaction in knowing that her black robes intimidated even the most powerful men. FitzAlan was no exception. He looked distinctly uncomfortable—and not just because the chair was far too small for his frame.

She suppressed a smile. Now that he had blustered his way in, it was apparent FitzAlan had no notion what to do next. He kept clasping his hands, as if about to speak. The gesture was familiar to her. Her husband had also been a man who found action easier than words.

She let him suffer, enjoying it to a degree that would require penance later. When a servant arrived with the wine and honey cakes, she took her time pouring.

"You've had a hard ride this morning," she said at last, her voice dripping with false sympathy. She offered him the plate of honey cakes. "I thought perhaps you did not take time for breakfast."

He rubbed his neck in growing discomfort. She was pleased to see he understood she was chastising him for stampeding through her gates and breaking the peace of the abbey.

"The cakes are warm," she said, encouraging him to eat. She watched him choke down two, from either politeness or extreme hunger, and wash them down with the wine. She really must assign the baking to someone other than Sister Katrina.

Seeing no reason to delay any longer, she asked, "Did you know your wife came here asking to take vows and remain with us permanently?"

"The housekeeper said as much," FitzAlan conceded.

His face colored in a most appealing way. She found herself beginning to like the man. Of course, she had noticed how handsome he was as soon as she laid eyes on him. Taking vows did not affect her eyesight.

"That an annulment could even be considered now suggests"—she paused deliberately—"relations are not as they should be between you."

The young man choked and appeared to be trying to speak, but she held up her hand. "Of course, Catherine's coming here in the middle of the night with only an elderly man as escort was quite sufficient to tell me that."

FitzAlan looked mortified, another hopeful sign. By now, he probably realized his wife had related more of his behavior the night before than he would wish.

"I know I frightened her," he confessed readily enough. "But I swear to you, I would never harm her."

"I do not speak plainly to embarrass you, Lord FitzAlan." It was only a partial falsehood. As it was in service of a worthy purpose, God would forgive her. "I have known Lady Catherine since she was a babe. Perhaps I can help you understand her."

"I would be most appreciative, Lady Abbess," FitzAlan said with a touch of desperation in his eyes.

"I understand you have been patient with Catherine." Giving him a pointed look, she added, "For the most part." It would not be wise to be too soft on the young man.

"I am not sure how much you know of her marriage to Rayburn." She could barely say that horrid man's name without spitting. "If Catherine's mother had been alive, she would have been able to guide Catherine's father and the king in choosing a better man to serve their purposes. Without her good influence, they chose a perfectly loathsome man who mistreated Catherine horribly.

"I, for one, was not surprised when Rayburn turned against the king." The abbess hoped she did not sound as if she thought the king deserved to suffer for his bad choice, though she did.

"Catherine got her loveliness from her mother." She sighed. "Before Rayburn, she had something more—a radiance about her, a light in her eyes. He took that from her."

She was frustrated at not being able to describe it more clearly, but FitzAlan nodded as though he understood.

"I counsel more patience. Give her time to trust you, and she will be a good wife to you."

"I want her to be content with me," FitzAlan said, "for the sake of our children, as much as for me."

Abbess Talcott sensed from the way he said this that he wanted something for his children he had not had himself. Aye, she was pleased with him. Very pleased, indeed.

"If you can bring that spark back into her eyes, I promise she will bring you joy—and many children." She hoped she had not winked at him, but old habits die hard.

"My wife's coming here could have caused difficulties for you and the abbey," FitzAlan said. "I apologize for that."

The abbess nodded. "I could not have allowed her to remain here. In her haste, Catherine forgot the king gave her but two choices—and one of them was not joining a nunnery."

The abbess signaled to Sister Matilde, who rose immediately and went to speak to someone just outside the door.

A few moments later, they heard light footsteps coming up the stairs. FitzAlan got to his feet, but the abbess signaled for him to wait where he was. She stepped outside the open door and met Catherine at the top of the stairs.

"Tell me," she asked in a low voice as she took Catherine's hands, "have you decided to comply with your marriage vows and go with your husband?"

Catherine nodded, her eyes cast down.

"Surely, it is God's will that you do."

Though FitzAlan was only a few yards away, Catherine did not even glance in his direction.

"Your new husband seems to be an honorable man who cares for your happiness. A woman cannot ask for more." His fine looks were certainly an added blessing, but the abbess did not say this aloud.

She embraced Catherine and took the opportunity to whisper in her ear. "I will soon learn what message the emissaries from the French court have brought to Owain Glyndwr."

"You will send me news when you have it?" Catherine whispered back.

"Aye." The abbess released her and said, "God bless you both."

She turned and went down the stairs with Sister Matilde, leaving Catherine alone to face her husband.

* * *

Catherine clasped her hands together to control their shaking and entered the parlor. Unable to look into her husband's face, she fixed her eyes on his boots and walked across the room to him. She'd practiced her apology in the chapel. But when she opened her mouth to give it, her throat closed.

William's face was suddenly in her line of vision. The saints have mercy, he'd dropped to his knee before her. She could not read the deep emotion in his amber eyes, but she could not look away if she tried.

"I apologize for frightening you last night," he said, enfolding her clasped hands in his. "I should not have come to you drunk…and…in that manner."

The apology was so unexpected that she could think of no reply.

"But you did not need to leave," he said more forcefully. "You had only to speak to make me stop." A look of unease flitted across his face. "In sooth, you might have had to shout, but I did not intend to hurt you."

Unsure what he expected of her, she murmured, "Thank you."

"I have come to take you back, but I will give you my promise." He spoke his next words slowly and deliberately, his eyes never leaving her face. "I swear to you, Mary Catherine FitzAlan, I will never harm you."

His apology and promise made, he rose to his feet and said, "That is not to say I think you are without fault in this."

Catherine felt her face color, thinking of her refusal to come willingly to the marriage bed. "I am most sorry for my failures, m'lord husband," she stammered. "I intended to ask your forgiveness as soon as I came in."

"You broke your word to me." He loomed over her, his fists clenched, his voice sharp with anger. "You agreed to tell no one our marriage was not consummated. Now I find you've told Abbess Talcott as well as the housekeeper."

"I am sorry," she said, surprised to learn this was what he was most angry about. "In my fright, I forgot my promise."

"You may as well have announced it in the hall," he said, raising his voice and spreading his arms wide. "Everyone you did not tell outright will know it when they hear you came here seeking *an annulment*!"

After a few moments of silence, he took a deep breath and ran his hands through his hair.

"We shall return at once," he said, his voice deadly calm now. "You will not leave Ross Castle without my permission again."

She nodded her agreement. Obediently, she took his proffered hand, but he made no move toward the door.

"You will keep your word to me in the future," he said, fixing her with a look that was as hard as granite. His words were both a demand and a warning. "I cannot abide deceit."

* * *

Catherine averted her eyes as William marched her past the half-dozen men waiting with their horses in the courtyard. He headed straight for Jacob, who stood alone a few yards away from the others.

"You should not have been party to this foolishness," William said, tapping a menacing forefinger on Jacob's chest. "You took a great chance with my wife and Jamie, traveling alone at night as you did. You and I shall come to an understanding, or you shall not remain in my service. The men at the gate who let you pass shall answer to me as well."

Catherine appreciated that William gave the reprimand out of the other men's hearing. She understood, too, why he said it in front of her. It had been reckless of her to travel with only the old man for protection. Old Jacob would do anything she asked, and she had taken advantage of that.

Hearing Jamie's shout, she turned around to see him break loose from the novice's hand and run across the courtyard toward them. Instead of coming to her, he barreled into William. He shrieked with pleasure as William caught him. Reminded of Abbess Talcott's reproof to be grateful for William's kindness toward her son, she felt ashamed.

William put the boy on Jacob's horse, gruffly telling the old man to take care with him. It was a sign Jacob would be forgiven. Catherine made herself turn to acknowledge the other men. None would meet her eyes. Forgiveness would not come so easily for her.

The ride back to Ross Castle was long and silent, broken only by Jamie's occasional question and Jacob's murmured reply. After a time, even Jamie picked up the somber mood and grew quiet. Finally, Ross Castle came into sight. The ordeal was almost over.

As soon as they were within the protective watch of the sentries on the walls, William sent the others ahead.

"There is something I must ask you," he said to her.

William lifted her down from her horse. He took her elbow and began walking with her, slowly and without direction. The ground was rough, and she had to watch her step.

Suddenly, he stopped and pulled her around to face him. "I want to know the nature of your relationship with the prince."

She raised her eyebrows in surprise. "What is it you wish to know?"

"I can think of no other way to say it, except bluntly." William looked off in the distance and then back at her, as if expecting her to discern his question without his asking it.

When she continued to look at him blankly, he said in a strained voice, "I must know if you have lain with him yet."

She did not immediately respond, because she simply *could not*.

"If you have," he said in a gruff voice, "it must stop."

Her hand went to her mouth, and she stepped back from him. "You would say such a thing to me!" she said, torn between shock and outrage. It was unthinkable. She turned on her heel to walk away from him, but he grabbed her arm.

"You betrayed your first husband while you shared his bed—a favor you have yet to grant me." His voice was caustic. "Why should I believe you would not betray me as well?"

Before now, the intensity of his desire for her had so overwhelmed her that she had failed to perceive the depth of his distrust of her. Why had he chosen to marry her?

"I see what you think of my character, husband," she said, spitting out the word *husband*. "But how could you believe it of Harry? He is selfless and righteous and honorable." She was ranting now, and she did not care whether

her defense of Harry was helping her case or not. "How could you think he would be a guest in your home and bed your wife?"

She jerked her arm from his grasp but remained facing him, defiant and angry.

"If you have not yet acted upon what is between you," he said, his eyes spitting fire, "then I am telling you now that you shall not."

She slapped him so hard that the stinging of her hand brought tears to her eyes. Seeing her handprint on his face brought visions of the marks Rayburn had left on her.

She covered her face and crumpled to the ground. She was both startled by her own uncontrolled rage and humiliated by William's accusations.

The future seemed very bleak, indeed.

Eventually her raging emotions receded, leaving a heavy tiredness that weighed down every bone and muscle. William knelt beside her, but she did not look at him. Staring, unseeing, into the distance, she made one last attempt to make him understand the impossibility of what he was suggesting.

"Harry does not think of me that way," she said. "He is like a younger brother to me and I an older sister to him."

William put his hands on either side of her face, forcing her to look at him. "My mother gave herself to whomever she pleased, regardless of the consequences to anyone else. I will not tolerate such behavior in my wife.

"We must have this understood between us." His eyes held hers with a burning intensity. "I will not share my wife with another man, whether he be prince or king or commoner. I keep what is mine."

* * *

As they remounted their horses and rode in silence to the gate, Catherine was grateful he had not asked the one question she could not answer honestly. She had one secret she would keep from him, no matter what his threats or her promises.

One secret she would never tell.

Chapter Nine

The tension was thick at the table. News of her flight had spread through the castle—and likely to everyone in the village below as well. William's men were restless. The servants gave her worried looks as they carried in jugs of wine and heaping trays of food. Beside her, William was as silent as the grave.

As soon as the interminable meal ended, Catherine made her escape.

"Jamie, come with me," she said, taking his hand. "I will tell you tales of King Arthur before you sleep." They were his favorites, so she knew he would not argue.

She sat beside Jamie on his bed and recited every Camelot story she knew. When she could no longer justify keeping him awake, she made him say his prayers and kissed him. With a nod to the nursemaid, she slipped out.

Jamie had slept in her bedchamber until Rayburn came home unexpectedly one night. That was the only time Jamie saw Rayburn hit her, but he was so upset by it she did not risk it again. The next day, she settled him into his own chamber on the floor above.

Her feet dragged as she went down the stairs. Knowing what she must do did not make doing it any easier. When did she become such a coward? William was not like Rayburn. As furious as he was with her today, he did not strike her. He might punish her by keeping her under lock and key, but his sense of honor would not permit him to physically harm her.

Perhaps sharing his bed would be no worse than unpleasant. Women all over England submitted to their husbands; most seemed none the worse for it. Aye, she would hope for the best.

Her maid was waiting for her in her bedchamber. "You may go now, Mary," she said after the woman had helped her out of her gown and into her night shift. "I shall not need you until morning."

Mary smiled and raised an eyebrow. "Of course, m'lady."

There were few secrets one could keep from one's maid.

"Tell Thomas he will not be needed either." Covering her embarrassment as best she could, she said, "I shall help my husband prepare for bed tonight."

The look of approval on Mary's face did not make Catherine feel any better.

Once she was alone, she went into William's bedchamber. She stood uncertainly before the bed. Remembering William liked her hair down, she loosened it from the braid the maid had just made and climbed up the step to the bed.

* * *

William sighed as he made his way up the stairs. Catherine had been as nervous as a cat at supper. Then she left in such haste, he could have no hope she would come to him tonight. Though he forced her to return, she did seem to accept she must fulfill her marriage vows to him.

If he had any reason to believe it would be tonight, he would be running up these stairs.

Making her so angry had not helped, of course. He was now inclined to believe her relationship with the prince was yet innocent. Still, he was glad he made it clear to her he would not tolerate infidelity. He knew from experience how lightly many noblewomen took their marriage vows.

He was not ready to face his empty bed, so he continued up the stairs to the upper floor. When he stepped into Jamie's chamber, he nodded to the startled nursemaid who sat in the corner stitching.

He watched the boy's face in the lamplight. Jamie, who was always in motion when awake, had the face of a cherub in the peace of sleep. The sweetness of his expression made William think of his brother John at that age. William had not been allowed to visit his mother's home often. But when he came, it was to see John.

"God protect you," he said, touching the top of the boy's head.

Having no more excuse for delay, he trudged down the stairs to his and Catherine's rooms. He gave yet another heavy sigh when he saw no light under her door. For the hundredth time that day, he reminded himself of the abbess's advice. He must give Catherine time to trust him.

Where was Thomas? God's beard, the man did not even light a lamp for him. Further punishment for his sins—as if he needed to be chastised by his manservant.

He felt his way in the dark to the table and lit the lamp. He yawned and stretched his arms wide as he turned toward the bed.

Catherine. Catherine was in his bed.

In three heartbeats, he went from dumbstruck to breathless. She was stunning, with her fair hair spilling over his pillow like a river of moonbeams. It was a long moment before he thought to drop his arms.

"You have come to me," he said, not quite believing it.

She clutched the bedclothes to her chin and nodded.

Now that she was here, he could show her she had nothing to fear in his bed. He uncurled her hand from the coverlet and pressed it to his lips.

"It pleases me very much that you are here." He squeezed her icy fingers to reassure her and kissed her cheek. "I will give you no cause to regret it."

He undressed quickly, dropping his clothes on the floor before lifting the bedclothes. Ignoring her sharp intake of breath, he slid in beside her.

She was wearing her tunic, but that meant he would have the pleasure of taking it off. He tentatively placed his hand on the flat of her stomach. Imagining the feel of the smooth skin beneath the cloth, he closed his eyes. He was determined to go slowly and not frighten her. But he wanted her so badly that would not be easy.

He had wanted her for such a long, long time.

"Turn toward me. I want to look into your face."

As she turned, his hand slid from her stomach to the dip of her waist. He smiled at her. He hoped his eyes did not have a predatory gleam. But he thought they might.

He held her eyes as he ran his hand up her side to the tantalizing swell of the side of her breast. Gritting his teeth, he reminded himself to go slow. He moved his hand back to her waist, then over the curve of her hip and down her thigh.

He was as tight as a bowstring.

His only thought now was that he had to touch her skin. He tugged at her tunic, but it was caught beneath her.

"Help me." He heard the desperate, pleading note to his voice, but he didn't care.

She rolled onto her back and lifted her hips, the saints be praised. Without touching her, he drew the shift up to her waist. His heart pounded in his ears. She lifted her shoulders and raised her arms as he eased it up and over her head. His hand shook as he reached to touch her. Then he shut his eyes, his whole being focused on the silky softness of her skin.

Repeating his earlier journey, he slid his hand along her side with exquisite slowness. When he brushed the still softer skin of the side of her breast, his breath caught. How long he had waited to touch her. No other woman felt this good.

In a daze of desire, he kissed her face, her hair, her neck. Against her ear, he murmured, "I have dreamed of this."

He pulled back to look at her again. Good Lord, she had her eyes squeezed shut and her arms clenched in front of her breasts. He pried one hand free and held it.

"What is it?" he asked as he looked at her across the pillow.

She did not speak or move. He pressed her hand against his cheek and turned to kiss her palm.

When she opened her eyes, he asked again, "What is wrong?"

Her eyes were wide, her lips parted. She seemed to have trouble finding her voice. "I did not know what to expect. Since you were ready at once, I . . . I thought it would be over quickly."

William guffawed. So, she had taken a good look at him as he climbed naked into bed.

Grinning, he pulled her into his arms and buried his face in her neck. "You have good cause to fear I will be much too quick this first time."

Her naked body felt glorious against him. As he moved his mouth down the curve of her neck, he whispered, "I promise I shall do better the second time. And still better the third."

He was lost in the feel of her. Her breasts against his chest, her legs against his thighs. And, oh yes, her stomach against the length of his erection.

"I have longed for this," he murmured, breathing in the scent of her skin. How could a woman smell this good?

It was no longer enough to feel her breasts against his chest; he had to touch them. The sensation of her breasts filling his hands was heaven itself. He trailed kisses down her throat to her breastbone. He turned his head to feel the softness of her skin against his cheek. The wild beating of her heart matched his own.

He kept one breast cupped in his hand as he dragged his tongue across to the other. When he reached her nipple and flicked it with his tongue, she squeaked. He smiled.

Intent on claiming every inch of her, he eased himself down her body. He ran his tongue along the undersides of her breasts and planted slow wet kisses across her flat belly. He fought the temptation to move farther down and taste her. Though the thought made his cock throb, he did not want to shock her. All things in good time.

Still he toyed with the temptation. He grazed the silky skin of her inner thigh with his fingertips as he kissed the inside of her knee. So close. Before he knew what he was doing, his hand was gripping her buttock and his mouth was where his fingers had been and was moving upward.

All he wanted in this life was to taste her and then drive into her until her screams rang in his ears.

He got up on his hands and knees and shook his head.

He looked down at her breasts and sighed. How long he'd

waited to see them. To touch them. He gave each nipple a light kiss, then wanted more. When he took the tip of one in his mouth and sucked, he was rewarded by her sharp intake of breath. He slid down to feel her body beneath him. She felt so good against his chest, his thighs, his shaft. All the while, he sucked her breast harder, losing himself in the sensation.

The urge to enter her was almost more than he could bear. Perhaps if she'd not kept him on edge every minute of the last week, he would not be so close to losing all control. He lifted his head and, breathing hard, tried to calm himself.

Dragging his gaze up from her breasts, he saw her perfect mouth. How had he missed kissing it? He desperately needed her kisses—deep, deep kisses—before he entered her. As he slid up her body to take her mouth, the sensation of skin rubbing against skin set his every nerve tingling.

She opened her legs as he moved, and he gasped as he unexpectedly found himself at the threshold. With all his being, he wanted to keep moving until he was deep inside her. One strong thrust. The urge almost overpowered him. And yet, he held back. He wanted her mouth on his first.

"Kate," he moaned as he lowered his mouth to hers.

He anticipated a warm joining of mouths and tongues as a prelude to the joining of their bodies. But she kept her lips firmly together. Something was wrong, terribly wrong. But he was sliding into her now. It was too late. He could not stop. The urge overwhelmed him, taking over his body. His mind was one with his body, set on the same goal.

He had to have her. He had to have her now.

At last. At last. At last.

He came in an explosion of pent-up lust and longing, hunger and desire. She was his. She was his.

When he was able to move, he rolled to his side, taking

her with him. He had not performed with such speed since his youth. Happy, but a little embarrassed, he held her close and kissed her face and hair.

"Sorry, Kate," he whispered, and kissed the tip of her nose. "I shall go slower next time."

"Slower?" she asked in a startled voice. She did not sound grateful for his good intentions.

He leaned up on one elbow to see her better, but he could not read her expression in the dim lamplight. Gently, he smoothed back her hair.

He hated to ask, but he had to know. "Did I hurt you?"

She shook her head and said in a soft voice, "It did not hurt at all this time."

"It hurt you before? With Rayburn?" He did not want to remember that she had belonged to another man and disliked even more having to mention the man's name here in his own bed.

Catherine tried to turn her head away, but he would not let her.

He rested his forehead lightly against hers and asked, "Did he never give you pleasure in bed?"

She drew her brows together.

This was worse than he had thought. He sighed and lay back down beside her. Perhaps he should have expected this. But he had not. In his vanity, he had never doubted that once he had her in bed, she would enjoy it.

He had heard, of course, of wives who considered going to their husbands' beds a duty to be suffered, an obligation necessary to meet their husbands' vulgar needs and produce heirs. All of his own experience, however, was with women who came to his bed for pleasure. They sought him out and returned for more.

His wife's voice brought him back abruptly to the present.

"May I go to my chamber now?"

"You are welcome to sleep here." He hoped she would.

"I am sure I could not sleep," she said, her brows going up in surprise. "And Jamie would not know where to find me. He has bad dreams sometimes."

"If you do not wish to stay tonight, I will not insist upon it," he said, still hoping she would change her mind.

Her foot was on the step beside the bed almost before the words left his mouth.

"Catherine," he said, grabbing her arm to delay her escape, "you have a husband now who wants you in his bed. You must tell Jamie he can find you here when you are not in your own bed."

As she raced out the door, he called after her, "But teach the boy to knock."

* * *

The succeeding nights were no better.

He told himself he would not take her if she did not also want him. But each night he did. As he moved inside her, he would close his eyes and think of the other Catherine. The girl who threw her head back laughing and reached for the stars.

She came to him each night without his asking. She told him she prayed daily for another child. Though he knew he did not take her against her will, he felt shamed by what he did. Each encounter left him feeling emptier than before.

Though she denied him nothing, she rejected him wholly. When she left his bed, as she always did, he told himself he hoped she would not return the next night.

But in his heart, he knew if Catherine did not come to him, he would go to her. He knew better than to want something from a woman she could not give. And yet he could not stop himself from wanting more from Catherine.

Other men kept mistresses. There were plenty of women who would gladly fill that role for him. Beautiful women. Eager women.

But he wanted no woman but Catherine.

Chapter Ten

Catherine could let her guard down, knowing she would not run into William as she went about her tasks. Early this morning, he received a report of raiders crossing the border and took a group of men to flush them out.

He seemed grateful for a reason to be away.

She met with Alys as usual. She approved the housekeeper's plan to send the household servants to do a thorough cleaning of the gatehouse while most of the men were out of the way. Next, she spoke with the cook. She wanted a hearty supper prepared for the men when they returned this evening.

At midmorning, she sent Jamie off with his nursemaid and settled herself gratefully into the quiet solitude of the solar with her embroidery. She felt confused and on edge. William's behavior bewildered her. When he looked at her with that weary sadness, she found herself wishing for the burning looks he used to give her.

She perceived she was somehow the source of his

wretchedness. But how had she failed him? She had every reason to hope he would get her with child soon. She went to his bed every night. It was not nearly as bad as she had expected. In sooth, she'd grown to like the way he kissed her face and hair...and some of the other things he did as well. Most of it was so unsettling, though, that she found it difficult to sleep afterward.

If only she had another woman to talk to! Her mother had said little about what went on between man and wife in the bedchamber beyond vague allusions to duty and perseverance. She had no sisters, no close female cousins. The only person she might have such a conversation with—though she blushed at the thought—was Abbess Talcott.

'Twas unlikely, however, that William would approve of a visit to the abbey any time soon.

She was startled from her thoughts by the crash of the solar door against the wall. Looking up, she was astonished to see Edmund Forrester filling her doorway.

"There you are!" He said it as though he'd caught her someplace she should not be. "I've been looking for you."

She could smell the strong wine on him from across the room.

"The servants know where I am," she said with a calmness she did not feel. "Any one of them could have brought a message to me."

He did not respond to her subtle reprimand for entering the family's private living quarters without invitation. Instead, he stared at her in a way that made her glad for the heavy table between them.

"What is it that you need, sir?"

With the household servants all working at the gatehouse, no one would hear her if she screamed. She chided herself for letting her imagination get away with her. She'd never felt easy with Edmund, but she had no reason to fear him.

She set down the embroidery frame she was clutching to her chest and posed her question again. "What is it that I may do for you?"

He turned and shut the door. She jumped at the sound of the bolt sliding home. Before she could gather her wits to look for something to use as a weapon, he pulled up a stool and sat across the table from her.

"There are any number of things you could do for me," he said with a broad smile. "But as you are my best friend's wife, I will not suggest them."

She fought the urge to wipe her damp palms on her skirts. She would not give him the satisfaction of seeing how frightened she was.

"I presume I have permission to use your given name?" he asked with false politeness.

She glared at him. "You do not."

"*Catherine.*" He drilled his fingers on the table, quite aware, she was sure, of the effect on her taut nerves. "You made a fool of William, claiming you could have an annulment a full week after your wedding night."

"How dare you speak to me of this?" she said, gripping the sides of her chair. "Leave my rooms at once."

"Everyone thought William unable to perform his husbandly duty." Edmund leaned forward and gave her a long, penetrating look. "But we know better, don't we, Catherine?"

Catherine folded her arms and fumed in silence, waiting for him to have his say and leave.

"You should have seen the ladies at court!" he said, leaning back and slapping the table. "I swear, the widows gave him no peace. Poor William developed the skills of a diplomat trying to keep the women with living husbands out of his bed."

Edmund dropped his smile and tapped his finger on the table. "If an annulment was yet possible, the defect was not William's."

Despite herself, her face flushed hot.

"At first, I did not believe it possible he had not taken his rights as a husband," Edmund said, rubbing his chin. "And yet, it explained much. He'd been on edge and foul-tempered ever since the wedding."

He narrowed his eyes at her. "How did you convince him not to touch you? Did you claim disease?"

Catherine stood, so angry now she was shaking. Putting her hands on the table for support, she leaned across it to make her own threat. "I shall tell my husband how you have spoken to me. I suggest you take yourself some distance from the castle when I do."

Edmund grabbed her wrist and held it. "Who do you think William will believe?" With his other hand, he slowly ran his finger up the length of her forearm. "A woman who deceived her first husband and sent him to his death? Or his best friend?"

When her gaze wavered, he said, "You may as well sit, for we are not yet done with our talk."

"If you leave marks on me," she said, looking pointedly at where he held her wrist, "William just may believe me."

When he released his grip, she hugged her arms to herself and sank back into her chair.

"I know he beds you now."

Her face grew hot again as she imagined the servants whispering each night she sent her maid away. It would be easy for Edmund to learn of it, if he had a mind to.

"Even William, tolerant as he seems to be of your antics,

would not risk having all the Marches laughing at him a second time."

She tried not to listen, tried to keep from hearing the offensive things he was saying to her. Surely he could not go on much longer.

"How is it, then," he said, his tone shifting from mocking amusement to accusation, "that William is even more miserable than before?"

She was stunned. How could Edmund be asking her the very question that troubled her?

She met his eyes without flinching and pointed to the door. "I will tolerate your insolence no longer. Get out."

Once again, he acted as though she had not spoken.

"Your husband was happy for an excuse to leave today," he said, raising his eyebrows. "Rumor of a few ragged men crossing the border was not sufficient cause for William to lead the party himself—unless he wanted badly to be gone."

The words stung and Edmund saw it.

"I have my suspicions as to the reason for William's misery," he said, watching her closely. "I wager you are as cold as stone in bed."

Cold?

"God's beard, that is it!" he said, slapping the table. He shook his head and gave a short laugh. "'Tis not enough for William to have a wife so beautiful that all the men lust after her. Nay, our William must have her warm and willing, too."

Edmund leaned forward, his humor gone. "You will never make him happy," he said, his eyes burning into her. "Leave before it is too late, before he gets you with child. You need a better plan this time. I can help you."

Catherine was stunned again. Edmund was sincere. In his

own way, he was trying to protect his friend. But from what? From her?

"William wants me to stay," she stammered. "I promised him I would not leave again."

"As if a promise matters to you!" he said, pounding the table. "William is not the first fool to trust you. Is destroying one husband not enough for you?"

His words were so harsh she felt as if he'd slapped her. It was useless to argue Rayburn deserved neither honesty nor loyalty.

"I'll not sit by while you bring William down," he said, shaking a finger at her. "Know I have my eye on you. Be warned, I will discover your secrets."

"I have no secrets." *At least none you will ever find out.*

Edmund barked a laugh and leaned back in his chair, his mood changing once again. "Perhaps another woman will divert him in time. If William wants a woman who takes pleasure in bed, there are many to oblige him."

She looked up, unable to hide the question in her eyes.

"Not yet, but he is bound to," he said with a grim smile. "If he gets another woman with child now that he is wed to you, he will hate himself. And he'll not forgive you for driving him to it. William wants no bastards."

In her mind's eye, she saw William as he was on that first night, his eyes burning with ferocious intensity. *I want children, and I will have them only with my wife.*

She lifted her chin. "No man hopes for children outside of marriage."

A look of surprise crossed his face, then shifted to smug satisfaction. He stood and leaned over the table.

"You do not know, do you, Catherine?" he said, a mocking smile on his face.

She glared up at him, refusing to ask what he meant.

"William has not told you who his father is, has he?"

"'Tis FitzAlan," she blurted out, "is it not?"

"If William has not told you who his true father is, then he has told you nothing that matters." He shook his head. "I feared lust had blinded his good judgment, but I was wrong. He trusts you not at all."

Edmund went to the door, then turned to give her his parting words. "'Tis an open secret who his father is," he said. "You must be the only one in the realm who does not know it."

* * *

Hours later, Catherine was still angry and upset about the encounter with Edmund as she sat in the kitchen garden watching Jamie. He was following a kitchen maid from plant to plant, asking questions as the girl gathered herbs.

How dare Edmund corner her and speak to her like that! She tried not to think about what he actually said. The hateful man. But she could not help it. Who was William's father? If all of England and Scotland knew, why would he keep it secret from her?

Jamie grew bored with the herbs and hopped around pretending to be a bunny. When he tired of that, he came over and tugged at her arm.

"Can we go up?" he said, pointing to the top of the wall. "Please?"

He wanted her to take him up to the walkway that ran along the top of the wall. Her spirits lifted at the suggestion. The weather was glorious, and the view of the Wye River curving through the lush green hills was breathtaking from up there.

"You must promise not to let go of my hand this time," she told him sternly. "Otherwise, I shall not take you."

As soon as they were up on the walkway, she felt herself relax. The light breeze and the late afternoon sun felt good on her skin. She could not remember a lovelier day.

She undid the circlet and net that held her hair and carefully set them on a low square of the crenellated wall. A married woman was required to keep her hair covered, but there was no one to see her. The men patrolling the wall were on the far side of the castle, near the gatehouse. William and the other men were not expected before dark.

It had been years since she felt the wind blow her hair. The sense of freedom it gave her made her want to sing with joy.

"Your hair looks pretty," Jamie said, beaming up at her.

She lifted him up and kissed him soundly.

They walked first along the south wall, facing the river. They took their time, stopping to look at birds and watch the peasants toiling in the fields. When they reached the west wall, the sun was low on the horizon over the hills. It cast a warm glow on the stone walls and the fields below.

She lifted Jamie onto a low part of the wall for a better look.

"There they are!" Jamie shouted.

She squinted against the sun and saw the line of men riding toward the castle. She could pick out William, riding at the front. As she watched, the riders veered from the path and rode across the field toward them.

Jamie waved and several of the men waved back.

What could be drawing them to this spot? As the men pulled their horses up below her, she leaned over the wall as far as she dared. She brushed away the hair blowing across her face. Then her eyes locked with William's. The burn of his gaze seared through her.

Her hair! She jumped back. Without a headdress, she felt exposed, half naked. She grabbed Jamie and ran to the closest set of steps down the wall. If she hurried, she could be inside the keep before the men rode through the gates.

* * *

A quarter hour after William saw her on the wall, Catherine arrived in the hall to greet him. Her color was high, and she was breathless from running.

The eyes of every man were on her as she swept across the room toward him. William was too spellbound himself to chastise his men for staring at her. As one, he and his men tried and failed to keep from staring at the rise and fall of her chest in the close-fitting gown.

The elaborate azure headdress made her eyes look a startling blue and emphasized her long, graceful neck. Though not a lock of hair showed, the image of her above him on the wall was seared into his mind. With her long tresses blowing about her, she'd looked like a fairy queen sent to enchant them. He suspected every man with him imagined the pale gold waves falling over naked shoulders and breasts.

But he was the only man who would see her like that.

"I am glad to see you home safe, husband," she said, dipping her head in greeting.

A slow smile spread across his face as he lifted her hand to his lips. "And I am glad to be home."

Chapter Eleven

After sending hot water up to William's chamber, Catherine went to the kitchen to make certain all was in order. The cook had everything well in hand, of course, but Catherine needed to keep busy.

She touched her headdress to be sure it was in place as she returned to the hall for supper. At least William did not chastise her in front of his men, as Rayburn would have. She smiled to herself, recalling the warmth in William's eyes when he kissed her hand. Perhaps he was not too angry with her.

At supper, she listened with half an ear to the men's talk of their fruitless search for rebels. Edmund's harsh words plagued her. What if he was right? Was it possible William was unhappy with what took place between them in the bedchamber?

What could be wrong? She had every reason to hope he would get her with child soon. William was able to perform each time. And he wanted to do it. Over and over.

He did seem to dawdle. Perhaps that was a sign of trouble. It made it harder and harder for her to keep her mind on something else. She sighed, at a loss.

The platters were not yet cleared from the table when William stood and announced he was tired and would retire. The men exchanged glances, and one or two smothered a laugh. They stopped when she looked at them sharply, trying to discern the source of their amusement.

When her gaze met Edmund's, he tapped his finger next to his eye as if to remind her he was watching her. Hateful, hateful man. Then he dropped his gaze to her chest and lifted his eyebrow, just to annoy her. She put her hand over her chest and glared at him.

"Catherine?" William was holding his hand out to her.

She took it, glad to leave. She'd rather be lectured about having her hair uncovered than remain in the same room with Edmund.

She had trouble keeping up with William's pace. He was not as tired as he claimed. As soon as they reached their rooms, he shouted at the maid to leave and pulled her into his bedchamber.

Belatedly, she realized he did not bring her upstairs to lecture her about headdresses.

He barred the door, which made her feel anxious and trapped. Though he made no move to touch her, her heart was racing.

"You looked so beautiful up on the wall, with your hair flying in the wind," he said in a wistful voice. "It was just like when—"

He stopped himself and did not finish the thought aloud. After a moment, he said, "'Twas nice to have a wife to greet me when I came home. It is new to me."

His kind words and soft voice calmed her a bit. He stepped

closer but still did not touch her. She had the disconcerting feeling that he was waiting for her, that he wanted her to do something.

"I want to be a good wife to you," she stammered. "I beg your pardon. I should not have been outside with my hair down like a young girl."

He put his hands on her shoulders. His breath was warm on her ear as he leaned down to whisper, "Take it down for me now."

She swallowed. "Unless you want me to call my maid, you will have to help me with the pins in the back."

He spun her around. With a deftness that showed experience she did not want to think about, he had the headdress off in no time. He shook her hair loose with his fingers; it felt good to have it down again. As he massaged her scalp, she closed her eyes. A small sigh escaped her.

She was helpless to unfasten the long row of buttons at the back of her close-fitting gown, so he did that, too. Though she assured him she could manage the rest alone, he continued to help her undress. When the last garment came off, she sidestepped out of his reach and slipped under the bedclothes.

She watched surreptitiously as he removed his own clothes. Except for his arousal—which she tried not to look at—he was quite beautiful. She liked the strong planes of his face; the long lines of his lean, muscled body; his large, capable hands. In the lamplight, the hair on his head and chest glinted gold and red.

As he slid into bed, she wondered if it was possible to ever get used to the feel of a naked man beside her, the tingly feeling of skin touching skin from head to foot. He pulled her into his arms and let her rest there, her head against his chest. She loved this part. She could lie with him like this forever.

She sighed—and immediately wished she had not. William took it as a sign he should begin what they were here for.

Damn that Edmund. It was so confusing! She let William touch her in all the ways he wanted. She refused him nothing. Yet, tonight she felt a tension, an expectation. William wanted something from her, but she did not know what it was.

William rolled on top of her, his weight on his elbows, and began kissing her face and neck. The warmth of his mouth and breath felt good on her skin. Should she tell him? But she remembered Rayburn slapping her so hard she saw stars when she had interrupted his efforts. And so she kept quiet.

"I cannot do it!" William said, pounding his fists against the mattress. Abruptly, he rolled off her.

Her shock was so great that at first she could do nothing. After a few moments of tense silence, she raised herself onto her elbow to look at him. He lay with his arms crossed over his face, as if warding off an attacker.

"William?" She touched his arm with her fingertip.

He rolled away from her and pounded his fist against the mattress again.

God help her, what could she have done to cause him to behave like this?

Sitting up, she gripped his shoulder and shook him. "William, what is it? What have I done?"

When he still did not answer, she used all her weight to pull him onto his back to face her.

"You must tell me, please," she pleaded, but he kept his arms over his face, unable or unwilling to speak to her. "Whatever it is, I am sorry with all my heart."

She ran her fingers over the side of his face, but he rolled away from her again. Pressing herself against his back, she rubbed her hands up and down his sides and kissed his neck and shoulders, attempting to comfort him. Still, he made no response. Desperate, she crawled over him and wriggled under his arm until she was burrowed against his chest.

She put her arm around his waist and patted his back. "It is all right. I am here," she murmured, just as she would with Jamie.

He took a long shuddering breath. She felt the tension of his muscles ease beneath her hands.

"I do not know why I displease you so much," she said against his chest. "You must tell me what I can do to remedy it."

William put his hand to her cheek and gave her a small smile that eased her heart. "I have wanted you to put your arms around me, and it feels as good as I imagined."

She blinked at him. "Is that all you require?"

"Nay, 'tis not all, but it is a start." His smile was slightly wider now.

"What else?"

"I want you to kiss me."

This, too, seemed a fairly simple task. She touched her lips to his, then looked at him expectantly.

"That is nice, but not quite what I want. Will you let me teach you how lovers kiss?" His smile had reached his eyes and was positively wicked now.

Her confidence faltered. She felt out of her depth, but she nodded. She wanted to please him.

His lips were soft and warm, and he kept them on hers for a long time. When she thought he was finally finished, he ran his tongue across her bottom lip. It was hard to breathe, and she opened her mouth. When he slipped his tongue inside, she gasped.

The next time, she knew what to expect and opened her

mouth to him. She had trouble thinking of anything except the kiss this time, though it went on even longer.

He pulled back to look into her eyes. "I don't want you to leave me this time."

She swallowed back the surge of hurt rising from her chest. Why would he bring that up now? She dropped her gaze to his chest and said, "I promised you I would not run away again."

"That is not what I mean." With a sigh, he pushed a strand of hair from her forehead. "When I take you to bed, you let me have your body, but your mind and spirit are elsewhere."

He lifted her chin with his finger. "I do not want to have you like that anymore, Kate. I want you with me. All of you."

Her breath caught as she finally understood what he wanted. She was not at all sure she could do what he asked.

"I had to, with Rayburn," she protested. "I had to. There would have been nothing left of me." A tear slipped from the corner of her eye, and he rubbed it away with his thumb.

"I know," he said, kissing her forehead. "But you have no need to protect yourself from me. You can trust me."

He believed he told her the truth. Resolving to believe it, too, she nodded.

He looked at her thoughtfully. Then, suddenly, he rolled onto his back. Was he giving up on her so soon?

"Sit up, sweetheart."

Feeling uneasy, she did as he asked. She felt embarrassed and exposed—until she saw that his eyes were closed.

"Give me your hand," he said, waving his arm blindly.

Curiosity vied with uncertainty as she gave him her hand. She felt his hot breath on her palm as he pressed it to his lips. Then he took her wrist and laid the flat of her hand on his chest.

"I want you to touch me."

He guided her hand in a slow circular motion over his chest. The feel of the rough hair under her palm sent an unexpected sensation up her arm, right to her stomach. He released his hold and let his arm fall to his side. With his eyes still closed, he lay still, waiting.

Hesitantly, she skimmed her fingertips over his chest. The corners of his mouth turned up. Encouraged, she shifted her weight so that she could use both hands. His breathing grew shallow as she ran her fingers in increasingly wider circles. She explored the textures of his skin, sliding her fingers over the dip below his collarbone, the coarse hair of his chest, the smooth skin at his sides.

Because he relinquished control to her, the urge to escape did not overtake her. In fact, she was surprised to discover she liked touching him. He seemed all golden muscle beneath her hands.

After assuring herself his eyes were still closed, she allowed herself a good look at his member. It was, after all, sticking out right in front of her. She kept her eyes on it as she drew her fingernails from his sides to the center of his belly. His sharp intake of breath startled her, and she looked up at his face.

"Feels good," he said on a long breath.

Feeling more confident, she trailed her fingers over his hip bones, on either side of his shaft. She smiled when he shivered, enjoying the power of her touch.

Leaning over him, she rubbed firm hands up over his chest and shoulders and sent featherlight strokes down his arms. His whispered, "God in heaven," told her what she needed to know.

She kissed his shoulder and was rewarded with a sigh. Pleased, she trailed kisses along his throat and rubbed her cheek against his chest. This time, it was she who sighed. Letting her hair drag over him, she inched her way down toward the flat of his stomach, dropping kisses along the way.

She felt William's hand rest lightly on her head, touching her for the first time since the start. As he ran his fingers through her hair, she rested her head against his hip, enjoying the sensation. Tentatively, she slid her finger over his shaft. He jolted half upright, jostling her head.

She sat up straight and stared at him.

"Sorry," he said, touching her cheek. "I was not expecting it."

Her face hot with embarrassment, she averted her eyes.

"Catherine, please," he said, taking her gently by the shoulders. "I would not have you feel shamed about what we do in bed, not ever. And certainly not for something that felt so good."

He gathered her into his arms and pulled her down to lay beside him. His breath was hot against her skin as he kissed her forehead, the side of her face, her hair. When he sucked on her earlobe and breathed in her ear, she pressed closer against him.

"Here, touch me again," he said, taking her hand.

Before she could pull away, her hand was on his shaft again. Gingerly, she explored the surprisingly silky skin over the firmness underneath. His breathing changed as she ran her hand up and down its length. Breathing a little hard herself, she did it again. And again.

He groaned and pressed his mouth to her neck, sucking against her skin. Her head fell back. Of its own accord, her body moved against his in rhythm with the movement of her hand.

He grabbed her wrist. "No more. I cannot—" He broke off, apparently unable to form more words.

She understood it was not displeasure that made him ask her to stop. If she had had any doubt, the deep kiss he gave her next removed it. She felt herself merging into him as she focused with every part of her being on that kiss, on his tongue sliding in and out of her mouth.

She held on to him as he rolled her on top of him. When she lifted her head to smile at him, her hair fell in a curtain around his face. He kissed the tip of her nose. The feel of his chest against her breasts and the hardness of his shaft against her belly made it difficult to breathe.

She closed her eyes as he stroked his hands up and down her back. When he moved them along the sides of her breasts, she felt it all the way to her center. She let him draw her into another long kiss before she forced herself to pull away.

Rising to her hands and knees above him, she said with mock severity, "I thought I was to do the touching."

Obligingly, he dropped his hands. "Do what you will with me."

She leaned down to run her tongue along his collarbone and gasped when the tips of her breasts rubbed against his chest. It felt so good she did it again. Slowly this time.

She forgot to reprimand him when large, warm hands covered her breasts. When he rubbed his thumbs over her nipples, the sensation that gripped her was so strong she had to rest her forehead on his chest.

She moaned in complaint when he stopped to lift her higher on the bed. Forgiveness came quickly as she felt the wetness of his tongue circle her nipple. At the same time, he took the other nipple between his thumb and forefinger. Her hips swayed as she was drawn into a swirl of sensation. When he took her breast in his mouth and sucked, she squeezed her eyes shut against the jolt it sent through her. Nothing, nothing, nothing felt as good as this.

Just when she thought nothing could divert her from the feeling of his mouth on her breast, she felt his fingers sliding up the inside of her thigh. He dragged his fingers up and down, each time coming closer to her center. The rampant sensations racing through her now were more than she could bear.

Her body tensed with anticipation. Closer, closer. When his hand brushed the hair between her legs, a shiver went through her. All her concentration was on willing him to touch her again. When he barely brushed her a second time, she wanted to pound her fist against the bed in frustration.

Finally, finally, he pressed his fingers to the aching spot. It was as if he had known all along exactly where she needed to be touched and how. Her body began to move against his hand.

He took hold of her hips. Every part of her skin that touched him tingled as he pulled her along his body. He eased her down until the sensitive place he had been rubbing with his hand touched the tip of his shaft.

She stiffened.

"You have trusted me this far," he said, his voice tight, strained. "Trust me for the rest."

Putting his hands on either side of her face, he pulled her into a kiss. Their tongues danced together in a rhythm her body knew. The kiss was wet and hot and not enough. This time when the tip of his shaft touched her, she pressed against it. She wanted to be touched there, to feel him hard against her.

"Do not leave me, Kate," he rasped in her ear. "Do not leave me."

As he slid inside her, she inhaled at the unexpected rush of pleasure. They lay nearly motionless, breathing hard. Her body was tight, tense, aware of every inch of him inside her.

He kissed her face and hair. She resisted when he pushed her up by her shoulders, regretting any distance between them.

"You are so beautiful." The strength of the desire in his voice wiped away any awkwardness she felt at finding herself sitting astride him. And the pressure inside her felt so good.

He grasped her hips again. As he showed her how to move, the heat in his eyes almost burned her skin. Soon, her body found its own rhythm, and she was moving helplessly against him.

She leaned over him, needing to kiss him now. The tips of her breasts brushed against his chest as their mouths joined. She pressed her hips against him as he pushed up against her. Finally, she had to break away to breathe. She leaned back, losing herself wholly to the movement, aware of nothing but the powerful sensations emanating from where their bodies were joined.

"Slower, Kate," he begged. "Slower, please."

But she ignored his plea. The sensations pulsed through her, nearly blinding her. As they overtook her, she fell forward and grabbed on to his shoulders. From a distance, she heard screaming as spasms of pleasure shook her.

"God have mercy!" she said as she collapsed over him.

He folded his arms around her and held her tightly against his chest. When she gasped, "I cannot breathe," he eased his hold and ran his fingers lightly over her back. Her skin was so sensitive that she shivered. Her body spasmed as she realized she could still feel the full length of him deep inside her.

As she listened to his rapid heartbeat against her ear, she tried to piece together what had just happened to her. A wave of embarrassment hit her.

"Was that me screaming?" she asked in a whisper.

With an inarticulate groan, he gripped her shoulders and

pressed himself deeper inside her. His answer came in huffs as he thrust against her. "Aye. Aye. Aye."

She pushed herself up to lean against him, arms extended, and moved with him. The ache inside her grew. His need, his urgency became hers. Faster and harder, he slammed against her. She felt it coming again and wanted to beg him not to stop. And then she felt him surge inside her and heard him cry her name. Triumphant, she went over the edge with him.

* * *

Catherine felt light-headed from lack of sleep as she lay awake, watching the sleeping form of her husband in the gray light of early dawn. She sighed in contentment. It had been a long and wondrous night.

William taught her the joy that is possible between a man and a woman, the miraculous giving and receiving of pleasure. But she also learned something he did not intend to teach her. Something, she was certain, he did not yet know himself.

"Do not leave me, do not leave me," he whispered each time he was deep inside her.

She sensed the core loneliness in him. She understood his words meant more than that he wanted her fully with him in bed.

This physical pleasure, astonishing as it was, was only the beginning of what he needed from her.

Chapter Twelve

For the first time in his life, William dreaded going to war. He did not want to be away from Catherine for a single night.

For now, King Henry and the prince were busy sweeping up the last remnants of the rebellion in the North. The Welsh had been quiet since their losses at Grosmont and Pwll Melyn in the spring. The lull in the fighting, however, would not last.

Soon, he would be off fighting the Welsh. Perhaps the French as well. Once the fighting began again, he might be gone for weeks. He tried not to think of it.

Still, he worked his men hard to keep their skills sharp so they would be prepared. He had only to catch a glimpse of Catherine, though, to be distracted. If she walked into the hall while he was talking with his men or crossed the bailey yard while they practiced with their weapons, he would stop in place and watch her until she passed from sight.

His men were amused by the change in him. They had

always respected him as a sure and talented commander, a skilled fighter, a man who kept his word. But they had never been at ease with him before. Now he laughed at jokes they would never have told him before. They even teased him about the cause of the new lightness in his step.

To a man, they were green with envy when Catherine left the hall on his arm each night. Truth be told, he suspected thcy weie all a little in love with her. Even so, they were all pleased for him.

All, that is, save for Edmund Forrester.

Edmund warned him to watch for the betrayal he was sure would come.

* * *

The next weeks passed in a blur of happiness for Catherine. She and William could not wait for night to come. As often as he could, he slipped away for an hour or two in the middle of the day to whisk her off to their rooms.

Jamie adored William and followed him around like a puppy. Every time she heard Jamie squeal with delight as William swung the boy onto his shoulders, she thanked God for her blessings. She would not have dared hope for so much only a few weeks before.

There was just one mar on her happiness: Her husband still did not trust her. Edmund's goading bothered her even more now that she bared her own soul to William every night.

"William, you have never told me about your family or your home in the North," she said as they lay in bed.

They had come to bed early, as had become their habit, and spent themselves making love. The summer evening sky was still light enough for her to see the outline of his strong features.

She decided that if he trusted her enough to share his secret with her, she would tell him about Edmund's behavior. She could be sure then that he would believe her.

She propped herself up on one elbow and rested her hand on his bare chest. "I want to know everything."

"Everything?" He waggled his eyebrows, trying to make a joke of it. "All the women as well?"

She narrowed her eyes at him. "Just the ugly ones."

He laughed and kissed her.

"Stop it!" she said between kisses. "You are trying to divert me."

He rolled her onto her back and pressed his erection against her hip. "Tell me I am succeeding."

He trailed kisses down her neck. When she gave in, she did so wholeheartedly.

She did not, however, forget her question. The next morning, she grabbed his arm as he was slipping out of bed.

"Why will you not tell me?"

"Tell you what?" he said, pretending not to understand.

"About your family."

"Must you badger me about this, woman?"

Hurt, she released his arm and said nothing more.

William began to dress. The silence was strained, but she was not going to be the one to break it. William picked up his boots and sat down to put them on.

"All right, Catherine." He expelled a deep breath, making no effort to hide his exasperation.

He jerked on one boot. "Like most boys, I was sent off for my training at an early age." He jerked on the other boot. "Perhaps I was a bit younger than most."

He stood and took his belt from the back of the chair. "I was never close to any of my family. Except for John."

She noticed how his voice changed when he mentioned John.

"He was my half brother, younger by three years," he said as he strapped on his sword. In a tone meant to convey the subject was closed, he said, "John is dead. Without him, there is nothing and no one for me in the North."

"What of your mother and father? Are they still living?"

William picked up his leather riding gloves from the chest where Thomas had set them out the evening before. "Will these be your parting words to me, Catherine? My men await me."

"Oh, you go to Hereford!" she cried, putting her hand to her mouth. "I had forgotten."

He was meeting with the other Marcher lords in Hereford and would be gone at least four days. She leapt out of the bed and into his arms. His clothes felt rough against her bare skin.

"I wish I could go with you," she said.

"That would be far too dangerous." He smiled and winked at her. "These Marcher lords are a conniving lot, so I must have my wits about me."

"But I know the whole conniving lot and could advise you," she said. "Watch out for Lord Grey. He has the land north of here and wants to add some of ours to his."

"The risk is too great to take you, since I travel with only a half-dozen men." He kissed her forehead. "I am leaving most of the men here to keep watch on this part of the border."

She leaned against him, knowing the argument was lost.

"You and Jamie will be safe here," he said, rubbing his hand up and down her back. "I am leaving Edmund in command."

"Not Edmund!" She said it before she knew it.

"He is the best man I have," William said. "I trust him to keep Ross Castle—and you—safe until I return."

She put her hand on her hip and pressed her lips together.

"That is more important to me than whether you like the man, Catherine. I do not know what you find so objectionable about him. Edmund is a good man."

She did not want to argue with William as he was leaving. Instead, she wound her arms around her husband's neck and gave him a kiss she hoped he would remember all the way to Hereford.

* * *

Catherine went out to the garden with Jamie, hoping the sunshine would lift the melancholy that settled over her after William's departure. She watched Jamie try to catch a grasshopper. Each time he brought his cupped hands over it, it leapt away just in time. It got away for good when William's manservant came into the garden and interrupted Jamie's concentration.

"What is it, Thomas?"

"M'lady, there are men at the gate. They've come from the North to see Lord FitzAlan." He hesitated, then added, "One of them is FitzAlan's brother."

"His brother?" She must have misheard Thomas. William just told her this morning that his brother was dead.

"He is only a youth, m'lady. A boy."

"But we were not expecting anyone," she said, unable to hide her surprise.

"I happened to be near the gate when they arrived." Thomas cleared his throat, looking uncomfortable. "One of the men escorting him recognized me and told me the boy's mother sent him."

She thought she heard Thomas say under his breath, "Saints preserve us."

"Thank you, Thomas. I will come at once." Trying to sound pleased, she said, "Come, Jamie, we have guests!"

She felt uneasy. 'Twas odd that they received no prior word of this visit. And why had William not seen fit to mention this younger—*living*—brother to her?

She hurried across the bailey with Thomas and Jamie in tow. On the way, she stopped a passing servant to give instructions.

"Jane, tell Cook we have guests and need refreshments brought to the hall at once. Tell Alys to have rooms prepared."

She did not recognize the livery of the dozen men waiting on the other side of the portcullis, but they had the look of Northerners. Perhaps it was all the ginger hair and beards, or the way they stood as though they owned the world and were almost hoping for a fight.

She signaled for the guards to open the gate and waited as the men rode in. A well-dressed youth of perhaps twelve or thirteen dismounted and stepped forward, fidgeting with his hat. He was a good-looking boy with auburn hair, warm brown eyes, and a smattering of freckles across his cheeks and the bridge of his nose. He looked not one whit like William.

The lad looked over her shoulder, as though expecting someone else. Realizing his rudeness, he colored.

Catherine had to stifle a smile as he gave her a beautiful, if rather dramatic, bow.

"I am Stephen Neville Carleton." His voice broke with nervousness as he said it. "I thought to find my brother, Lord William Neville FitzAlan, here. If you would kindly tell him I am here, m'lady, I would be most grateful."

"I'm afraid Lord FitzAlan has been called away," she told him. "I do not know if you received news of your brother's marriage, but I am Lady Catherine, your new sister-in-law."

She gave him a warm smile. Though she did not know it, from that moment, young Stephen was hers.

"Welcome to Ross Castle," she said to the men who accompanied Stephen. "I am sure Lord FitzAlan will be as grateful to you as I am for bringing his brother to us safely."

The men took turns bowing and introducing themselves.

"The servants will take care of your horses," she said, bidding them to follow her. "We have refreshments for you in the hall."

She took Stephen's arm and walked with him toward the keep. They were of a height so that her face was close to his as she asked him about his journey. He had an appealing, almost pretty face, with large dark eyes, a straight nose, and full rosy lips. As he got older and his looks turned more masculine, he would have the ladies sighing.

As they passed through the second gate to the inner bailey, Edmund came running down the steps of the keep two at a time. He shouted greetings at a couple of the Northerners who came with Stephen.

"So this is young Stephen," Edmund said, thumping him on the back. "I would not have known you. You were crawling on all fours and smelling of piss when last I saw you."

Stephen scrunched his shoulders and made a face, but Edmund did not appear to notice.

"This will be quite a surprise for William," Edmund said.

It sounded like a warning; from the wary look on Stephen's face, the lad took it as such.

As soon as she had the visitors settled at table with wine and ale, Edmund appeared at her side.

"Pardon us a moment," he said to the others. His smile was polite, but his grip on her arm was unyielding. "The lady and I have an urgent matter to discuss."

He marched her into the corridor outside the hall.

"Why was I not called?" he demanded. "William made me responsible for the safety of this castle. You should not have ordered the gate open without my permission!"

"I do not need your permission to admit guests here," she said between clenched teeth. "I admitted no dangerous men, only my lord's young brother and his escort."

"God's beard, how could you be sure it was his brother? And a man's brother may also be his enemy. William can tell you that, if you do not know it."

"But you know these men," she argued, "and that boy is surely no threat."

"My God, woman, we are in the midst of rebellion," he said, raising his hands in the air. "You shall not act so foolishly again while I am in charge."

Catherine was too angry to concede anything. "You hear me well, Edmund Forrester," she said, shaking a finger in his face. "I have been the mistress of this castle since I was twelve years old. You may order the men about, but you shall not give orders to me."

She jerked her arm from his hold and left him there, wishing she had a door to slam.

* * *

Thomas watched Edmund take Lady Catherine from the hall. He did not like it. Not at all. Hearing their raised voices, he grew more concerned. He drummed his fingers as he thought of an excuse to interrupt them.

The door was flung open, and Lady Catherine entered, eyes blazing and silk skirts flowing out behind her. The men in the hall stopped, their cups midair, to watch her.

She looked for all the world like a beautiful avenging angel. Thomas shook his head in wonder. Surely, God had found the perfect woman for William. A woman strong enough to break through his barriers, to demand his heart, to heal his wounds.

Chapter Thirteen

William ended his business in Hereford early and set a fast pace for home. Home. It struck him that Ross Castle was the first place he had ever thought of as his home.

His mother's house was never that. His very existence had been a source of strain. As soon as his mother could convince Northumberland to take him into his household, she sent him. William's status on Northumberland's vast estates was complex and uncertain. No one knew whether to treat him as a poor relation of Northumberland's first wife, which he was, or as the great man's son.

William's true relationship to Northumberland was an open secret. God's truth, it would have been difficult to deny he was a Percy. He looked like a younger version of Hotspur.

Although Northumberland never claimed him, he assumed William's fealty. Likely he thought William should be grateful just for being brought into his service to train for knighthood.

In time, Northumberland let him lead a few men in the frequent skirmishes along the Scottish border. William proved able and rose in the ranks. After a few years, Northumberland gave him command of a portion of his army. Remnants of that force still served under William.

This past spring, Northumberland sent him to fight against the Welsh rebels. The great man saw no need to tell William he was sent as a diversion, a false show of Percy loyalty. While William fought with the king, his father was in York hatching another conspiracy.

When Northumberland made his move against the king, he ordered William to return to the North with all possible speed. William ignored the call. He'd sworn his oath to King Henry. All he had of value was his honor—and his fighting skills. While his father took up arms against the king in the North, William fought rebels in Wales.

William pushed aside his memories of that difficult time. At the next rise in the road, Ross Castle appeared on the horizon, and his thoughts returned to Catherine. She was the reason he left Hereford in such a hurry.

But Edmund's words of warning came back to him.

"What man would not want such a woman in his bed? But for God's sake, do not trust her," Edmund harped at him. "Have a care, or one day you'll find she's opened the gates to rebels—or made false accusations about you to the prince."

Trust came hard to a man who grew up having uncertain ties and no true place in the world. While William did not truly believe Catherine would betray him, he kept his guard up.

He tried to, anyway. His resolve was slipping day by day.

His anticipation grew as he approached the gate. He looked up at the ramparts, half expecting to see her there watching for him. 'Twas foolish to be disappointed. She did not expect him for another day.

Who would have thought three days could seem so long? All he wanted was to get her alone in their bedchamber, to feel her naked against his skin.

He threw his reins to a stable boy and left his men without a word. Ignoring their ribald remarks, he ran ahead to the keep. He looked up at the sun. Almost noon. He would find her with the rest of the household at dinner in the hall.

He burst through the doors, and she was there, just where he expected to find her. She stood and called his name, pleasure radiating from her face. His heart leapt in his chest as he strode across the room to her, intent on sweeping her into his arms and kissing her senseless.

He did hold her tantalizingly close before she put a firm hand against his chest and offered her cheek.

"William, we have guests," she whispered in his ear.

Damn, damn, damn. Grudgingly, he released her and turned to see what fool had the poor sense to visit today.

He looked around the table, taking in each man. With a sinking feeling, he recognized the livery of Carleton, his mother's latest husband. He supposed he should stop thinking of Carleton as her "latest," since she'd been married to him for a dozen years or more.

It never ceased to amaze him how his conniving mother managed to end up with men who had a knack for choosing the losing side of every major political intrigue. Carleton had sided with Northumberland in this latest debacle. The man lost most of his lands—but was lucky to keep his head.

William nodded at the men he recognized as his gaze moved from man to man along the table. When he came to the boy sitting next to Catherine, he started. The resemblance to his mother was striking. This boy had to be Eleanor's youngest son.

The boy stood and gave him a bow. Looking at William with their mother's bold brown eyes, he said, "Greetings, sir. I am Stephen Neville Carleton."

"Aye, I can see that is who you are." William neither smiled nor moved to greet the boy. "How is it that you find yourself here at Ross Castle?"

"William!" He heard Catherine's whispered reproach but ignored it.

The boy blushed, but he held William's gaze. "Our mother insisted on sending me."

"There is no thwarting her," William said, shaking his head. "Sit down, Stephen."

He could hardly send the boy away in the middle of his dinner. While William washed his hands in the basin a servant brought to him, Catherine filled his trencher. It had been hours since he rode out of Hereford, and he was ravenous.

"Where is Jamie?" he asked Catherine as he stabbed a hunk of roasted pork.

"He was worn out from trying to keep up with Stephen. His nursemaid took him up for a rest as soon as he finished eating."

After William ate enough to take the edge off his hunger, he leaned forward to address Stephen, who sat on the other side of Catherine.

"So, how old are you, Stephen Carleton?"

"Twelve, sir."

"Tell me, what is Lady Eleanor's intent in sending you here?" He pointed his eating knife at the boy. "I want to hear both what she told you and what you believe is her true purpose."

The boy raised his eyebrows in a manner so reminiscent of their mother that William could not keep the sarcastic edge from his voice. "You cannot have lived with her for twelve years and not know the two are different."

Stephen paused as if considering his answer, then said, "Mother said it was past time we knew each other." After a quick sideways glance at Catherine, he added, "And she wants me to tell her of your new wife."

Catherine gave the boy a reassuring smile and patted his arm.

"I believe she spoke the truth," Stephen said. "But those were not her only reasons."

"What else does she want?" William asked.

"Although she said this was a visit, I believe she intends for you to take me into your household." Stephen shrugged his shoulder. "You are the only one of us in the king's good graces."

That rang true. But William sensed the boy was holding something back. "Tell me. Out with it now."

"'Tis possible she wants you to arrange a marriage for me," the boy said, blushing furiously. "Not that she would wish me to marry now, but she wants a betrothal."

Stephen looked pained. "She gave me a letter for you. I expect she instructs—ah, asks—you to use your influence to get me betrothed to a wealthy heiress."

William could not help but feel some sympathy for the boy. With both him and John beyond her reach, their mother's ambition would all fall on her youngest. The woman could be relentless.

"I appreciate your candor," William said. "You are not as much like our mother as you look."

William took a drink of wine, then asked, "So tell me, Stephen Carleton, is wealth all you want in a wife?"

"Not all," the boy mumbled, giving Catherine a furtive glance. He colored again and fixed his eyes on the table.

William rubbed his hands over his face. He had not seen this young brother since Stephen had been a babe—and not for long then. Truth be told, he'd forgotten all about him. Now that the lad was here, what was he going to do with him? Should he send him back? Leave him at the mercy of their mother?

He would have to think on it long and hard.

"You can stay until I decide what to do with you," he said, and stood up. "Now I must speak with my wife."

"I have matters to report to you, things you must hear," Edmund said, also rising.

"All seems safe and sound, Edmund. I will find you later," William said, keeping his eyes on Catherine. "Come, m'lady wife," he said, offering her his hand.

As soon as they were out the doorway, he pulled her around the corner. He kissed her long and hard, not caring if a passing servant saw them.

When he moved his hand to her breast, she said, "Not here, William!"

He took her by the wrist and led her up the stairs to the solar. As soon as he closed the door, he had her up against it.

"It seems like three months, not three days," he said amidst a frenzy of kisses.

He wanted to touch her everywhere at once. With a hunger of her own, she met him kiss for kiss and touch for touch. Her little moans of pleasure increased the urgency of his desire. Unfastening the endless line of buttons was beyond him. He sucked on her breast through the bodice of her gown until he felt her nipple harden through the layers of cloth.

His cock was so hard it pained him. He would die if he didn't have her soon.

He worked her skirts up until, at last, he felt bare thighs above her stockings. Groaning with pleasure, he slid his hands along her warm skin. She caught his face in her hands and locked her mouth on his, hot and wet and urgent. When she sucked his tongue, he felt it to his toes. He thought he would explode.

He cupped her bare buttocks, lifting her off the ground, and ground against her. His need was mindless, pulsing.

Afraid of frightening her with the violence of his passion, he leaned over her shoulder to rest his forehead against the door. He closed his eyes and tried to slow his breathing. His effort at control was severely challenged when she wrapped her legs around him.

"Catherine, if you want me to stop, you must drop your legs," he said in a ragged voice. He did not ease his pressure holding her against the door. "If you leave them around me like this, I cannot be sure I will hear you if you tell me later."

Her breath in his ear was as hard and fast as his own.

"I want you inside me. Now."

The saints preserve him! With one hand, he loosed the ties that held his leggings as he kissed her fiercely. Then, in one strong thrust, he was deep inside her. The only place he wanted to be. Sweet Jesus! He hoped she would forgive him, but he could not go slowly. Not this time. As he pumped into her, her high gasping breaths sent him to the very edge. She screamed in his ear, and he went over with her.

Afterward, his legs were so weak he was afraid he would topple to the floor with her. He leaned one arm against the door until he could get his balance. With her legs still wrapped around him, he managed to carry her into the bed-chamber and collapse with her on the bed.

Good God! He was light-headed and out of breath. Never in his life had he wanted a woman that badly.

They lay side by side, barely touching, staring at the

ceiling. When she still said nothing, he thought uneasily of the night he caused her to flee to the abbey. Though he was not drunk this time, his behavior was no less aggressive, no less coarse. Nay, he was worse this time.

God's beard. He had taken her against the wall, faster than lightning, without so much as a greeting.

What had he been thinking? The truth, of course, was that he had not been thinking at all.

"I did not intend to misuse you," he said. "I just wanted you so much."

She took his hand and squeezed it. "And I you."

Hearing no censure in her voice, he sighed with relief. "So you will not be packing off to join a nunnery the moment I close my eyes?" He was only half joking.

She laughed. "'Tis much too late for that!"

"Aye," he agreed, smiling back at her. "No one who has seen us these past weeks would believe this marriage was not consummated."

His heart turned in his chest as he looked into her face. The spark was back in Catherine's eyes, as the abbess said. He meant to keep it there.

"Do you think I could be with child already?"

He heard the hopefulness in her voice and felt an unfamiliar joy rise in him. She would be the mother of his children. He had no words to tell her what this meant to him. Hoping to show her how grateful he was, he pulled her into his arms and gave her a long, gentle kiss.

One kiss led to another. This time, he took her with a slowness that nearly drove them both mad. When they finished, he lay sprawled across the bed. He felt suffused with well-being and peace.

He was jarred from this pleasant state when Catherine sat up and burst into convulsive weeping.

"What is it?" he asked, jolting upright. "What could be wrong?"

He had half expected something like this earlier, after he'd taken her against the door. But, God in heaven, why was she upset now? The second time, he'd been slow and gentle. She had certainly seemed to appreciate his efforts.

"I do not mean to weep," she said, wiping her tears away with her hands.

Her shoulders shook again, and she tried to turn away from him, but he put his arms around her and held her.

"Kate," he said into her hair. "Tell me."

She took a shaky breath. "It is just that I feel so close to you when we are like this."

He kissed her fingers and looked into her wet eyes, waiting for her to make sense of this for him.

"But I know it is an illusion." She wiped her hand under her nose. "'Tis all false."

He had never felt so close to a woman before, but he was not sure how to tell her that. Or whether he should. Instead, he asked, "Why do you think it false?"

"Because you do not trust me at all."

There was a long silence between them. When he did not take the opportunity she gave him to confess, she laid out her complaint in full.

"You have told me nothing. Nothing. Nothing of your family, your life. Imagine my surprise at finding a boy at our gate claiming to be your brother, when the only brother you mentioned to me is dead."

Once she started, she was going to say it all.

"I have to learn from a twelve-year-old boy that Northumberland is your father! That Hotspur was your brother!" She was sputtering now, her anger gaining ground. "I am your wife, and everyone knows this but me.

"You distrusted me because I fought my husband's treachery. Yet, I did not go against my own blood as you did." She gestured wildly as she spoke, pressing her hand to her chest each time she referred to herself.

"You fought on the king's side when it was your own father and brother who led the Northern rebels." She shook her finger at him. "Do not tell me your brother and father did not expect you to join them or that they did not feel betrayed when you did not."

William let her talk until she ran out of words. His reasons for not telling her no longer seemed important. He had hurt her, and he did not want to do that anymore.

"Where would you like me to start?"

* * *

Catherine listened as William told her his story.

"My mother played a high-stakes game and lost," he began. "Northumberland took his time looking for a second wife after the death of his first wife, Margaret Neville Percy. He had three sons by Margaret, so he could bide his time.

"My mother was Margaret's niece and visited often." In an indifferent tone, he added, "She is quite beautiful.

"She was married to an elderly man named FitzAlan. She might have looked forward to life as a wealthy widow if FitzAlan had not crossed King Richard. When most of FitzAlan's lands were seized, she anticipated the need for a second husband. She set her sights high.

"She toyed with Northumberland, putting him off until FitzAlan was on his deathbed," he continued. "When she found herself with child a few weeks after the funeral, she expected Northumberland to marry her.

"What my mother could not anticipate was that Robert

Umfraville, Earl of Angus, would die at just that time, leaving his titles and vast wealth to his widow, Maud. Maud was a widow but two weeks before Northumberland wed her. My mother was left to make the pretense that FitzAlan miraculously conceived a child on his deathbed. That is how I came to bear his name.

"Northumberland arranged for her to be married to one of his knights. Everyone knew I was the result of Northumberland's dalliance with my mother—most especially her new husband."

Catherine understood from this that, even as a very young child, William was aware of his stepfather's resentment.

"She sent me to live in Northumberland's household when I was six."

He spoke with little emotion, but Catherine sensed the great bitterness he harbored against his mother.

She ventured to ask, "How old was your mother when she had her affair with Northumberland?"

He shrugged. "She was married to FitzAlan at fifteen, so I suppose she was about sixteen."

"And yet you believe it was she who seduced him?" she asked. "Northumberland must have been, what, forty? And he was a very powerful man. It may have been difficult for her to refuse him."

When he did not respond, she said in a soft voice, "I cannot help thinking you judge her harshly."

William folded his arms. "You do not know her."

"You as much as called her deceitful and manipulative at table today," she said as gently as she could. "You should consider the effect of your words on Stephen. He is just a boy."

"Stephen seems to have her measure." After a moment, he took a deep breath and said, "Perhaps I should take more care with him. He looks so much like her that it is difficult for me to remember he is an innocent."

Their conversation was interrupted by a furious knocking at the door.

"Who is it?" William demanded in a booming voice.

The words were indistinguishable, but the high-pitched voice on the other side of the door was Jamie's.

She and William scrambled to the floor for their clothes. Catherine slipped her gown over her head and jumped back into the bed just as William reached the door.

"Jamie!" William called out in greeting. Scooping Jamie up with one arm, he brought him over to the bed.

"Did Mother make you take a rest, too?" Jamie asked, rubbing his eye with his fist.

William nodded. "I suspect she will make me go to bed early tonight as well."

"'Tis best to just do what she wants," Jamie said, his blue eyes wide and knowing.

William could not keep back his smile. "I will do everything she asks." He caught Catherine's eye over the boy's head. "And then I will do it all again, just to be sure I've got it right."

Chapter Fourteen

The next morning, Catherine suggested they take Stephen riding to show him some of the nearby area. It was another lovely summer day, and it felt good to be outside the confines of the castle walls. She maneuvered her horse so that she and William rode behind the others.

"Stephen is a charming lad," she said.

"Charming?" William said in a sour tone. "What good is that?"

She laughed. "Stephen will need it! Something about him tells me he has a talent for getting into trouble. He's already gone into the village without telling anyone."

"That seems harmless."

"The illness we had at the castle earlier in the summer spread to the village," she explained. "I thought it had run its course, but two villagers died of it just this week."

"Stephen seems healthy enough."

She nodded and went back to what she had been saying before. "Stephen may have more charm than is good for him, but he has a good heart. He has been very kind to Jamie." She turned to smile at William. "Just as you are."

Unable to help herself, she added, "Truly, your mother cannot be as bad as you say to have raised two such sons."

"If either of us has a soft heart toward children," he said, staring straight ahead, "do not credit it to her."

Mentioning his mother was a mistake. She regretted letting herself get diverted from her purpose.

"So, William, what are your plans for your brother?"

"I have not yet decided, but I take it you have an opinion, m'lady wife?" Before she could answer, he asked, "Tell me, do you think most wives offer their opinions on all manner of things to their husbands?"

"Aye, most certainly, to both questions," she replied so quickly that William laughed.

"All right," he said, in full good humor now. "Tell me what you've been planning to say from the start."

"Stephen should stay with us," she said without hesitation. "There is no one better to train him for knighthood than you." 'Twas blatant flattery but true nonetheless. "And Stephen will need a steady man like you to fish him out of trouble from time to time."

"I was happy to settle here in the Marches precisely because it is far away from the Percys, my mother, and all the rest. I don't want to renew those ties. Besides, if I give in to my mother on this, she will ask for more."

"If she is so horrid," Catherine countered, "how can you leave Stephen in her hands?"

* * *

"Send that boy home to his mother," Edmund warned, "before the king catches wind of his being here."

"The king knows my loyalty," William replied evenly.

"And you know the king," Edmund said. "Carleton's support for the Northern rebels makes any connection with his son too risky for you."

"There is some risk," William agreed. With rebellions on both borders, Henry tended to see threats everywhere he looked.

"The king fears that the next time Northumberland calls for you, you may come," Edmund said in a low voice. "It would take little to raise his suspicions."

"Then ask the king's permission to keep Stephen here."

Both men whirled around at the sound of Catherine's voice.

"What are you doing sneaking up behind us!" Edmund shouted, his face red with anger.

"Perhaps you need to improve your skills," Catherine replied with equal anger, "if a woman can surprise you in broad daylight in the middle of the bailey yard."

"Catherine—" William began, but stopped when she turned her glare to him.

"Stephen is twelve years old. The king will not hold him accountable for his father's treachery." She arched an eyebrow at William. "He has been known to separate a father's guilt from his son."

With that, she turned on her heel and left them staring after her.

"You must do something about that woman," Edmund said in a taut voice. "She interferes in men's affairs. She does as she pleases, and she will take you down."

"I know you mean well." The cold anger in William's voice got Edmund's full attention. "But she is my wife, and you will not speak to her as you did."

"Fine, just tell me you'll not start taking her advice," Edmund said. "For God's sake, remember what she did to her first husband and watch your back."

"Rayburn deserved what he got," William bit out.

"Aye, but at his wife's hands?" Edmund said. "How long did she deceive him? Five years?"

"The past is past."

"You are thinking with what's between your legs, man. Can't you see she has blinded you?"

"Then I'm a happy blind man." William grabbed Edmund by the front of his tunic and looked him hard in the eye. "Find a way to get along with her. If I must choose between you, have no doubt I will choose her."

William was tired of this conflict between the two of them. He left Edmund and marched to the keep, intent on having words with Catherine as well. When he reached the hall, one of the servants informed him that Lady FitzAlan was in Stephen's chamber on the third floor.

Puzzled more than angry now, he went up the stairs to one of the previously unoccupied chambers next to Jamie's. He found Stephen in bed and Catherine hovering over him, wiping his face with a damp cloth.

She looked up and saw him in the doorway. "He has the fever. That is what I came to the bailey to tell you."

* * *

"Let one of the servants sit with Stephen tonight," William urged Catherine when she came to bid him good night. "You must get some rest. You are exhausted."

For the last three days and nights, Catherine had shared the watch with Alys. Even when it was Alys's turn, William would wake to find Catherine had left their bed to check on him.

The lad was ill, indeed. When William looked in on him earlier, Stephen's skin was so pale that the blue veins showed through it. He'd looked unbearably young lying on the bed.

"The fever should peak tonight, so it is the most dangerous time." She gave him a tired smile. "Once the fever breaks, I will rest, and gladly."

"I'll come with you," William said, throwing the bedclothes back.

"You will only be in the way," she said, putting her hand out to stop him. Although her tone was teasing, he knew she meant it. She kissed him distractedly and left.

Hours later, he awoke to find her side of the bed still empty. He dressed quickly in the faint first light of dawn. The keep was eerily quiet as he made his way up the stairs to Stephen's chamber.

The door was slightly ajar. He eased it open.

A surge of relief swamped him when he saw Stephen. The lad lay on the bed, wan but awake, with a slight smile on his face.

Lying beside him, fully dressed on top of the bedclothes, was Catherine. She was fast asleep and holding Stephen's hand.

William walked softly to the side of the bed and put his hand on Stephen's forehead.

"I see your fever has broken," he said in a hushed voice.

Stephen nodded.

With a wry smile, William said, "Then perhaps I can have my wife back."

They were quiet for a few moments; then Stephen said, "I can tell you what I want now."

William raised his eyebrows. What was the boy talking about?

"In a bride. If you arrange a betrothal for me."

William nodded, recalling the conversation.

Stephen cast a sideways look at Catherine sleeping soundly next to him on the bed.

"I want one like her—like your lady wife."

Stephen's grin was sheepish, but the sparkle in his eyes was anything but. And the boy was only twelve! William drew in a deep breath and shook his head. His wife was right. Stephen was the sort to get himself into trouble.

He made his decision.

"There is not another woman like Catherine, but I will do my best for you," he promised. "I'll send a message to your mother telling her you shall remain here at Ross Castle."

Stephen's smile grew wide at the news. William did not return the smile. It was time for the lessons to begin.

"Let this be the last time," he said, tapping his finger against Stephen's chest, "I find you in bed with another man's wife."

Chapter Fifteen

Stephen recovered his health quickly. He was a good-humored lad, and William enjoyed his company.

Truth be told, he felt more content with his new life with each passing day. He felt he had a family, with Catherine, Jamie, and Stephen. He was not sure how it happened, but he'd come to trust his wife.

He had even told her about Hotspur's death at the Battle of Shrewsbury and what happened after. King Henry had had the grace—or perhaps the wisdom—not to ask William to fight against Hotspur that day. Instead, William was sent off to keep watch for the approach of Glyndwr's forces. He returned in time to see Hotspur fighting his way through the melee. Hotspur killed two decoys dressed to look like the king and nearly reached the king himself before he was cut down.

Hotspur died a true warrior's death.

William accepted that Hotspur should lose his life for taking up arms against the king. But he could not reconcile himself to what the king did after.

When the people refused to believe the famous warrior was dead, the king had Hotspur's body dug up and drawn and quartered. On fast horses, the four parts were taken to be displayed in the four corners of the kingdom. The bloody head was delivered to Hotspur's poor wife.

William did not change his allegiance, but he lost a large measure of respect for his king that day.

Hotspur never once spoke to him with warmth, never once acknowledged their blood tie. Yet, William had been plagued by guilt ever since Shrewsbury. Only after he spoke of the events with Catherine did those feelings ease. She seemed to understand both why he sided with the king and what the choice had cost him.

* * *

Catherine paced the solar, debating with herself. Now that she had badgered William into telling her all, she felt guilty for the one secret she kept from him. His fierce words to her at the abbey came back to her again and again.

I cannot abide deceit.

Though she had told him no lie, neither had she been fully honest with him. Was she wrong not to have faith in him? Not to believe he would understand? She rubbed her temples. She had a blazing headache.

She did not like to admit it, but there was another reason to tell William. Although she dismissed it at first, Edmund's threat to discover her secrets nagged at her. What if someone had seen her that day? She did not think so, but it was possible one of the servants had been there in the hall. None of them would speak against her. But Edmund had already shown he could wheedle information out of them.

She jumped when the door opened.

"What are you doing here?" she snapped.

William's eyes twinkled in amusement. "I like to visit my lady wife in the middle of the afternoon. I come often enough; I did not think to give you such a start."

Catherine let out her breath and attempted to return his smile. "I am sorry. I was lost in my thoughts."

"Then I hope your thoughts were the same as mine."

He pulled her into his arms. It felt so good that she was sorely tempted to put off telling him once again. Her conscience got the better of her.

"William, I have something to tell you."

His light mood was gone in an instant.

"All right," he said, releasing her and stepping back.

She took his hand and led him to the window seat. Sensing his tension, she feared their new bond was too fragile for this revelation. She took a moment to get her courage up.

"Come, Catherine, it cannot be as bad as that," he said, and patted her hand. "Tell me what worries you."

The anxiety in his dark honey eyes belied his soft tone. Keeping him waiting would only cause him to think of darker and darker possibilities.

"You know Rayburn hurt me." She fixed her eyes on William's hand over hers as she began her tale; it still was not easy for her to talk about how Rayburn mistreated her. "He wanted an heir, but he had difficulty...performing the task." She cleared her throat. "Sometimes he did manage it, but I did not conceive. He was becoming more and more violent.

"I was young and very frightened." She gave William a furtive glance, hoping he understood how dire her situation was. "I thought it would not be long before he killed me."

She ran her tongue over her dry lips. "There was a young man," she said, barely above a whisper. "He saved me."

"Saved you?" William said, a note of suspicion creeping into his voice. "Just how did he save you?"

"He took care of me when I was injured."

She closed her eyes and remembered that day, more than four years ago. Prince Harry had stopped overnight. Rayburn was leaving with him the next day to fight the rebels. Since Rayburn might be gone for weeks, he came to her that night for another attempt. He hurt her badly that time.

The next morning, she waited to go down to the hall until Rayburn and the other men were gone. She forgot about the young knight Harry left behind to carry a message to the king. The moment she entered the hall, the young man rushed to her side. When she refused to let him call anyone to help her, he carried her upstairs and took care of her injuries himself.

"He was very kind and courteous," she said aloud.

She remembered how the young man's face and even his ears turned red when he eased the hem of her gown up to wrap the linen strips around her injured ankle. His fingers were unexpectedly gentle.

"He wrapped my ankle for me," she murmured. "He told me he learned his skills from the monks at a monastery near his home. He said he once hoped to join their order."

William made an indecipherable sound. Still, she did not look at him.

"When he helped me to my bed, my sleeve fell back. He saw the bruises on my arm."

After his careful treatment, she was startled when he held her wrist and pushed her sleeve up to her shoulder. She remembered how the dark purple and blue of the new bruises stood out against the fading yellow ones. The young man's eyes were full of compassion when he looked into her face again.

"He saw that my injuries were not from a fall, as I had told him—and that this was not the first time," she said. "He pressed me to tell him who was hurting me and why."

It was the memory of the young knight who took her riding before her wedding that led her to trust in the kindness in this young man's eyes. And that was what saved her.

"I told him everything. That there was no hope for me. That my husband could not get me with child and that he would not stop hurting me until I conceived."

The young man put his arms around her and made shushing noises into her hair. She remembered leaning into the comfort of his embrace and weeping until she fell into an exhausted sleep. By the time she awoke, he had worked out a solution to her problem.

"He said that to save my life, I must let another man get me with child." Her voice was so low that William leaned forward to hear her. "He said letting Rayburn murder me would be a greater sin than adultery."

Catherine let the silence stretch. Nothing could have made her look at William now. She could feel him next to her, fairly vibrating with violent emotion.

Finally, she made herself say it: "I asked him to do that favor for me."

"You what!"

"He refused at first," she said. William was gripping her hand so hard now that it hurt. "He was offended that I might think he carried me upstairs with the intent of seducing me."

"That is precisely what he intended!"

"He did not," she protested, looking up. "It was not like that."

"Just how was it, Catherine?" William's amber eyes were hard and narrowed, and she saw the warning in them.

"In sooth, it was not easy to persuade him." Her voice dropped to a whisper. "But there was no one else to ask, no one else I could trust."

She felt herself blush, remembering how she pulled her gown off before she could lose her courage. The young man's eyes traveled slowly down her naked body. In a breathy voice, he asked, "Are you very, very sure?"

She knew then she had won.

"Do not tell me how you convinced him," William spat out, as if reading her thoughts. "I thought you never enjoyed having a man in your bed before me."

"It was not like it is with us," she said, surprised he might think so. "He did not hurt me, but it was nothing like what happens between us."

The memory came back to her slowly. With a gentleness she could not have imagined, the young man kissed her cheek, her forehead, her throat. He caressed her with the softest touches, all the while murmuring soothing words to her. A great calmness settled over her.

She sensed a power held back to protect her, and she was grateful. Weak, barely able to move, she gave herself over to him. He seemed to understand she was hurt in spirit even more than in body and expected nothing from her.

The young knight gave her a glimpse that day of what her life could have been like with a different man, a kind man. It had been almost more than she could bear.

* * *

A jagged knife ripped through William's heart as he watched her thinking of her lover.

He always hated thinking of her with Rayburn, but the man had been her husband. It helped to know she had felt neither lust nor affection for the man. But Catherine taking a lover was something altogether different.

A terrible coldness swept over him. He stood up. He had to get out of this room, to get away. He could not be here.

But there were things he had to know before he could allow himself to escape.

"This knight is Jamie's father?"

She nodded.

"How long was he your lover?"

When Catherine's answer was too slow, he demanded, "Is he your lover still?"

Her eyes went wide. "He is not! He could not be! One time was all—I swear it."

"One time?" His voice was heavy with skepticism. "Quite the miracle."

She had the nerve to say, "I've always thought so."

He ground his teeth, trying to control the rage pounding through him. "Where is your lover now?"

He would track the man down and kill him.

"I learned he died of a fever," she said, and the sadness in her voice wrenched him. "It was not long after..."

She had the sense not to say after *what,* but the vision of her writhing under the man burned across his mind.

"I can see you think I was wrong to do it," she said, standing up and clenching her fists. "But I cannot regret it. I cannot! Rayburn would have killed me if I did not conceive. And you cannot ask me to wish Jamie had not been born."

William had watched her face soften as she spoke of her lover. The man she had "persuaded" to take her to bed. He knew all he needed to know; he could stand no more.

"What I regret, William FitzAlan, is that I was foolish enough to tell you!" She was shouting at him now, tears streaking down her face. "I trusted that you would understand, that you would not think these hateful thoughts of me."

He barely heard her.

The last thing he saw before he slammed the door was Catherine standing in the middle of the room with her hands over her face, weeping. Weeping for her dead lover.

What a fool he had been to trust her.

* * *

Edmund and Stephen jumped back as William stormed past them down the steps of the keep. William was in such a fury that he did not even seem to see them. But Stephen, who missed nothing, saw the slow smile on Edmund's face. And he wondered why.

Chapter Sixteen

Catherine was too upset after her disastrous conversation with William to venture from their rooms. An hour before supper, Alys came to find her.

"M'lady," Alys said, giving her a quick curtsy, "there is a group of minstrels at the gate. The guards want to know if they may let them in. As Lord FitzAlan has gone hunting, I told them I would ask you."

"Do we know these troubadours?"

"Aye, we do! We've enjoyed their music many a time." Alys frowned and tilted her head. "I believe the last time was not long before Lord FitzAlan came to us."

Aye, Catherine knew them. One of them she knew very well, indeed.

"Do say yes, m'lady. It will help make up for not having musicians at your wedding feast." With barely suppressed excitement, Alys added, "And they always bring news, traveling as they do."

"That they do," Catherine agreed. "I shall tell the guards to open the gates myself."

As she and Alys crossed the bailey toward the main gate, she heard Stephen call her name. She turned to see him running headlong down the steps from the castle's outer wall.

"There are traveling musicians at the gate!" he said as he fell into step beside her.

"I swear, Stephen, you hear news faster than anyone in Ross Castle," she said, shaking her head. "No secret could be kept from you for long."

She looked at him sideways without slackening her pace. "How do you do it?"

She meant it as a rhetorical question, but Stephen answered.

"I make friends with the servants, fetch drinks for the guards." He paused, then added, "And I listen."

"Behind doors?"

Stephen would not lie to her, but he opened his eyes wide with feigned innocence.

"Have a care," she scolded. "One day you may hear something you should not, and it could cost you dearly."

When they reached the gate, she recognized the faces and colorful clothing of the band of troubadours. For longer than she could remember, this troupe had come to Ross Castle and received warm welcome here. She recalled how her mother loved the ballads, especially the "chansons d'amour."

She signaled to the guards to raise the portcullis and stepped forward, calling, "Welcome! Welcome!" She greeted each man with a smile as they bowed to her in turn.

Robert Fass kissed her hand and gave her a rakish grin. The devil looked as handsome as ever with his sea-green eyes and unfashionably long blond hair.

Robert joined the troupe three years before. No one knew where he came from, nor would he say, but he could mimic any accent and spoke French, English, and Welsh equally well. And he had a voice to make the angels cry.

The female angels, at least.

She'd seen serving women trip over sleeping dogs, because they could not take their eyes off him. She sighed and shook her head. They would fight for his favors, and the hard feelings would cause her trouble for weeks to come.

From hints Robert gave, highborn ladies took him into their beds as often as the maids did. She suspected that was how he got his best information.

She was anxious to have a private word with him. With Stephen's sharp ears close by, it was not possible to talk now. She would have to wait and seek him out later.

* * *

Catherine could feel William's anger as he sat stiffly beside her at supper. He barely spoke, and not a word to her.

Fine. She was angry, too. Her disappointment in him dragged her spirits down as much as his hostility.

Thank heaven the musicians were here to provide a diversion. She sincerely regretted her decision to delay the surprise until the end of supper.

She waited until the last course of stewed fruits, sugared nuts, tarts, and cakes was brought to the table. At her nod, two servants posted at the entrance swung open the massive doors. The troubadours swept into the hall in a burst of song to the music harp and flute.

The hall erupted in cheers and clapping.

As she hoped, the musicians provided the household a welcome respite from the tedium of waiting for the next major confrontation with the rebels. Even William seemed to put aside his ill humor and enjoy the music for a time.

That was short-lived, however.

Robert stood to give the final ballad and waited until the room fell into a hushed silence.

"I sing this song for the fairest lady of the Marches." Robert bowed low in her direction and gave her that wicked smile of his.

She could have throttled him.

He settled back onto his stool and took up his harp. The moment he began to sing, she forgot her annoyance with him.

From the first note to the last, no one made a sound to interrupt the soaring voice that filled the room. They hung on every word as he sang. It was a well-known ballad, a sad tale of a young man's undying love for a beautiful maid. As she listened to the familiar words, Catherine closed her eyes and let the music take her into the story.

Her eyes flew open as the words of the final verse came to her. In horror, she listened to Robert sing of the maid being forced to wed another. His voice filled the hall with the young man's lament: He must meet his love in secret, and his child will have another man's name.

William clenched his fist around his eating knife so tightly his knuckles were white. She did not dare steal a glance at his face. His rage was so palpable that it made her skin prickle.

The sudden, jubilant applause brought her attention abruptly back to the musicians. As Robert took his bow, he caught her eye and gave her another devilish grin. Could the fool not see William was ready to take him by the throat?

She left the table before the applause died. In the corridor just outside the hall, she found the musicians chatting and putting away their instruments.

"A wonderful performance!" she said. "Cook has supper waiting for you in the kitchens."

She grabbed Robert's arm as he attempted to file out behind the others. When he put his hand over hers, she snatched it back.

"Must you embarrass me?" she said in a harsh whisper.

Robert threw his head back and laughed. "Most women are flattered when I sing a love song to them. It's your annoyance that makes it so irresistible."

"You had best find a way to resist, or my new husband may murder you! How is it that no husband has killed you yet?"

"I usually take care not to look at the married women when I sing love songs—if their husbands are present." He winked at her. "But tonight I could not help myself."

"I tire of your jokes, Robert." Chastising him was useless, and she wanted to talk of other matters. She leaned close and lowered her voice. "Tell me, what news have you?"

All humor left his face. "A French army is expected to land on the southwest coast of Wales, at Milford Haven, within the week."

"What!" The French had taken so long in meeting their promise to Glyndwr that she had ceased to believe they would come at all. "How many men do they bring?"

"I cannot say for certain, but it is a large force. Perhaps as many as twenty-five hundred men."

Catherine was so dismayed that Robert put his hand on her shoulder to soothe her. "From what I hear of FitzAlan, you can trust him to defend Ross Castle. Praise God, you no longer have that worthless scum Rayburn for a husband."

"I am forever grateful to you for taking my messages to the prince." With less warmth, she added, "You know the extent of my gratitude, for you take great advantage of it."

"I mean no harm." His smile was gentle this time.

"I know," she said, touching his hand where it rested on

her shoulder. She knew that beneath his flirting and joking, he felt a genuine friendship for her.

"There is more," he said, lowering his voice again. "The French do not come just to help Glyndwr take the castles in South Wales. They intend to march into England itself."

"No." Catherine put her hand to her chest. "They would not dare!"

"We shall see," Robert said, giving his characteristic shrug. "I have only heard a whisper of it."

A whisper in bed, no doubt.

Robert's gaze shifted from her face to fix on something behind her. She whirled around, alarmed that someone may have overheard their conversation.

She was relieved to see it was only William. When she turned back to Robert to make the introductions, Robert was several paces away and heading for the door.

"I shall find that supper now, Lady FitzAlan," he called out just before the door banged closed.

Robert had experience with hasty exits.

* * *

William was almost blind with rage. He let the troubadour go. For now. Fists clenched at his sides, he stepped forward to confront his wife. He stopped just inches from her, not daring to touch her for fear of what he might do.

"Is he Jamie's father?" he demanded. "The man you would have me believe is dead?"

She looked up at him with eyes as blue and innocent as periwinkles. He was torn between wanting to shake her until her teeth rattled and howling out in pain.

"What?" she said, as if she had not heard him. "Jamie's father? I did not even know Robert then."

Her response did nothing to calm him.

"So Jamie's father was not your only lover?" He thought his head would explode from the pressure. Enunciating each word distinctly, he said, "How many have there been, Catherine? I want their names."

He could see she was frightened now, but she stood her ground.

"I took no lover, save for the one I told you about," she said, looking him in the eye. "And only the one time."

The thought nagged at him that she would not have been so inexperienced if the two had been lovers. He sincerely doubted there would be much left to teach a woman after she'd been with the troubadour.

"Swear to God," he demanded. "Swear to God you have not lain with him."

She became calmer, as if she saw a means of escape.

She grasped the cross at her neck and said in an unwavering voice, "I swear before God and all that is holy, I have not lain with him."

He did not know what to believe. While the bard had been singing, William pictured the two of them together, naked and entwined. Any doubts he had were swept away when he saw them, touching and whispering, alone in the dark corridor.

But, she swore before God. Either Catherine was telling the truth or she did not fear even God's wrath.

"If you speak the truth," he said, "then what reason could you have for whispering in secret with him?"

"I—"

"Now that you know a man can give you pleasure, you want to try another. Is that it? Confess, you were planning a tryst with him!"

"I would not! Robert behaves that way to tease me, truly. 'Tis a game to him."

"A game to seduce my wife?" he shouted. "I swear, I shall tear him limb from limb."

He brushed past her, charging for the door, but she grabbed his arm and clung to him.

"Do not touch him, William," she pleaded. "He is innocent."

"Innocent, you say?" he said, incredulous. "There is not a man alive who would believe that troubadour is innocent."

In a quieter voice, he asked, "But what of you, wife? Am I to believe you are innocent? What explanation can you give for what I saw here?"

"That is what I must tell you, if you will but listen," she said. "Robert gave me news of the French. We must send word to the king at once."

"You would have me believe your tête-à-tête was of politics?"

He pushed her away in disgust, and she dropped to the floor.

Standing over her, he said in a low growl, "I will get the truth from this troubadour of yours. I will put him on the rack if I have to."

She rose to her knees and grabbed his leg. "Please, William, do not hurt him!"

He watched her groveling on the floor, begging for her lover, and felt a crushing pain in his chest.

"Did what passed between us mean nothing to you?" he asked. He heard the plaintive note in his voice and hated himself for his weakness.

He turned his back on her and went out the door. The rush of cold night air could not cool his burning skin. Not since his mother sent him away as a child of six had he felt such an aching, overpowering sense of desolation. For the second time in his life, his world crashed down around him.

He loved her. Only now did he realize it. The girl he met in the stables years before touched his imagination and filled his dreams. But it was the woman, his most reluctant wife, who stole his heart. And she did it without his even knowing it.

He was used to deciding what he wanted and setting a course to get it. But he could not begin to think what he should do about Catherine and his feelings for her.

Tonight, however, he would find this too-handsome troubadour and send him packing.

* * *

Catherine sent her maid away and barred the door. Not that it would keep William out if he was determined to come in. She paced the floor, waiting for him to pound on her door and demand to know where Robert was hiding. Thank God she had shown Robert the secret tunnel and hidden boat long ago. With luck, he would be well down the river by now.

William did not come. Exhausted from the ordeal, she pushed the heavy chest in front of the door and went to bed. She slept fitfully and awoke in the morning feeling bone-tired.

"The men have left the hall, m'lady," her maid called through the door. "Shall I help you dress now?"

Catherine heaved the trunk aside and let Mary in.

"I shall rest a while longer," she said, sitting down on the trunk. "My stomach is a touch uneasy."

"I shall bring you sop, m'lady," Mary said. "There is nothing like bread soaked in warm milk and a touch of honey for belly trouble."

Though Catherine felt well again before the midday meal,

she sent word down that she was ill and would take her dinner in her rooms. She was not ready to see William. Also, she needed time to figure out how to get the news of the French invasion to Harry. Clearly, William would not do it for her.

Could she be sure enough of Robert's information to risk sending word to Harry? She did not like sending him a message of such import until she heard it from two sources. She was always cautious; it would hurt the prince's standing with the king and his council if the information later proved false.

Prince Harry and the king were on the Northern border. With the royal armies so distant from Wales, it was all the more urgent to get news to them of the imminent arrival of the French. If only she could be sure! Even if she could confirm it, how would she get a message to Harry?

She heard a light knock, and an auburn head popped around the door. In spite of her troubles, Catherine gave Stephen a warm smile.

"How do you fare?" the boy asked, drawing his dark brows together. "I heard you were not well."

"I am better, thank you," she replied, feeling guilty her deception had caused him concern.

"A message arrived for you from the abbey," he said, handing her a sealed parchment.

Leaving Stephen to fidget behind her, she stepped inside the doorway of her bedchamber. With her back to the open door, she broke the seal. She found two letters, one rolled inside the other. She read the hidden one quickly, with a rising sense of urgency.

The abbess, too, had received word of the imminent arrival of a French army.

God was with her. No sooner had she slipped the secret

missive through the slit in her gown and into the small pouch she wore underneath than William burst into the solar.

She held the other letter in her hand as she went to join him. It gave her a good deal of satisfaction to see he did not look as if he'd slept any better than she had.

"Edmund told me you received a message," he said without greeting her. He held out his hand for it.

"'Tis from Abbess Talcott," she said coolly, and dropped it into his hand.

If he was surprised to see it was, indeed, from the abbess, he did not show it.

"As you can see, m'lord husband, the abbess hopes I may come see her soon. It has been some time since..." She faltered for just a moment. "Since I visited."

"Perhaps you would benefit from spending time on your knees with holy women," William said in a hard voice. He narrowed his eyes and jabbed his finger against her chest. "But you shall not go outside these castle walls without me or Edmund Forrester. I will not have my wife sneaking off for some tryst."

Before she knew it, Stephen was between them.

"You shall not say such vile things to her!" Stephen shouted.

William's harsh words hurt and humiliated her, but it was Stephen's futile gallantry that pushed her to the edge of tears.

"Stephen, I am sending your escort home today," William said in a cold voice. "Go or stay, as you will."

With that, he turned and stomped out of the room.

Stephen's fair skin had gone blotchy, and his deep brown eyes showed confusion and hurt.

"William does want you here," Catherine said, touching his arm. "He is just angry now."

Stephen shrugged and hung his head.

She took his face in her hands and looked him in the eyes. "You have a home at Ross Castle as long as I am here," she said. "I want you here, and so does Jamie."

"I would rather face William's wrath than my mother's disappointment," Stephen said, attempting a smile. "She is not a woman to cross."

Catherine smiled back. "Whatever the reason, I am glad you will stay."

"Edmund told me why William is so vexed with you," he said, looking away and blushing faintly. "My brother is a fool, and I shall tell him so."

It should not surprise her that Stephen knew more than he should.

"So you would slay dragons for me, Sir Stephen?" she said, touched by the boy's blind faith in her. "You are good to offer, but I don't think you can help me with your brother."

"Surely there is something I can do for you? I would do anything you asked."

She narrowed her eyes, considering.

"Aye, Stephen, there is something."

* * *

An hour later, the men of Stephen's escort rode out of the castle, headed for the North. Unbeknownst to William, they carried a message from Catherine to the prince. When Prince Harry brought it to the king, the king snatched the parchment from his hands and tore it to bits in his face.

"You expect me to move my armies across the length of England," he fumed, "based on a woman's gossip?"

Within days, the king would sorely regret that he had not.

Chapter Seventeen

Catherine did not show her face at table for three days. William knew their rift was the talk of the castle. From the looks the servants gave him when they thought he was not looking, it was evident they thought him the vilest of criminals. His men, on the other hand, were embarrassed for him. Even Edmund would not meet his eyes.

Stephen was firmly in the servants' camp and vocal in his recriminations. How could William fault the lad for being a fool for Catherine? Even after discovering her cavorting in the dark with the troubadour, William's desire for her was unabated. He lay awake at night, wanting her past bearing. He swore he could almost hear her breathing.

Even in the daytime, he caught himself imagining her trailing kisses down his body or remembering how her breath caught when he entered her. He would soon go mad with frustration.

He told himself he would be justified in taking her to bed again. She was his wife. He had a right. A duty. A man needed an heir. And a godly man must avoid the sin of adultery. Unless he wanted a life of celibacy, he must bed his wife.

If he was honest with himself, it was not only bedding her that he missed. He felt her absence beside him at table and longed to hear her laugh at Jamie's antics or Stephen's jokes. Sadness settled over him when he thought of the long rides they used to take.

He missed it all.

In the end, it was pure desire that drove him to stand beside her bed in the middle of the night. Though she lay perfectly still, he knew damned well she was awake.

"You can refuse me," he said, his voice hard and clear in the darkness. The tension hummed through his naked body, every muscle drawn taut, as he waited for her response. Her silence was answer enough for him.

When he lifted the bedclothes to crawl in beside her, she did not cry out in protest. He felt her move on the bed, then heard the soft swoosh of her tunic hitting the floor. He turned toward her and, at long last, felt her naked body next to his.

In an instant, he had her in his arms, every part of her pressed against him. His hands moved over her as he kissed her hair, her face, her throat. Rolling her onto her back, he buried his face between her breasts and breathed in her scent. He sucked her breasts, first one and then the other, until her breath came in sharp gasps.

He tried to fill the yawning emptiness inside him with his passion, the feel of her smooth skin, the smell of her hair, the sensation of her body responding to his. Driven to possess her in every way, he lowered himself until his head was between her legs.

If this was sin, he was long past caring. He tasted her as he wanted to. As he'd wanted to from the first time. When she gasped in surprise, he tightened his hold around her thighs. She would have to make her protest loud and certain if she wanted him to stop. No other woman tasted like this, smelled like this. He licked and sucked and slid his finger inside her.

She writhed and moaned, but he would not be satisfied until he made her cry out. When she did, he surged up on his knees and pulled her hips against him, thrusting, fast and hard, fast and hard, until they cried out together.

He collapsed forward, panting, his weight on his outstretched arms, his forehead resting on her chest.

Neither had spoken a single word.

He lifted himself up and dropped beside her, spent.

Surely that frenzied coupling had satisfied the aching hunger inside him. But when her fingers brushed his cheek, he knew it had not. He wanted far more from her than he could trust her to give.

He lay on his back, staring into the darkness. Her fear in the first days of their marriage had been real. He was almost sure of that. But had she feigned the tenderness in the weeks that followed? Had she?

He was about to get up to return to his own bed when she moved beside him. The breath went out of him as her hand came to rest on the flat of his stomach. Then she leaned over him, her hair sliding over his skin.

And he was lost again.

* * *

She did not come to his bed as she used to. But each night he went to hers, and they made love. Silent, frantic, all need and want and anger. Afterward, he would leave her, unable to bear the intimacy of sleeping with her.

Though she let him into her bed each night, she avoided him during the daylight hours. Against his will, he watched for her all day. He caught only glimpses of her—leaving a room, walking on the ramparts with Stephen, running across the bailey yard with Jamie.

He knew it could not go on like this.

When she once again did not come to the hall to take her breakfast, he decided enough was enough. He took the stairs two at a time and entered the solar.

He stood outside the closed door to her bedchamber, asking himself why he was there. He did not know whether he could trust her. Whether her feelings were true. The hard truth was, none of that changed what he wanted. He wanted their relationship to be as it had been before.

Through the door, he heard her retching. He pushed the door open to find her vomiting into a basin. As she wiped her mouth on a cloth, she looked up. The apprehension that came into her eyes when she saw him took him aback.

"Are you ill?" he asked from the doorway.

"'Tis nothing. Just an uneasy stomach."

His anger drained out of him. She looked so frail and vulnerable in her night shift, with her slim ankles and delicate feet showing below. Despite everything, a feeling of tenderness swept over him.

He took the basin and towel from her and set them aside. Taking her hand, he said, "Catherine, I want us—"

Before he could say more, there was a loud banging at the solar door. *Damnation.*

"What is it?" he shouted as he stomped into the solar.

To his surprise, it was not a servant waiting outside the door but one of his men.

"Lord FitzAlan," the man said, "we have reports the French have landed a force." He was breathless from running.

"What else do you know? Where are they?"

"They landed at Milford Haven," the man said. "'Tis a disaster, m'lord. The castles at Haverfordwest, Cardigan, Tenby, and Carmarthen have all been taken. The French are now sweeping across the south of Wales to Cardiff."

"God in heaven," William swore, "the king and his army are in the North."

"I was told messengers are on their way to both London and the king."

"We must make haste to be ready when the king calls."

William followed the man out. What he had to say to Catherine would have to wait.

* * *

The castle bustled with activity as the men prepared to leave for war. There would be a major battle when the two armies met, so William would take most of the men with him. Luckily, Ross Castle could be defended with a small number of men. The most serious threat was siege. William had worked hard, however, to ensure the castle's stores were adequate.

As soon as the news reached the king, he would race his army south. He would send word to the Marcher lords, telling them where to join him for the confrontation.

The call would come soon. As soon as tomorrow.

At supper, he asked Catherine to wait up for him. He did not know if a full reconciliation was possible, but he wanted to come to some understanding with her before he left. He still had much to do, so it was late before he finally made his way up to their rooms.

He found her asleep on the window seat in the solar. The candle on the table was nearly gone. He pulled up a stool, glad for the opportunity to watch her unobserved.

Starting with her shining hair and the delicate features of her face, he let his gaze travel over her. His throat tightened as he took in the curves of her breasts, her waist, her hips, and then the long line of her legs. When he reached her feet, so small and graceful, he felt an unexpected sting at the back of his eyes.

What was he to do with her? He could not say, but he did not want to leave things as they were. He picked up her hand and rubbed his thumb over it. Its very smallness made him feel protective.

Her eyes fluttered open.

"You were smiling in your sleep," he said. "What were you dreaming?"

Still only half awake, she said, "A dream I often have about something that happened long ago."

"Tell me about it."

She sat up and ran her fingers through her hair. Awake now, she gave him a wary look and shook her head. "It will only make you angry."

"Please, I want to hear."

After more prodding and assurances, she gave in.

His heart turned in his chest as she began to tell of the ride they took the night before her wedding to Rayburn.

"A young man was sleeping in the stable, and he went with me." She cast a nervous glance at William and added, "He was an honorable young man who wished to protect me."

William nodded, which seemed to reassure her. He kept quiet and let her tell the tale.

At the end, she said in a wistful voice, "That night I felt safe and happy and free all at once."

He swallowed hard, regretting that he'd never made her feel that way again.

"I've dreamed of that night often," she said, looking off

into the distance. "The dream seems to come to me when I am worried or unhappy."

He felt worse, knowing he was the cause of her unhappiness tonight.

"Is your dream always the same?" he asked. "Do you dream it just as it happened that night?"

She looked down at her hands and took her time in answering. "It has always been so, until tonight. This time, the young man became you in the dream."

William felt as if a fist gripped his heart. Taking both her hands, he asked, "Do you remember in whose service this young knight was?"

She jerked her hands away. "You are not going to chase him down and threaten his life, are you?"

"I swear, I will not."

She seemed to take him at his word, for she put her hand to her chin and paused to think. "I am certain he did tell me. . . . He was on an errand for someone important. . . ."

Her eyes widened. "It was Northumberland."

"Aye, it was."

She stared at him a long while, a question forming in her eyes.

"My hair was long then, and I wore a beard," he said in a quiet voice. "At that age, my pride at being able to grow one was greater than my annoyance at how much it made me look like Hotspur."

Her jaw dropped.

"It was you?"

He nodded.

She scrutinized him through narrowed eyes. "'Tis true, between the beard and the darkness I could see little of the man's face," she said slowly. "But the difference is in more than your appearance."

"I am changed?" he asked, though he was not sure he wanted to hear.

"You are used to command now, and it shows," she said in a tentative voice. "Back then, you were...you were...more trusting."

"What do you mean?"

She bit her lip, hesitant.

"You can tell me," he pressed.

"You did not know me, yet you took every word I said on faith."

He saw the hurt in her eyes. And the accusation.

"I thought you had forgotten that night," he said, his heart in his hand. "I dream of it as well. But in my dreams, I always rescue you." It made him feel vulnerable to tell her, but he made himself continue. "I chastised myself for not finding a way to help you that night. I think that is one reason the dreams would not leave me."

"You could not know how Rayburn would mistreat me," she said without a hint of hesitation. "And there was nothing you could do. Rayburn was the king's choice."

He shrugged. Practical considerations did not release a man from what honor required.

"How long have you known I was that girl?" she asked, an edge to her voice now. "Did you know even before you came to take Ross Castle?"

"I did not know until I saw you on the drawbridge." He closed his eyes as he recalled how he had ridden his horse up to her in a fit of rage. "It was when you fainted."

They were silent for a time, each lost in their own thoughts.

"Guilt was not the only reason I dreamed of you." He wanted to tell her all of it now, before he left for battle. "There have been other women. But from the night I rode with you in the moonlight, it was always you I wanted."

The confession was hard to make. He expected it to please her. Instead, her expression grew melancholy.

"At times in these last weeks, I believed you cared for me." She sighed and shook her head. "But it was never me you cared for. You were in love with a girl in a dream."

He came to her tonight hoping to bridge the rift between them. Even though he had doubts about her, still he came. He confessed he had wanted her—*dreamed* of her—for years.

And yet, she dismissed all this as nothing.

"You have hurt me more than Rayburn ever did," she said.

There was nothing she could have said that would have surprised or offended him more.

"I've never taken my hand to you," he snapped.

"Rayburn battered my body, but he could not touch my heart. He was predictably cruel, never once to be trusted." She looked hard at him as she spoke, her eyes revealing both hurt and anger. "But you, William, you are so kind to me that I trust you—and then you rage at me.

"You made me ache with your tenderness," she continued, her voice beginning to quaver. "And then you come to me in lust only, taking me and then leaving me more alone than I have ever been before."

"You could have refused me," he said in a choked whisper. "I told you that you could." It was his only defense.

"I missed your touch," she said, her smile bittersweet. "Each time, I hoped what we did would bring you close to me again. That it would be as it was before between us."

William covered his face with his hands, overwhelmed with emotion. When he heard her rise, he dropped them and looked up at her.

"It is you I need rescuing from now, William, for you are breaking my heart," she said, her eyes wet with unshed tears. "You bring me misery of a kind Rayburn never could."

He grabbed her wrist to stop her from leaving.

"I am sorry with all my heart for hurting you," he said, pleading. "I am sorry for it all."

"You did not even believe me when I tried to warn you of the French landing," she flung at him, her voice bitter.

He did not care if she chastised him so long as she stayed.

"I should have listened to you." The fact that the troubadour brought her news of war did not mean the man was not also trying to seduce her, but William did not say that.

"Please, Catherine, I do not want to leave with this unhappiness between us."

She knew the risk that he might not return from battle without him having to say it. It was unfair to play on her sympathy in this way, but he was too desperate to care.

All he wanted was to have that closeness between them again. The joy. She was not like other women, not like his mother. If he could make Catherine happy, she would not leave him.

He pressed her open hand against his cheek. "I know I cannot mend it all tonight," he said, looking up at her. "But could you pretend to forgive me for this one night? We cannot know when we will have another."

When he kissed her palm, she closed her eyes as if bracing herself. He put his arms around her waist and rested his head against her.

"I promise I will be a better husband to you when I return." He meant it with all his heart.

She ran her fingers through his hair, then kissed the top of his head. The miracle of her kindness washed over him.

He knew he must not fail her again.

He rose to his feet and lifted her in his arms. He looked into her face, waiting for her answer. After a long, long moment, she nodded. He carried her to his bedchamber before she could change her mind.

Tonight he would take her with a tenderness he hoped might begin to heal her heart.

He set her on the edge of the bed and lit a single candle. When he came to sit beside her, she moved away so that they did not touch. He had a long way to go to earn her trust back.

He turned her away from him and began massaging her neck and shoulders. Her muscles were tense under his hands; he worked them until he felt her relax.

He kissed her along the curve of her neck. When he reached her ear, he whispered, "Lie down for me, Kate."

She let him ease her down onto her belly.

He undid her braid and ran his fingers through the long, silky strands. As always, he was mesmerized by the hundred shades of gold reflected in the candlelight. Sweeping her hair to one side, he leaned over and pressed his lips to her cheek.

He rubbed her scalp and temples with his fingertips until she closed her eyes. Then he moved down to her shoulders and back, massaging through the thin night shift. By the time he worked his way to her fingers, her hands were limp.

"Are you cold?" he asked, and smiled at her muffled grunt in response.

He turned his attention to her feet, rubbing first the soles and then each toe in turn. The curve of her lips told him she was enjoying his ministrations. He bent her leg so that her foot rested against his chest while he massaged her calf. He stopped to kiss her foot, her toes, to run his tongue along the sole of her foot.

He laid her foot on the bed and kissed the back of her knee. As he kissed it, he eased her night shift up her thighs.

The room was warm.

Sweat broke out on his forehead as he massaged her thighs.

Slowly but steadily, he worked his way upward. When he got to the juncture between leg and buttock, he traced the delectable curve with his tongue. When she shivered in response, he gently bit her with his teeth. Once, twice, three times.

He lifted his head and gave it a shake, reminding himself that this was for her. He tried to slow his breathing.

He returned to his work with renewed resolve. As he pulled her shift up, she lifted her hips and then her chest and head. He had her naked at last.

God have mercy, his wife was beautiful.

His wife.

He straddled her to rub her back. With slow deliberation, he worked his way over every inch. Then he ran his fingers in light circles over her back. He felt himself grow harder and harder with anticipation as he swept his hands closer and closer, until at last his fingers touched the soft, full curve of the sides of her breasts.

Feeling her stir at the touch, he clenched his jaw until it ached. He wanted to feel her breasts in his hands, her nipples hard beneath his palms.

He took a deep breath.

Hoping he could keep himself in check, he leaned on his forearms to kiss her neck. His chest brushed against her back, sending a jolt of hot lust through him. He squeezed his eyes shut against the urge to rub his throbbing cock against her backside. If he did, he would never last.

For a long moment, he remained poised over her, his breath coming hard and fast. All he could think of was lifting her hips and entering her from behind.

He opened his eyes as she rolled over to face him. Her amused smile told him she knew exactly what he'd been thinking. Eyes twinkling, she shook her head at him. He was pleased to see a hint of the playfulness she used to show him in bed.

"Aye, 'tis much too soon," he agreed. Sighing dramatically, he fell beside her and took her in his arms.

"It is good to be here with you like this," he said, and kissed the tip of her nose.

"Mmmm," she murmured, squeezing closer.

She gave him an openmouthed kiss that made him forget his name. As they kissed, he slid his hands between her legs. It took the breath out of him when he felt how hot and wet she was. She would kill him for certain. She pressed against him as if wanting to melt into him.

Keeping his hand on her, he eased himself down on the bed until he could take her breast in his mouth. When he did, he heard her sharp intake of breath. He loved to hear the sounds she made. He slowly slid his finger in and out of her as he flicked his tongue over her nipple, listening to the change in her breathing.

His heart pounded in his ears as he sucked harder, and she moaned and moved against his hand. At first, he ignored her insistent pull on his shoulders. He was set on bringing her to release the first time before he entered her. But when she persisted, he obeyed.

Hovering over her, he gave her a long wet kiss. When she wrapped her legs around him, the battle was lost. He slid deep inside her in one forceful stroke.

Good God! The rush that went through him blinded him and left him shuddering. It was all he could do to stop himself from spilling his seed at once. He found her mouth. Their tongues slid together as he moved back and forth against her as slowly as he could bear.

When she increased the rhythm, he could not find his voice to tell her she must stop. She was relentless and he loved it. She arched her back, letting her head fall over the side of the bed. Her breath came in short gasps as he felt her tighten around his shaft.

And then she called his name. She was his. She was his.

With her cries ringing in his ears, urging him on, he pounded into her, again and again, until sight and sound were obliterated in an explosion that was near death.

He could barely keep from collapsing with his full weight on top of her. Breathing hard and dripping with sweat, he let his forehead rest on the bed beside her head.

"God in heaven, what have you done to me, Catherine?"

When he heard her low chuckle, a wave of tenderness swept over him. How long since he had made her laugh? He pulled her into his arms as he sank down beside her.

He lay with his face buried in her hair.

"I wish I did not have to leave you so soon," he whispered.

He needed more time. Time to heal her, to heal himself, to be with her like this. With a sense of desperation, he turned to her again and again in the night. In the heat of passion, Catherine told him she loved him.

But William—though he tried to show her with his every touch—could not yet confess his love aloud.

Chapter Eighteen

The men of Ross Castle were gathered near the gate, their armor shining bright in the August sun. Shielding her eyes with her hand, Catherine took in each man and prayed for his safe return.

The news came an hour ago. The French-Welsh army was nearing the English border, marching toward Worcester. Glyndwr's move was both unexpected and brilliant. Taking an English town for even a short time would be a devastating blow to English pride. A blow that King Henry, already hanging on to the throne by his fingernails, could ill afford.

Caught by surprise, the king was racing his army headlong across the length of England to save Worcester. William and the other Marcher lords were commanded to await him there with their men-at-arms. If Henry could reach Worcester in time, the major battle between the two armies would be there.

Catherine swallowed hard to keep back the tears. One

night was not enough to recover the closeness they had before. She could not forget so soon how much he'd hurt her. Nor did she believe he'd overcome his mistrust of her. Still, it was a magical night, and she was hopeful. Very hopeful.

She caught sight of Edmund, talking with several of the men.

"Why is Edmund not in armor?" she asked William, tightening her grip on his arm.

"Edmund is staying here with a few of the men," William said. "Glyndwr has his army moving fast, hoping to take Worcester before the king can reach it. There is almost no danger of an attack on the castle; still, I cannot leave it completely undefended."

"I have been left in charge of this castle many times," Catherine said. "I neither need nor want Edmund Forrester here."

William ran a hand through his hair, looking uncomfortable. "I am sure you managed well enough on your own, but Edmund has years of fighting experience."

She was unmoved by his argument and did not hide it.

"I warned Edmund that if he does anything to offend you, I'll not keep him in my service." He held her face in his hands and kissed her forehead. "Please, Catherine, I do not want to argue with you as I leave. I need to know my best man is protecting you if I'm to keep my mind on what is before me."

She ceased to argue. It was dangerous for a man to be distracted when he fought. For this same reason, she was waiting to tell him about her pregnancy until he returned.

Stephen appeared beside them with Jamie in tow.

"You were fighting Scots at my age," Stephen said to William, his eyes bright with anger. "You treat me like a child!"

Catherine grabbed Stephen's arm and hauled him a few feet away where William would not overhear her.

"With William gone, I need you here," she told him in a low, fierce voice. "Do not abandon me." She held his eyes until she was sure he understood she meant it.

When she rejoined William, he whispered in her ear, "What did you do, promise to marry the lad if I do not return? He's puffed up like a peacock!" He squeezed her hand. "Whatever it was, I thank you."

The men were mounting their horses, so William threw Jamie into the air one more time and ruffled the boy's hair.

Next, he turned to say farewell to Stephen. With a nod toward Catherine and Jamie, he said, "Keep them safe, brother."

Finally, he gathered Catherine in his arms and kissed her hard on the mouth in front of everyone.

He mounted his horse. "You will be safe here," he said, looking down at her. "I promise you."

"Promise only that you will come back to us."

"You need not worry for me," he said, flashing her a wide smile. "I will always come back for you, Kate. Always."

* * *

Those left behind at Ross Castle waited for news. They heard, first, that King Henry reached Worcester faster than anyone thought possible—and not an hour too soon. Since his arrival, however, the two great armies had been in a standoff.

While the commanders decided what to do, individual knights met in single combat on the field between the armies. This served no purpose, except to relieve the boredom. The stakes were too high to be decided by knightly challenges.

Catherine's tension over the coming battle grew as the days of waiting continued. Having Edmund unclothe her with his eyes every time she crossed his path did not help. He was, however, careful to speak politely and show her every other courtesy.

The memory of how he cornered her in the solar still rankled. While he would not dare harm her, neither did she want to be caught alone with him again. With Stephen here, there was little chance of that.

Stephen took William's admonition to keep her safe to heart. The first night, she found him sleeping in front of her chamber door. Her promises to have her maid sleep with her and bar her door were not enough to dissuade him. Only when she showed him the blade under her pillow did he finally agree to return to his own chamber.

"I would like to visit Abbess Talcott today," she announced at the midday meal, pushing her food away.

"I will be your escort," Stephen said.

Edmund shook his head. "I doubt that is what your brother had in mind when he told me to provide a proper escort for his lady wife." To Catherine, he said, "I will take you myself, since that is what William would wish. I have an errand in the village today, but I'll gladly take you tomorrow."

"Thank you," she said, thinking William must have lectured Edmund to accommodate her.

"I'll come, too," Stephen said.

Edmund took one look at the stubborn set of Stephen's jaw and shrugged. "I cannot spare another man to go with us, but there isn't much danger with the whole of the rebel army at Worcester. You are both fine riders, so we should be able to outrun any other kind of trouble."

Edmund took a piece of roasted pork with his eating

knife. "All the same," he said, pointing his knife at her as he chewed, "I would not take your son along."

Much as Catherine hated to admit it, Edmund was right. It was safer to leave Jamie at the castle. He would be fine with his nursemaid for the day.

* * *

"Did you get your business done in the village yesterday?" Catherine asked Edmund. Now that they were on their way, she could afford to be friendly.

"Aye." Edmund's reply was curt.

She had to admit Edmund took his responsibility to protect her seriously. Riding in front of her, he kept a sharp watch, constantly moving his head from side to side. She turned in her saddle and found Stephen doing the same behind her. In the North, boys learned to watch for raiders from a young age.

Catherine blinked as they rode into a copse of wood, and her eyes adjusted from bright sun to dappled light. The green canopy overhead was lovely. She was leaning back to look for birds when she heard the sound of hoof-beats. In another moment, a half-dozen men on horses burst into view around the bend ahead.

Edmund turned and shouted, "Ride hard back to the castle! I will hold them as long as I can."

Catherine was unable to tear her eyes from the men galloping toward them. She watched Edmund spur his horse forward to meet them, his broadsword ready in his hand.

"Now, Catherine!" Stephen shouted. He grabbed her horse's bridle, turned her around, and slapped her horse's hindquarters. It took off with a jerk.

Over her shoulder, she saw Edmund fighting off two of

the men. As she watched, four other riders rode past the swinging swords without breaking their speed. The four charged toward her and Stephen.

Too late, she spurred her horse. As she left the copse for the open field, two horses came thundering beside her, pinning her between them. One of the riders leaned down and snatched up her reins.

As the man pulled her horse to a jarring halt, she tried to keep her eyes on Stephen. He was sweeping across the field ahead of his two pursuers. Praise God, he was going to outrun them. But then Stephen looked back and saw her.

"No, Stephen, no!" she shouted as he turned his horse in a wide arc to evade the two men and head back toward her. To her horror, he was brandishing his sword as if he meant to take them all on to rescue her.

She turned to the dark, fierce-looking man holding her horse's reins. "Please, sir, do not hurt him!"

The man squinted against the sun and watched Stephen's progress without giving any sign he heard her.

Frantic, she turned to the man on her other side. "Please, he is only a boy!"

The man flashed her a smile. "If you can convince the lad to put down his sword, I can promise his safety."

Stephen came thundering down on them, and the man who had just spoken was forced to fend off his attack. Though Stephen was skilled with a sword for his age, the man easily parried his thrusts. The silent man who held her horse watched them, looking unconcerned.

"M'lady?" the man fighting Stephen called out. "I need your help."

"Stephen, put down your sword!"

Her shout caused Stephen to glance toward her. The man

took advantage of Stephen's momentary distraction to take his sword.

"Listen to the lady," he said, "and you shall not be harmed."

Stephen reached for the dagger at his belt, but the man anticipated the move. Holding Stephen's forearm, he reached across Stephen's body and took the dagger.

Without taking his hands off Stephen, he said to the other man, "Rhys, do you think that is all?"

The man called Rhys flicked his eyes to Stephen's foot. At this silent signal, the first man checked both of Stephen's boots. When he had removed the hidden blade, he glanced again at Rhys. Rhys nodded, apparently satisfied Stephen was disarmed.

Ignoring the men, Stephen said to Catherine, "I am sorry I failed you."

"You could not have done more." Even in the midst of their danger, it hurt her to see Stephen look so defeated. "I do not believe these men mean to harm me," she added, and regretted the note of uncertainty that crept into her voice.

"Most assuredly we do not, dear lady," the handsome man who disarmed Stephen spoke up.

The two riders who chased Stephen had joined them by now. Catherine examined their four captors closely. They looked as though they had been traveling rough, but their clothes were finely made. She guessed they were Welsh noblemen. If she was right, their intent was likely ransom, not rape and murder.

"You are Welsh rebels?" she asked.

"Aye, that we are, Lady FitzAlan," the handsome one answered.

They knew her name. That meant they did not just happen upon her, notice her fine clothes and horse, and take advantage of a chance opportunity.

"My name is Maredudd ap Tudor," the man said, bowing his head. "These two"—he pointed to the two young men who had chased Stephen—"are my brothers, Owen and Maddog."

Both young men nodded politely. She could see the family resemblance, though neither was quite as good-looking as their dashing older brother.

Tudors? She had heard the name. She knew she had. Were they not close kinsmen of Owain Glyndwr, the rebel leader?

And then it came to her.

"Are you the same Tudors who violated holy Good Friday to take Conwy Castle?"

"That would be our elder brothers," Maredudd said, and all three Tudor men grinned.

God have mercy, she was a captive of the wily Tudors!

"The church decree to shed no blood on the holy day was not violated," one of the younger Tudors put in. With a wink, he added, "The castle guards were strangled."

The story of the unexpected attack was told up and down England. The rebels took the castle easily, since the entire garrison was at Mass in the nearby village.

"And the man holding your horse," Maredudd ap Tudor continued, "is Rhys Gethin."

Upon hearing the name, Catherine gasped aloud and brought a hand to her chest.

"I see you have heard of him," Maredudd said with an amused smile. "Then you will know why we call him 'Gethin.' It means 'the Fierce' in Welsh."

Rhys Gethin had led the Welsh forces in their great bloody victory at Bryn Glas three years before. Against overwhelming odds, the Welsh killed nearly eleven hundred Englishmen. It was said that at the end of the battle, the field was knee-deep in English blood.

"I am surprised men of such importance have come on such a lowly errand," she said, trying to keep the quaver out of her voice. She risked a glance at Stephen, hoping he would not contradict her. "You go to much trouble for little, I fear. It is unlikely my husband will pay much for my ransom."

Maredudd Tudor threw his head back and laughed. "Faith, m'lady, a man would pay a good deal for the return of so fair a woman. The rumors of your beauty hardly—"

"Enough!" Rhys Gethin's deep voice cut Maredudd off. "We delay too long. Glyndwr needs us at Worcester."

With that, he tossed her horse's reins to Maredudd and spurred his own horse forward. Maredudd tied her horse to his and fell into line behind him. The two younger Tudors followed with Stephen between them.

Catherine looked over her shoulder at the copse of wood, hoping Edmund got away.

* * *

They rode for hours, stopping only once to allow her to stretch her legs and relieve herself. Toward evening, small groups of men appeared out of the woods and joined them. Now she understood why English soldiers claimed the Welsh came and disappeared like fairies, with the help of magic.

At nightfall, they stopped in a heavy wood to make camp. Her legs were so weak that Maredudd had to catch her to keep her from falling when she dismounted. He led her to sit on a fallen log, holding her a bit more tightly than necessary.

"Lady FitzAlan, I would have your promise you will not try to escape," he said as he sat down next to her on the log. "You would only get lost, and I am too tired to go chasing about the woods for you tonight."

There was no point in trying. The woods were unfamiliar, and in the dark, she had no idea in which direction to go.

"If you make an attempt, I will catch you. And then you will sleep tied to me." His face broke into a wide smile. Giving her a wink, he said, "Perhaps you should try after all."

"With such charm, sir, how is it that some maid has not yet captured you?"

"Ah, but one has," he replied genially. "I am married to a remarkable woman named Marged."

"She is remarkably trusting to let you out of her sight." She surprised them both by speaking the thought aloud.

"I do enjoy your company," Maredudd said, slapping his thigh. "Marged knows I am devoted to her. Fortunately, she has the wisdom not to expect the impossible from me. In sooth," he added with a twinkle in his eye, "she is quite content with me."

Catherine wanted to roll her eyes at the man's vanity, though she suspected he spoke the truth. Maredudd Tudor was charming and devilishly handsome. Despite the circumstances, she also trusted him to protect her in this camp of armed men.

"May I speak with my young friend now?" She was anxious to talk with Stephen.

"We know the lad is Stephen Carleton, FitzAlan's half-brother," Maredudd said.

They could have guessed who she was. They found her near Ross Castle, and her family was well known in the Marches. But how did they know Stephen?

"Do not fret over the lad. He'll be returned safe and sound," Maredudd said. "If it had not been plain the boy would follow us, we would have left him where we found him."

At the sound of a scuffle, she peered through the growing darkness. A moment later, the younger Tudor brothers

appeared with Stephen kicking and twisting furiously between them.

"God's beard, can you not see the lady is well?" one of
them shouted at Stephen.

"We Welshmen are not the savages Englishmen are," the
other complained. "Besides, no man here will dare touch her
while she is under the protection of a Tudor."

Stephen saw her and ceased to struggle. The men dropped
him to the ground.

"He does not believe you will be safe, m'lady," one of the
brothers explained, "unless he is the one who guards you."

She saw the flash of Maredudd's white teeth in the rapidly
falling darkness. "It is encouraging to find chivalry still lives
in at least one young Englishman," he said. "Stephen, you
can make your bed next to the fair lady. That will make it
easier to keep watch over the two of you."

Leaving them in the care of his brothers, Maredudd left to
talk with some of the other men. Catherine and Stephen sat
huddled together while the younger Tudors cooked a supper
of small game over the fire. The two men were too near,
however, for them to speak freely.

They waited until after they had eaten and lay down on
the blankets spread for them close to the fire.

"The Welsh commanders fear their army is too strung out,"
Stephen whispered. "Gethin and the Tudors backtracked
from Worcester to make sure the king did not send part of
his army behind them, to cut them off from their base."

Catherine was not surprised Stephen had managed to
overhear so much.

"They did not come for you," Stephen continued. "But
when they caught wind you would be outside the castle this
morning, you were too great a prize to miss."

This made much more sense than that the Tudors and

Rhys Gethin would leave Worcester to take a single captive for ransom.

"Did you hear them say how they knew I would be outside the castle walls today?" She still could not understand this part.

"Nay, but it must mean we have a traitor at the castle," he whispered. "Who do you think it is?"

Who, indeed.

Chapter Nineteen

*C*atherine awoke with the prickling sensation that someone was watching her. She opened her eyes to find Maredudd standing over her.

"Good morning," he said, and nodded toward Stephen. "I see your gallant protector gave up the fight and took his rest."

Embarrassed to be talking with Maredudd while lying down, she sat up. Shivering, she pulled her blanket tightly around her shoulders. The early morning air held a chill.

"We are near Worcester, a few minutes' ride from where Glyndwr is encamped," Maredudd told her. "I sent word last night that I would bring you to him as soon as we break our fast."

She had not expected to be taken to Glyndwr himself. Unconsciously, she reached up to touch her hair. With no maid— or even a comb—she did not know how she could make herself presentable to the man the Welsh called their prince.

"Glyndwr understands rough travel. He'll not think it

amiss that you did not have a maid to dress your hair," Maredudd said with a smile. "'Tis a sin that custom requires such lovely hair be hidden."

He squatted down and shook Stephen's shoulder. "Come, lad. Prince Glyndwr has much on his mind, and I do not wish to keep him waiting."

Catherine picked up the ornate headdress she wore yesterday. Stephen had helped her remove it last night, but there was no hope of getting it back on today.

She heaved a sigh. There was nothing for it but to make do as best she could. After painstakingly detaching the gold mesh and circlet from the headdress, she combed her hair with her fingers and plaited it into a single braid down her back. Then she put the mesh over her hair and fixed the circlet across her forehead to hold it in place. The makeshift covering left too much hair exposed, but that was that.

She looked down at the dismal state of her gown. Working methodically, she began brushing the dirt from it, top to bottom. She was so absorbed in her task that she was startled when she looked up to find Stephen and all three Tudors staring at her, slack-jawed.

She narrowed her eyes at them. "How long have you been watching me?"

There was a general shrugging of shoulders.

"Do you men have nothing better to do?" she asked, her irritation evident in her tone.

Stephen had the grace to look away. The three Tudors, however, just shook their heads and smiled.

* * *

The other men were breaking camp when Catherine and Stephen rode off with the Tudors. Praise God her captors brought her here, rather than into Wales. William was in Worcester. She could be ransomed and delivered to him this very day.

"Can you see the old Celtic fort at the top of that hill?" Maredudd said, pointing ahead. "That is where we and the French are encamped."

Catherine dragged her thoughts from her reunion with William to prepare herself to meet the rebel leader. Quickly, she reviewed what she knew of Owain Glyndwr. He was a Welsh nobleman, close kinsman to the Tudors. Before the rebellion, his home was known as a center of Welsh culture, where troubadours and musicians were always welcome.

A man who liked music, she told herself, could not be completely heartless. The common folk claimed he used magic to call up terrible storms. There were other stories she could not dismiss so easily. She had ridden out after rebel raids. She had seen the smoldering villages and heard the women weeping.

Before she knew it, they were riding through the gates of the old fort. The bailey was teeming with soldiers. They rode through the chaos of men and horses and carts to the main building. After helping her from her horse, Maredudd led her up the steps with Stephen and the two brothers following on their heels.

The guards inside the entry nodded to the Tudors and opened the second set of heavy doors. Once her eyes adjusted, Catherine saw they were in a dark, cavernous hall. There was a huge hearth against one of the long walls and trestle tables set up along the other. A number of men were in the room, talking in groups or cleaning weapons.

Only one man drew her attention, however. He was watching her from the far end of the hall.

With his hand firmly on her arm, Maredudd walked her

across the room to him. Catherine dropped into the low curtsy reserved for monarchs and kept her head down until a deep voice told her to rise.

When she did, she got her first good look at the famous rebel whose name had been on everyone's lips for the past five years. Owain Glyndwr looked to be in his late forties. His sternly handsome face was lined, and the dark hair that fell to his shoulders was streaked iron gray. Catherine had the impression of long limbs and a powerful body beneath his robes. The riveting black eyes held hers.

"Lady FitzAlan, you have done great harm to me and my people." Glyndwr's words carried through the hall and reverberated off the walls.

Taken aback, Catherine could make no reply. What did he think she had done?

"I wondered for a long time who passed the information that led to my son and his men being caught unawares at Pwll Melyn," Glyndwr said. "In the end, I decided it could only be you."

How had he known? King Henry did not believe she was the one, even when the prince had told him.

"I am sorry, Your Grace," she stammered. "It was my duty."

"Prince Harry took three hundred Welshmen prisoner at Pwll Melyn," he said. "He executed them all, save one."

Involuntarily, she put her hand to her mouth. She had heard something of this before but had not believed it.

"At least young Harry does not kill for sport or revenge. He kills ruthlessly in pursuit of his aims, as a great commander must." Glyndwr's face looked suddenly weary as he turned to gaze into the hearth fire. "The difference, however, matters not to the widows and orphans.

"He executed them all, save for my son Gruffydd, who was taken to London in chains." Glyndwr paused and pressed his lips together. "He is tortured, I am told. After he was caught attempting to escape, the king had his eyes put out."

Catherine felt the sting of tears at the back of her eyes. The truth of Glyndwr's words was etched in the pain on his face. She did not want to believe her king capable of such barbarism. Yet, in her heart, she knew he was. For the first time, she wondered if what she had done was right. Should she have told Harry he could catch the Welsh unprepared that day? Would she have, if she could have foreseen the consequences?

"I hear you have a son, Lady FitzAlan," Glyndwr said, jolting her attention back to the present. "So you will understand that I will do what I can to get my son out of my enemy's hands."

Catherine held her breath, waiting for Glyndwr to reveal his purpose in telling her this.

"You shall be my son's deliverance. His life is the ransom I will claim for your return."

Dismay and confusion warred within her. "I fear you mistake my importance, Your Grace," she said, clutching her hands together. "The king would never trade your son for me. He is not...a sentimental man."

She gave up trying to find a diplomatic way to explain it and said, "The king would sacrifice me without a second thought."

She felt disloyal for her frankness, but she saw what looked like appreciation in Glyndwr's eyes.

"Rayburn was a fool not to realize he had such a perceptive wife. You are right, of course. Henry would not, on his own, make a sacrifice for you."

"My husband will not be able to persuade him otherwise," she said. "I believe Lord FitzAlan would, however, be willing to pay a handsome ransom for me." She no longer cared how much William had to pay, just that he pay it quickly.

"I will not make my demand to FitzAlan," Glyndwr said, "but to the king's son."

Catherine was stunned. "To Harry?"

"I have heard troubadours sing of your beauty, Lady FitzAlan." Glyndwr smiled at her for the first time. "'Tis no wonder you have a prince besotted with you."

Catherine opened her mouth to speak, but no words came out.

"I will send a message informing Prince Harry I will take no payment but my son in exchange for his lover."

"But I am not the prince's lover!" Catherine said, finally finding her voice.

When Glyndwr looked at her skeptically, she attempted to explain. "We were childhood friends. We are friends yet. Besides, I am a married woman." Her face flushing hot with embarrassment, she said, "He would never... he would not..."

"Surely you do not believe your wedded state would stop a man from wanting you," Glyndwr said, raising an eyebrow. "And an English prince would never think such rules applied to him."

Glyndwr looked past her and nodded. Maredudd, whose presence she had forgotten, came to her side.

"Let us hope you are as precious to the prince as I've heard," Glyndwr said, dismissing her. "For you will not see your home again unless he persuades the king to release my son."

Maredudd touched her elbow and whispered, "Make your curtsy."

She did so numbly and let him lead her out to where Stephen and the other Tudors waited.

When the doors to the hall shut behind them, she broke down into sobs. "I fear I shall never see my son or my home again!"

"You shall," Maredudd said, putting his hands on her shoulders. "All will be well in the end, you will see."

"Your prince misunderstands everything!" She clenched her fists and cried out in frustration, "This ransom demand to Prince Harry will make my husband believe I have been unfaithful."

"Nay, he will not," Maredudd said, squeezing her shoulders. "He will just be happy to have you back."

She shook her head. "You know *nothing* of my husband."

* * *

Maredudd escorted her up crumbling stairs to a room crowded with chests—probably pillaged from the town. Through the open window, she saw soldiers gathering in the yard below.

"Will the battle be today?" she asked anxiously.

"I don't know," Maredudd said as he came to stand beside her at the window. "We've been at a standstill for a week. I cannot see it lasting much longer."

"What do you think will happen?"

"We have a slight advantage in numbers, though both armies are large," he said matter-of-factly. "And the English are tired, coming from weeks of hard fighting in the North. Still, anything can happen. All I can say for certain is that there will be a great many deaths on both sides."

He excused himself to join the men below.

She watched the soldiers ride out the gate, looking magnificent in their full armor. As she watched, she thought of the three hundred Welshmen whose capture and execution Glyndwr blamed on her, and she wept for them.

And what of the fate of the English soldiers today? Of William? And Harry?

"Please, God, protect them," she prayed over and over.

For hours, she paced between the trunks of the cramped room. At long last, the gates were thrown open and the men rode back in, looking none the worse. There was no blood on their armor, no wounded comrades slung over their saddles.

She collapsed onto one of the trunks and put her head in her hands. There was still time. Before long, she heard a knock and Maredudd poked his head through the door.

She waved him in, impatient for news. "There was no battle today?"

He shook his head and sank wearily onto a trunk by the window. "God's beard, this waiting is tedious."

"Maredudd, you must ask for an audience with Prince Glyndwr for me," she said. "There is something I must tell him."

"God in heaven, what can it be? He is busy consulting with his commanders."

Seeing her recalcitrant look, he sighed. "Perhaps I can tell him whatever it is you want him to know."

"I must speak with him myself."

Stifling another oath, Maredudd put his hands on his knees and hoisted himself up. "Your servant," he said, sweeping her a low bow.

An hour later, a woman came to her room carrying a basin of water and a cloth.

"One of the Tudor men sent me. He says to tell you Prince Glyndwr will see you in an hour."

The woman was no ladies' maid. From her rouged lips and revealing bodice, Catherine suspected her usual duties involved providing service of quite a different sort.

The woman put her hands on her hips and looked Catherine up and down. "You're a bit worse for wear, you are. Perhaps we can find you a clean gown in one of these trunks."

Catherine glanced down at her bedraggled gown.

"Aye, let us take a look."

The two women opened trunks and pawed through tunics, leggings, and shirts until they were both hot and red-faced. Near the bottom of one, they found an elegant silk gown of robin' s-egg blue with delicate silver trim.

The woman helped Catherine into it. Though it was a bit tight through the bodice, it fit well enough. The woman stuck her head back in the trunk and popped back out, proudly holding up a matching headdress and slippers.

When Catherine was dressed and ready, her helper beamed at her, proud as a peacock. She gave Catherine a broad wink and said, "You look like a princess."

Regal might be just what she needed for this performance, Catherine thought grimly as she started down the stairs. Maredudd was waiting for her at the bottom, just outside the entrance to the hall. When he caught sight of her, he ran his eyes over her from head to toe.

"I see conquering one prince is not enough," he said in a low voice as she took his arm, "but you must set your sights on ensnaring a second."

"I don't know what you mean," she snapped.

"I warn you, our prince is no boy to do your bidding like young Harry," he said, his tone serious. "Do not attempt to play games with him. Glyndwr will know if you tell him lies."

The guards opened the doors, and she saw that the men inside were gathered around a large map rolled out on a trestle table. They turned to stare at her as she entered.

Glyndwr moved away from the others and motioned for her and Maredudd to join him by the hearth.

"What is it you wish to tell me, Lady FitzAlan?" Glyndwr asked at once. He was not a man with time to waste on pleasantries.

It seemed best to start with the truth.

"I have thought hard on what you said about the three hundred men who died because of what I did." Her hands were sweating, but she kept them still. "I regret their deaths."

Glyndwr waited, his gaze unrelenting.

"I fear many more men will die in this battle," she said. "So I prayed to God, asking if it would be a sin to tell you what I know when it might prevent more bloodshed."

"And God answered you?" Glyndwr did not sound as though he thought it likely.

"Not clearly, no." The distress in her voice was genuine.

"So you decided to tell me without the benefit of divine guidance. What is it, Lady FitzAlan? My time is short."

Now for her lie.

"Part of the English army waits near Monmouth Castle." She looked straight into his eyes and made herself believe it as she said it. "They plan to attack you from behind and cut your army off from Wales."

After a pause, Glyndwr asked, "Who leads these men?"

"Prince Harry." She knew from what he said in their first meeting that he respected Harry's military skills.

"But the prince is here at Worcester," Glyndwr said with a smile. "He is easy to pick out on the field."

"Remember Shrewsbury?" she said, her tone challenging.

Anger flashed in his eyes. There were rumors Glyndwr arrived late at Shrewsbury and watched from the woods as the Northern rebel army folded.

"At Shrewsbury, the king employed decoys—knights dressed in the king's armor and mounted on horses like his own," she said. "Hotspur killed two of them before he was cut down."

Catherine kept her eyes steady on Glyndwr as she told her next lie. "The prince uses the same device to fool you now. It was a false prince you saw today. The true one waits to cut off your retreat and attack you from behind."

"Why should I believe you?" he said, his black eyes searching for the truth in her soul. "Why would you come to the rebel cause now, after what you did before?"

"I do not take the rebel side," she said, on the firm ground of truth again. "But I do not want to have more blood on my hands, English or Welsh."

"So you regret betraying your husband to his death?"

"No!" She blurted her answer without stopping to think.

He nodded, and she saw that the frankness of her response lent credibility to her story.

For a reason she could not explain, she wanted to give Glyndwr the truth about Rayburn, at least.

"Rayburn gave you no true allegiance, Prince Glyndwr," she said in a quiet voice. "He would have sold you to the devil to save himself."

"You tell me nothing I did not know." With a bittersweet smile, he added, "In sooth, his lady wife would have been the better ally."

He stepped closer to her. The penetrating look he gave her sent a shiver through her, but she could not look away from the intense dark eyes. There was a magnetism about this man. She understood Maredudd's warning now. A woman might risk a great deal to be near a man who emanated such power, in the hope he might direct some of that dark passion toward her. She would have to be a brave woman, though.

"Please, let me go home," she said. "I want to see my son."

Glyndwr's eyes went flat, and he looked away from her. "As do I, Lady FitzAlan. As do I."

Guilt stabbed her for reminding him of his pain.

But she had told her lies well. She could only pray she had been right to tell them.

Chapter Twenty

The English commanders awoke to find the Welsh-French army had disappeared during the night. None could explain the unexpected withdrawal. William, for one, was glad to save his men to fight another day. No good could have come from the battle for the English. Even if they prevailed, the field would have been awash with English blood. The loss of men would have made them more vulnerable to the French, their real enemy.

However, it was hard to understand why the other army had withdrawn. A French-Welsh victory on English soil might well have forced King Henry to sacrifice his claim on Wales.

William bid the king farewell and headed for home. Prince Harry rode with him as far as Monmouth. Until it was certain the French were retreating all the way to their ships, the prince would remain in the Welsh Marches.

William had come to like Prince Harry well enough, but

he was glad when they parted ways. He was tired of talking of military matters. Riding in blessed silence, he tried to resolve the mystery that was his wife.

Would he always find her in hallways, sharing secrets with princes and troubadours? Good Lord, she even admitted to passing her lover's child off as her husband's. Yet, this same woman welcomed William's young brother into her household with an open heart. She forgave William his harsh words, his lack of trust, and accepted on faith his promise to do better.

And she said she loved him.

Though he did not fully understand her, he knew for certain he could never be content without her.

A sense of well-being came over him when he saw Ross Castle in the distance. Even now, the lookouts would be reporting his arrival to the household. He looked forward to seeing Jamie and Stephen as well. He had grown attached to the boys.

He shook his head. Odd how life could change so quickly. Two months ago, he came here with no real ties. Now, for the first time in his life, he felt as if he had something to lose.

He remembered Catherine's uneasy stomach the day before he left and felt anxious. He spurred his horse ahead of his men and rode through the open gate.

Most of the men he had left at the castle were waiting for him in the bailey. Catherine was not. Scanning the group, he saw that Stephen was missing, too. And where the devil was Edmund?

As he dismounted, a small figure shot out from between the men. He tossed his reins to a waiting stable boy and lifted Jamie into the air.

"Where's your mother, big boy?"

"Didn't you find her?"

Fear ran like ice through his veins.

"Lord FitzAlan." He turned to see Hugh Stratton, one of the men he left with Edmund.

"What has happened?" William said, his heart beating wildly in his chest. "Where is my wife?"

"Lady FitzAlan wished to go to the abbey," Hugh said. "Edmund and Stephen escorted her."

William sagged with relief. His relief dissolved a moment later when Hugh could not meet his eyes.

"What is it? Out with it, man!"

"They were attacked."

God, no!

"When they did not return when expected, we went out looking for them. We found Edmund, but he's in bad shape."

"What of Catherine and Stephen?" Would the fool not tell him if they were alive or dead?

"They must have been taken captive. Except where Edmund was, we found no blood, no piece of torn clothing..."

God have mercy. "When was this?"

"Two days ago. I had the men out searching for them all of yesterday and today," Hugh said. "Edmund can speak now, if you wish to see him. Alys put a bed up for him in the keep."

William was so intent on questioning Hugh that he forgot the boy in his arms until Jamie yelled, "I want my mother!"

Jamie looked at him with eyes big and wet with tears. "I want Stephen, too."

"I shall bring them home," William promised. *And if either one is harmed, I will track the villains down and kill every one of them.*

Jamie leaned heavily against his chest as William carried

him to the keep. After handing the boy off to his nursemaid, William went with Hugh to see Edmund.

William paused at the door. He'd seen more than his share of wounded men. But, God's blood, Edmund looked as if he'd been trampled by horses. Everywhere he wasn't bandaged, he was black and blue.

When William knelt beside the cot, Edmund opened one eye. The other was swollen shut.

"I did my best, but there were six of them," Edmund croaked. "I killed one before another caught me from behind."

"What sort of men were they?"

"Welshmen, highborn," Edmund said, and closed his eye.

Praise God they were not rabble! Noblemen were as violent as any men, but rarely so with women of their own class. If Catherine's captors were indeed noblemen, it was likely they took her for ransom and would treat her reasonably well.

He turned and asked Hugh, "Has a ransom message come?"

Hugh shook his head.

When William started to get up, Edmund tried to speak again. William put his hand on Edmund's arm and leaned over to hear him better.

"They were expecting us," Edmund said in a hoarse whisper. "I heard them say her name."

William left Edmund and took his men out to search for Catherine and Stephen. Though the kidnappers would have them deep in Wales by now, he ordered his men to search every wood and hut. They found no sign of Catherine, Stephen, or the men who took them. He continued searching alone long after dark.

When he returned, he was too dispirited to face his empty bed. Instead, he went up to Jamie's bedchamber where he startled the poor nursemaid from her pallet. As soon as she scurried into the adjoining room, he slumped into the chair by the bed. Somehow, it soothed his troubled soul to watch the boy's face, relaxed and peaceful in sleep.

He awoke at dawn, stiff from sleeping in the chair.

Chapter Twenty-one

Stephen felt the lookouts' eyes tracking him as he rode across the empty fields toward Monmouth Castle in the bright moonlight. As soon as the gate was opened, he was surrounded by a dozen armed men.

"I have a message for the prince's eyes only," Stephen said to each man who questioned him as he was passed up the chain of command. "The prince will want to see it tonight."

It was well past midnight when Stephen was finally delivered to the prince's private rooms. To his relief, Prince Harry did not look as if he had been roused from bed. Stephen bowed low, as his mother had taught him.

"So, young Carleton, what brings you to travel alone at this late hour to see me?"

"Lady Catherine and I were taken captive by Welsh rebels, Your Highness," Stephen said.

"Lady Catherine?" The prince gripped the arms of his chair. "They've taken Catherine?"

"Aye, they have. They released me to bring you this message." Stephen pulled it from his belt and handed it over. "I was told to put it in no one's hands but yours."

The prince broke the seal and scanned it quickly. With an impatient wave, he sent his manservant from the room. He did not speak until the door was shut again.

"You've had a rough journey and must be hungry." The prince gestured to a platter piled high with bread, cheese, and fruit on the table next to him. "Come, sit and eat."

Stephen took the chair on the other side of the small table and accepted the cup of mulled wine the prince poured from an ornate silver decanter.

"They treated you well?"

Stephen nodded and took a long drink from the cup.

"I must consult FitzAlan on this matter," the prince said. "Lady Catherine is, after all, his wife."

Stephen's mouth was full, so he nodded vigorously. "I'll go with you," he said as soon as he swallowed. "'Tis best you don't go alone to speak with my brother."

The prince raised an eyebrow. "You know the content of the message?"

Stephen nodded again.

"These rebels are bold," the prince said. "Can you tell me why they sent a ransom demand to me, rather than FitzAlan?"

Stephen fidgeted in his chair and looked toward the door.

"Out with it," the prince commanded. "I shall not blame the messenger."

Stephen shifted his gaze back to the prince and tried to discern if he meant what he said.

"Owain Glyndwr has heard you are fond of Lady Catherine." Stephen really did not want to say this, but he saw no way around it. "More than fond."

When the prince did not react, Stephen began to wonder if he was a little slow in the head. He judged the distance to the door again, then decided to get it over with.

"Glyndwr believes Catherine is your mistress."

He watched the prince, waiting for a violent reaction.

Prince Harry rested his chin on his clasped hands. "This is unfortunate," he said quite calmly. "Glyndwr is mistaken if he thinks the king would release her for my sake, no matter what she is to me."

The prince appeared to be lost in thought for a moment.

"There must be talk about Lady Catherine and me for Glyndwr to have heard this." He looked at Stephen and lifted an eyebrow. "Tell me, Stephen Carleton, what do you believe?"

"Lady Catherine is an honorable lady," Stephen said at once. "She would never do it."

The prince smiled. "I am glad to hear you share my high opinion of her."

Forgetting his earlier caution, Stephen added, "But I did hear talk among the men at Ross Castle. It is well known the two of you are close."

"Damnation," the prince muttered.

After that, the prince made Stephen recount every detail of their capture and the events since. By the time Prince Harry dismissed him, Stephen was dizzy with fatigue.

Stephen paused at the door. "If we both tell William it is not true—about you and Lady Catherine—perhaps he will believe us."

The prince smiled. "You are a brave man, Stephen. I shall be glad to have you at my back."

* * *

Why did the men who took Catherine and Stephen not send a message yet? William was nearly mad with worry and frustrated past bearing.

Edmund was more alert today. Though he was not out of danger, he seemed likely to survive. William pressed him about why he thought their attackers did not just happen upon them.

"Why would a half-dozen well-armed men on good horses be on that quiet path to the abbey at just that time?" Edmund asked.

Men of that ilk should have been at Worcester, whether they be Welsh or English.

"I tell you, William, they knew her name."

"But I've questioned every man, woman, and child in the castle," William said, pacing the sickroom in frustration. "If we have a traitor in the castle who passed the word you were taking her to the abbey, someone should have heard or seen something."

After a long pause, Edmund said in a low voice, "She's run from you before."

William stopped his pacing. *She's run from you before.* The words were like a knife in his belly.

He turned slowly to face Edmund, clenching and unclenching his fists. "Are you suggesting Catherine arranged this herself?"

"All I'm saying, 'tis peculiar," Edmund said.

He remembered what she said the night before he left for Worcester. *It is you I need rescuing from now, William. You bring me misery of a kind Rayburn never could.*

"She wouldn't leave Jamie," William said.

"She meant to take the boy, but I told her no."

"You've been against her from the start!" he shouted. "I tell you, she wouldn't do it."

"You would not let her leave the castle on her own," Edmund persisted, "so she might have used the kidnap as a ruse to get away."

If Edmund wasn't bandaged from head to foot, he'd pick him up and slam him against the wall.

"There is another explanation," he ground out through clenched teeth. "There has to be."

She promised she would not leave again. She gave her word.

"She deceived her last husband for years," Edmund said. "You've known her, what, three months?"

Less than that. But he knew her. He loved her. And she loved him. Didn't she?

He looked at the crusted blood on the bandage around Edmund's head and the seeping wound on his neck. "If you think so little of her, why would you nearly get yourself killed trying to protect her?"

"Out of loyalty to you, of course," Edmund said in his croaking voice. "You entrusted her to my protection, and I have an inkling of what she means to you."

Edmund could have no notion of what she meant to him.

"I will pay whatever ransom they ask," he said more to himself than to Edmund. "There is nothing I will not do to get her back. Nothing."

"Women are fickle. Perhaps she'll change her mind and return," Edmund said. "Or the men she trusted to take her away will play her false and hold her for ransom."

"Enough of your poison tongue!" William said, shaking with anger. "I swear to you, Edmund, injured or not, I will throw you out if you speak another word against her."

"What do I know about women?" Edmund's breathing was labored now, and his words were punctuated by long pauses. "I'm sorry...I won't say it again...No one will be happier than I...to be proved wrong about her. I..."

William couldn't berate an unconscious man, so he left.

He tried to push what Edmund said out of his head. But the damage was done. Against his will, the doubts and questions came. They raced through his mind, around and around. Was Jamie's father not dead after all? Did she go to him? Was he one of the rebels? Or that damn troubadour?

Nay, it could not be true. Surely she would not have taken Stephen with her?

William was in a poor state by the time the prince and Stephen arrived. The moment Stephen slid down from his horse, William took hold of him. It was the first time he had embraced this young brother of his.

"Your lady wife is well," Stephen said.

"Who has her? Where is she?" William demanded.

"The Tudors will take good care of her," Stephen said in a rush. "They are good men, for rebels."

"Sweet lamb of God!" William thundered. "The Tudors! Are you saying the Tudors have her?"

The prince stepped forward and put a hand on William's arm.

"Let us go inside," he said, and cast his eyes meaningfully toward the men and servants gathered around them. "We will tell you all we know, but it is a tale too long for the bailey yard."

William escorted Prince Harry and Stephen into the keep and upstairs to the family's private rooms. As soon as they were seated in the solar with the door closed, William looked at them expectantly.

"Tell FitzAlan what happened when you and Lady Catherine were captured," Prince Harry directed Stephen. "Give him the shortened version now. Later, he will want to hear it with all the detail you can remember."

Stephen's abbreviated recounting of events relieved

William's worst fears. In his darkest moments, he had imagined his wife lying raped and murdered in a wood somewhere.

He had so many questions, he did not know where to start. "Why did they take you to Monmouth?"

Stephen looked uneasily at the prince.

"I was as surprised as you," Prince Harry said, pulling a letter from a pouch at his belt and handing it to William. "This is the message they sent with Stephen."

He noticed the prince and Stephen exchange glances before he began to read. As he read the message, signed by Owain Glyndwr himself, the blood drained from his head.

"Can you please tell me," he addressed Prince Harry in a coldly polite tone, "why my wife's captors would present a demand to you, rather than seek ransom from me, her husband?"

Prince Harry met William's eyes with a hard look of his own. "I am your prince, FitzAlan. I answer to no man, save the king. Still, I will tell you what you want to know. But listen well, for I'll not speak of it again.

"I care too deeply for your lady wife to dishonor her by making her my mistress," the prince said, enunciating every word clearly. "And Catherine would never consent to it. She respects me as her future king, but she loves me as a brother. A *younger* brother."

"And you, sire?" William asked in a tight voice. "May I ask the nature of your feelings for my wife?"

"I will not tell you I've never felt desire for her," Prince Harry said, meeting his eyes with a steady gaze. "But I have known since I was twelve I could not marry her. While a woman as astute as Catherine would be an asset, I must make a marriage that is an alliance for England.

"Since I could not make Catherine my queen, and I would

not make her my mistress," the prince said, "I remain her friend. And happily so."

With his speech finished, Prince Harry considered the question settled and the subject closed. He moved at once to the problem before them.

"'Tis useless to ask the king to trade Gruffydd for her," the prince said, rubbing his chin. "I am not certain my father would give up Glyndwr's son even if it were me the rebels held."

William did not disagree.

"So we must think of another means to gain her safe return," the prince said. "Stephen says she remained with Glyndwr's army, traveling west, when the Tudors split off to deliver him to Monmouth."

In the end, they agreed Prince Harry would send a message to the rebel leader advising him that the king could not be persuaded to release Gruffydd. The prince would enclose a letter from William offering a monetary ransom.

"In the meantime, we must discover where Catherine is being held," William said. "Glyndwr may refuse to ransom her. I cannot rescue her if I do not know where she is."

Prince Harry made the astonishing suggestion that William talk with Abbess Talcott.

"You never know," Prince Harry said with a smile, "what news might come to the good abbess."

* * *

Like most Northerners, William was related to half the nobility—and knew the rest—on both sides of the Scots-English border. Hostage-taking was so common in that region that it was almost a sport. If his wife had been kidnapped there, he could have found out where she was being held in half a day.

But he was at a loss as to how to find her in Wales. The language was different, the people hostile. Hostages taken deep into that country were not found until their ransoms were paid.

He did not know how a nun in an isolated abbey could help him discover where Catherine was, but he had no other notion what to do. He and Stephen set off for the abbey as soon as the prince was out the gates.

As they made the short ride, William could not help thinking of the last time he had ridden this path: the day he retrieved his bride from the abbey. Had he driven her to run from him again?

"Please, God, keep her safe," he prayed. "Whether she went willingly or not, bring her back."

This time, he entered the abbey grounds quietly and waited in the courtyard for one of the nuns to escort him and Stephen up to the abbess's private rooms. When he reached the doorway to her parlor, he was too surprised to speak.

It could not be! There, chatting amiably with the abbess, his long legs stretched out before him, sat Catherine's troubadour.

"Good afternoon, Lord FitzAlan," the abbess greeted him.

William stared at the troubadour as Abbess Talcott exchanged greetings with Stephen.

Gesturing toward the troubadour, she said, "May I present Robert Fass?"

"We have met," William bit out.

"After a fashion," Robert said, an amused smile lifting the corners of his mouth. The man evidently was counting on William's forbearance while on abbey grounds.

Abbess Talcott invited them to sit and passed around a tray of honey cakes. To William, she said in a low voice, "I've assigned another sister the task of baking."

All the same, William waited until Stephen devoured two with no obvious ill effects before taking one himself.

When the abbess made no move to send the troubadour away so they could speak privately, he stated his business. "My wife has been taken hostage by the rebels. She was captured while on her way to visit you here, at the abbey."

The abbess's face showed deep concern but not surprise. "I only just heard the news from Robert."

"In God's name, how did he know of it?"

"Remember where you are," the abbess reprimanded him. "It hardly matters how Robert learned of it."

"Do you know where she is?" William asked the troubadour. He was willing to overlook the man's transgressions if only he would tell him where to find her.

"Not yet," the abbess answered for him. She patted the troubadour's arm and said, "But my friend Robert is our best hope of finding out."

Holding back the oath that had been on his lips, William asked, "How would you learn of my wife's whereabouts?"

"Despite the rebellion, my troupe travels freely in both Wales and the Marches," Robert said. "I can take my troupe into Wales and look for her without being suspected."

"And why would you go to such trouble for my wife?"

Robert's eyes danced with amusement. "We are great friends. Did she not tell you?"

"Don't be foolish," the abbess chided. "Lord FitzAlan, tell us what you can about what happened."

Stephen and William told them all they knew. Robert asked a number of questions. He had the good sense, however, not to remark on the unusual nature of the ransom demand.

"The possibilities are not good," Robert said, shaking his head. "Let us hope Glyndwr doesn't send her to the Continent with the French forces for safekeeping. It would be as bad, though, if he takes her to Aberystwyth or Harlech castles."

God help him if Glyndwr held her at either of those castles. They were on the west coast of Wales, far from English soil. Both castles were considered impregnable, or very nearly so.

"I will follow Glyndwr's trail until I hear news of her," Robert said. "I will be discreet, of course."

Spying appeared to come easily to this itinerant bard. He hid a fine mind behind that handsome face and glib demeanor.

William looked back and forth between Robert and the abbess and raised an eyebrow. "The two of you helped Catherine with her spying?"

They smiled with the look of well-fed cats.

"Rayburn did not have a chance," William said.

"That devil's spawn did not deserve one," Robert said, showing a flash of anger for the first time.

William wondered who this singer of ballads truly was. The man was not raised by a peasant or tradesman, to be sure. He showed too much ease conversing with an abbess and a lord. Whoever he was, William was profoundly grateful for his help.

"The part we occasionally play in the conflict must remain a secret," the abbess advised William. "Robert can be of no help if his collaboration is suspected."

"We will tell no one," William promised. He gave Stephen a severe look to be sure his brother understood.

"Not even Edmund," Stephen said.

Chapter Twenty-two

Catherine felt very much alone traveling in the midst of a Welsh-French army of thousands. Even the Tudor brothers would have been a welcome sight to her now.

She certainly would have felt safer under their protection.

She braved a glance at Rhys Gethin, whose heavily muscled thigh was uncomfortably close to hers as he rode at her side. He'd taken Maredudd's place as her primary keeper. "The Fierce One," as she had come to think of him, had neither the fine looks nor the courtly manners of the Tudors.

Everything about the man was rough, from the well-worn tunic that reeked of sweat and horses to the long hair that fell to his shoulders in matted knots. He was built like an ox, with a broad chest and thick neck. Though he rarely spoke, the other Welshmen paid heed when he did.

He turned and fixed his intense gaze on her. With eyes as black as his soul, he was the most frightening man she had ever met.

"What is it, sir?" she asked sharply, though it was she who had stared at him first.

He nodded ahead to where the path narrowed and grunted something she took to mean he wanted her to ride in front. She spurred her horse, grateful to put a little distance between them. A shiver crept up her spine. When she looked over her shoulder, his eyes were on her like hot burning coals.

At least she was free of The Fierce One at night. Rhys Gethin camped out with the army, while Catherine was taken into Welsh homes as Glyndwr's guest. The homes were humble, but at least she had a roof over her head.

When they reached Milford Haven, the French soldiers and horses were loaded onto the ships waiting in the harbor. After the ships disembarked, Glyndwr disbursed most of his army. The fighting season was over. Only a core contingent of men rode north with them along the west coast.

Catherine's breath caught at the sight of Aberystwyth, a magnificent castle with concentric walls built in the shape of a diamond on the very edge of the roiling sea. It was one of the iron ring of fortresses Edward I built around the perimeter of Wales to demonstrate English power over the subjugated Welsh.

After little more than a hundred years, Aberystwyth was crumbling under the assault of pounding sea, wind, and rain. Catherine looked around as they rode into the castle's huge outer bailey. The main gate and drawbridge were falling down, but its rings of thick walls still made it formidable. Glyndwr had been able to take it only because King Henry diverted men to fight the Scots and left the castle inadequately defended.

From the moment they turned north, Catherine had feared Glyndwr would bring her here—or worse, to Harlech Castle. Her chances of escape or rescue from either were dismal.

Still, they were better here at crumbling Aberystwyth than at Harlech.

When Rhys lifted her from her saddle, she held her breath against the smell of him. She tried not to show how much it distressed her to have him touch her.

She slept that night in a chamber high in a tower overlooking the sea. The guards outside her door seemed an unnecessary precaution. Tense and uneasy, she barred her door and fell asleep to the sound of waves crashing on the shore.

In the morning, a maid came to help her dress and to tell her she would ride with Prince Glyndwr today. Aberystwyth, then, was not their final destination.

When Gethin helped her mount her horse, she noticed he did not smell quite so bad and that someone had made an attempt to brush his clothes. Silent as usual, he escorted her to where Glyndwr waited.

"I was going to send you to France," Glyndwr said as they rode out the gate heading north.

Catherine nearly gasped aloud. England's conflict with France was unending. If she was taken there, she might be held for years and years.

"I want to go home," she said, "but I prefer the wild beauty of Wales to France."

"Then you can thank Rhys Gethin, for he was adamant I keep you here. He mistrusts our French allies."

"So, where are you taking me?"

"To Harlech Castle, where I live with my family."

Her heart plummeted.

"Your King Edward—may he rot in hell—did not make the mistake he made at Aberystwyth by building Harlech too near the sea." There was pride in his voice as he added, "There was never a castle better built for defense."

Prince Harry said the same of Harlech.

"There will be gowns and the other things you need at Harlech. I am sorry I neglected to provide better for you, but I did not foresee I would have a lady traveling with my army."

Gowns were the least of her concerns.

"You managed the rough travel well," he said with an approving glance. "Gethin says you are made of tougher stock than your first husband. But then, he thought even less of Rayburn than he does of our French allies. He dislikes men who betray their own."

He signaled to the nearest men to ride farther back.

"Rhys Gethin has made a request of me," he said. "If King Henry refuses to release my son, he wants me to give you to him to be his wife."

Catherine could not have been more stunned.

Of all the objections she could make, what she said was, "But the man dislikes me!"

"Nay, he is captivated." Glyndwr smiled with rare amusement. "He surprises us both."

"Does he not have a wife?"

"She died many years ago," Glyndwr said. "He did not seem to mind the lack of one until now."

No doubt he terrorizes the serving girls, Catherine thought to herself.

"But, Your Grace, I am already married."

"If King Henry will not yield what I ask, I may relieve you of your husband."

Catherine looked at him in horror. "If you think to make me a widow, you underestimate my husband. He is a skilled fighter."

"You are right to praise FitzAlan's skills," Glyndwr said, unperturbed. "I was disappointed when Northumberland could not persuade him to join our cause. But I was not speaking of FitzAlan's death—only of an annulment of your marriage."

"That is not possible," she said, feeling herself color. "Our marriage was consummated."

Glyndwr dismissed this difficulty with a wave of his hand.

They rode in silence for a time. Then, with seeming indifference, he asked, "Are you with child?"

She sensed it was to ask this single question that Glyndwr chose to ride with her today. Without pausing a heartbeat to consider her response, she looked directly into his eyes and said, "Sadly, I am not."

She was getting better at lying all the time.

"Good, then an annulment is possible," he said, but Catherine did not think he was pleased by her answer.

* * *

Harlech Castle served as both Glyndwr's court and his base of military operations. With the fighting season over and the autumn rains setting in, the castle was crawling with soldiers with little to do. Catherine was not left unguarded for a moment.

Guarding her must be a singularly tedious assignment. She spent most of her time alone in her chamber or praying in the chapel. Since she could not bear to feel The Fierce One's eyes on her while she ate, she rarely took her meals in the great hall. Besides, observing Glyndwr's happy family life only served to make her feel more despondent.

She had been at Harlech a week when she was summoned to the great hall for an audience with Glyndwr. Here in his court, Glyndwr maintained the outward trappings of his princely status. She bowed low before a severe-looking

Glyndwr dressed in ermine-trimmed robes and sitting on a gilded throne.

"Lady FitzAlan, I have received Prince Harry's reply to my ransom demand," he announced. "He advises me that the king will not release my son in exchange for your safe return."

Since Glyndwr's son was blind and could not fight, Catherine thought the king was only keeping him for spite.

"It is as I expected, Your Grace," she said in a low voice. "I am sorry he will not return your son."

"I believe you are," Glyndwr said, his eyes softening.

He came down from the dais and led her to sit with him before the roaring fire in the hearth.

"I served with King Henry in Scotland twenty years ago," Glyndwr remarked. "He was just 'Bolingbroke' then."

"I believe he has changed a good deal since then—since he gained the throne," she said, throwing caution to the wind.

Glyndwr raised an eyebrow and nodded for her to continue.

"These rebellions have made our king mistrustful." She ventured a sideways glance at him. "And unforgiving. He will not show mercy, even when it costs him nothing."

Was it wise to speak of her king like this to Glyndwr? Was it treason? She did not know, but she wanted to give Glyndwr the truth with regard to his son, if nothing else.

"If you wish to have your son back, you must give the king something he holds very dear." She gave him the only suggestion she had. "He would exchange Gruffydd for Harlech."

Glyndwr shook his head. "You know I cannot put my son above the interests of my people."

"Then your best hope is to arrange for Gruffydd to escape," she said. "It has been done before. Perhaps you could bribe a guard?"

"My son was blinded for his first attempt to escape," Glyndwr said. "I would not have him risk so much again."

Catherine looked away from the pain she saw on the great man's face.

"When Harry takes his father's place," she said in a quiet voice, "I am certain he will pardon your son and release him." It was a paltry offering.

"I fear Gruffydd will not survive long in the Tower."

They sat in silence, staring at the fire.

After a few moments, he said, "Prince Harry enclosed a letter from your husband with his message."

She sat up straight. "A letter from William? What does he say?"

Glyndwr leaned forward and tapped his forefingers against his pursed lips before answering. "FitzAlan offers a large monetary ransom."

Catherine closed her eyes. God be praised! After the utter bleakness she had felt since arriving at Harlech, she was afraid of the hope that sprang inside her.

Her voice quavered as she put the question to Glyndwr. "Will you take the ransom my husband offers?"

Glyndwr's expression was hard now. He was no longer father, but prince.

"I will send another message, reiterating my price," he said, his voice stern. "If Prince Harry still does not comply, I have a commander who would benefit from having a wife with the political skills he lacks."

Glyndwr was no fool, so she wondered how he believed he could have her marriage annulled.

"I am considering recognizing the French pope in Avignon."

His words struck her like a thunderbolt. God chose Saint Peter's successor on Earth. A ruler who supported the alternative pope risked damnation not only for himself, but also for all his people. Even in her shock, Catherine was awed by Glyndwr's boldness.

"I will demand concessions in return, of course," he said, more to himself than to her. "Independence for the Welsh church. A guarantee that only men who speak Welsh will be appointed bishops and priests. The end of payments to English monasteries and colleges.

"It would be a small matter to add a request for the annulment of one marriage." He turned and focused his eyes on her again. "Particularly when that marriage was made without proper banns and on the very day of the first husband's murder."

Cold fear gripped her heart. As a last resort, she could reveal her pregnancy. Surely even the French pope would not grant an annulment if he knew she was with child.

* * *

Catherine paced her chamber, as she often did since her conversation with Glyndwr. If she could only have something to give her hope!

She jumped at the knock on her door. Opening the door a crack, she saw that one of her guards wanted to speak to her.

"Prince Glyndwr requests your presence in the hall this evening," the young man said. "He wants you to enjoy the music of the traveling musicians who've just arrived."

"Thank you, I will come." She closed the door and leaned against it. *God, please, let it be Robert.*

That evening, she sat at the table, every muscle taut, waiting for the musicians. Even having Rhys Gethin sit beside her—and, God help her, share a trencher with her—could not divert her. When the musicians finally came into the hall, she nearly burst into tears.

Robert had come. With his dazzling good looks and striking blond hair, he stood out like a white crane in the midst of crows.

Robert did not let his gaze fall on her directly, but she knew he saw her, too. She wanted desperately to talk with him, to hear news of home. But how could they find a way to meet with guards dogging her every step?

She listened through the long evening for a message or a signal of some kind. It finally came in his last ballad, a familiar song about secret lovers. As Robert sang the final refrain in which the man asks his beloved where she will meet him, he put his hands together as if in prayer and glanced in her direction.

Catherine put her hands together and nodded, hoping she understood his meaning.

Her guards had spent many hours standing in the doorway of the chapel while she prayed. They were not surprised, then, when she told them she wished to go there before retiring to her chamber. She caught the annoyed look that passed between them, but they could hardly complain that their prisoner prayed too much.

She was on her knees on the cold stone floor for an hour before someone in priest's robes entered. She glanced over her shoulder to be sure her guards' soft snores were not feigned.

Robert sank to his knees beside her.

"Before you ask," he whispered close to her ear, "William, Jamie, and Stephen are all well, though they miss you."

"Praise God," she said, crossing herself. "You cannot know how glad I am to see you! How did you find me?"

"There is no time to tell you now. We must be brief. Do

you know if Glyndwr plans to keep you here at Harlech? Will he accept William's ransom?"

"Glyndwr yet holds a thread of hope that Harry will secure his son's release." She reached for Robert's hand. "When he loses that hope, it will be still worse for me."

Robert held a finger to his lips, and she realized her voice had risen in her distress.

"Glyndwr says he will have my marriage to William annulled," she whispered. "He talks of marrying me to one of his men—to Rhys Gethin! Robert, I cannot bear it!"

Robert contemplated this in silence for a moment. "Aye, we must get you out. But annulments are never quick, so we have time to make a plan."

"I cannot wait much longer—"

"I must go," he whispered. "I will look for you here tomorrow night at the same time."

"If something happens and we do not meet again," she said, gripping his hand, "tell my family I love them and miss them with all my heart."

"We shall meet tomorrow," he said, giving her hand one last squeeze.

She waited until Robert was safely out of the chapel. After saying one more prayer, she rose on stiff legs to wake her guards. They escorted her to her chamber, where she bid them good night and barred the door.

Her mind was still on her conversation with Robert as she turned from the door. A shriek caught in her throat. In the moonlight from the narrow window, she could see the outline of a man sprawled on the chair beside her bed.

"Did you enjoy the music?" Maredudd Tudor asked.

Chapter Twenty-three

Catherine was so tired of riding that she was sure she would never be able to walk normally again. She lost her headdress days ago. Her hair hung in a tangled mess. Her gown was so filthy that if they did not reach their destination soon, she just might rip it off and ride naked.

Maredudd said he was taking her to his home on the island of Anglesey on the northwest coast. After establishing a false trail to the south, he took her inland and headed north, across countless streams and through endless forests. He apologized for the rough travel, explaining that Glyndwr ordered him to take every precaution. Even his own people must not learn where she went or with whom she traveled.

Catherine longed with all her heart to wash, to sleep in fresh sheets, and to eat a meal prepared by anyone other than Maredudd Tudor. The only benefit to her physical misery was that it diverted her from dwelling on how much she missed William, Jamie, and Stephen.

They crossed the isthmus onto Anglesey at low tide. A few miles farther, they reached Plas Penmynydd, the large fortified manor that was the Tudor home. When Maredudd lifted her from her horse before the entrance to the house, he had to hold on to her to keep her from falling.

Still clutching his arm, Catherine looked up into the hostile gray eyes of a pretty dark-haired woman. She was well rounded, almost plump, and a few years older than Catherine.

What caught Catherine's attention, however, was the lady's apricot silk gown. All her life, Catherine had taken her fine gowns for granted, but at this moment, she coveted this one with a piercing envy. It was so very *clean.*

"Marged, come greet me properly, love, and meet our guest," Maredudd called out.

So, this angry woman in apricot was Maredudd's wife. Catherine suddenly felt aware of her own disheveled appearance.

In that moment, a boy of about five ran out of the house and barreled into Maredudd. He lifted the boy up, laughing, and settled him on his hip. When the boy turned his head to look at her, Catherine was taken aback by the sheer beauty of the child.

"Who is the lady, Father?" the boy asked.

"This is Lady Catherine FitzAlan. She will be our guest for a time," he said, ruffling the boy's hair. "Lady Catherine, meet my lovely wife, Marged, and my son Owain, lead troublemaker of Plas Penmynydd."

Catherine nodded politely at Marged, then turned back to the boy. "To be lead troublemaker among the Tudor men," she said with a smile, "is quite a feat."

* * *

Catherine remembered almost nothing of her first evening at Penmynydd. She was taken to a bedchamber, stripped of her filthy gown, and soaked in a tub of steaming water until her skin puckered. She was asleep on her feet as the maid dried her and helped her into a plain shift for bed.

The smells from a waiting tray roused her long enough to eat. The food was so delicious she nearly cried with pleasure.

The sun was high when she awoke the next day. Sadness weighed upon her heart like a stone. How would William ever find her here in Anglesey? Would she ever see her home again? And what of the child she carried? Tears fell down the sides of her face and into her hair, but she was too bone-weary to lift her arms and wipe them away.

Sometime later, a maid peeked through her door. "I'm to help you dress, m'lady."

Catherine was about to object that she had nothing to wear, when the maid held out a lovely, pale green gown.

She decided that with God's help and a clean gown, she could face what came.

A few minutes later, she followed the maid down the stairs to the main floor of the house. The hall was empty, save for Marged Tudor and a couple of servants.

"Good afternoon, Lady FitzAlan," Marged greeted her. "I understand you had a hard journey."

The woman smiled kindly at her, all the hostility of yesterday gone.

"I do not like this business of taking a woman from her home and family," Marged said, shaking her head. "Until you can be returned to your own home, I want you to be comfortable in ours."

"I appreciate your kindness," Catherine said. "And thank you for the use of this gown."

"I am afraid yours could not be saved," Marged said. "I gave it to one of the servants to cut for rags."

"Good. I never want to see it again."

"You must call me Marged. We must not be formal, since you may be our guest for some weeks."

"Weeks?" Catherine sank onto the bench beside Marged.

Marged patted her arm. "If it were up to my Maredudd, this would be resolved quickly. But Glyndwr … well, you know what he thinks. These foolish men! Just looking at you, I can see you are not the kind of woman to commit adultery."

Catherine wondered how but did not ask.

"Still, I will admit," Marged said, "when I first laid eyes on you yesterday, you gave me quite a fright."

Catherine could not help but laugh. "You should have made me wash in the yard!"

"That is not what I meant," Marged protested. "You looked like a wood nymph with your hair all wild about you and that lovely face of yours. I thought my husband had the gall to bring home a mistress!"

Catherine looked at her, startled.

"But Maredudd let me know last night how much he missed me," Marged said, her eyes twinkling. "I should have known, but a woman needs to be shown sometimes."

Marged paused to wave a servant over with a platter of food for Catherine. "Maredudd was worried bringing you on such a hard journey, but he was afraid to leave you at Harlech."

Catherine raised her eyebrows. "He thinks Glyndwr would harm me?"

"Of course not," Marged said. "But he says that if Prince Glyndwr discovers you are with child, he will never agree to release you."

"Maredudd knows I am with child?"

Marged laughed. "You were sick in the morning. 'Twas the same with me when I carried Owain."

"Why would Glyndwr not let me go if he knew?" The answer came to Catherine even before Marged spoke.

"To hold the prince's lover as hostage is one thing; to hold the prince's son is quite another," Marged said. "In exchange for the only child of the heir to the English throne, Glyndwr might ask anything—even an independent Wales."

"But this is not Harry's child!" Catherine closed her eyes and put her head on the table.

"Glyndwr would want to believe it was," Marged said, resting her hand on Catherine's back. "And that is what matters."

Chapter Twenty-four

Catherine, where are you?

William stared across the distance, as if he could find her if only he looked hard enough. From the top of this hill, he could see across the border into Wales. He rode out here when he needed to be alone.

As the weeks passed, he began to fear he might never get her back. He was a man of action. The frustration of waiting wore his nerves raw. There were days when foolish action seemed better than none, and he rode out blindly into Wales.

Other days, he lost himself in regret and self-recrimination. He made promises to God. If God would return his wife to him, he would protect her always. If God would grant this one request, he would do whatever it took to make her want to stay.

Things remained cool between him and Edmund. Although Edmund seemed to sincerely regret all he'd said about Catherine, the sight of him reminded William of how quickly he himself had questioned her loyalty. In sooth, Edmund had done little more than express the same doubts he had. All the same, William spent more of his time with Stephen and Jamie these days. He liked to keep the boys close.

He took Stephen with him whenever he went to the abbey to hear the cryptic messages Robert sent to the abbess through the hands of monks, musicians, and itinerant workers. The messages relayed Robert's journey as he trailed Catherine along the south coast of Wales, then north to Aberystwyth. Their hopes soared when, at long last, he sent word he had found her—then fell again when they read she disappeared again.

It was almost December. There had been no word from Robert for weeks.

At the sound of a horse crashing through the trees behind, William turned and pulled his sword. He sheathed it when he saw who the rider was.

"How the devil did you know where to find me?" he called out to Stephen.

"The abbess sent word she has news!" Stephen said as he drew his horse up.

"Praise God!"

They galloped all the way to the abbey. When they burst into the abbess's private parlor, they found it was not a message waiting for them this time. It was the troubadour himself.

"Heaven above," William said, clapping Robert on the back, "who would have thought I would be so glad to see you!"

When Robert laughed, William noticed the lines of fatigue etched on his handsome face.

"I have found where she is," Robert said. "It will not be easy, but there is hope we can get her out."

"God bless you, Robert," William said as he squeezed Stephen's shoulder. "I am forever in your debt."

"I was able to speak with her briefly at Harlech," Robert said. "She was well and sent her love."

William ran his hands through his hair, overcome with emotion.

"The next day she was gone," Robert said. "No one—except Glyndwr himself—knew where she went or who took her.

"Eventually, I heard a whisper that someone had seen Maredudd Tudor in the castle the night she went missing," Robert continued. "Glyndwr loves music, so it was another week before I could leave Harlech without raising suspicion.

"I followed Maredudd's trail to the south, until it disappeared. On a hunch, I went north again. I did not catch wind of an English lady again until I was all the way to Beaumaris Castle."

"Beaumaris is a fortress on the coast of Anglesey," William explained to Stephen. "It is still in English hands."

"I sought news among the Welsh servants at Beaumaris," Robert said, picking up his tale again. "I found a maid whose sister works for the Tudors at their manor house, Plas Penmynydd. From her, I learned a beautiful Englishwoman is living with the Tudors."

Robert leaned forward. "William, the house is but *five miles from Beaumaris*."

"You know this for certain?"

"I do." Robert stretched out his long legs and folded his hands on his stomach. "Believe me, I had to work hard to get the information. That Welsh maid is homely, but energetic."

"Robert!" the abbess said, but her lips twitched with amusement.

"As I see it, there are two ways to do this," William said. "I can surprise the Tudors and take her by force. Or, I can approach this Maredudd Tudor and see if he is willing to give her up for a price."

"If you parlay with him first," Stephen interjected, "you lose the advantage of surprise."

William nodded and turned to Robert. "Do you think it worth the risk?"

Robert would understand, as he did, that there was a greater chance of Catherine coming to harm in an attack.

"I will go to Plas Penmynydd and find out," Robert said.

When William started to object, the abbess put her hand on his arm. "Robert can gain entry to the household without alerting them to your plans."

"You can take your men and wait at Beaumaris," Robert said. "Catherine has been in the household for weeks and can tell me whether Maredudd Tudor will negotiate. If she says nay, I can forewarn her to be ready for the attack."

Chapter Twenty-five

*M*arged frowned as she came into the solar and saw Owain asleep on Catherine's lap.

"Owain is too big for that," she said, resting her hand on Catherine's shoulder.

"Please, Marged, it comforts me to hold him," Catherine said. "I miss my own son so very much."

The two women watched the sleeping child in silence for a time.

"One thinks of beauty as an advantage in finding a good match for a daughter," Catherine said, teasing her friend, "but I swear this boy of yours will marry up. Some wealthy widow will decide she must have him."

Marged laughed. "He has his father's charm as well as his looks, so God help the woman he sets his sights on. I only hope it is an heiress and not a milkmaid."

Marged pulled a stool next to Catherine's and pushed a loose strand of hair from her face. "Perhaps we will have good news soon. It's been a fortnight since Maredudd wrote to Prince Glyndwr urging him to take your husband's ransom."

"What if Glyndwr tells Maredudd to take me back to Harlech?"

"Maredudd will find a way out before then," Marged said in a soothing voice.

Catherine did not argue, but she did not expect Maredudd to defy his prince. Though Maredudd was fond of her, he would put his family first. She could not fault him that.

She rubbed her cheek against Owain's head. "Do you think Jamie has forgotten me?"

"I am sure your husband speaks of you often," Marged said. "The boy will not forget."

Catherine did not share the other worry that plagued her. Had she been gone so long that William had stopped caring for her? Did he ever, truly, care?

"William wanted a child so very much, and he does not even know." She shifted Owain on her lap so she could rest a hand on her belly. "I want to birth this child at home."

"You're not far along," Marged said. "There's plenty of time yet."

"Are you coddling that boy again?" Maredudd called from the doorway. He was grinning from ear to ear. "Just as well he's having a rest, for it will be a late night for all of us."

He came over and shook Owain's shoulder. "Owain! A troupe of musicians is here!"

Owain awoke wide-eyed and wiggled off Catherine's lap.

"They've just come through the gate." As Owain scampered off to look, Maredudd stooped to kiss his wife. "This should cheer up my beautiful ladies."

"'Tis a long time since a troupe has come this far," Marged said, smiling up at him.

"The musicians say they've traveled across the whole of Wales this autumn, so they should carry much news."

Catherine closed her eyes to make a silent prayer. A moment later, the players entered the hall. Her prayer was answered. It took all the self-control she possessed not to run to Robert and throw her arms around him. His eyes held no surprise; Robert expected to find her here.

With her thoughts spinning wildly in her head, she did not hear Marged speak to her at first. She blinked at her friend, having no notion what she had asked.

Marged laughed and took her hand. "Come with me to talk with the cook. I want a special meal prepared for this evening."

As Catherine got to her feet, Robert gave what was meant to be a casual glance in her direction. As good as he was, he stared a moment too long at her belly.

The Welsh loved music, and the Tudor household was no exception. They kept the musicians playing late into the night. Catherine sat through it as long as she could. When she could bear the strain no longer, she put her hand on her belly and whispered to Marged that she must go to bed.

In her bedchamber, she paced the floor. At long last, the music died and she heard the sounds of feet on the stairs and doors closing. The house finally settled into silence.

She never doubted Robert would learn which room was hers. When she heard the faint tapping she was waiting for, she unbarred her door and Robert slipped in.

"I was almost without hope," she said into his shoulder as he held her. Leaning back, she asked, "Are they all well? William and the boys?"

"They are," he said, and kissed her forehead.

"Where is William? Has he not come for me?"

"The devil could not keep him away," Robert said. "He is waiting nearby, at Beaumaris Castle."

"It's been so long that I feared he did not seek my return," she confessed. Only now did she admit to herself how deep her doubts had grown.

"You will be happy to know your husband looks quite ill with worry," Robert said, lifting her chin with his finger. "I doubt he's had a full night's sleep since you were taken."

It was wrong to feel so pleased that William suffered, too. Of course, Robert could be lying.

"I see you have news for him," Robert said, letting his eyes drop to the slight swell of her gown.

She smiled. "Aye, the babe should come after Easter."

Robert turned to the business at hand. "We have two possible plans for getting you released."

When she heard them, her response was adamant. "He must talk with Maredudd. I will not have harm come to—"

She stopped at the sound of the door creaking. With growing horror, she realized that she had failed to bar the door behind Robert. She watched helplessly as it eased open.

Marged's head peeked through the opening. Her eyes bulged almost comically, then she leapt into the room and closed the door behind her.

She fixed her gaze on Catherine and began speaking in a rush. "I beg you, do not do it! I know you fear you shall never see your husband again, but I promise you shall. And when you do, you will regret what you are about to do."

Marged stopped her lecture long enough to cast a good long look at Robert. "I can see the temptation." It was evident she could, from the way she flushed. "Truly, I can."

Marged could not seem to drag her eyes away from Robert. Her color deepened when Robert brazenly winked at her.

"'Tis true, in your condition you need not worry about

bringing another man's babe home to your husband, but..."
Marged's will to argue her point seemed to fade the longer
she stared at Robert.

"Marged!" Catherine said sharply. "This man has not
come to bed me! How could you think it?"

Catherine turned to Robert. "You must see we cannot
wait. We have to tell her and Maredudd now."

Robert said in a low voice, "Are you sure this is wise,
Catherine?"

She took Marged's arm. "Robert is a friend who has brought
a message from my husband," she explained as she walked
Marged to the door. "Go wake Maredudd and bring him here
so we may talk in private while the servants sleep."

Once Catherine finally convinced Marged to fetch her
husband, she turned and found Robert leaning out the
window.

"Unless you are certain this Tudor is willing to come to
terms with your husband," he said over his shoulder, "we
should make our escape now, before the lady wakes him."

Though Maredudd's easy manner might fool some into
believing he was not a careful man, Catherine knew better.
Robert may not see the guards outside, but they were there.

"What I am certain of," she said, "is that we would not
make the gate."

Chapter Twenty-six

A harsh wind blew the rain against William's face in icy pellets. He'd been keeping watch on the ramparts of the outer curtain wall of Beaumaris Castle since dawn, and he was chilled to the bone. He paced back and forth to keep warm. At each turn, he stopped to squint through the driving rain toward the west.

He looked again. In the dull gray light of the dismal morning, he picked out a lone figure riding toward the castle.

The troubadour was back.

A quarter hour later, he and Robert were conferring in his room in one of the sixteen towers along the outer wall.

"She has been treated well," Robert assured him again.

William narrowed his eyes at Robert. There was something he was not telling him.

"In sooth, she has grown quite fond of her captors," Robert said. "She made it clear she wants none of them harmed."

"She thinks it worth the risk, then, of approaching Maredudd Tudor?"

"I would say so, since she has already done it."

"She what!" William sighed and shook his head. "She has not changed, I see. Catherine would step right into it, once she decided that was the thing to do."

"I was shaking in my boots for fear she misjudged the man," Robert admitted with a grin.

"Since you returned alive, I take it this Tudor is willing to make a deal?"

"So he says, and your lady wife believes him," Robert replied with a shrug. "He will meet you in a wood along the road between here and Plas Penmynydd to give you his terms. He says he will come alone, and you must do the same. He wants to keep this quiet so Glyndwr does not catch wind of it."

Robert paused, then said, "You know this could be a trap."

"Aye, but I have no choice," William said. "When are we to meet?"

"On the morrow, an hour past dawn."

It was still cold when William set out the next morning, but the rain had lessened to a light drizzle. As directed, he traveled alone and put his fate in the hands of God. And Maredudd Tudor. He thought of Jamie and Stephen and prayed he could bring Catherine home to them soon.

As he came to the copse beside the dip in the road that Robert described as the meeting place, a hooded rider crested the hill before him.

"FitzAlan?" the rider called out.

William started. The voice was a woman's. As she pulled her horse up, he saw that the voice belonged to a pretty dark-haired woman.

"I am FitzAlan. Are you here for Maredudd Tudor?"

"I am his wife, Marged," she said.

What sort of man was this Tudor to send his wife out alone on such an errand?

"Maredudd went with the men who are taking Catherine to Harlech."

"What!" he exploded. "The devil's spawn is taking her to Harlech?"

"There is little time, so listen," she snapped. "A dozen men rode up to our gate this morning with orders from Glyndwr to take Catherine."

William told himself he had plenty of time to catch up to them. The ride to Harlech was long.

"What route did they travel? How far ahead are they?"

"They left not more than half an hour ago, but they are taking her by sea! Their ship is to the west, eight or nine miles from here."

Beaumaris was in the opposite direction. There was no time to ride back for his men. Even if he rode straight to the ship, he might not catch them.

"Maredudd will try to stall them, but you'd best ride hard." She quickly gave him directions.

"Are you safe riding back to Plas Penmynydd alone?"

She smiled. "Aye, these are Tudor lands."

"God bless you, dear lady."

He spurred his horse and rode like the wind. He had to get to the ship before it set sail. His heart seemed to beat in time with the pounding of his horse's hooves. Faster, faster, faster.

After what seemed like hours, he reached the coast. A half mile north, he found the manor house where Marged Tudor said Glyndwr's men had borrowed horses. He spotted the ship offshore, just visible in the morning fog.

He turned his horse off the road and pulled up in the low trees to count the figures on the beach. One man in the water, guiding a rowboat to shore. Two in the rowboat. Eight on the shore. He narrowed his eyes, searching for Catherine.

Two more men emerged from the wood dragging a woman between them. She struggled against them as they hauled her toward the rowboat.

Catherine. He'd found his wife.

The frustrating weeks of waiting were behind him. Patience, negotiation, money offers—none of it had brought her back. Now he could do what he was born to do, what he'd been trained to do, what he did best.

Percy blood ran through his veins. He was son of Northumberland the King-maker, brother to the legendary fighter Hotspur. None could touch him. It would not matter if there were ten men or twenty or sixty between him and Catherine. He would get to her.

"AAARRRRRRHHHHH!" He shouted his battle cry as he burst through the brush.

He rode to the edge of the sea where his horse could get better purchase and galloped along the shoreline. Brandishing his broadsword, he rode straight at the men on the beach, striking fear into every heart.

* * *

An unearthly cry in the distance sent a shiver up Catherine's spine. She turned toward the sound and heard hoofbeats pounding up the shore. Everyone on the beach stopped in place to peer through the fog in the direction of the sound.

As they watched, a horse and rider emerged through the fog charging toward them at a full gallop. Horse and rider lifted and then sailed over a log as if the horse had wings. The men scattered as the rider bore down on them, sword swinging and screaming his battle cry.

William had come to save her.

She had heard stories of his feats in battle. She'd watched

him practice countless times. None of it prepared her for seeing him like this. He fought with a grace and power that was both terrible and utterly magnificent.

The first two men were dead before they could draw their swords. The sword of a third went flying through the air. The man ran for the woods as William turned his horse to take another pass. At least two more fell. Then William dropped from his horse onto one man and came up swinging his sword into another. He whirled to face the remaining men, broadswords in both hands now.

"Your husband, I presume," Maredudd said in her ear. "Let us get off the beach before one of these men thinks to grab you and hold a knife to your throat."

She and Maredudd watched the rest of the fight from behind the low bushes that grew back from the shore. It was over soon. Two men were in the water, swimming toward the ship. Others had run from the beach and disappeared into the trees.

"Catherine! Catherine!" William's voice echoed as he looked up and down the shore shouting her name.

* * *

William looked up and down the beach, frantic.

Then he saw her standing alone in the tall grass at the edge of the beach. Catherine. An angel come to earth.

He stood for a long moment, frozen in place, not breathing. Then he slid his sword into its scabbard and ran to her. His hands shook as he cupped her beloved face. Never had she looked more beautiful. He kissed each cheek, pink with the cold.

"I praise God you are safe!" he said, closing his eyes and letting his forehead touch hers.

He had promised himself that this time he would give her the choice. This time, she would come to him willingly, or she would not come.

"I failed in my duty to protect you. If you cannot forgive me, if you do not wish to live with me again," he said, his heart pounding in his chest, "I will make other arrangements for you."

He waited for her to speak, to rail at him for failing her. But she was silent. She would hear him out.

"I hope with all my heart you will choose to live with me. If you will, I promise I shall do all I can to protect you and be a good husband to you."

Catherine rested her palms against his chest and looked up at him with vivid blue eyes that saw the truth in his heart.

"Thank you for coming for me." She leaned her head against his chest. "Take me home, William. Take me home."

He wrapped his arms around her. "How I have missed you!"

God be praised, she was his again.

"Greetings, FitzAlan."

William pushed Catherine behind him and pulled his sword as the man who spoke stepped out from behind the bushes.

"'Tis all right," Catherine said, grabbing his sword arm. "This is Maredudd Tudor. He has been very good to me."

"Not good enough to send you home," William said, staring hard into the man's sharp hazel eyes.

"If not for Maredudd, I might still be at Harlech," she said. "He did his best to protect me."

Maredudd Tudor gave him a broad smile full of humor. William would not trust the man farther than he could throw him. Still, he felt he owed some debt to him.

"What were you going to ask in exchange for my wife, before Glyndwr's men changed your plan today?" William asked.

Maredudd Tudor went still. "I sought a promise for a later time."

William nodded for him to continue.

"Under Glyndwr's leadership, we have succeeded in taking control of all of Wales, save for a handful of castles. Still, I fear we will not be able to maintain our hold."

"You won't," William said. "You cannot prevail against us without the help of the French. The French will promise, but they'll not send their army again."

Maredudd Tudor nodded. "Even without the French, we might outlast King Henry. His enemies are many and they divert him. But Prince Harry is another matter. He will defeat us in the end."

William sensed what this admission cost the proud rebel. He waited for the man to make his request.

"Before the rebellion, we Tudors held high offices in the service of English kings. When this is over, I want my son Owain to be able to make his way in the English world. What I intended to ask was your pledge to assist him when the time comes."

William respected the man for seeking a means to protect his son in an uncertain world. He gave his promise.

"When you call on me, I will help your son."

"I am grateful," Maredudd Tudor said with a stiff nod. Then he said, "This is yet Welsh rebel country, so you'd best be gone before the men you chased off raise the alarm."

William turned to Catherine. "He's right. We must make haste."

"Thank you," Catherine said, throwing herself at Maredudd. "You were the best of wardens, Maredudd Tudor."

Both of them were laughing as she stepped back.

"Give my love to Marged and Owain," she said.

"We shall miss you, Catherine. Go with God."

It began to drizzle again soon after they set off for Beaumaris. The last few miles, it turned into a cold rain.

When they reached Beaumaris, Robert was waiting for them at the gatehouse. William was anxious to get Catherine out of the rain and hustled her through the side door Robert held open.

"Sweet Lamb of God, what took you so long?" Robert said. "I expected you hours ago."

"We'll tell you the story later," William said, stepping in front of Robert, who was about to greet Catherine with a kiss. "I must get her before a fire."

He was grateful for all Robert had done, but the man did try his patience.

"You'll take the horses, Robert?"

Without waiting for Robert's answer, he took Catherine's icy hand, grabbed a torch, and led her into the dark corridor that connected the towers and gatehouse through the castle wall.

Chapter Twenty-seven

As soon as they reached his chamber, William sat her on a bench before the dwindling fire and began to add kindling to it.

Catherine was content to watch the firelight play across the planes of his face and spark gold in his hair as he built the fire. How she had missed the sight of him! She smiled at him each time he glanced over his shoulder. She understood his need to reassure himself she was truly here, for she felt the same.

Once the roaring blaze drove the dank chill from the room, she stood to remove her damp cloak. William looked up as she turned and slipped it off. He stared openmouthed at her belly. Though she was not very big yet, anyone looking that closely could see she was with child.

She saw searing pain distort his face before he masked it. It hit her like a blow. How could she have been so mistaken? She had feared William might not be glad to see her. But the child? She never doubted for a moment he would be pleased about the child.

He came to her and took her hands. "You must not worry for the child. I will claim him and raise him as my own," he said in a gentle voice. "I place no blame on you. You had every reason to fear I would never obtain your release."

She was so shocked she could not speak.

"Did you love the man?" he asked in a choked voice. He swallowed, and then added, "Do you love him still?"

She did not know whether to slap him or weep.

"This child was conceived in summer, before I was taken," she said in a voice as cold as ice.

"The child is mine?" William said, breaking into a grin.

"Of course the child is yours," she snapped. "And I pray to God he does not become a horse's ass like his father!"

"Then we must hope it is a girl," he said, scooping her up off the bench. Holding her across his chest, he twirled in a circle, laughing.

He stopped and covered her face with kisses. Gently then, he set her on her feet and took her hands.

"My happiness this day makes up for all the days of sadness since you were taken from me," he said, his eyes shining. "God punished me for my pigheadedness. But now I am doubly blessed."

Unable to hang on to her anger in the face of his joy, she wrapped her arms around him. She would not let the mistake he made in that moment of surprise ruin this reunion. After all, he had accepted her at her word as soon as she told him.

"I love you to the depths of my soul," he said into her hair. "I do not know how I lived these months without you."

She pulled his head down to press her lips to his. In an instant, his kiss turned hungry, demanding. His hands were all over her, rubbing up and down her back, over her buttocks, pressing her against him.

Abruptly, he pulled away. "Are we hurting the babe?"

Feeling dazed from his kisses, she blinked at him for a moment before she understood.

"The babe is fine," she said, smiling. "Marged tells me that if a woman is healthy, she can share her husband's bed almost until the child is born."

She rose on her tiptoes and put her mouth to his ear. "I am exceedingly healthy, William."

He needed no further encouragement. They were on the bed pulling each other's clothes off without knowing how they got there.

Once he had her naked, he leaned back to run his eyes over her. In a ragged voice, he said, "You are even more beautiful than I remembered."

"With this belly?" she said, putting her hand on it as she smiled up at him.

"You are more rounded now, love. Not just your belly, but also"—he gave her a wicked smile—"your breasts."

As if unable to resist, he leaned down and nuzzled his face between them.

"I hope you do not prefer me like this," she protested, "for I will not always be with child."

He lifted his head and said, "You are my Kate and beautiful to me in all ways."

Her pulse quickened at the desire she saw in his eyes.

"How I have longed for you," he murmured as he pressed his face into the curve of her neck. "Night after night, and day after day."

"I, too," she whispered back as he trailed slow wet kisses up and down her throat.

"I lay awake nights thinking of doing this," he said, then circled her nipple with his tongue with tantalizing slowness. "And this," he murmured, and took it into his mouth.

At last. She closed her eyes.

After a time, he worked his way down to her belly. She watched as he pressed tender kisses over it.

With his eyes on hers, he ran his hand up the inside of her thigh. "Shall I show you the other things I longed to do?"

She swallowed and nodded.

He trailed kisses all the way down her leg to her toes. Then ever so slowly, he worked his way back up again. Her heart raced and her breath came fast in anticipation. His hand moved ahead of his mouth, up the inside of her thigh. Finally, his fingers reached the spot where she was aching for him to touch her.

Even as her body responded to the circling motion of his hand between her legs, she was aware of his lips and tongue inching up the inside of her leg. She forgot to breathe as he moved closer and closer to her center.

When his mouth replaced his hand, new sensations rocked through her. It felt so good. *Oh God, oh God, oh God.* Had she said that aloud? Fleetingly, she hoped she would not be struck by lightning for her blasphemy. Then that thought, along with all others, left her. All she knew was his tongue moving over her. And then he was sliding his finger in and out of her and sucking.

As the tension grew inside her, she tossed her head from side to side. She wanted to tell him, "Don't stop, don't stop, don't stop," but she could not form the words. Every muscle was taut; every part of her was focused on his tongue, his mouth. The tension grew and grew until she wanted to scream in frustration.

Then her body convulsed in waves of pleasure so intense she thought she might never recover. After, she lay limp, her limbs boneless.

When he came to lie beside her, she rolled weakly to her

side. He enveloped her in his arms from behind. She heard his harsh breathing in her ear.

"I love you," he said, and pressed a kiss to her shoulder.

He ran his fingers lightly over her skin, sending tingles through her. He kissed her neck, her cheek, her hair. When he reached around to cup her breast, she felt his erection against her bottom, and she moved closer. He pressed more insistently against her, and she wanted to feel him inside her again.

His hand was between her legs, his breath hot in her ear.

"You are the only one, Kate. The only one I want. The only one I'll ever want."

When he entered her, she was engulfed in his warmth, his desire. She could no longer tell where he ended and she began. They moved as one; they were one. When he cried out, his cry was her cry, too, and she was swept away with him.

She dozed with his arms wrapped around her, happy and at peace. He wanted her back. He loved her.

When she awoke, she turned in his arms to look at him. In the firelight, he was all sharp angles, golden skin, and long sinewy muscles. How she missed seeing him like this. He was so beautiful he took her breath away.

He cupped her cheek with his hand. His dark honey eyes were intense, serious, as they gazed deep into hers.

"It almost killed me to lose you," he whispered. "I could not bear it again."

She put her arms around him and buried her head in his neck, wanting to comfort and reassure him.

Soon they were kissing. Warm, long, wet kisses. Melding, merging, deep, deep kisses. Then he was inside her again, and they were moving together. This time, the intensity of emotion between them was almost overwhelming. Catherine let down every barrier. She gave herself up to him utterly, absolutely, holding nothing back. She let his passion and love surround her, complete her, and make her whole.

She awoke hours later to a gush of cold air. She stretched and sat up as William came through the door with a heaping platter of food and a heavy pitcher. She smiled at him as she pulled the bedclothes up around her shoulders.

"The weather has turned bad," he said, draping his wet cloak over a chair by the fire. "I was told Robert left yesterday to beat the storm."

The smell of warm bread and roasted meat set her stomach rumbling as she joined him at the small table. Judging by the way he fell to his breakfast, William was as ravenous as she. They ate in silence for some minutes before he spoke again.

"I know you are anxious to be home and see Jamie," he said, "but we shall have to wait another day for this storm to pass."

She pressed her lips together and nodded.

"Will you be angry if I confess I am glad to have my wife to myself for another day?" He leaned across the table to give her a slow, lingering kiss. "Tomorrow is soon enough for putting on clothes and traveling with the men."

* * *

William had not wanted to ask questions—or hear answers—that might spoil the complete happiness between them while they were ensconced in their bedchamber at Beaumaris. Lost in their passion, they spoke little there beyond love talk.

So it was not until they started on the long ride home to Ross Castle that they began to share details of their time apart. William gave her the mundane news of Ross Castle first. Gradually, he turned the conversation to her weeks of captivity.

He asked first about her time with the Tudors, since he knew she had not suffered unduly there. For a time, she entertained him with stories of the antics of little Owain. Then her face grew serious.

"If you had come a day later, I would be back at Harlech." She clutched her cloak tightly about her as she rode and stared off at the horizon. "It was a close thing."

He asked about Glyndwr. From the way she spoke of him, it was clear she admired the rebel leader.

"Maredudd told me Glyndwr can always tell a falsehood, but I managed it." She gave a light laugh, and he heard the pride in her voice. "I got better each time. When I told him I was not with child, I looked straight into his eyes—and this man has eyes that see right into your soul.

"Of course," she said, her face turning grave again, "if I had returned to Harlech, he would have seen I am with child and never believed me again."

It was midday, so William called his men to halt so they could eat and let their horses drink in the nearby stream. He took Catherine's hand and drew her away from the others. They found a flat boulder to sit on in a sheltered spot at the stream's edge to have their meal. The sun was out, but it was still cold. Huddling close to him, she took the cup of mead he poured for them to share.

"Glyndwr would have thought you carried the prince's child?" he asked as he laid out dried meat, bread, and cheese on a cloth. The question was an awkward one, so perhaps he should not have asked it.

"Glyndwr began to doubt what he'd been told about the prince and me," she replied thoughtfully. "However, on the chance he held the only child of the heir to the English throne, he would have kept me and the child under lock and key."

If that had happened, William might not have gotten her back until this miserable rebellion was crushed.

"William, you are hurting my hand."

Startled, he eased his grip. He kissed her fingers, saying, "Sorry, love."

"Edmund was badly injured when they took you," he said. Her eyes went wide. "He was?"

"'Twas a long recovery," he said. "But he has his strength back now, except in one leg."

They sat in silence while William got up his courage to ask the question that had tormented him for months. He heard the rustle and clatter of his men packing up their things, but he ignored their restlessness. He needed to ask this question face-to-face; he could not wait and ask it as they rode.

"Edmund and Stephen both say that the Welshmen who took you that morning..." He paused, struggling to find a way to ask what he wanted to know without sounding as though he were accusing or blaming her. "Well, they thought the men knew they would find you riding to the abbey then."

"'Tis true! I have given it much thought," she said, putting her hand on his arm and leaning forward. "We must have a traitor at Ross Castle—or in the village."

Unbidden, the image came to him of his wife laughing as she told him how well she lied to Glyndwr.

"I asked Maredudd how they knew," she said. "He said he did not meet our traitor but that Rhys Gethin did."

William was not sure what she had done, or if she had done anything at all. But he wanted her to know she did not need to lie to him. Not about this or anything, ever.

"I want honesty between us now," he said, resting his hand on her knee. "You told me I hurt you even more than

Rayburn had. So perhaps you wanted to leave, to get away from me, and later changed your mind. If that is how it was, I would understand. Nay, I would be grateful you changed your mind."

He took one look at the shock and fury on her face and started backtracking as fast as he could. "I am not saying that is what happened," he said, holding up his hands. "What I mean to say is that I do not care how it happened or what you did, so long as you will stay with me now. Nothing else matters."

Catherine threw the full cup of mead in his face and jumped to her feet. "That is *not* all that matters!" Her eyes were narrowed to slits, and her voice was low and threatening.

He had seen her angry before, but never like this. Fleetingly he thought of the blade she usually carried and hoped her Welsh captors had disarmed her.

"Honesty! You ask for honesty between us?" Her voice was seething. "You bed me for two days, all the while thinking I arranged my own kidnapping? What, did you think I went willingly, and only came to regret it when Glyndwr threatened to marry me off to the Fierce One?"

"He did what?" William said, rising to his feet.

He would have been impressed by the string of oaths Catherine rained on him if he was not quite so intent on getting an answer to his question. When she turned on her heel and stomped off, he ran after her and caught her arm.

"Who is this man you call 'The Fierce One'?"

She turned and shoved his chest hard with both her hands. "You insult me with these horrid accusations, and all you can say to me is, 'Who is the Fierce One?'"

Belatedly, he realized that if she had played no part in her kidnapping, he had committed a very grave error by asking if she had. Why could he never think clearly when it came to this woman? He would never have committed such a blunder with anyone else.

"I am so very, very sorry, Catherine," he stumbled. "I...I just could not find another explanation. And I wanted you to know that I love you, no matter what."

"I don't want you to love me *in spite of* who I am and what I've done," she ranted at him. "I want you to love me *because* of it. If you think I am someone who commits treason and breaks promises to those I care about—or, worst of all, abandons her child—then you do not know me at all.

"I do not know who you think you are in love with, William FitzAlan," she finished, "but it surely is not me."

* * *

Beneath her anger, Catherine's heart was breaking with hurt and bitter, bitter disappointment. While she had pined for William over those long months apart, he was thinking unspeakably low thoughts of her.

She marched over to the man holding her horse and grabbed the reins from him. Waving off his attempt to help her up, she mounted and set off down the road at a gallop.

Let them catch up to her if they could. She had dallied long enough. Her son was waiting for her.

Chapter Twenty-eight

William was beside her almost before she reached the road. Soon after, she heard the other horses following at a safe distance behind. William's men were brave soldiers, but they would let him face this kind of trouble alone.

He tried to speak to her, but she fixed her eyes on the road before her and ignored him. Eventually, he ceased to try.

At some point during the long ride, she resolved not to let her anger and resentment toward William spoil her homecoming. She had waited too long for this. When Ross Castle came into sight at long last, she thought her heart would burst. She leaned forward and spurred her horse into a full gallop.

"Is it wise to ride so hard in your condition?" William called out as he raced beside her.

She did not spare him a glance. She would be damned if she would walk her horse the last mile home. A figure on the wall next to the gatehouse jumped up and down, waving. It had to be Stephen. She waved back.

A surge of emotion had her weeping as she rode through the open gate. All the household was running across the bailey to meet her. Stephen flew down the stairs from the wall and reached her first.

She pulled her horse up and almost fell into his arms.

"I missed you so much!" She stepped back to look at him. "Why, you've grown half a foot! And you are even more handsome than before."

Stephen's face turned crimson in embarrassed pleasure.

"Where is Jamie—"

"Mother!"

She turned to see Jamie running toward her and dropped to one knee to catch him in her arms. The force of his greeting nearly toppled her. When he buried his face in her neck and clung to her, she knew Marged was right. Her son had not forgotten her.

All evening, they fussed over her. Alys insisted she sit close to the hearth and wrapped a blanket around her shoulders. Thomas put a stool under her feet. Others brought her cakes and hot spiced wine. Tears stung Catherine's eyes; she was so grateful to be home and among her own household.

While the servants ministered to her, William stood close by, silent and watchful. After a time, he signaled for them to leave, saying, "Lady Catherine is tired from her journey."

At his words, she felt the weight of her exhaustion. She held her arms out to Jamie. He crawled into her lap and soon was fast asleep against her chest.

He felt so good against her. As she watched his sweet face, slack with sleep, she saw it had lost some of its plumpness in her absence. His hair was longer and darker, too. She brushed it back and sighed for all she had missed.

Still, she had her son in her arms now. She was home.

She must have dozed, for she awoke with a start when William touched her arm.

"The two of you should be in bed," he said, lifting the sleeping boy from her lap.

A rush of cool air replaced the warm weight, and she felt the loss acutely. Looking up, she saw that William had Jamie on one shoulder. He was holding his other hand out to her. She took it and let him help her up.

As they climbed the stairs, he squeezed her hand and said, "When you were gone, I would carry Jamie up to bed and imagine you were with us, just like this."

He was trying to make up to her, but she was not yet ready. They continued up the stairs in silence, past their own rooms, to Jamie's. After William laid Jamie on his bed, she pulled the bedclothes up and kissed her son good night.

"Father," Jamie called in a sleepy voice as he stretched out his arms to William.

William embraced the boy and kissed his cheek. Jamie was asleep before they slipped outside his chamber door.

"Jamie started calling me that some weeks ago," William said, sounding defensive. "I saw no reason he should not."

"I would never criticize you for that."

In truth, the warm bond between Jamie and William made her wish she could forgive William his other transgressions. Her anger had dulled, but she was a long way from forgetting. The disappointment of learning he thought so little of her left her with an ache in her chest.

"I'll sleep here with Jamie tonight," she said.

She would not meet his eyes. She did not want to see the hurt she knew was there. What he offered her was good. It just was not all she hoped for. She understood she needed to accept it and be grateful. But she was not ready to make that compromise tonight, not when the hurt was so fresh.

He did not argue but leaned down to kiss her cheek. When she felt the warmth of his breath and smelled the wood smoke in his hair, she was tempted to lean into him. But her heart was too bruised to give in. In time, she would be strong enough to be with him and still protect that true part of herself she valued most. The part he could not see.

But not tonight.

When Jamie's nursemaid appeared, Catherine asked her to help her undress and then sent her away for the night.

She crawled into bed next to her son and breathed in his scent: damp earth, dogs, and the barest hint of his baby smell. For the hundredth time that day, she prayed her thanks to God for bringing her home and keeping her son safe.

She lay awake thinking of the changes in her household. Not only was the bond between William and Jamie stronger, but there was also an easy closeness between him and Stephen that was not there before.

The servants' attitude toward William had changed as well. Alys, in particular, seemed to have developed a strong affection for him. She complained repeatedly how he had lost weight.

The problem was not that Catherine did not recognize and appreciate her husband's many good qualities—but that he did not recognize hers. She sighed and rested her cheek against Jamie's hair. Unbidden, the abbess's words from last summer came back to her. She should be grateful her husband was an honorable man who treated her son well. That should be enough. It must.

Hours later, she felt William slide into bed behind her, fully clothed. She was too drowsy to complain. Instead, she let herself sink into the comfort of her cocoon. With her husband's arms wrapped around her and her own wrapped around Jamie, she fell into deep sleep.

When she awoke in the morning, William was gone. She rubbed her hand over the indentation where he had slept, but there was no trace of his warmth. With a sigh, she dropped a kiss on her sleeping son's head and then climbed out of bed.

She slipped her robe over her shift and headed down the stairs to dress for the day.

She was one step from the landing before she saw Edmund outside the solar door. Instinctively, she put one foot back on the step behind her, ready to retreat. But Edmund had already seen her.

She meant to ask about his health, to tell him she was sorry for his injuries. But his gaze moved down her body with deliberate rudeness, making her conscious that her hair was loose and her robe hung open. She jerked the robe around her and glared at him.

She noticed his limp as Edmund walked toward her. He did not stop until his feet touched the step on which she stood. She did not back away, though he was so close she could smell him and feel his breath on her face.

"It is curious," he said, his eyes level with hers, "that after such a long time apart, you do not sleep with your husband."

"Get out of my way."

"Is it because you carry another man's child that William will not have you?" he asked in a harsh whisper. "Or is it you who turns your husband away? Perhaps you cannot appreciate a good man after whoring with Welshmen."

He caught her arm as she swung to slap him. They stood glaring at each other, neither one backing down.

"Which is it, Edmund? One time you say I must be as cold as ice, another you call me whore." She narrowed her eyes at him and hissed, "But we both know the true reason you resent me."

"And what, pray tell, is that?"

"'Tis because you will never have me," she said. "Do you suppose I don't know you've lusted after me from the first?"

From the way Edmund's eyelids twitched, she knew she hit her mark dead-on. She let the satisfaction show in her eyes.

"If my husband knew how you look at me, he would rip your eyes out." Thrusting her shoulder against his chest, she shoved past him.

"Then why do you not tell him?" Edmund called out behind her. "He would not believe you, would he?"

Yesterday, before the ride home, she would have told William. But now? William believed she deceived him in things more important than this.

The solar door opened. Her husband's dark amber eyes swept over her, taking in her crimson face, loose hair, nightclothes, and bare feet. Then they shifted past her to Edmund.

"You have embarrassed my wife, catching her before she is dressed for the day," William said. "Next time, wait for me in the hall."

William gave her a nod and headed down the stairs. Before Edmund followed, he ran his eyes up and down her. She wanted to throw something after him. Slamming the solar door was not nearly enough to satisfy her.

Pulsing with anger, she paced the room. She could no longer pretend Edmund was merely an annoyance. Though she was not certain he was truly dangerous, he was her enemy. One way or another, she intended to get him out of her home.

* * *

The abbess must have left the abbey as soon as she received William's message telling her of Catherine's return. She arrived just as they were sitting down to the midday meal.

"You are with child!" Abbess Talcott said as Catherine rose from the table to embrace her. "What a happy surprise. William did not tell me you were blessed."

"He did not know of it," Catherine said. "I discovered I was with child after my capture."

William caught the unease in Catherine's voice and wondered if she spoke the truth. Had she known she carried his child before she left and not told him?

The abbess sat next to Catherine and squeezed her hand. "It was a charity William did not know. The poor man would have only suffered more."

"I see William has won you over as well," Catherine teased. "Even Alys adores him now. I swear, the woman goes on about poor William turning away his favorite foods. Forget that I was in the wilds of Wales, sleeping on the hard ground and growing a babe on food prepared by a rebel who could not cook!"

Catherine meant to make a joke of it, but the abbess gripped Catherine's hand and asked, "Was it as bad as that? We were so very worried about you."

"Nay, 'twas not," Catherine assured her friend. "The travel was a bit hard, for we covered long distances over rough roads. So long as I was with Glyndwr, though, I always slept in houses. It was only later, when I traveled alone with Maredudd Tudor, that we slept outside—and I had to eat his dreadful cooking!"

William listened intently; this was the first he had heard in detail of the rough travel his wife had endured. Her attempt to make light of it did not deceive him.

"Maredudd dragged me all over western Wales before taking me to his home," she said with a slight smile and shook her head. "When we finally headed toward Anglesey, we traveled on back trails through the Snowdon Mountains."

"Oh, dear," the abbess said, patting her arm, "that must have been terrible."

"Though I would have bargained with the devil for a bath and a clean gown," Catherine said, her voice losing its light tone, "I never felt afraid with Maredudd."

The pulse at William's temples throbbed as the darkness of his guilt engulfed him. Somehow, he had never let himself think of her as being truly in fear of her captors.

Catherine had gone white. Belatedly, the abbess saw that her questions were causing Catherine distress and changed the subject.

"Now that you are safely back," she said, "perhaps we can devote our attention to the question of Stephen's betrothal."

One look at Stephen's scarlet face, and Catherine was on her feet. "Shall we go to the solar, Lady Abbess? It is pleasant there when the sun is out, as it is today."

As the ladies left the room, the abbess's voice carried back to the men at the table. "I've made a list of all the heiresses of an appropriate age in the Marches. I assume you do want him nearby. . . ."

Stephen sent William a terrified look.

"Don't worry, little brother," William said with more confidence than he felt. "I will have the final say."

* * *

William was on edge. In spite of having every reason to be happy, things between him and Catherine had gone horribly wrong. Their time at Beaumaris had been everything he had hoped for. And more. Somehow, he lost it all with a single question.

Catherine did not even want to sleep with him on her first

night at home. At least she did not kick him out when he slipped in beside her during the night. He wanted to believe it was a sign she was warming to him, but he suspected she had been just too tired to argue.

He hoped to talk with her after the abbess left, but there seemed no opportunity. The servants hung about, waiting on her hand and foot, and he could hardly send Stephen and Jamie away. He understood too well that they needed the reassurance of having her near.

Even if he got Catherine alone, what would he say to her?

As he went into supper that evening, Stephen sidled up to him. "What have you done?" Stephen hissed in his ear.

"Now that you are all of thirteen," William said, "you believe you can counsel me?"

"No one has thrown a cup of mead in my face."

If this young brother of his did not learn to watch his tongue, it would be the death of him.

"How did you hear of that?" he demanded.

Stephen shrugged. The boy seemed to hear everything, but he never revealed his sources.

"I would hate to have Lady Catherine cross with me," Stephen said. "If I were you, I would do whatever she wants to make amends."

"So, you advise complete capitulation in dealing with women?"

"'Tis what Mother taught me," Stephen replied with a grin. "But Lady Catherine is so much nicer, I would think you would want to make her happy."

"It is all I want," William said, his eyes on Catherine, who was entering the hall. "All I want in this world."

After supper, Catherine turned to him and said in a low voice, "I cannot bear having the servants smother me again tonight. I am taking Jamie up to the solar."

She did not invite him, but neither did she ask him not to come. He followed her up, with Stephen on his heels. No doubt Stephen was coming along to whisper more helpful guidance in his ear, should he need it.

The four of them spent a pleasant hour together, and William began to relax. Then Catherine announced she was going upstairs with the boys to put Jamie to bed.

Would she return, or would she sleep in Jamie's bed again?

His shoulders sagged with relief when he heard her light steps coming down the stairs. Watching her hesitate at the doorway, he knew the decision to return had not been easy for her.

He hurried across the room to her, intent on making sure she did not regret her decision, and took her hand.

"Thank you," he said as he raised it to his lips.

Keeping his eyes on hers, he turned her hand and kissed her palm. When she did not pull back, he told himself it was going to be all right.

With his tongue, he lightly circled her palm. He felt the pulse at her wrist quicken. In bed, at least, he could make her happy. From the way she was looking at him, he suspected she was going to let him take her there.

She did. He was so intoxicated by the feel of her skin against his, the way her body responded to his every touch, the sound of her crying his name as he moved inside her, that he did not notice. Or did not let himself notice.

But after it was over, he knew. He felt so suffused with love for her that he fought against the dawning recognition. But as he clasped her to him, both of them still breathing hard, he knew. Something had changed since the last time they made love. Something was different.

Missing.

For those two days at Beaumaris, she gave herself to him

wholly, holding nothing back. He felt as if he held her heart in his hands. As she held his. If not for Beaumaris, he might not know she withheld a part of herself from him now.

In the nights that followed, he made love to her again and again, trying to break down her barriers. Unable to find words that might bring her back to him, he used the strength of his love and desire to draw her. But no matter how deep their passion, there was a part of her he could not reach. A wall he could not climb. A place she guarded from him.

He satisfied her body, even pleased her. He knew he did. But when he told her he loved her, she became upset. So upset, he stopped saying it.

Except sometimes, when he was deep inside her, he could not hold back the words. *I love you, I love you, I love you.*

She did not say them back.

Chapter Twenty-nine

Catherine, you must help me understand the rebel leaders so that I can end this rebellion more quickly," Prince Harry said. "This conflict with our Welsh brothers only weakens us for the war we must inevitably wage with France."

At William's request, the prince had given Catherine a week to recover before coming to Ross Castle to question her.

"Glyndwr is a good man," Catherine told him. "He wants what is best for his people."

"What he has brought them is razed villages and ruined crops!" the prince said with irritation. "That is all this rebellion will ever bring them. They cannot prevail, so their suffering is for naught."

"Glyndwr believes God supports him, just as you do," she said in a reasonable voice. "He will not give up easily."

William listened as Prince Harry pressed Catherine for every bit of information she had gleaned during her capture. He asked her everything from the character of the rebel leaders to Glyndwr's intentions regarding the French pope to the number of armed men defending Aberystwyth and Harlech. The two discussed the Tudors at length.

Observing their interaction, William was struck by the prince's obvious faith in the accuracy of her reports. It was easy to believe he had drawn up battle plans based on information she provided.

"What can you tell me about Rhys Gethin?" Prince Harry asked.

William sat forward and watched his wife closely. He'd been afraid to ask about this rebel—or any of her experiences with the rebels—since their disastrous conversation on the way home from Beaumaris.

"I know Rhys Gethin is a fearless and skilled commander," the prince continued, "but what is he like as a man?"

For the first time, Catherine seemed reluctant to answer.

"Gethin is a rougher man than Glyndwr or the Tudors," she finally said, looking away from the prince as she spoke. She paused, then said, "I thought him the most dangerous of all."

Keeping her eyes focused on some distant point, she said, "Glyndwr threatened to have my marriage annulled by the false pope so he could wed me to Rhys Gethin."

So Gethin was "The Fierce One." The blood pounded in William's head at the thought of her being treated like chattel and traded for favors.

"Glyndwr let Maredudd Tudor take me from Harlech to remove me from Gethin's sight," she said. "He feared Gethin might carry me off to be 'married' by a village priest with a knife pricking his back."

"So Glyndwr wanted to protect you from Gethin?" the prince asked.

"It was more that Glyndwr would not permit Gethin to force his hand," she said with a rueful smile. "You see, Glyndwr had not yet decided what to do with me."

A chill went up William's spine as he thought of how close he had come to losing her. Catherine's pale, pinched face told him the discussion of Rhys Gethin had distressed her as well.

"My wife is tired," he said before Prince Harry could press her with more questions.

"Forgive me, Kate," the prince said, hopping to his feet. He dropped his gaze to her belly for the briefest moment and blushed faintly. "I did not realize how long I droned on."

The prince was a leader of armies, a battle-hardened commander. It was easy to forget he was also a young man of eighteen, inexperienced in other ways.

Catherine touched his arm and smiled up at him. "I am not ill, Harry, only with child."

"You feel well, then?" he asked in an uncertain tone.

"In sooth, I feel extremely well these days," she said, her smile broadening. "So much better than the first weeks, when I was nauseous and bone-tired."

From the look on the prince's face, this was more than he wanted to hear. He bid Catherine a quick good night and excused himself to speak to his men.

William's stomach clenched as he thought of Catherine, ill with her pregnancy, traveling hundreds of miles over rough roads. Sleeping out of doors in the rain and mud, for God's sake. As long as he lived, he would never forgive himself.

Stifling an urge to carry her, he helped her to her feet and escorted her up the stairs. Once he had her in their bedchamber, he resolutely ignored her protests and tucked her into bed.

He sat on the edge of the bed and rubbed his knuckles against her cheek. "I am sorry I was not there to protect you or ease your discomfort."

"I do not blame you," she assured him, but he could not accept her absolution for his gross failure.

"I also apologize for suggesting you could have helped bring about your capture."

She narrowed her eyes at him, weighing the sincerity of his words. After a long moment, she said, "I want to know who gave me up, William. Someone did. Someone told the rebels I was going to the abbey that day."

She could not absolve him, but perhaps she had given him a means to partially redeem himself.

"I will do my best to find the man who betrayed you." *And make him pay dearly for her suffering.* "I'll question everyone in the castle and the village again."

"Ask about the tenant Tyler," she said. "I always suspected he carried messages to the rebels for Rayburn."

If Tyler had a hand in this, he will not see another sunset.

William kissed her forehead and left her to rest.

Back in the hall, he and Prince Harry talked by the hearth until late, going over the information Catherine had shared.

"What a woman!" the prince said, shaking his head and grinning.

"Aye," William agreed quietly.

"No prince ever had a more perfect spy," Harry gloated. "She is courageous and daring—and her loyalty is boundless.

"Boundless, I tell you," he repeated, swinging his arms wide. "By the saints, she can lie through her teeth to an enemy, make him believe every word. Yet, she could not lie to me or to you to save her life!"

William winced. Though Harry did not intend to chastise him, the young man's absolute faith in Catherine made William feel like a worm for doubting her.

"As you know, the king is keeping his Christmas court at Eltham Castle this year," the prince said. "Come to Monmouth and we'll ride there together."

The prince was reminding him that he was expected to make an appearance. With Northumberland still spouting rebellion from Scotland, the king required reassurance of William's loyalty. Reluctantly, he agreed to meet the prince at Monmouth in two days' time.

* * *

"Tyler was the man."

Catherine looked up to find William in the solar doorway.

He came to sit beside her and took her hand. "After the prince left this morning, I went to the village. I heard from several folk that Tyler bought a cow a few weeks ago. No one knew where he found the money."

"That is suspicious."

"Aye. And now he's disappeared, which only confirms it. No one has seen him since the day you returned. Likely he feared you may have learned of his role from your captors."

"Or else he knew I would suspect he was involved."

"I've sent men out looking for him," William said. "Eventually they'll find him and bring him back."

She had expected this news to set her mind to rest more than it did. William, too, still seemed uneasy.

"What is it?" she asked.

"I intend to take Stephen with me to Eltham."

"I am so pleased," she said. "It will be good to have the king and others see him as William FitzAlan's brother and not just as Carleton's son."

Her smile faded when she noticed William was not meeting her eyes.

"As always, I'll be leaving Edmund in charge of the castle's defense while I am gone."

She put her hand on her hip and glared at him. "You did not want to tell me, because you knew full well I would not like it."

"He is my second in command," he said. "I leave him in charge because I have confidence in him. It would be a grave insult to him if I did not."

The patience in his voice grated on her nerves.

"I do not trust him," she said, making no effort to hide her irritation. "I do not wish to be in his care."

"How can you say that when he nearly died trying to protect you?" William said. "He would do it again without hesitation. He takes the trust I put in him seriously."

"What of the other men? Surely you can put one of them in charge and take Edmund with you."

He reached to brush back a strand of hair that had escaped from her headdress. She slapped his hand away.

"I have other good men, but Edmund is by far the best fighter among them." He softened his voice and said, "He's sworn to try to make amends with you. Why do you object to him so much?"

"I told you already I do not trust him." She gave him a sideways glance and saw that was not enough for her stubborn husband. Against her better judgment, she said, "I do not like the way he looks at me."

He gave a deep sigh and spread his arms out. "Catherine, I cannot send men away for looking at you, or I will have none left. All the men look at you. They cannot help it."

Anger surging in her veins, she got to her feet so she could glare down at him. "You misunderstand me, and I begin to wonder if it is deliberate." She shook a finger in his face. "I tell you, husband, if you saw how Edmund looks at me, you would not like it either."

His nostrils flared and an icy coldness came into his

eyes. In a quiet, dangerous voice, he asked, "Has he touched you?"

Edmund had not touched her, except for that one time months ago. Even then, all he truly did was slide his finger down her forearm. She was not prepared to see him dead for these offenses—yet. Grudgingly, she pressed her lips together and shook her head.

William's expression relaxed. "I will warn Edmund not to do or say anything that might offend you."

"But you will still leave him here?" She could barely keep herself from stamping her foot like a child.

"When I cannot be here, I must leave my best man in my stead. I do it to keep my promise to protect you."

"You failed to keep that promise once already." She blurted the words out in anger before she knew what she said. They burned hot in the air between them.

"I did not mean that." Although she regretted her hurtful words, she was still so angry her hands shook. "But it distresses me beyond bearing that you dismiss my opinion on a matter so important to me."

"The king trusts me in matters of military defense," he said, a note of pleading in his voice. "Why can you not?"

"Perhaps you should trust me more than you do Edmund," she snapped. "But then, you've never trusted me, have you?"

With that, she marched into her bedchamber and slammed the door behind her.

* * *

William tapped at her door. When she did not answer, he called out, "I will send Edmund away."

She opened the door a crack. "When?"

"He'll be gone today."

She opened the door no farther. "If you think I don't know why you are doing this, you are sorely mistaken."

"I'm showing I respect your wishes."

"You are doing this so I will not be too angry to come to your bed tonight."

Should he admit that was part of it? Probably not.

"If it makes you unhappy to have Edmund here, I want him gone."

The door banged shut. Apparently, he'd given the wrong answer. God help him! He hovered outside her door, trying to think of what else he could say, but he could think of nothing.

With a long sigh, he went down to write a message and have his talk with Edmund.

"You've upset my wife," he told Edmund a short time later.

"Pregnant women are known to get strange notions," Edmund said with a shrug. "Who knows why?"

"I am recommending you for service with the king's brother, Thomas Beaufort. He's a good man and close to both the king and Prince Harry."

"After all our years together, all we've been through, you will throw me out for her!"

"I warned you that if I had to choose between you, I would choose her," William said. "And I'm not throwing you out; I'm finding you a better position. 'Tis an honor to serve Thomas Beaufort."

"She's ruined you. Can't you see it? She's a lying who—"

He grabbed Edmund by the throat. "Don't say it if you want to live."

The blood was pounding in William's ears he was so angry. If Edmund ever spoke to Catherine like this, why had she not told him?

Edmund put his hands up, croaking, "All right, all right!"

William waited a long moment before he released him.

Edmund rubbed his throat as he tried to get his breath back. "You are right," he said when he could speak again. "I did not mean to offend her, but you must put your wife first. Your offer to find me a place with Thomas Beaufort is generous."

"I want you gone today." William slapped the sealed parchment he'd written for Beaufort into Edmund's hand. "You'll find Beaufort attending Christmas court at Eltham."

"I hope we can part as friends," Edmund said.

"Mind what you say about my wife in the future, or I'll see that Beaufort dismisses you," William said. "If I don't kill you first."

The business with Edmund left him in a sour mood. It was followed by a miserable night alone in his bedchamber. With only the solar between them, Catherine seemed as far away as when she was held at Harlech Castle.

He was still in a foul mood when he arrived at Monmouth the next morning.

Chapter Thirty

Catherine was relieved that Edmund was gone—and she felt guilty at the same time. Perhaps she was too hard on William. The wound from what he said to her on the way home from Beaumaris was still raw. That he dismissed her judgment regarding Edmund only added salt to the wound. He gave in to keep the peace with her, not because he trusted her opinion.

What was keeping Jamie? Jacob took him to see a litter of new kittens in the stable, but they should have been back by now. It was almost time for supper.

She paused in her sewing and cocked her head. What was that noise? She heard a crash and a bloodcurdling scream, followed by more screams and shouts. She sprang to her feet. Before she reached the door, it opened.

Edmund filled the doorway. Panic closed her throat. She backed up slowly. With the door open, the shouts and clatter coming from below were louder.

Edmund closed the door and leaned against it. "Thought you were rid of me, did you?" he said with a wide smile.

Her breath came in short, shallow gasps, making her feel light-headed.

Edmund went to the table and poured wine from his flask into an empty cup he found there.

"Come, Catherine, drink to my success," he said, waving her toward one of the two chairs.

When she took the seat he indicated, he pushed the cup toward her and raised his flask. She touched the cup to her lips as he took a long pull from the flask.

She forced herself to take several slow, deep breaths before speaking. "May I ask what we are celebrating?"

She did not know what his game was, but she must play along to give herself time to think.

"I've taken the castle."

She couldn't help gasping, though she had guessed as much.

"As soon as my men finish locking up the servants, they'll carry one of your barrels of ale to the hall," Edmund said. "But I wanted to have a private celebration with you."

It did not reassure her that the noise below had died down. She prayed God Jacob had found somewhere to hide with Jamie.

"I thought you were on your way to see Thomas Beaufort."

"I paid a visit to Lord Grey instead," Edmund said, and winked at her. "That old fox has wanted a piece of these lands since the day he was born. He was happy to pay for the rabble downstairs."

She could well believe it of Grey. At dawn tomorrow, Grey would attempt to take as much of their lands as he dared.

"How did you take the castle?" She needed time, and she was counting on his vanity.

"Since the men know me as William's right-hand man, they opened the gate to me. I slit a throat or two, and in no time we had most of the guard chained in the gatehouse."

"You cannot think the king will let you keep Ross Castle," Catherine said.

"Nay, but neither will he give it back to William," Edmund said, his voice full of bitter anger. "You think he will be in the king's favor after losing his castle within six months? Ha!"

William would be lucky not to be drawn and quartered.

"Besides losing his castle, William will have lost his wife—not once, but twice!" Edmund gave a harsh laugh and slapped the table. "The king will have no respect for him after this. No one will."

"But why? Why would you do it?"

"After all I've done for him, he kicks me out! Sends me away like a dog with his tail between his legs. So I've taken his castle and ruined him."

Without taking his eyes off her, he backed up to the door and put his hand behind him. She heard the scrape of the bar sliding into place.

"And now I'm going to take his wife."

* * *

William cooled his heels Efor half a day at Monmouth while Prince Harry dealt with some unexpected business. Damn. He was anxious to get this appearance at the king's Christmas court over with and get back home. It was midafternoon before the prince was finally ready to start the journey to Eltham.

"What an hour to get started," William grumbled to Stephen. "We'll have to stop for the night in a couple of hours."

As they mounted their horses, two score of men-at-arms bearing the Lancaster lion banner pounded through the main gate.

The prince watched them with narrowed eyes. "'Tis my uncle Beaufort."

William dismounted. They wouldn't be going to Eltham today. He scanned Beaufort's men but did not see Edmund.

After greetings were exchanged, William said to Beaufort, "I sent a man to you yesterday. If you came on the London road, you should have crossed paths."

"We traveled on it all the way from Eltham," Beaufort said. "We passed a few men but none stopped us."

An uneasy feeling settled in the pit of William's stomach.

"We are difficult to miss," Beaufort said. "Are you sure your man took the London road?"

It was the only road Edmund could take to Eltham Castle.

William tried to tell himself something could have happened to waylay Edmund. His horse took lame. Bandits attacked him. He got drunk and found a woman along the way.

William had fought beside Edmund for ten years. He'd trusted the man with his life more times than he could count. And yet, all he could hear were Catherine's words: *I do not trust him.*

He remembered the night he met her here at Monmouth Castle. She had told him her betrothed was not a man to be trusted. As an inexperienced girl of sixteen, Catherine had seen Rayburn for what he was. No one else had.

His heart thundered in his chest as he mounted his horse.

"Catherine may be in danger," he said to Prince Harry. "Make my excuses to the king."

He did not wait to hear the prince's reply.

He signaled to his men to follow and galloped out the gate.

Chapter Thirty-one

"$\mathcal{W}$as it you who arranged my kidnapping?" Catherine asked in an attempt to divert Edmund.

"Aye, I did it to save him," he said. "William was a fool for you from the start. I could see you would be the ruin of him, bedding every man from prince to troubadour right under his nose."

Edmund sat in the chair on the other side of the small table and took another long drink from his flask.

"The Welsh wanted you as soon as I told them Prince Harry would pay any price for you," he said with a cold smile. "Then I made William believe you'd run off with a lover. Believe me, I just had to plant the seed."

She felt the smoldering anger beneath his taunting humor.

"I expected the ransom demand to the prince to remove any doubt about the sort of woman you are," he said, shaking his head. "After that, William should have been happy to leave you to rot in Wales.

"I meant to cure him of you. If the Welsh offered me

money to sweeten the pot, why not?" Edmund slammed his fist on the table. "William got his land and wealth. By heaven, did I not deserve something as well?"

His shifting moods were frightening her as much as his words.

"But instead of paying me the rest of my money, that bastard Rhys Gethin had his men try to kill me!"

Rhys Gethin had the sense not to trust a man who betrayed his own.

"But how could you do that to William?" she asked. "You were his friend. His second in command. He trusted you."

He turned to gaze out the window at the dark sky. "I loved him like a brother," he said, nodding. "'Twas a time we had everything in common. We were the best of soldiers, but landless, with no bonds of family."

She heard the plaintive longing in his voice.

"There was freedom in the life we had. And always plenty of women. William drew them like flies." Edmund blew out a deep breath and shook his head. "But William was never content with it. Nay, he always wanted what he did not have."

He lifted his flask and, finding it empty, tossed it aside. He picked up her cup and took a deep drink. Though he showed little outward sign, she thought he must be drunk.

"Then the king hands him a castle, lands, and a title—and all for nothing more than refusing to follow his father into treason." Tiny drops of spittle hit the table as Edmund spoke. "Truly, his bounty was too much!"

"You understand him well enough to know what he truly desired was not wealth or lands," she said in a soft voice. "What he wanted was a family of his own, a home."

"I would not have begrudged William his good fortune," he said, fixing her with a look that burned right through her.

"But then, in addition to all else, he got you. And for you, he had to pay no price at all."

Edmund's words sent a wave of panic through her that threatened to swamp her.

"No matter what you were, what you looked like," Edmund said, "he would have married you because you needed saving. You see, William lacks his parents' pragmatism when it comes to honor. I could have forgiven him the rest of his good fortune if he had to take an ugly heiress into the bargain.

"Instead, the whore's son got a woman who puts all the others to shame," he said, his voice thick with bitterness. "It was more than one man deserved."

Her years with Rayburn gave her the sharp instincts of the hunted. She sensed Edmund was on the verge of attacking her.

"What about Tyler?" she asked, hoping to divert him again.

"Tyler knew some of the rebels. He served as my go-between with Rhys Gethin."

"What happened to him?" she asked, though she could guess.

"When William brought you back, I knew he would figure out someone here betrayed you. I gave him Tyler." He shrugged. "I suspect they'll find his body in the spring."

With an edge to her voice, she asked, "How is it you are not concerned William will come after you?"

"Well might you ask!" He laughed as he said it, but she heard unease in his laughter. "Believe me, I plan to be far, far away before William returns."

Praise God, he was going to take his rabble and leave soon. She narrowed her eyes at him. "You might want to get started."

"I have three days, maybe more, before the news reaches

him and he returns. All the same, we'll leave in the morning."

She just had to survive until morning.

"You do know I'm taking you with me?" he said.

She did not look down soon enough to hide the terror in her eyes, and he smiled with satisfaction.

"You bewitch men at every turn. One of them is sure to pay," he said. "I'll send ransom demands to them all and sell you to the highest bidder.

"Mind you, I'd make Gethin pay twice as much as the others, after what he did to me." He took another drink of wine and narrowed his eyes to slits. "But even if William could find the money after he loses Ross Castle, I'd never let him buy you back."

Catherine felt such a surge of rage it left her shaking. But then the child rolled in her belly, and her thoughts turned cold and clear. She would save herself and her baby.

"It would be a shame to give you to a man like Rhys Gethin. I suspect he has no refinement in bed," he said, leaving no doubt as to the direction of his thoughts. "He probably makes love the same as he fights—charges straight for the prize with all speed."

He leaned across the table and took her chin in his hand. She sat still, every muscle taut.

"Perhaps I'll give up the money and keep you for myself." His eyes were shining, and he was breathing hard. "Believe me, Catherine, I could make you call out my name and beg for more."

She was too late in wiping the revulsion from her face. He released her chin and grabbed her wrist.

"Then you shall go to that vulgar Welshman, who will use you as roughly as a whore and give away your child."

She felt his anger like the edge of a blade against her skin.

She tried to pull her hand out of his grasp, but he held it in an iron grip.

"But I shall have you first," he said, jerking her to her feet. "I want William to come home and smell another man on your sheets."

Chapter Thirty-two

William and his men raced in silence through the increasingly gray afternoon light. All the while, he prayed he was wrong. Prayed she was safe. Prayed Edmund feared him enough not to do it. Edmund must know William would follow him across the earth and into hell to kill him if he...

The sun dipped below the horizon, and the air turned bitter cold. It was not the cold, however, but a sense of foreboding that sent a shiver up his spine.

At long last, the outline of Ross Castle was dimly visible in the early darkness of the winter evening. William pushed his tired horse harder over the last stretch and reached the gate ahead of his men. When he roared at the guards, nothing happened. They neither called back nor dropped the drawbridge. He looked at the gatehouse and the towers. No torchlight. All was dark, as if the castle were abandoned, empty of every living soul.

God help him. They took his castle. His wife and Jamie were inside. The protection of every member of the household was his responsibility. Somehow, he had to get inside. He thought of all his work, strengthening the castle's defenses. He could see the storage rooms filled with sacks of grain to withstand weeks, even months, of siege.

It would take him at least two days to get a siege tower here. Too much could happen in two days. He could not wait that long. He heard the trampling and snorting of the other horses as his men joined him.

"Ropes," he shouted at them, panic rising in his throat. "We need ropes to climb the walls."

The men were silent. One or two might carry a bit of rope, but it was unlikely to be long enough to scale the curtain wall.

"William."

He turned toward his brother's voice in the darkness.

"I know a way."

* * *

Catherine screamed as Edmund dragged her across the solar toward the threshold to the bedchamber.

"No one will come," he shouted over her screams.

As he carried her toward the high bed, memories of Rayburn came crashing down on her. She kicked and screamed and clawed at his face. She would not be taken against her will again without a fight.

He pushed her onto the bed and straddled her. Holding her wrists over her head, he leaned down close to her face. "We can do this rough or not," he rasped, breathing hard. "The choice is yours, but I will have you one way or the other."

She struggled against him, but he held her fast. Holding her with one hand, he reached inside his tunic and pulled out a length of rope.

God help her, he meant to tie her down!

He put his mouth against her ear and said, "Aye, Catherine, I will do it."

He pulled back to look at her, but he was still close enough for her to feel his breath on her face. It smelled of sour wine.

"You may as well cooperate and enjoy yourself," he said, his voice almost playful. "Then you can tell me if I am better than William."

He put his palm to her cheek and rubbed his thumb across her bottom lip. "What say you, Catherine? How shall it be?"

It was difficult to think with him holding her down, but she could not let him tie her. She must have her hands free to have any chance at all.

"Will you promise to be careful of my baby?" Her voice came out faint and high-pitched.

"Very, very careful," he purred.

She swallowed and nodded. "All right, I will do it willingly. But you frightened me badly. You must give me time to calm myself…if…if I am to enjoy myself."

"I've had enough of waiting. Waiting and watching while you carried on with William, the prince, even that troubadour."

His eyes fixed on her mouth. Oh God, she could not take it if he kissed her mouth. Without releasing her wrists, he leaned down and kissed her throat. She bit her lip to keep from screaming at him to stop.

"But I am an understanding man," he said with a thin smile. "I will give you as much time as it takes for me to remove my boots."

He lifted her to the floor with him.

"Light a candle while I take my boots off," he said. "It's getting dark, and I want to see you."

Her hands shook as she lit the candle stub. As she did it, she listened for sounds from below. She heard no sound of guards fighting their way into the keep to save her, only the soft rumble of male voices and hoots of laughter. If she was to be saved, she must do it herself.

Feeling his eyes on her back, she turned to find Edmund sitting on the bench holding his boots midair.

"You are beautiful," he said, raking his eyes over her. "I gave you your time. Now I want to see you naked."

She took two steps back but could go no farther. Her back was against the bed. Somehow, she had to slow him down and gain control of the situation.

"What about you?" She let a faint smile lift the corners of her mouth. "If you want me to enjoy myself, you will have to take your clothes off as well."

She fluttered her eyelashes and tilted her head to the side. "And you will most definitely have to take your time."

Praise God, he was even drunker than she thought! Judging from the way his mouth gaped like a fish out of water, he believed her act. Or he wanted badly to pretend he did.

"You did say we have until dawn, did you not?" she asked, drawing out each word. "That is a long, long time."

Edmund dropped his boots to the floor and stood up. Without a word, he methodically removed every article of his clothing. Apparently, he had not listened to the part about taking his time.

She tried to tell herself this was going well, but he was standing naked before her, fully aroused. Fortunately, he was a vain man and misinterpreted the cause of her flushed cheeks.

As he came toward her, she dropped her gaze so he would not see her rising panic. When he ran his hands down her arms and kissed her neck, she thought for sure he would notice she was trembling and clammy with fear.

She need not have worried.

He turned her around and pressed himself against her. She felt the hardness of his erection through the layers of her clothing as he moved against her, groaning.

"I thought your growing belly would decrease my desire for you," he said, breathing hard against her ear. "But I want you more than ever."

This was going much too fast! She needed time, more time.

He kissed her neck as he undid the tiny buttons down the back of her gown.

"Please, I'm cold," she said, clutching her arms across her chest to keep the gown from falling.

"Then I shall keep you warm, for I am hot as fire."

In one quick movement, he pried her hands loose and jerked the gown down. It hung for a moment on her swollen belly and hips, then slid to her feet. She was left standing in only the thin tunic she wore underneath.

He lifted her in his arms and looked down at her.

"I promise you, Catherine, we shall make the most of our time together."

Chapter Thirty-three

$\mathcal{E}$dmund laid Catherine down on the bed with unexpected gentleness. Taking care not to put his weight on her belly, he lay naked against her side. He threw one leg over hers, pinning her down. She felt trapped, surrounded by his smell, his heat, his male body.

No matter what he did, she told herself, she had suffered worse at Rayburn's hands when she was just a girl of sixteen. She was a more formidable opponent now.

Edmund brought a fistful of her hair to his face and breathed in deeply. "From the moment I saw you on the drawbridge that first day, I knew you were not like any other woman."

He rubbed his cheek against the hair he clutched and closed his eyes. Her muscles tensed in readiness. But she held back. It was too soon. She would have but one chance.

"I desired you from the start," he murmured as he kissed the side of her face. "But when I saw you on the castle wall that day with your hair blowing all about you, I knew I would take you under William's very nose if we both remained in the castle."

He rose up on one elbow and ran his finger down the side of her face and along her throat. As his eyes followed the line his finger traveled to the neck of her tunic, his breathing quickened, and she sensed his mood change. He leaned down and kissed her where his finger stopped, at the lowest point of the neckline of her tunic.

And still, she waited.

She drew in a sharp breath when he cupped her breast. Misunderstanding her reaction, he groaned with pleasure. He ran kisses along her collarbone, his breath hot and damp against her skin.

This was nothing like with Rayburn. It was a shock to realize Edmund wanted to make love to her, to give her pleasure. She felt violated nonetheless. Clenching her fists, she closed her eyes and counted.

The next thing she knew, Edmund was on his hands and knees above her, and his tongue was in her ear. Panic nearly overtook her reason; it took all her resolve not to scream and beat her fists against his chest.

He moved down her body, murmuring her name. When she felt the wet of his tongue touch her nipple through the thin fabric, she fought the urge to grab him by the hair and jerk his head away. That would not save her.

Slowly, she reached her arms up behind her head and under her pillow until she felt her dagger. The movement made her back arch slightly.

"Aye, aye," he moaned, and clamped his mouth painfully over her breast. He was moving against her now, pressing his erection against her hip and suckling her breast.

Holding the sheath of her knife with one hand, she pulled on the hilt with the other. She had the blade free. She was ready.

* * *

William and the other men followed Stephen through the brush and tall grass along the river side of the castle wall. The mud sucked at his boot as he stepped in a hole of icy water.

"Old Jacob told me about the tunnel," Stephen said in a low voice over his shoulder. "It's been here since the castle was built."

William would never criticize his brother for prying secrets from anyone again.

"No one knows about it but him and Catherine," Stephen said. "And Robert."

Of course.

"The tunnel comes up in a storeroom near the kitchen," Stephen said. "We're close to the opening now."

William felt along the wall. Behind a sprawling bush, he found the break low on the wall.

"Follow me," he called. "Silence in the tunnel and have your swords ready. Stephen, I want you last."

The tunnel was dank and pitch-black. The entrance was no more than two feet high, but once he crawled through it, the tunnel was large enough for him to walk upright. Animals scurried away as he felt his way along in the dark. After several yards, he came to the end of the tunnel and felt above his head. Wood, not stone. The trapdoor. He put his dagger between his teeth and pushed it up.

There was a crack of light coming from under the door to the room. He could see pots and sacks of grain. He climbed out and helped the next man, then went to listen at the door. When half a dozen of his men were crowded in the small room, he eased the door open. The thrush lamp in the sconce was lit, but no one was in sight.

He moved quickly down the corridor, sword in hand. As he passed the kitchen, he heard muffled sounds. Somehow he knew Edmund would not lock Catherine in the kitchen with the servants.

"Get the door open," he whispered to the man behind him. "But tell them to stay put and keep quiet until we come back for them."

He heard men's voices in the hall above as he took the stairs two at a time. He hit the room at a run, his sword in one hand and his dagger in the other. The drunken fools were falling over each other trying to get to their weapons. His men would make short work of these. He had no time to stop and help.

Catherine was not here. And neither was Edmund.

He ran for the stairs. He sliced through one man who tried to stop him and tossed another over his shoulder without breaking his stride.

* * *

Once, when they were children, Harry showed her where to slide a blade into a man to reach his heart. She hesitated, trying to remember. Perhaps it was enough to injure him.

Suddenly, Edmund was pulling feverishly at her tunic. She could wait no longer. Swinging her arm down with all her strength, she sank the sharp blade deep into his shoulder. Somehow she managed to wrench it free before he flung his arms out and arched back, howling in pain.

Seeing the murderous rage distorting his face, she knew she had made a grave mistake. She should have killed him.

He rose up on his knees and reached his arm across his chest to feel the stab wound in his shoulder. When he brought his hand back, it was covered with blood. He stared at his bloody hand and then at her with bulging eyes. Then he drew his arm back and slapped her so hard she saw stars.

Before her vision cleared, he grabbed the front of her tunic and wrenched it in two. The effort cost him, and he bent forward, clutching his arms high across his chest. She would never know whether he failed to see she still held the knife or whether he believed he had incapacitated her with the blow.

This time, she did not hesitate. Gripping the hilt with both hands, she plunged the blade straight up under his breast-bone. The room reverberated with his single scream.

For one long and terrifying moment, he hung suspended above her, an expression of surprise on his face. Blood seeped in a thin line from between his lips. It gushed down her arms from where her knife was planted below his chest.

He fell forward on top of her, his chest on her face. The hilt of her blade pressed painfully into her shoulder, and she could not breathe. Frantically, she pushed against him with the strength of a madwoman to get his weight off her belly.

Grunting with the effort, she rolled him off her, only to find him lying face-to-face beside her. His cold dead eyes stared into hers. Screaming and weeping, she shoved at him with both her arms and legs until she sent his body over the edge of the bed. She heard the hard thud as it hit the floor.

Drawing her knees up, she curled her body into a protective circle around her baby. Only then did she let the darkness take her.

Chapter Thirty-four

*H*is heart racing with terror, William ran up the stairs to the family's private rooms. *Please, God, let me not be too late!* As he climbed, he heard the shouts and clatter of swords of the men fighting below. He hit the solar door running and slammed against it. It would not open. Howling with frustration, he rammed his shoulder against it again and again.

He was pounding it with his fists and calling her name when Stephen shouted, "William, move aside!"

He turned to see Stephen and three other men with a log from the hearth to use as a battering ram. He stepped back.

On their third run at the door, the hinges gave way and the heavy wooden door scraped against the floor. William was through the gap before they set the log down. He stood in the center of the solar, frantically looking back and forth in the near blackness. *Where is she? Where is she?*

Stephen pushed past him and lit the lamp on the table. William swept his eyes over the empty room, searching for clues. An empty flask on its side on the table. Catherine's embroidery frame on the floor. *Please, God, no.* His eyes went to the open door to her bedchamber.

She was in there; he knew it.

And he could smell blood.

He never felt fear in battle. When he fought, a cold determination settled over him, and his mind was sharp and clear. But he felt fear now. In every fiber of his body and deep in his bones. It took more courage than anything he'd ever done to walk toward the darkness beyond that open door.

He took the candle Stephen thrust into his hand and waved his brother back. Ignoring the signal, Stephen followed hard on his heels with the lamp. As soon as he entered Catherine's bedchamber, he saw Edmund's body sprawled across the floor in a dark pool of blood.

Stephen knelt beside the corpse, but Edmund was of no concern to William now. He couldn't kill a dead man.

His eyes traveled slowly from the inert body to the blood-smeared sheet that hung down the side of the bed. He followed the sheet up to the high bed, where the light from Stephen's lamp did not reach.

He caught the glint of a single strand of golden hair curling over the side of the bed. Unable to move, he strained to see into the shadows of the rumpled bedclothes. There was a form on the bed. A form that was much, much too still.

Oh God, oh God, oh God. The candle fell from his hand as he cried out her name. In another moment, he was holding her lifeless body against his chest and keening over her.

She was dead. Catherine was dead.

* * *

At the sound of his brother's harrowing cry, Stephen jumped to his feet and ran to the bed. He sucked in his breath. At the sight of so much blood, he nearly dropped the lamp. It was everywhere. Dark swaths of it covered the bed—and the limp body cradled in William's arms.

Casting a look back toward the door, he saw the men who crowded into the room behind them were backing out. He turned back to the bed and saw what they saw: William hunched over Catherine, weeping; Catherine's head lolling over his arm; her blood-soaked tunic ripped asunder, gaping open.

Swiftly, Stephen swung his cape off and draped it over her exposed breasts and swollen belly.

"Thank you," William whispered.

The misery in his brother's eyes when he lifted his gaze for that brief moment would haunt Stephen always.

"Is she alive?" Stephen's voice came out as a croak.

When William did not answer, he asked the question again, more insistently. Still, his brother did not respond.

Stephen reached out and touched Catherine's cheek with the back of his fingers. A dead person should not feel so warm. Edmund did not. With growing hope, he found her hand under the cloak and felt for a pulse at her wrist.

"She is alive!" When William stared blankly at him, Stephen gripped his arm and said in a louder voice, "William, I tell you, Lady Catherine lives!"

Stephen turned to the men in the doorway. "Find Alys and bring her here. She will know what to do."

Several of the men rushed from the room.

Stephen was used to his older brother taking charge, but it was obvious William would be of no help. He'd seen his mother and Catherine deal with household illness and injury countless times. Biting his lip, he tried to recall what they did.

"Tell the servants to bring warm water and strips of clean

cloth," he told the other men. "I'm not sure which we'll need, so have them bring both spirits and hot broth."

The men rushed out almost before he had the words out.

Relief washed over him when Alys burst into the room, raining curses on Edmund.

"That devil's spawn locked us all in the kitchen!"

She took command the moment she entered. Ignoring the body on the floor, she hurried to where William still held Catherine on the bed. She ran quick hands over Catherine.

"No wound!" she announced.

She left them to give direction to the servants setting up the washing tub in the solar. In no time, Stephen heard her shooing the servants, "Out with you now, out, out."

As she bustled back into the bedchamber, she called over her shoulder, "And shut that door behind you!"

"Lord FitzAlan, I need you to carry her to the solar," she said in her no-nonsense voice. "I must wash the blood off and get a better look at her."

William cradled Catherine in his arms, rocking her as though he had not heard.

Alys got up on the step to the bed and put her face in front of his. "M'lord, this is not your wife's blood. 'Tis only the blood of that bastard friend of yours."

When he only blinked at her, she raised her voice. "M'lord, you must get off your backside and help me. Now!"

Stephen could almost see the words penetrating William's skull as he looked from Alys to Stephen and back again. When William rose with Catherine from the bed, Stephen felt some of the tension go out of his shoulders.

The saints be praised, William was back with them.

In the solar, William sat on a bench next to the tub with Catherine on his lap. At Alys's direction, Stephen picked up the cup of broth from the table and knelt in front of Catherine.

Holding the cup under her nose, he watched her draw in a deep breath of the steam. He wanted to shout for joy when she opened her eyes a crack and took a small sip.

The broth seemed to revive her, for she took another sip and another. He darted a look at Alys, who smiled and nodded.

Catherine lifted her hand to touch his wrist and whispered, "Thank you."

Stephen took her hand and kissed it, trying not to cry.

"Jamie?" Catherine asked.

"He is safe," Stephen said. "He and Jacob hid in the stable."

"Out with you now, Stephen," Alys said. When he turned, prepared to argue, she said, "We must get her in the bath."

Stephen leapt to his feet so quickly he nearly knocked over the bowl of broth. "I'll be just outside if you need me."

As soon as Stephen was gone, Alys directed William to put Catherine's feet into the tub. "'Tis important we keep her warm."

She began a thorough inspection then, washing off blood as she worked her way up Catherine's legs. She nodded and murmured, "Good, good," as she went.

"The blood is not mine," Catherine said in a voice so low William had to strain to hear it. "I do not think I am injured."

He pressed his cheek against hers and closed his eyes. *Praise God. Praise God.*

"Shhh, do not talk yet, dear," Alys crooned. "Now let us get this dirty gown off you and get you in this nice hot bath. That, and another cup of broth, and you'll feel much better."

He lifted Catherine from his lap so Alys could pull the torn gown off, then eased her into the steaming tub of water before she could get chilled. After tucking a folded linen cloth behind Catherine's head, Alys refilled the cup of broth. She held Catherine's hands around the cup until she was sure Catherine could hold it on her own.

Alys touched his arm and jerked her head to the side. Reluctantly, he stood and stepped away with her.

"I see no outward injuries except the bruises around her wrists and the one on her cheek," Alys said in a low voice. "Now I must find out if the man forced himself upon her."

"We find her in bed, covered in blood," he hissed through clenched teeth, "and you doubt he did it?"

"What we know is that he tried," Alys said in a calm voice. "Remember, it was him we found dead on the floor— and with her blade in his heart."

Alys cleared her throat and said, "Now, m'lord, 'tis best you leave for a bit. If the man did take her violently, she will have injuries I must treat. And I need to check the babe."

William rubbed his hands over his face, as if he could push the horrible thoughts away. "I am staying unless she wants me to go."

Alys did not look pleased, but she did not argue when he took his seat beside his wife. He held Catherine's hand under the water while Alys spoke to her in a low voice.

When he felt Catherine's fingers tighten on his hand, he said, "I will go if you wish."

She gripped the side of the tub with her free hand and leaned toward him. "Nay, do not leave me!"

Choked with emotion, he could not speak at first. That she wanted him with her, in spite of how badly he had failed her, was more than he had any right to hope. More than he deserved.

He lifted her hand from the water and kissed her wet fingers. "I will stay as long as you will have me."

His penance for his sins against his wife began in earnest

then. He held her hand and stared out the window into the blackness of the night as Alys asked her terrible questions. Did Edmund strike her anywhere other than her face? Did he throw her to the ground? Was she sure she suffered no blow to her belly?

Eventually, in her straightforward way, Alys asked if Edmund raped her.

Catherine's answer, when she gave it, was indirect. "If I had been a virgin, I would yet have my maidenhood."

William let out the breath he had been holding, though her careful answer left him worried about what did happen. Alys, however, asked no more questions. Instead, she put her hands on Catherine's rounded belly. After a time, she looked at Catherine and then at William, a broad smile on her face.

"The babe is well!"

"God be praised!" William said, squeezing Catherine's hand.

All the way to Ross Castle, he had prayed God would protect his wife, never once sparing a prayer for their unborn child. But God, in his grace, had preserved the babe as well.

"Try to think of all you have to look forward to," Alys said, touching Catherine's cheek. "You have a fine husband and child, and soon you shall have another babe in your arms."

Catherine pressed her lips together and nodded.

"Active as this one is, I'll wager it's another boy," Alys said as she got stiffly to her feet. "Now, it is off to bed with you. Sleep is the best healer."

Before she left, Alys pulled William aside once more. "Your lady is stronger than you know. She's been through as bad as this and worse before." With a last pat on his arm, she said, "'Tis a blessing she has you to help her this time."

William was grateful to be left alone to care for his wife. As he helped her out of the tub, he dried her quickly and pulled a tunic over her head. He carried her to the bed in her chamber. After covering her, he shed his own clothes and crawled in beside her. He wrapped his arms around her and held her close.

He stayed awake most of the night, listening to her steady breathing. No matter how many years God gave them, he would be thankful for every night his wife fell asleep in his arms.

Chapter Thirty-five

Catherine awoke to the sound of voices outside the bed-chamber door. She heard the low rumble of William's voice, followed by Jamie's loud wail of complaint. Shivering as her bare feet hit the cold floor, she grabbed her robe and hurried to the door.

When she opened it, she found her four-year-old and her husband glaring at each other, hands on hips in identical poses. Stephen, who was standing on the other side of them, caught her eye, making no effort to hide his amusement.

"Jamie!"

The boy flew at her and threw his arms around her legs. Laughing, she sank to her knees to embrace him.

"Be easy with your mother," William said sharply, and took Catherine's arm to help her up. "I am sorry. I tried to make him wait until you were awake."

She smiled at Jamie to let him know it was all right.

"I will meet you all for breakfast as soon as I have dressed," she told them. "I had only broth for supper last night and am near starved."

The normalcy of sitting at table with her family soothed her soul. Although the others had long since eaten, the cook sent out platters heaped high with bread and meats and bowls of stewed apricots and sugared nuts. While she ate, Jamie told her about hiding with Jacob and the new kittens in the straw. To her relief, Jamie had thought it all a game.

At William's signal, Jamie's nursemaid collected her charge. "The dogs are jealous of the kittens now," she told him. "They are so unhappy they've ceased to wag their tails."

"They have not!" Jamie protested, but he jumped up to go with her all the same.

"I thought it best not to tell the boy too much," William said when they had gone.

Catherine nodded. Jamie needed no reassurance beyond seeing her. From the dark circles under William's eyes and the pinched skin between his brows, it was apparent her husband would need more.

Waving down William's objections, she asked Stephen to recount their part of what happened the day before.

"You were clever to remember the tunnel," she said when he had finished.

Stephen blushed at the compliment.

She patted his arm. "And cleverer still to get the secret out of Jacob. I'm sure no one has before."

Still blushing, Stephen cast a sidelong glance at his brother. William jerked his head meaningfully toward the door. Taking the hint, Stephen got to his feet.

"It brings me joy to see you safe and well," Stephen

said, sweeping her an elaborate bow. With that, he left the room.

Catherine shook her head, smiling. "That boy has enough gallantry and charm for two. Heaven help us."

William had no interest in discussing his brother.

"Time for you to rest." He stood and offered his hands to her. "Come, I'll help you back upstairs."

"But I have not been up an hour," she protested.

In the end, she gave in and let him take her upstairs, but she adamantly refused to get into bed. He settled her on the window seat with a stool propped under her feet and a blanket tucked tightly around her.

She tugged one arm free and patted the space beside her. "Sit with me a while."

She leaned into the comfort of his arms and rested her head on his shoulder. After a time, she said, "You must want to know the rest."

She looked at the hard planes of his face and watched the muscles of his jaw tighten and release.

"Only if you wish to speak of it," he said, his eyes fixed straight ahead. "And only when you are ready—not now."

"I cannot help but think of it now," she said. "Telling you may help me put it behind me."

He nodded and took her hand. "If it will help."

Once she began, she could not stop. She recounted the entire horror of it: every word, every look, every touch. The telling was cathartic for her—and torture for William. She understood that he had to hear it. Reliving the nightmare with her was a penance he needed to make before he could begin to forgive himself.

He kept his rage behind a careful mask. But when she told him what Edmund was doing to her when she stabbed him the first time and then how terrified she was when he backhanded her, William jumped to his feet. Clenching his fists, he paced the room, letting loose a rain of curses.

Then he collapsed beside her and covered his face in his hands. "I saw Edmund fight many, many times," he whispered. "I do not know another who gave him a second chance and survived."

He pulled her into his arms again. "I was arrogant and foolish to ignore your concerns about him."

Aye, he should have listened to her.

"Edmund was your friend," she said, leaning back to look at him. "You could not know he would do this."

"I pledged to protect you, and I failed—not once, but twice." He faltered for a moment, then said, "I do not know how you can ever forgive me."

"I am glad I saved myself."

"Please, Catherine. You don't need to lie to excuse my failings."

She bit her lip, trying to think how to explain it so he would understand. "The worst part with Rayburn was how helpless I felt. It was different with Edmund. Though I was frightened, I was never powerless. I believed I could get the better of him, and I was determined to do it.

"I am proud I was strong enough and clever enough to save myself," she continued. "That will make it easier to get over what happened and not be afraid."

She let her head fall against William's shoulder. Recounting the traumatic events of the day before had tired her. He kissed the top of her head and held her securely in his arms.

"I'm glad you are my husband, William," she murmured.

Only after her breathing became soft and regular against his chest did William give his reply.

"And yet, you had to save yourself."

* * *

After a couple days of rest, Catherine resumed her routine tasks. Edmund's attack would always be a bad memory, but she damn well was not going to let it rule her. She enjoyed managing the castle household. It was, however, a good deal of work. And now, every time she turned around, there was William, getting in the way and telling her to rest.

For the first day or two, it was reassuring to see him every time she looked up. But after several days, she was sure he would drive her mad with his hovering. He was unwilling to let her out of his sight for a moment.

She came upstairs this afternoon to do her sewing just to get away from him for an hour. At the sound of the door, she dropped her embroidery in her lap. It was William, of course.

"You do not need to keep watch over me from dawn till dusk," she said, not even trying to keep the edge from her voice. "Go out hunting or take the boys riding—or something!"

"I am happy to be here with you," he answered, the soul of patience.

"Well, I am tired of it, husband," she responded sharply, then sighed in exasperation at hearing herself sound like a shrew. "I know you mean well, but you act as though I will fall to pieces if you relax your guard for a moment. You will not even touch me at night."

There, she'd said it, and she would not be sorry for it.

"I was afraid it would remind you of—" He stopped himself, and she knew he could not bear to think of what that swine Edmund had done to her.

"I thought it too soon," he finished lamely.

"Too soon for whom, William?" she demanded. "Is it that you cannot touch me without thinking of Edmund's hands on me?"

She flung her embroidery on the table and stormed into her bedchamber, slamming the door behind her. He was still standing there staring at the door when she opened it again.

"It is not good for the babe to upset me like this!" she shouted at him and slammed the door again.

* * *

Mother of God, what had he done? William sank down onto the bench, which, thankfully, was just behind him. Propping his elbows on his knees, he ran his hands through his hair and over his face.

Should he go in to her now or leave her alone? Whichever he did was bound to be wrong.

A soft rapping at the solar door interrupted his thoughts.

"Blast it!" he said under his breath. He jerked the door open, ready to take his frustration out on whoever was there.

"Have you no sense at all?" he said, glaring down at Stephen. "Catherine could be resting!"

His tone would have put the fear of God into anyone else, but not this brother of his. He paused to take a better look at him. Stephen was fidgeting with his clothing and shifting his feet from side to side.

This was not like Stephen.

"What is it?" he asked.

Stephen fidgeted some more until William thought he might have to shake the answer out of him.

"We have a visitor," Stephen said at last.

"Catherine is not ready for visitors," he replied curtly.

"Send them away." He started to shut the door but stopped when Stephen made no move to leave.

Pinning Stephen with a hard look, he said, "What is the problem, brother?"

"I cannot send her away."

"And why is that?" William asked through clenched teeth.

"Because the visitor is our mother."

Chapter Thirty-six

William grabbed Stephen's wrist and pulled him into the solar. "What did you say?"

"Our mother is here in the hall," Stephen said. "She says she's come to meet your bride."

William's head was pounding with a sudden headache that was so bad it made his eyes hurt. His mother had never troubled herself to visit him before. But he should have expected her. Aye, she would come now that he was a man of property and in the king's favor.

"I kept her waiting as long as I could," Stephen said, "but you really must come down and see her now."

Better to strike quickly, William told himself. He marched out the door, ready to do battle.

* * *

Because Catherine's ear was pressed firmly to the door, she learned as soon as William did of Lady Eleanor's arrival. The anger and irritation that plagued her since Edmund's attack were displaced, for the moment, by fervent curiosity. And a spark of excitement.

Her mother-in-law was an enigma to her. Both William and Stephan painted Lady Eleanor as strong-willed, even manipulative. But while William professed to dislike and mistrust her, Stephen had strong affection for their mother.

Catherine was inclined to think well of the lady. No matter what her failings might be, she bore two fine sons whom Catherine loved with all her heart.

She could not wait to meet her! As soon as she heard the door close behind William, she called her maid to help her change. The challenge was to look her best—without looking as though she had taken any special care.

She decided on a new velvet gown of a silvery blue that brought out the color of her eyes. The gown, which had just been made to accommodate her growing size, fell over her protruding belly in soft folds from a tightly fitting bodice. Silver ribbon trimmed the neckline, sleeves, and high waist. The headdress was of the same silvery blue, with silver mesh encasing the braids on either side of her face.

After a last glance in her polished steel mirror, she hurried down the stairs. She paused to listen outside the entrance to the hall to gauge the tone of the conversation.

"Your visit comes at a most inopportune time." William's voice was politely formal but held a hard edge.

"Stephen told me of the recent misfortunes here." The woman's voice was rich and low. "I am most sorry to hear of them. How is your wife?"

Taking her cue, Catherine made her entrance.

"Lady Eleanor," she began, but stopped before she finished her words of welcome. Putting her hand to her chest, she said instead, "But... you are so beautiful!"

Catherine had never seen such a breathtaking woman. Lady Eleanor's rich brown eyes, auburn hair, and creamy skin matched Stephen's coloring, but her features were more delicate, more feminine. The lady had to be in her midforties, but she looked ten—even fifteen—years younger. Her close-fitting gown showed off curves that must turn heads.

Catherine realized she had spoken the words aloud and flushed as she curtsied. "'Tis good to meet you at last," she said, giving Lady Eleanor a warm smile despite her embarrassment. "I am so glad you've come."

Lady Eleanor laughed and put her hands out to Catherine. "Thank you, my dear," she said, kissing Catherine's cheeks. "You do make me wonder how my sons describe me." Flicking her eyes toward William, she said, "Odious and overbearing?"

Catherine turned to look at William and Stephen. To her dismay, William stood with his arms folded, fairly seething with hostility. And Stephen might catch fire, backed up almost into the hearth.

"I wish you congratulations on your marriage," Lady Eleanor said. After sweeping her gaze over Catherine, she added, "And on your upcoming blessing! I am pleased to see such a bloom of health in your cheeks. You look lovely, dear."

"Thank you, I could not feel better."

"I was just telling Lady Eleanor that this is not a good time for us to receive visitors," William interrupted.

His rudeness shocked her. "I must disagree," she said, giving him a look meant to convey her disapproval. "It could not be a better time, with Advent here."

"It would be a burden on you to entertain guests when you are yet recovering from your ordeal." Dropping his gaze to her belly, he added, "You must take care of your health."

"Your mother will be no burden at all," she said with a

tight smile. Turning to Eleanor, she said, "Your visit will divert me from my recent troubles. I shall enjoy having another woman for company."

William was outmaneuvered. From the look of resignation on his face, he knew it.

* * *

If William wanted to see his wife, he could not avoid his mother. Much to his surprise, the two women appeared to enjoy each other's company enormously. He had to admit Eleanor's presence had a soothing effect on Catherine. He often heard them sharing a laugh as he passed by.

Catherine's irritation with him, however, continued unabated. Knowing he deserved the sharp edge of her anger, he took it without complaint. And yet, he could not understand why she became more vexed with him with each passing day. He was doing everything he could to make her feel safe and protected.

He sent his men to remove Grey from his lands. He had not left the castle since finding Catherine limp on the bed, covered in blood. That image would never leave him. He lived in fear someone would snatch her away again if he relaxed his vigilance for a single moment.

Between his mother's presence and the tension with Catherine, he was in an unrelentingly sour mood. Lack of sleep did not help. And it was not just guilt and worry that kept him awake at night. Lord in heaven, he wanted his wife!

He wanted her with an aching need, a longing past bearing. But he did bear it. He was afraid touching her would revive her memories of that night. Although Catherine gave broad hints she was ready to resume marital relations, he could not bring himself to risk it.

Late one evening, he found her alone in the hall after the rest of the household had gone to bed. He was pleased to catch her without Eleanor for once.

He approached cautiously. "You look a little tired," he said, trying to show his concern for her. "Perhaps you should retire?"

"I am not in the least bit tired," she snapped.

He sat down on the bench beside her and tried to think of something else to say.

"It has been too long since I visited the tenants," she announced. "I want you to take me for a ride around the estates tomorrow."

Her suggestion was so unexpected, he forgot his resolve to keep his patience and not rile her.

"I shall not permit it," he said flatly. "There are too many dangers outside the castle walls."

She slammed closed the prayer book she had been reading and banged it down on the table.

"Will you keep me under lock and key in my chamber, husband?" she demanded, her eyes burning holes into him. "You are a worse jailor than my Welsh captors!"

Her eyes flicked to the table. Before he knew it, she picked up a pitcher and threw it at him. She stormed out of the hall, so angry she did not appear to see Eleanor near the entrance.

He caught the pitcher, but cider splashed onto his clothes and was dripping from his hands. As he shook his hands, he looked up to see Eleanor watching him from across the room. She arched an eyebrow at him.

"How long have you been there?" he asked.

"Long enough to see you are going about this all wrong."

She walked over and handed him a cloth from the table. "Perhaps I did send you off to your father too soon," she said, shaking her head. "It is remarkable how little you know about women—at least about the woman who is your wife."

William wiped himself off as best he could and tossed the cloth on the table.

"Come, sit down," Eleanor said, gesturing to the chairs near the hearth. "Let me help you."

His mother had made colossal mistakes with her own life. So far, she'd caused nothing but pain and trouble in his. It was a sign of how desperate he was that he was willing to listen to her advice.

"You are forgetting whom you married," she said once they were settled by the fire. "A woman who would cross her husband to spy for the prince is not like other women."

"Of course she's not like other women," he grunted.

"You did not marry a demure child, so you should not expect your wife to like it when you treat her as one."

"I do not treat her like a child," he said through clenched teeth. "I merely wish to keep her safe."

"What you do not seem to understand is that Catherine takes pride in her strength," Eleanor said. "It is important to her that you value that in her as well."

"Are you suggesting I let her ride alone—pregnant as she is—all over the countryside at her whim?"

His mother sighed deeply to let him know he was trying her patience. "What I am saying is that you mustn't cosset her. If you do, she will find a way to defy you. Or worse, she will comply and become a different woman from the one you love. Either way, you will make her unhappy."

William thought back to when he arrived to take the castle. Catherine was magnificent that day, bold as brass, coming out alone on the drawbridge to meet them.

"I admired her courage from the start," he said.

"Then you must let her know that," his mother said. "A

woman enjoys having her looks and charm appreciated, but she wants to be loved for what is best in her, for what she values in herself.

"Go to her now," she said, patting his knee. "She loves you, so it should not take much to set things aright."

For the first time since he was a very small boy, William kissed his mother's cheek. Long after he had gone, Eleanor gazed into the fire, her fingers stroking the place where her son's lips had touched her.

* * *

William searched their rooms, but Catherine was nowhere to be found. With his mother's warning that Catherine would defy him ringing in his ears, he looked about her bedchamber more carefully. There was no sign of hurried packing. No open chest with gowns hanging over the side, as when she had run off to the abbey. Praise God.

What a fool he was. She must be up in Jamie's chamber. He turned to go, then turned back. Everything was in its place....

Her riding boots were missing.

He grabbed his cloak and ran down the stairs two at a time. As he raced across the bailey, his breath came out in white puffs in the cold night air. How long had it been since she left the hall? He prayed it was not time enough for her to escape.

As he slipped through the stable door, he saw the glow of a lamp in the far corner. He was not too late.

When he saw her hooded shadow, the memory of their first meeting at Monmouth swept over him. As he thought of the straightforward and determined girl he found in the stable that night, it struck him with sudden clarity that his mother was right.

He was a wiser man back then. Though he was young

and she a stranger to him, he had understood her intuitively. That night, they managed to find a compromise between her determination to do what she felt she must and his equal resolve to keep her safe.

It gave him hope they could do so again.

Taking care not to make a sound, he crossed the stable. When he stood just behind her, he said, "I see you still have not learned to saddle a horse in the dark."

She let out a short scream and whirled around to face him.

After a long moment, she cocked an eyebrow and said, "I suppose I should be grateful you did not knock me to the ground this time."

"Just as I am grateful you do not have a blade aimed at my heart." Tilting his head, he added, "Though I suspect you wish you did."

"I pray you do not drive me to it." Her tone made William hope she had left her blade behind.

Without another word, she turned to take her horse's bridle from its hook.

He clasped his hand over hers. In a quiet voice, he said, "Let me do that for you."

She looked at him sharply. But as she examined him, her expression softened. "You will go with me?"

"I shall go with you, or you shall not go," he said. "Just as before."

His heart felt tight in his chest when she responded with the first genuine smile she had bestowed on him in much too long.

The men at the gate were not able to cover their surprise when he ordered them to open it. Telling himself it was safe enough, he stifled the impulse to grab her reins and turn around. God's beard, even rebels had more sense than to be out on a night as cold as this.

She led the way around the castle to the path by the river.

He was relieved to see that, in deference to her pregnancy, she kept her horse at a walk. Despite the fact that she had him out riding at midnight on a December night, he must try to remember she was usually a sensible woman.

They dismounted and walked up the bank overlooking the dark river. The moon and stars were bright in the night sky. William wrapped his cloak around them both and held her close against him.

"Are you warm enough?" he asked.

"Mmm," she murmured, leaning back against him.

"I know why you came riding with me that night at Monmouth," she said. "You were afraid of what would happen if you carried me kicking and screaming to the keep."

"Aye, that was one reason." He chuckled, remembering, and rubbed his chin against the top of her head.

"But later, after just one kiss, I wanted to forget my honor and steal you away." He closed his eyes and tightened his arms around her. "That is what made it so hard for me to believe about Jamie's father. If I'd had you in bed even once, I could not have left you as he did. I would have killed Rayburn and defied the king if need be, but I could never have let another man have you after that."

After a time, she asked, "Why did you come with me this time? What made you change your mind about keeping me in the castle?"

He took a deep breath and let it out. "I wasn't hovering over you because I thought you were weak," he said, though it was hard to admit. "I did it because I knew I was."

She turned around to face him. "You don't have a weak bone in your body, William FitzAlan. What can you be talking about?"

"I never felt true fear until I knew Edmund had you behind that barred door. And then, when I saw you covered in blood and believed you were dead..." He swallowed hard against the memory. "I was lost in a darkness so deep I thought I would never come out of it. And I did not care if I did."

She took his hand and held it against her cheek. "I should have realized how it was for you to find me like that."

"I would not change you from the strong, bold woman I love, but you must help me find my way," he said, wanting to make her understand. "Twice I have nearly lost you. I live in fear another disaster will befall you—and that when it does, I shall fail you again."

"You are a good man, William. A man of honor." She slipped her arms around his waist and rested her head against his chest. "I do not know why God chose to bless me by making you my husband, but I am very grateful."

Later, as they rode back to the castle, William felt light, as if a burden was lifted from him. A feeling of happiness welled up inside him. They pulled their horses up in a clearing to take a last look at the river. When Catherine suddenly threw her arms up to the heavens and laughed with the same joy he felt, he knew he had all he ever wanted.

* * *

They stopped in the hall to warm their hands before the hearth. As soon as Catherine could feel her fingers and toes again, she raised an eyebrow at William and cocked her head toward the stairs.

When they reached the solar, he removed her cloak and wrapped a blanket around her shoulders.

"'Tis late," he said, and kissed her forehead. "You must be tired."

She pulled away from him and went to the door to slide the bolt. Then she turned and gave him her best wicked smile.

"What is it?" William asked.

She nearly rolled her eyes, the man was so thick.

Keeping her eyes fixed on his, she dropped the blanket at her feet. She began undoing the buttons at the back of her gown. When he rushed over to help her, she grabbed the front of his tunic and pulled him against her.

"Kiss me." It was not a request.

He gave her a slow smile, then leaned down and brushed his lips against hers.

She was having none of that. Clasping her hands behind his neck, she gave him a kiss to remember. When they finally came up for air, she grabbed his belt before he could get away. She unfastened it and slipped her hands under his tunic and shirt. When her fingers touched warm skin and rough hair, she smiled.

Victory was within her grasp.

William grabbed her wrists to stop her. "What are you doing?"

"You did tell me I would have to help you find your way," she said, fighting a grin, "but I thought you would remember this part."

He released her wrists and took her face in his hands. "I do not think you are ready for this, love."

"Oh, but I am." She tilted her head back for another kiss, confident he was losing his will to fight her.

When she felt him melt into the kiss, she ran her hand along his erect shaft. He sucked in his breath and tried to pull back. She drew him deeper into the kiss and lifted his hand to her breast.

Thankfully, he did not need further direction.

She was breathless when he turned her and lifted her hair to finish unfastening her gown. He kissed her neck, sending thrills down her spine.

"Are you sure?" he whispered against her skin.

"Aye," she sighed as he worked on the buttons, "I have grown weary of waiting for you."

He chuckled and eased the gown down to kiss her shoulder. Impatient, she tugged the gown down to her waist.

No more hesitation, no more light humor. His passion exploded. He pulled her hard against him, his mouth hot and wet on her neck, his hands cupping her breasts. She closed her eyes and dropped her head back to rest against his shoulder. This is what she needed to wipe away the memory of Edmund's touch.

William scooped her up in his arms and carried her into the bedchamber. Again and again through the night he told her he loved her.

And now, Catherine believed him.

Epilogue

1417

William ran his finger up her arm. "We have the afternoon without the children underfoot. Do you wish to spend it *all* discussing them?"

Catherine laughed and squeezed his hand. After a dozen years, their love and their passion for each other remained strong.

"God has truly blessed us," she said.

"His blessing today is that the children are gone," he said as he pulled her to her feet.

Before they reached the stairs, Catherine heard male laughter behind them, and Stephen and Jamie burst into the hall.

"This is a happy surprise!" she said as she crossed the room to greet them. "We did not expect you for another fortnight."

"We missed you too much to wait," Stephen said as he leaned down to kiss her cheek.

"I suppose the ladies at court believe all your lies," she chided. "You must tell me later what truly brought you home early."

She settled the men by the hearth and sent for wine.

"I am certain the king intends to return the Carleton family lands to you," William said, "so there is no reason to delay arranging a betrothal for you."

She sighed. Did William have to raise the subject even before the wine was poured? She and William were in perfect accord on the need for Stephen to be settled, but she would have waited for a quiet moment to speak with Stephen alone.

"There is no cause to hurry either," Stephen said. His tone was light, but she caught the obstinate look in his eyes.

"Still," she put in, "there can be no harm in discussing it."

"I have presents for the little ones," Stephen said in a blatant attempt to divert her. "Where have you hidden them?"

"They are visiting the abbess." She folded her arms. "Now Stephen—"

"Truly, Catherine, every young lady you've asked me to consider is exceedingly dull." To annoy her, he turned to Jamie and said in a loud whisper, "And pliant in all the wrong ways."

"You should have let us arrange this betrothal long ago," William said. "Now Mother and Abbess Talcott have put their minds to it."

"I thought Mother's new husband would keep her better occupied," Stephen grumbled. Lady Eleanor had married a man a dozen years her junior after the death of Stephen's father.

William's eyes gleamed with amusement. "I suggest you settle the matter soon, or those two are sure to trap you in some scheme of their own."

"I told you a long time ago," Stephen said, winking at Catherine, "if you can find me a woman like yours, I'll be wed as soon as the banns can be posted."

Catherine rolled her eyes and waved her hand in a dismissive gesture. "Save your false flattery for the foolish women I hear you spend your time with."

As the men continued talking, she bit her lip and stared into the fire. She should have known the young girls of marriageable age would bore him. Perhaps a foreign bride would pique Stephen's interest. Or a young widow...

When she looked back at Stephen, something in her expression caused his smile to falter. She was a more formidable opponent than his mother and the abbess combined, and he knew it.

"We have news," Jamie said. "Maredudd Tudor has come forward to be pardoned."

"Praise God!" Catherine said, putting a hand to her chest. Maredudd went into hiding eight years ago when Harlech fell and the rebellion was crushed. "Poor Marged. How difficult these years must have been for her."

"He waited long enough," Stephen said. "Harry offered Glyndwr and all the Welsh rebels pardons when he was crowned four years ago."

"If Maredudd wants to help that son of his, he should send him on campaign with us to Normandy," William said. "Fighting the French would go a long way toward demonstrating his loyalty to the Crown."

Catherine put her hand on William's arm. "Will that be soon? I hoped Harry would wait another year before making a second expedition."

"The king has been preparing all winter," William said in a soft voice. "He'll not let another summer pass before returning to fight for the lands our prior kings lost to France."

"Everyone at court was talking of it," Jamie said, his eyes alight. "We came home to tell you the king has commanded all the men to gather in a few weeks."

Catherine closed her eyes. It had been so hard when they went on the first expedition two years ago.

"Jamie," Stephen said in a low voice, "let us go collect your brothers and sisters from the abbey."

Their footsteps echoed in the hall as they made their escape.

William pulled her onto his lap. "No harm will come to us," he said, lifting her chin with his finger. "You forget what a fearsome trio we make. The French will run like rabbits when they see us."

Please, God, let my men come home from this war.

She thought of how the course of her life had been changed, more than once, by the events of a single day. No matter how much William tried to protect her, it could all change again.

But for now, she would count her blessings and be grateful for the time she and William had together.

She would not waste a day of it.

"William, take me upstairs." She stood and held her hand out to her husband.

Much later, as she lay with her head on William's chest, she heard their children entering the hall below. She took comfort in their laughter and in the strong, steady beating of her husband's heart.

Historical Note

𝒯he more I read about the great Welsh rebellion of six hundred years ago, the more I came to admire both Prince Owain Glyndwr (rhymes with *endure*), the Welsh rebel leader, and young Prince Harry, who spent much of his youth putting down the rebellion.

Glyndwr took control of all of Wales, inspired a ten-year rebellion, won recognition from foreign countries, and pressed a forward-thinking reform agenda. My natural inclination would be to take the rebel side, but history was against them.

Henry V (Prince Harry in this book) was also a leader of stunning accomplishments. In writing about him as a young man, I could not see him as the frivolous youth Shakespeare depicted. At eighteen, he was already an experienced commander in charge of the English forces fighting the Welsh. As king, he appears to have devoted every waking moment to his duties. After the disastrous reigns of Richard II and Henry IV, he united England as both beloved warrior king and a skilled and tireless administrator. He reconciled the noble factions, fostered nationalism across the classes by making English the language of his court, and decisively turned the tide in the Hundred Years' War with France.

Another interesting historical character in this book is the child Owain (or Owen) Tudor, son of a Welsh rebel. After Henry V died in 1422, Owain held the lowly position of clerk of the queen's wardrobe. He had an affair with the king's young widow that sent the Lancasters into apoplexy—and resulted in five children. It is ironic that the grandson of this Welsh rebel and Henry V's French princess would usurp the throne in 1485 and begin the Tudor dynasty.

I drew personality traits for these and other historical figures from the information I had—and made up the rest. I apologize to descendants of the Welsh rebel Rhys Gethin, in particular, for giving him unappealing characteristics to serve my story.

Acknowledgments

A first book requires a lot of thank-yous. I am tremendously grateful to my agent, Kevan Lyon, for her grace, wisdom, and unflagging support. Many thanks to the folks at Grand Central for taking a chance on a new author. Alex Logan deserves a prize for guiding me through the publishing process. Both she and Amy Pierpont provided thoughtful comments that made this a much better book. Thanks also to Claire Brown for the gorgeous cover. I would not have made it to publication without the guidance and support of other romance writers. Thank you to the members of the Olympia and the Greater Seattle RWA chapters, volunteer contest judges, presenters at the Emerald City Conferences, and my critique buddies.

I am grateful to my father, who taught me all about heroes. Some men are honorable because of the example set for them. Others, like my father and the hero of this book, choose to be honorable in spite of it. Thanks also to my mother, who is probably the reason all my female characters are strong.

I appreciate all the friends and family who were amazingly supportive when I decided to change careers and take up the uncertain life of a writer. Special thanks go to Cathy, Sharon, Nancy, Laurie, and Ginny for reading manuscript drafts before I had a clue what I was doing. Most of all, I thank my husband. When I wanted to quit my job to write just as the first college tuition payments came due, he told me, "Whatever you want, honey." They don't come better than that.

Knight
of Pleasure

For my parents,
Norman and Audrey Brown,
who gave me my love of history,
books, and foreign places.

Prologue

Northumberland, England
1409

"Which of you brave Knights of the Round Table will fight me?" Isobel called out.

"Me! Choose me! Isobel, choose me!"

Isobel ignored the shouts of the boys jumping up and down around her and rose up on her toes, searching for her brother. Where was Geoffrey? When she spotted him in the tall grass, she dropped to her heels and sighed. Her brother was gazing at the sky, a smile on his face, happily talking to himself.

She pointed instead to a frail-looking boy at the back of the circle. "You shall be Gawain."

The other boys groaned as Gawain stepped forward, dragging his wooden sword behind him.

"Sir Gawain," Isobel said, giving him a low bow. "I am the evil Black Knight who has captured Queen Guinevere."

The little boy scrunched up his face. "Why do you not play Queen Gui-, Gui-, Gui-"

"Because I am the Black Knight." At thirteen, she was the eldest here and got to set the rules.

She glared up at the gray stone walls of Hume Castle. The boys her age were inside, practicing with real swords in the castle's bailey yard. 'Twas so unfair! For no cause at all, her father forbade her to go off with the boys—or touch a sword—while they were at this gathering. She was to sit quietly and keep her gown clean.

She turned back to Gawain and raised her sword. "Will you not fight to save your queen?"

Gawain stood frozen, his eyes round with panic.

Quickly, she leaned down and cupped her hand to the boy's ear. "The Knight of the Round Table *always* prevails, I promise."

She did her best to make his clumsy swings look skilled. When that proved hopeless, she jumped about, making faces and acting the fool. Soon, even Gawain was laughing. She finished with a most worthy death, moaning and clutching her chest before sprawling full length on the ground.

She lay, sweaty and breathless, listening to the boys' cheers. The rare sunshine felt good on her face. When a shadow passed over her, she opened her eyes. She squinted at the tall figure looming over her and groaned. Would Bartholomew Graham not leave her alone? He plagued her!

"Go away, calf brain," she said and stuck her tongue out.

She pushed herself up onto her elbows. More ill luck. All the older boys had come out to watch.

"You've changed since last summer," Bartholomew Graham said. He moved his eyes deliberately to her chest.

"'Tis a shame you have not." She batted away the hand

he offered and scrambled to her feet. "Or have you ceased to cheat at games and bully the younger boys?"

"I have a real sword, pretty Isobel," he said with a wink. "If you'll go into the wood with me, I'll let you play with it."

The older boys guffawed at this witless remark. Praise God, she would marry none of them! Her father would find a young man as noble and worthy as Galahad for her.

"Isobel!"

The boys' laughter died as her father's voice boomed out across the field. Isobel was the apple of her father's eye, and woe to any boy caught offending her. Boys, big and small, began slipping away through the field. All save one. Her brother looked about him as though awakened from a dream.

"Geoffrey, go!" she hissed at him. "It will not help to have you in trouble, as well."

Isobel waved to her father. Ah, she was in luck. The man lumbering beside him with a gait like a pregnant cow was their host, Lord Hume. Her father would keep his temper around the old man. All the same, she opened her other hand and let the wooden sword slip to the ground beside her.

When the men finally reached her, she gave Lord Hume her best curtsy. She wanted to make a good impression, since her father said Lord Hume could help them regain their lands.

"I am most sorry for your loss," she said, pleased with herself for remembering the recent death of his wife.

What an old man he was! 'Twas hard to look at him with all that loose skin hanging from his neck and those puffy bags under his eyes drooping halfway down his cheeks. But he must be wealthy. As wealthy as her father said, to own a jeweled belt that could reach around that immense belly of his.

"Your daughter is the image of your lovely wife," Hume said. "And she has spirit enough to keep a man young."

How often did her father say she would make him old before his time? A smile tugged at the corners of her mouth as she slid a look at him, hoping to catch his eye.

"Aye, she is a lively girl," her father said.

The cheerfulness of his reply gave Isobel hope she might escape a scolding for her swordplay with the boys. While the men talked on and on about some event that would take place in the autumn, she grew bored and tried not to fidget.

"'Tis settled then," Lord Hume said, taking his leave at last. "You will want to speak to your daughter now."

Lord Hume took hold of her hand before she could hide it behind her back. She tried not to make a face as he slavered on it. As soon as his back was turned, though, she wiped it on her gown.

She stood beside her father, waiting to be chastised about swords and dirty gowns. When Hume finally hobbled through the castle gate, she turned to face her father.

To her amazement, he was hopping from foot to foot, doing a little dance!

"Father, what has happened?"

He picked her up and swung her in a circle. Then he did his little dance again. Seeing him so gloriously happy made her heart swell with pleasure.

"Tell me, tell me!" she said, laughing.

He raised his hands toward the heavens and shouted, "God forgive me for ever wishing you were a boy!"

Her father grinned down at her, eyes shining, as if she had just handed him the moon and stars.

"Isobel, my girl, I have such good news!"

Chapter One

Northumberland, England
September 1417

The cold from the chapel's stone floor seeped through Isobel's knees. Her every bone and muscle ached with it. 'Twas not the cold, however, that caused her to pause in her prayers. Once again, she ran her eyes over the shrouded corpse surrounded by tall, flickering candles.

When her gaze reached the corpse's belly, high and wide beneath the cloth, a small sigh escaped her. The body was, indeed, Lord Hume's.

This need for reassurance was childish. Chastising herself for her lapse, Isobel returned to her prayers. She would fulfill this last duty to her husband.

And then she would be free of him.

When next she opened her eyes, it was to find the pinched face of the castle chaplain leaning over her.

"I must speak with you," he said without apology.

She nodded and held her breath until he straightened. Did the man never bathe? He smelled almost as bad as Hume.

Whatever the priest had to tell her must be important. As her husband's confessor, he had reason to know Hume's soul was in need of every prayer. Still, she was reluctant to leave the servants to keep vigil without her. Despite the extra coin she gave them, they would cease their prayers the moment the door closed behind her.

Hume had not been a well-loved lord.

When she attempted to rise, her legs failed her, and the priest had to grasp her arm to keep her from falling. She let him lead her out of the tower that housed the castle's small chapel. As she stepped out into the bailey yard, a gush of wind cut through her cloak and gown. She waited, shivering, while Father Dunne fought the wind to close the heavy wooden door.

As soon as he joined her in the yard, she asked, "What is it, Father Dunne?"

Father Dunne pulled his hood low over his face, took her arm, and started walking her toward the keep. "Please, let us wait to speak until we are inside."

"Of course."

The frozen ground crunched beneath their feet. Thinking of the blazing hearth in the hall, Isobel quickened her steps. Food would do her good, as well. She'd missed the midday meal.

As they went up the steps of the keep, she noticed two of them were cracked. She added the repair to the list in her head. The castle was hers now. No more begging Hume's permission to take care of what needed to be done.

As she entered the hall, she saw their nearest neighbor warming his hands at the hearth. She gave Father Dunne a sharp look. The priest was sorely mistaken if he thought the arrival of Bartholomew Graham was good cause to draw her from her vigil.

"Isobel!"

It set her teeth on edge to hear Graham address her by her Christian name, despite her repeated requests that he not.

"My most sincere regrets at Lord Hume's passing," Graham said as he rushed toward her, arms extended.

She offered her hand to prevent his coming closer. Fixing fine gray eyes on her, he pressed his lips to it. He lingered unnecessarily. As he always did.

She should not have been shocked when Graham pursued her during her marriage. After all, he'd been a liar and a cheat as a boy. But how he could still not know his good looks and easy charm were lost on her—that was a mystery.

"Thank you for your concern, but I must speak with Father Dunne now," she said, tugging her hand from Graham's grip.

She clenched her jaw to keep from snapping at him. Usually, she handled Graham's attentions with more grace, but she was tired and her patience short. The last days of Hume's illness had not been easy.

"If you wish to wait," she made herself say, "I will have some refreshment brought."

Father Dunne cleared his throat. "Forgive me, Lady Hume, but I must ask that he join us." Her face must have shown her irritation, for Father Dunne hastened to add, "I have good cause, as you shall see."

She could not very well argue with the castle chaplain in front of the servants in the hall. Biting back her temper, she turned and led the two men up the circular stairs to the family's private rooms on the floor above.

She added replacing the castle chaplain to her list.

Once they were in the privacy of the family solar, she did not bother to keep the sharpness from her tone. "Now, Father Dunne, what is so important that you have seen fit to call me away from my prayers for my husband's soul?"

The chaplain bristled. "I felt it my duty to inform you of a document your husband entrusted into my care."

"A document?" She felt a pang of anxiety in the pit of her stomach. "What sort of document?"

"'Tis a conveyance of certain properties."

Just how large a sum had Hume given to the Cistercian monks at Melrose Abbey to say Masses for him? She did not begrudge the monks, but she hoped there would be sufficient funds left to make the long-neglected repairs to the castle.

"You speak of his will?" she asked.

"A will could not serve this purpose," Father Dunne said in his ponderous voice. "A man may give his gold, his horse, and his armor to whomever he chooses in his will—but not his lands. Upon his death, his lands pass to his heirs."

Father Dunne coughed, looking uneasy for the first time. "To give his lands to anyone else," he said, drawing a rolled parchment from inside his robe, "a man must do it *before* his death."

Isobel had tried for months to convince her husband to let Jamieson buy the small plot he worked so he could marry the miller's daughter. With death knocking at his door, Hume must have finally done it. Good deeds, like prayers, could reduce his time in purgatory.

This must be what the priest was fussing about. She smiled and reached her hand out. "Let me see it, then."

Father Dunne stepped back, clutching the document to his chest. "I suggest you sit first, Lady Hume."

Isobel folded her arms and tapped her foot. "I prefer to stand." Truly, the man did bring out the worst in her.

The priest tightened his mouth and began unrolling the parchment. "'Tis a simple document," he said, still not giving it to her. "In essence, it grants all of Lord Hume's lands, including this castle, to Bartholomew Graham."

The priest had to be mistaken. Or lying. Still, the smug look on his face sent a wave of fear through her.

She ripped the parchment from his hands and scanned the words. She read them a second time, more slowly. And then again, a third time. She looked up, unseeing, and tried to take in the enormity of what her husband had done to her. Surely he would not do this. Could not do it. Not after all she had given up, all she had done for him.

For eight long years she was at the beck and call of a peckish old man who wore her down with his whining and constant demands. Day after day after day. Listening to his tedious conversation. Trying not to watch as food and drink dribbled down his chins and onto his fine clothes.

And then there were the nights.

She put her hand to her chest, fighting the feeling of suffocation. Once again, she saw him huffing and puffing over her, red-faced and sweating. God's mercy! How she feared he would fall dead on top of her and trap her beneath his enormous weight. After years without conceiving, she finally convinced him the risk to his health was too great.

She resented every day, every hour, of her marriage. Still, she had done her duty by her husband.

"It must be a forgery," she murmured, looking down at the parchment again. She recognized the script as the priest's, but that meant nothing. With shaking hands, she uncurled the final roll of the document.

She ran numb fingertips over the familiar seal.

She watched as the parchment slipped from her hand and

fluttered to the floor. The ground shifted beneath her feet. As she reached out to catch herself, the room went black.

Isobel awoke to the nightmarish sight of Graham and that weasel of a priest hovering over her. Before she could gather her wits, Graham lifted her to the bench, his hands touching her in more places than necessary for the task.

As she looked down, a deep red drop hit the bodice of her gown. Bewildered, she touched her finger to it.

"You struck your head on the bench when you fell," Father Dunne said, handing her a cloth. "I did warn you to sit."

"Leave us, Father Dunne," Graham said, as if he were already lord of the castle.

The priest's eyes darted back and forth between them as he backed out of the room. Isobel suspected he went no farther than the other side of the door.

She glared up at Graham as she dabbed at the cut on her forehead. "How did you get Hume to do it?"

Graham dropped next to her on the bench, sitting so close that his thigh touched hers. Too light-headed to stand, she slid to the edge of the bench.

"Hume came to believe I was his son," Graham said, smiling at her. "You know how much he wanted one."

"So you lied to him!"

"Well, it certainly *could* be true," he said with a shrug. "Fortunately, the conveyance is not dependent upon it."

Graham's mother had been a wealthy widow, notorious in this part of the Borders. When she became pregnant, more than one man stepped forward, claiming to be the father and offering to marry her. She disappointed them all by keeping her property—and the secret of her son's parentage—to herself.

"I gave my husband no cause to punish me," Isobel murmured to herself. She could not believe Hume would leave her destitute.

"In sooth, the old man was most concerned for your welfare." Graham stretched his legs out and crossed his arms behind his head. "It gave him great comfort to know I would wed you after his death."

"You would do what?" She must have misheard him.

"Finally, you shall have a man who can please you." His hot breath was in her ear, but she was too stunned to move. "I've wanted you since you were a girl, still playing at sword fighting with the boys."

Coming back to her senses, she slapped at the hand creeping up her thigh. "What would make you believe I would agree to marry you?"

"You would prefer," he said in an amused tone, "to return to your father's house?"

The blood drained from her head. 'Twas true. If she could not remain at Hume Castle, she had no place else to go. She sank against the stone wall behind her and closed her eyes.

"Do not fret—your father would not keep you long," Graham said, patting her knee. "Though you are no longer an untouched girl, he'll have no trouble finding another old man to pay to have such a beauty in his bed."

She swung her arm to slap him, but he caught her wrist.

"'Tis always exciting to be with you, Isobel." With his eyes hot on hers, he pried her fist open and ran his tongue over her palm, sending a quiver of revulsion through her.

All these years, she had sorely misjudged him. She had considered him a mere annoyance, fool that she was. Only now did she see he was not merely shallow and selfish, but ruthless and cunning. The handsome face and easy manner hid a man without honor.

A man who would take what he wanted.

"I shall return in a few days to take my place here," he said.

Isobel's limbs went weak with relief as he rose to go.

At the door, he turned. "Send a message," he said, giving her a wink, "if you cannot wait so long."

Chapter Two

As soon as Graham was out the door, she raced to it and slid the bar across. Rage pulsed through her now, blurring her vision. She paced the room, clenching her fists until her nails cut into her palms. What could she do? Surely there must be some way to challenge the theft of her property. But how would she go about it? Who could help her?

The only person she trusted was her brother. But Geoffrey was in Normandy with the king's army. She covered her face in her hands, not wanting to think now how worried she was about him. Her sweet, dreamy brother was no soldier. Sending him off to fight was one more thing she would not forgive her father.

Her father. In this alone he would be her ally. He would care if she lost her property.

In the end, she sent for him, for she had no one else to ask.

An hour later, her maid poked her head through the solar door. "M'lady, Sir Edward awaits you in the hall."

Her father must have set out as soon as he received her message.

Isobel hurried down the stairs to the hall. At the entrance she halted, caught off guard by the wave of loss that hit her at the sight of the familiar bullish frame. Her father stood half turned from her, surveying the imposing hall with a smile of satisfaction on his face. After all these years, it should not hurt this much to see him.

With a growing tightness in her chest, she remembered how she used to think he caused the sun to shine. She was the favored child, the adored daughter he took with him everywhere. If it had been otherwise, she would not have felt so betrayed.

What a foolish girl she was. She had believed her father delayed betrothing her because he could not find a man he deemed worthy. Galahads are hard to come by.

Then he sold her like cattle. To a man like Hume.

She recalled how her legs shook and her breath came in gasping hiccups as she climbed down from Hume's high bed to wash that first night. Behind the screen, she lit a candle and poured water into the basin. As she wiped the blood smeared along the inside of her thigh, it struck her: her father knew what Hume would do to her. He knew, and yet he gave her to the man anyway.

"Isobel, 'tis good to see you!" Her father's booming voice jarred her back to the present.

When he came toward her as though he would embrace her, she stopped him with a lift of her hand.

"'Tis a shame," he said, "it took your husband's death for you to receive me in your home."

Isobel resented both the criticism and the hurt in his voice. "Come, we must speak in private."

With no further greeting, she turned and led him up the stairs to the solar. Here, too, he looked about with a proprietary air, admiring the rich tapestries and costly glass window.

"Who would have thought the old man would live so long?" he said, his good cheer restored. "But now this fine castle and all the Hume lands are yours! I told you marriage was a woman's path to power."

Before Isobel could step back, he took hold of her arms. "With what Hume has left you," he said, his eyes alight, "who knows how high you may reach next time?"

Isobel could only stare at him in horror. Could her father truly believe she would let him plan a second marriage for her?

"I know 'twas not easy," he said, his voice softer. "But now you shall reap the reward for your sacrifice."

"My 'sacrifice,' as you call it, has been for naught—at least, naught for me!" Isobel was so choked with emotion, she could barcly get the words out. "Hume gave you what you wanted the day the marriage was consummated, but he's left me with nothing."

"He what?"

As she looked into her father's face, her rage returned full force. "My lord husband gave away all the lands I was to inherit." She wanted to pound her fists against her father's chest like the willful child she once was. "You promised I would have my independence once he died. You promised me!"

His fingers dug painfully into her arms. "You are mistaken. Hume had no children; his lands must come to you."

"He has given it all to Bartholomew Graham!" she shouted at him. "My home. My lands. Every last parcel."

"The devil take him!" her father exploded. "What reason could Hume have?"

Isobel covered her face with her hands. "Graham tricked the old fool into believing he was his son."

"This will not stand!" Her father stormed up and down the room, eyes bulging and hands flying in the air. "We will take this up with Bishop Beaufort. Then we shall see! Surely the king's uncle can cure this fraud. I swear, Isobel, we shall see young Graham imprisoned for this."

Before the last shovel of dirt covered Hume's body, Isobel and her father set out for Alnwick Castle. Bishop Beaufort was at the castle on business for the king.

Isobel pulled her horse up at the bridge and eyed the sprawling stone fortress above her. As a child, she had come here often. But that was in the days when Alnwick was home to the Earl of Northumberland—before Northumberland attempted to wrest the crown from Henry Lancaster.

Northumberland escaped to Scotland. The more important of his co-conspirators were beheaded, the lesser dispossessed. Foolish men, every one of them, to take on the Lancasters.

Her father, heedless as ever, spurred his horse over the river that served as Alnwick Castle's first line of defense. Isobel followed more slowly. Bishop Beaufort was the wiliest of all the Lancasters.

"I hear Beaufort is the richest man in all of England," her father said as they neared the gatehouse. "God's beard, he's loaned the crown vast sums for the king's expedition to Normandy."

"Hush!" she whispered. "Do not forgot he was half brother to our last king." *The king you committed treason against.*

"I have my pardon from young King Henry," he said, but he was not as confident as he pretended. Beads of sweat stood out on his forehead as they rode through the barbican, the narrow passage designed to trap an enemy inside the main gate.

They were escorted into the keep and shut in a small

anteroom to await the bishop's pleasure. Almost at once, an immaculately dressed servant came to usher her father into the great hall for an audience. Isobel was left to stew while two men discussed her fate.

She was surprised when the servant returned a short time later without her father.

"His Grace the Bishop wishes to see you now, m'lady." She must have been too slow to rise to her feet, for he arched an eyebrow and said, "His Grace is a busy man."

She walked through the massive wooden door he held open for her and entered an enormous hall with high ceilings that drew the eye ever upward like a church.

There was no mistaking the man behind the heavy wooden table near the hearth. She would have known Bishop Beaufort by the power he exuded, even if he had not worn the vestments of his office—a gold silk chasuble over a snowy white linen alb with apparels worked in silk and gold at the wrists.

The bishop did not look up from his papers as she crossed the room. When she took her place before the table beside her father, she saw that the parchment in the bishop's hands was her copy of Hume's property conveyance.

Her father poked his elbow in her side and winked. His conversation with the bishop must have gone well, praise God!

"I do not believe," the bishop said, his eyes still on the document, "the transfer of Hume's property can be challenged."

Stunned by the bishop's swift dismissal of her cause, she shot a look at her father. His nod did not reassure her.

"Your father suggests a reasonable solution," the bishop said, snapping her attention back to him. "Under the circumstances, the only honorable course open to Graham is to wed you. I shall see that he makes the offer."

The bishop picked up a new sheaf of papers, dismissing both her and her problem.

"But I have already refused him." Her voice seemed to echo in the cavernous hall. "I do not mean to be ungrateful for your kind assistance, Your Grace," she added hastily. "But I could not marry the man who stole my property. He is wholly without honor."

The bishop set his papers aside and truly looked at her for the first time. Powerful as he was, he could not move her; she met his eyes so he would know it. Instead of irritation, she saw keen interest in the sharp gaze he leveled at her.

"Let me speak alone with your daughter," he said without taking his eyes from hers. Though spoken politely enough, it was not a request.

When the door closed behind her father, the bishop motioned for her to sit. She sat, hands clasped in her lap, and willed herself to stay calm as the bishop inspected her.

"Let us review your choices, Lady Hume," he said, touching his steepled fingers to his chin. "First, you can accept Graham. With him, you keep your home, maintain your position."

She opened her mouth to object and snapped it closed again.

"Second, you can return to your father's care. With the generous dowry your father will provide"—the pointed look he gave her made it clear he knew the humiliating terms of her first marriage—"I am confident the next husband he finds for you will be as suitable as the last."

He paused, as though to give her time to consider. Time, however, could improve neither choice.

Please God, is there no escape for me? None at all?

"I can offer you a third choice," the bishop said in a slow, deliberate voice. He reached out and rested his long, tapered fingers on a rolled parchment at the side of his table. "I just received a letter from my nephew. He has taken Caen."

"God preserve him," she murmured. Desperately, she tried to think of what reason he could have for telling her of King Henry's progress in reclaiming English lands in Normandy. The bishop did not seem like a man to speak without purpose.

"The king is anxious to strengthen the ties between England and Normandy. Come spring, Parliament will offer incentives to English merchants to settle there."

Merchants? What could this have to do with her?

"Alliances among the nobility are even more important." He tapped the rolled parchment with his forefinger. "The king asks for my assistance in making such...arrangements."

Her thoughts seemed thick and slow as she struggled to understand the import of his words.

"I offer you the opportunity to enter into a marriage advantageous to you," he said. "And to England."

Her breath caught. "In Normandy?"

"You must marry someone," the bishop said, turning his palm up on the table. He leaned forward a fraction and narrowed his eyes. "I think perhaps you are a woman who would prefer the devil you do not know over the devil you do."

Knowing she was being played by a master did not help her one whit.

The bishop drummed his fingers lightly on the table.

She tried to think it through. A stranger could hardly be worse than Graham. And if she were in Normandy, she could watch over her brother. But how could she agree to wed a man she knew nothing about?

The bishop drummed his fingers again.

"Would I be permitted to meet the French 'devil' first, before committing to marry him?"

An appreciative smile briefly touched the bishop's lips, but he shook his head. "Even if you leave before a betrothal can be arranged, you will be bound by your pledge to the king." He arched one thin eyebrow. "Do you have some...*requirement*...you wish me to pass on to the king?"

A knight, brave and true, good and kind. The description of a Camelot knight came to her, quite inexplicably. Flushing, she shook her head.

"After your father's...misjudgments...of the past," the bishop said, his nostrils flaring ever so slightly, "such a marriage would do much to restore your family to the king's good graces."

"May I have time to consider, Your Grace?"

"Of course." With a glimmer in his eye he said, "Soon the crossing will be impossible until spring, but I am sure you wish to spend the long winter months here, with your father."

Oh, he was a clever man.

The bishop rose to his feet. "I leave for Westminster in three days. Until then, you may send a message to me here."

With no further word, he swept out of the room.

Chapter Three

Duchy of Normandy
October 1417

Sir Stephen Carleton awoke to a blinding headache. He lay still, listening to the distant sound of wind and rain, and tried to recall where he was. Aye, he was with King Henry's army in Normandy. In the town of Caen, in fact.

But where, precisely, in Caen?

Giving up, he slit one eye open and winced at the dim light. It came through an arrow slit, so he was somewhere in the castle. But this was not his bedchamber. And what was he doing in bed when it was yet daylight—

He groaned. Gingerly, he turned his head for confirmation. Upon seeing the bare shoulder and tousled blond hair, he squeezed his eyes shut again. Marie de Lisieux. God help him, she was a lot of woman to forget.

He edged his arm out from under her, taking great care not

to disturb her. Pleased at his success, he sat up and swung his legs over the side of the bed—much, much too quickly.

Resting his head in his hands to recover, he looked down at his limp member and wondered if it would ever rise again. The woman was insatiable. No wonder her husband turned a blind eye to her infidelities; the man was grateful for the respite.

How had he ended up in bed with her again? A wave of self-loathing washed over him, making him desperate for a drink. Ironic, since drink was what had gotten him here. But drink kept at bay the visions that plagued him.

Aye, drink helped. And women, of course.

There were plenty of men to drink with in a town overrun with soldiers. And, for him, there were always willing women. Which one hardly mattered. He had even less expectation of finding a woman who could make him happy than he did of achieving knightly glory in this wretched war.

He wondered what it would be like to be with a woman who was strong and brave and clever. A woman who would not settle for him being less than the man he could be.

Could she save him? Was he worth saving?

He knew only one woman like that, and he did not expect to meet another. Still, he enjoyed women. Talking with them. Flirting with them. Bedding them. He did not have to be fully sober, however, to know the one asleep beside him was a mistake.

Keeping a watchful eye on Marie's still form, he eased himself down from the bed. She slept like the dead, the saints be praised. When he leaned over to gather his clothes, his head throbbed so violently he feared he would be sick. He waited for his stomach to settle before pulling the shirt and tunic over his head. Teetering on one foot, he nearly fell as he struggled into his leggings.

He grabbed his boots in one hand, his belt and sword in the other, and made his escape.

God's beard, the corridor was freezing!

He could see now he was in the castle's keep. But whose bedchamber was that? It would be just like Marie to take him to another lover's bed. The woman thrived on trouble.

Caen Castle was huge, with numerous buildings scattered across acres of bailey yard. The walk to the main gate was almost long enough to clear his head. When he finally crossed the bridge into the Old Town, he entered the first public house he found.

He was still there hours later, drinking with a boisterous group of soldiers, when he felt eyes upon him. The familiar form of his half brother, Lord William FitzAlan, filled the doorway. When the other men noticed the great commander, they fumbled to their feet and offered to make room. William kept his gaze on Stephen.

Stephen poured more wine into his cup and ignored his brother. When one of his companions called out, "May God bring us more victories," he did not raise his cup with the others. But he drank it down all the same.

He poured another and decided to make his own toast.

"God grant us victory," he said, clutching the edge of the table, "even if we must starve women and children to achieve it."

Before he saw William move, his brother had an iron grip on his arm and was leading him out the door. Outside, William slammed him up against the wall.

William cupped Stephen's chin and jaw in his hand. With his face so close their noses nearly touched, he said, "God in heaven, Stephen, what am I to do with you?"

Drunk or sober, Stephen would not let any other man lay hands on him. But this was William. "'Tis a long time since I've been your responsibility, big brother."

"I have served as both father and brother to you for far too many years to stand by and let you do this to yourself!"

William released his hold and leaned heavily against the wall beside Stephen. In a quiet voice he said, "We did what we could. You must try to put it behind you."

Stephen did not want to talk about what happened the day the siege of Caen broke and the English army swarmed through the town. By the time he and William reached the market square, English soldiers were massacring the crowd of women, children, and old men gathered there. He and William rode through the melee, swinging their swords in the air, shouting and pushing, until at last the order to halt was heard and obeyed.

The images of that day would not leave him.

When it was over, Stephen walked through the carnage in the square. The wails of women filled his ears, and the smell of blood choked him as he stepped over broken bodies of children and old men. When he looked down, a child's severed arm lay before his bloody boot. He leaned against a wall and vomited until his knees were weak.

"This is not the path to glory I expected when we came to fight the French," he said.

"King Henry's army slaughtering old men, women, and children!" William said, his voice hard with anger. "I never thought to see it."

"You must have known. Why else did you order Jamie to remain outside the city walls that day?" Despite the accusation in his voice, Stephen was immensely grateful his nephew did not witness the slaughter in the square.

"The lad is only fifteen," William objected. "'Tis true I suspected trouble, though not as foul as that. The men were full of bloodlust after our knight was burned to death."

The city defenders had thrown bales of burning straw onto

the knight, who lay injured in the ditch at the base of the wall. Unable to reach their man, listening to his screams, the English sat by their campfires in frustrated rage.

"And the king?" Stephen asked, though he knew the answer.

"He believes the people brought the wrath of God upon themselves," William said in a grim voice. "They had only to submit to him as their rightful sovereign to escape their fate."

"The women and children had no part in the city's decision to hold out against us."

"The killing was against the king's orders, and he'll not allow it to happen again." William took in a deep breath and let it out. "The other towns will fall quickly now."

"So the slaughter served a purpose," Stephen said, his voice tight. "Our king is nothing if not strategic."

"You are incautious with your opinions," William said, though without much force. "If the people here had the sense God gave them, they would welcome us. The French nobility are a blight upon the land. Both Burgundy and Armagnac factions pillage the countryside for their own enrichment."

"'Tis a shame the French armies will not fight us. I hoped to win great battles for England." Embarrassed, Stephen elbowed William and tried for a lighter tone. "Like my famous brother."

"By God, I never thought I would miss fighting the Scots," William said as he heaved himself away from the wall. "Come, I'll walk with you to the castle. You need to get your sleep—you have an appointment with the king early on the morrow."

Stephen felt the remaining effects of the drink drain out of him. "Called in a favor for your feckless little brother, have you?"

"Feckless perhaps, but hardly little." William clouted him on the back. "And I called in no favors. God knows why, but the king has seen something special in you since you were a lad. He says he has an assignment for you."

"What is it?"

William shrugged. "He did not say."

They walked in companionable silence through the castle gate and into the castle grounds. During the day the bailey yard was busy with soldiers, but it was peaceful this time of night. They were nearly to the Old Palace, where Stephen shared a chamber with his nephew, before William spoke again.

"You should ask the king's permission to return to Northumberland. 'Tis time you claimed the Carleton lands."

"I am not so foolish as that! Mother and Catherine will be relentless, once I have the property, to make a good match." Why was his unmarried state such a thorn in their sides?

"They want to see you settled before you fall into serious trouble over some woman." William shook his head. "And they are right. 'Tis bound to happen."

Stephen ignored the remark; he'd heard it before.

After a time, William said, "There is much to be said for a life with wife and children, on lands of one's own. God knows, Catherine is the source of all my happiness."

"As I've always told you," Stephen said, forcing a laugh, "if you find me a woman like her, I'll be wed as soon as the banns can be posted."

Catherine was beautiful, courageous, full of opinions and laughter. He'd adored her from the age of twelve, when his mother sent him to live with William and his new wife.

"I wish to God Catherine were here now," William said, his tone sour. "You would not behave like this if she were here to see it."

Stephen shrugged, acknowledging the truth of it. In his youth, it had always been easier to face William's anger than Catherine's disappointment. Even now, he would do anything to please her.

Well, almost anything. At least here in Normandy, he was free of her attempts to get him betrothed to some pliant and exceedingly dull young lady of good family and fortune.

Aye, he knew he must marry. But he was only five and twenty! With luck, he could put that duty off for many years.

Stephen sat in the Great Hall of the Exchequer, drumming his fingers. Damn. He should have risen early enough to join the king for Mass in the chapel.

At the sound of boots, he jumped to his feet. King Henry swept into the hall, trailed by several soldiers who served as his personal guard. With a curt nod, the king released Stephen from his bow.

Stephen sighed inwardly as the king scrutinized him in the long silence that followed. Though he had taken care in dressing for this ungodly early appointment, there was naught he could do about his bloodshot eyes. King Henry indulged in neither women nor drink; he had little tolerance for those who did.

"How can I be of service to you, sire?" Stephen smiled and gave a deferential nod to temper his boldness in speaking first.

"Perhaps you could explain to me," the king said, clasping his hands behind his back, "why a man who is so easily amused must devote so much time to seeking amusement."

Stephen dropped the smile. Had he been so indiscreet that word of his behavior had reached even the king's ears?

"I have better use for your talents, Stephen Carleton."

Stephen detected no trace of sarcasm in the king's tone. A good sign, perhaps. "I am, as always, at your disposal, sire."

He wondered again what assignment the king had for him. He desperately wanted a military command, but he would be satisfied with rounding up renegades. Anything, so long as it was dangerous and diverting.

"My subjects here must see that I come not to conquer, but to rule as their rightful sovereign. 'Tis time to establish order and good governance in the lands we have thus far reclaimed. To that end, I have appointed Sir John Popham as bailli of Caen. I want you to assist him."

Stephen could not believe what he was hearing. "You want me to be…to be…" He had to grope for the word, and it felt distasteful in his mouth when he found it. "An *administrator?* But I am a skilled knight, sire."

"You would make a fine commander, as well," the king said in a flat voice. "But until a French army is willing to face us in battle, I have more commanders than I need."

Two years before, the English army decimated the cream of French chivalry at the Battle of Agincourt in a defeat so resounding it would be remembered through the ages. The French commanders had studiously avoided fighting the young English king head-to-head ever since.

"What I need is a man of wit and charm who can earn the people's trust," the king said. "Your charge is to hear their complaints, resolve their disputes fairly, and convince them they are better off under English rule."

Sweet Lamb of God. "I am glad to be of service, sire."

"Leave us," the king called out. When the heavy doors closed behind the soldiers keeping guard at the entrance, the king said, "I knew I chose the right man. No one would guess from your countenance you are seething."

The smile on the king's face brought to mind a cat with an injured bird under his paw.

"That deceptive charm," the king continued, "and your much-lauded talent for learning secrets, will prove valuable in your second assignment, as well."

It was a family joke that no secret was safe from him. Stephen tried to guess which of his loved ones saw fit to share this with the king. His musings were stopped dead as a panel in the wall behind the king swung open. When a tall, elegantly dressed man with distinctive white-blond hair stepped through the opening, Stephen re-sheathed his sword.

"Robert!" Stephen shouted. "What are you doing in Normandy? Does William know?"

He and Robert thumped each other on the back, then stepped back to look more closely at each other. Though Robert's face showed a few more laugh lines, Stephen didn't doubt women fell at his feet—and into his bed—with the same regularity.

"*Sir* Robert now," the king said. "After twenty years, our friend has given up the guise of traveling musician. He has returned to claim his rightful place as a nobleman of Normandy."

"You are full of surprises," Stephen said, laughing.

Robert grinned back. "How it would grieve my uncle to know I've inherited his estates! I went into hiding because he was determined to have me murdered." Robert leaned close to Stephen and whispered, "His second wife favored me a bit too much."

"Despite his change in circumstances," the king said, "Robert has agreed to continue his service to me."

Steven knew what that "service" was. As a troubadour, Robert traveled widely and was welcomed everywhere. That had made him a useful spy in the years when England was roiled in rebellion and King Henry was yet Prince Harry.

"I cannot tell you how many evenings the family spent speculating about who you truly were," Stephen said.

Robert's eyes crinkled with good humor. "We can speak more of that another time. Now we must discuss the king's plans for you. We shall be working together, my friend."

* * *

When the king dismissed Stephen and signaled for him to remain, Robert felt no sense of alarm, no foreboding. Though they were very different men, their relationship was one of long-standing and mutual respect.

"Order and good government will not be enough to bind Normandy to England," Harry began. "We must have marriage alliances among the nobility, as well."

Apprehension crept up Robert's spine. Marriage alliances? Could the king mean—good God, the saints protect him!

"I received a letter today from my uncle, Bishop Beaufort, regarding one such young lady. If the weather holds, she could arrive any day."

A drop of sweat trickled down Robert's back. "A young lady, sire? How young?" Please God, not some young innocent. He was years and years too old for that.

"She is a widow of two and twenty."

Better than fifteen or sixteen. But only slightly. He must think of an excuse, but what? Blast it, if he were yet just a troubadour, the king would never ask this of him.

"I want your advice," Harry said, touching the points of his steepled fingers to his chin. "Which of the French noblemen who have pledged loyalty to me should I bind more closely through a marriage alliance?"

Praise God! Relief coursed through Robert's body. He hoped it did not show in his face.

"The only city that lies between my army and Paris is Rouen," the king said. "I want a man with influence in that city. A man who might convince them it is in their interest to surrender quickly."

Robert sucked in a breath to steady himself and set his mind to the king's question.

"Philippe de Roche," he said, glad the answer was so easy. "He is a powerful man in Rouen. And, as a member of the Burgundy faction, he is allied with us for the time being. From what I hear, his only true loyalty is to himself."

"Then he is no different from most of these French nobles," the king said, disapproval heavy in his voice.

"De Roche will not wish to bind himself to an English lady," Robert said, "until he is certain which way the wind blows."

"Since most of his lands are under our control, he will agree to the marriage," the king said with a smile. "But will it keep him loyal?"

Robert shrugged. "It will, at least, preclude him from making a marriage alliance unfavorable to us."

"I have reason to hope for more," the king said. "My uncle reports that this particular lady is blessed with both a strong will and great beauty."

Robert had no interest in the young widow's attributes.

"Perhaps you met her in your travels?" the king said. "Her name is Lady Isobel Hume—her father is Sir Edward Dobson."

The blood drained from Robert's head so rapidly he swayed on his feet. Margaret's daughter. The king was speaking of Margaret's daughter. Coming here. To Caen.

"'Tis many years since I traveled to the north," Robert

said, struggling to keep his features smooth. "But I believe my troupe did perform for her father's household once or twice."

Pretty little Isobel, so like her mother. She sat at his feet for hours listening to him sing ballads and recite tales. Her favorites were those of King Arthur.

"She was a lovely child," he said and regretted the wistful tone that crept into his voice.

"Well, she is no child now," the king snapped. "I do not know what I shall do with her until the marriage can be arranged. There are no English noblewomen here into whose care I may put her. She has a brother with Gloucester's army, but it will take time to bring him to Caen."

"Put her into my care until the brother comes." The words were out of Robert's mouth before he thought them.

"A young lady? In your care? Do you take me for a fool!"

"Believe me, I do not want this burden," Robert said, putting his hands up. "If you had anyone else, I would not own up to my obligation."

"Obligation?" the king demanded. "What obligation?"

Obligations. Consequences. What lad of sixteen considers these when he believes himself in love? That summer in Flanders, he and Margaret sneaked off every chance they got.

"We are distant relation, through our families in Flanders," Robert said, knowing bits of truth always improve a falsehood. "If you doubt it, ask Lady Hume if she has a Flemish grandmother."

The king narrowed his eyes at Robert, considering.

"She is a widow, not a young girl," Robert reminded him. "She does not need a guardian."

"Still, I must do something with her," the king grumbled.

"I give you my pledge, the lady will be safe with me."

The king nodded; Harry always did like a pledge.

"But you shall watch over her," the king said, shaking his finger in Robert's face, "as a father watches over a daughter."

Robert's throat tightened. God knew, he was late to the task. And wholly unsuited.

But he would do his best.

Chapter Four

November 1417

Stephen strode through the bailey yard, his thoughts sour after spending an entire morning resolving a dispute between two whining merchants. Praise God, he had the afternoon free to train with William and Jamie. He needed to wield a sword until his muscles ached and the sweat poured from his skin.

This evening, like all his evenings now, belonged to Robert. God help him, his king valued him for the secrets he could wheedle out of people. What honor was there in that?

The king should be pleased to learn Stephen was employing his "special talents." So far, there was no shortage of local men who wished to drink with him or women who wished to bed him.

"Stephen!"

He did not see Marie de Lisieux until he had to grab her to keep from knocking her to the ground. God in heaven, the woman was always underfoot. She pursued him with a persistence that had long since ceased to be flattering.

Marie pressed her hand to her ample bosom. "You must come sit with me while I recover."

The spark in her eyes told him sitting was not what the lady had in mind. Keeping her marriage vows was just the beginning of the scruples the voluptuous Marie de Lisieux did not have. The woman was trouble. But who was he to deny the king's command to "insinuate" himself with the local nobility?

"I cannot now." Over her shoulder, he saw William and Jamie coming across the bailey yard. Robert was with them.

Marie tugged on his arm. "Then when?"

"Saturday," he said and waved to the others.

"But that is days away!"

Her perfume was so strong it made his eyes water. Odd he never noticed before.

"Tonight," she insisted. "You must come to me tonight."

"Late," he said, prying her fingers from his tunic. He gave her a wink and ran off to join the others.

His mood lifted as the four of them walked in the direction of the Old Palace. Between it and the Exchequer was an open space where they usually practiced.

"I am pleased you are joining us," he said, clamping his hand on Robert's shoulder. "After all you've done for me, I shall make it my personal duty to keep you in fighting shape."

Robert laughed. "I should enjoy the challenge, but I cannot today. I've come to ask a favor."

Stephen threw him a black look. "What is it?"

"A noblewoman from Northumberland arrived by ship this morning," Robert said, turning to address William and Jamie, as well. "The king has put her in my care. Since she is here without friend or family, it would be a kindness if you would talk with her."

The back of Stephen's neck prickled. He could think of only one explanation for the arrival of a lone English lady in Caen.

"If this is some foolish girl my mother and Catherine have sent, I will send her back. No matter the consequences." His suspicion shifted quickly to outrage. "Robert, how could you be party to this scheme of theirs?"

"Afore God, I am innocent!" Robert said, putting his hand over his heart and laughing. "This lady is here to make a political marriage. Believe me, I shall have to answer to the king if anything more than friendly talk occurs between you."

Stephen's good humor returned at once. "What was the king thinking, putting her into your care?"

"As it happens, her mother is a distant cousin of mine."

"The king believed that?" Stephen said, grinning. "What of her betrothed? Surely the man does not know you, to allow it."

"The lady is safe in my hands," Robert said. "As for the man, he is in Rouen—and has yet to learn of his impending betrothal."

* * *

Isobel tried to ignore her maid's fidgeting as she watched for Sir Robert. From their bench in front of the Old Palace, she could see most of the buildings enclosed within the castle's outer walls. The Exchequer Hall, where Sir Robert said King Henry held court, was to her right. If she leaned forward and looked the other way, she could see past the curtain wall of the keep all the way to the eastern gate, Porte des Champs.

Soldiers were everywhere she looked.

"There are so many men here," her maid said. "Are we safe, m'lady?" The woman's eyes flitted from side to side, as though she expected to be attacked at any moment.

"Hush!" Isobel was exasperated with the woman's endless questions. Since she had no servants of her own now, she was forced to bring this silly woman from her father's household. "The men guarding us wear the king's livery. We could not be safer."

The unease that gnawed at her stomach had nothing to do with finding herself in the midst of hundreds of armed men. All her anxiety centered on one man.

"But where is your intended?" the maid asked. "When will he come for you?"

"You know very well Sir Robert has gone to ask for news of him." So long as her Frenchman was not here, she did not care where he was. *Please, God, let him never come.*

"Have you ever seen a man so handsome?"

Isobel knew the maid was no longer speaking of her intended, but of Sir Robert. The woman was so agog when he met them at the ship that Isobel had to give her a firm shove to get her down the ship's ramp.

"He is more beautiful than handsome," Isobel said, more to herself than the maid. "Like the angel Gabriel."

"Just so, m'lady!"

He'd been kind as an angel, too. After making sure she was comfortably settled into a chamber in the keep, he devoted the rest of his morning to walking her about the castle grounds.

'Twas odd, though. Bits of song kept coming into her head when he spoke. As she puzzled over it, she gazed at the lovely chapel dedicated to Saint George that stood midway between her bench and the main gate, Porte Saint-Pierre.

Her jaw dropped when she saw Robert striding toward

her with three other men. Like the waters of the Red Sea, the crowds of soldiers parted before them, leaving her with a clear view. The four tall, formidable, well-built men looked as if they stepped out of the magical tales of her childhood.

One of them was of an age with Sir Robert and looked precisely as she always imagined King Arthur: dark golden, commanding, grave. Next to him was a dark-haired youth of perhaps sixteen.

She shifted her gaze to the last man, who was talking with great animation. Judging from how the others turned their heads to listen, it was a good story he was telling. All four men were handsome, but there was something about this one that held her attention.

That rich auburn hair, which he wore to his shoulders, must be the envy of every woman who saw it. She liked his long, lithe frame and the way he walked with an easy, catlike grace despite the wild gestures he was making.

"M'lady, could one of these fine men be your intended?"

Isobel turned to stare at her maid. Could it be true? Could he have arrived already? Alarm coursed through her limbs and settled in a knot in her belly.

"One of them is the right age, aye?" the maid persisted.

Sir Robert said her Frenchman was but a few years older than she.

When she turned back to look at the men again, her throat closed in panic. They were nearly upon her!

"See, m'lady, the one on the end with the lovely hair—"

Out of the corner of her eye, she saw the maid's arm rising and grabbed it before the woman could point.

She was not ready to meet him, she was not, she was not. She busied herself brushing her gown, trying desperately to calm herself.

With a burst of male laughter, the men surrounded her.

Robert greeted her with a warm smile and helped her to her feet. Tilting his head toward the man who looked like King Arthur, he said, "Lady Hume, let me present Lord William FitzAlan."

FitzAlan looked as though he slayed dragons for breakfast. But when he greeted her, she saw kindness in his eyes.

"And this is FitzAlan's son, Jamie Rayburn," Robert said, turning to the dark-haired youth.

Young Jamie Rayburn seemed unable to keep his eyes from running over her, head to foot, despite the fact that it caused him to blush furiously.

She had no time to wonder how it might be that father and son had different family names before the third man eased the youth aside. All else faded away as she looked into the face of the man she was to marry.

Could it be true? Could this man with the laughing eyes be her new husband?

She'd prayed for a man who did not disgust her. Never did she dare hope for this. The man was so handsome he took her breath away. Every feature was pleasing: the black slash eyebrows; the hard planes of cheek and jaw; the strong, straight nose; the wide, mobile mouth.

But his eyes would always be her favorite part. Amazing how the color almost matched his hair—just a few shades darker and more deep brown than chestnut.

And his voice. So melodic.

As she listened to it, she imagined a row of pretty children with the warm brown eyes of puppies.

And almost failed to catch his words.

"...a delight to meet you. I am Sir Stephen Carleton."

She blinked at him. "But that is an English name."

"Aye, 'tis," he said with a grin that drew her gaze to his even white teeth. "I am from Northumberland, just as you are."

Northumberland? But…good heavens! She felt herself blush to her roots, mortified by her mistake. What must the man think?

"I've spent little time in Northumberland since I was twelve," Carleton continued, smooth as silk. "Still, I expect we have some acquaintances in common."

She caught the devilish twinkle in his eyes, and her humiliation was complete. Did he guess she mistook him for her Frenchman? Or was he merely amused by her wide-open stare?

What had come over her? She thought she gave up those childish dreams of Knights of the Round Table a long, long time ago.

In sooth, this Stephen Carleton was as handsome as any of the knights of legend. She was quite sure, however, none of the Camelot knights had the mischief she saw in the eyes of the man grinning down at her.

Unbidden, the image of Bartholomew Graham flitted across her mind. A reminder that good looks and easy charm could hide a very black heart.

* * *

Stephen watched, amused, as Jamie gawked helplessly at the dark-haired beauty. His nephew appeared incapable of speech. Before the poor boy could embarrass himself further, Stephen stepped forward to introduce himself.

He did not anticipate the effect those green eyes would have on him when the lady shifted her gaze to him. God in heaven, she was looking at him as though he were the answer to her prayers. It made him almost wish he were.

The undisguised longing in her eyes sent a bolt of desire scorching through him. The look was gone so quickly he might have imagined it.

Except he knew he had not.

Hoping to strike the spark again, he gave her the smile that usually got him what he wanted. Cool as ice, she turned and took up conversation with Robert.

He found himself behaving as badly as Jamie, taking her in from head to toe. The braids wound in gold mesh attached to her headdress were dark. She had pale skin and lovely delicate features that made her appear fragile. But there was something about the way she held herself that told him she did not consider herself weak or in need of protection.

He followed the elegant line of her neck. Breathing hard, he worked his way down her slender, shapely form. He was grateful for the unseasonably warm weather that had led her to remove her cloak. Grateful, indeed.

His slow, thorough perusal was interrupted by a hard jab to the ribs. When he sent a questioning sideways glance at the offender, William gave his head an almost imperceptible shake and mouthed, "Nay."

Stephen almost laughed aloud. Aye, there were many reasons he should not look at Lady Hume like that. That she was to make a political marriage for the king was reason enough for a wise man to keep his distance.

He bit back a smile, considering the dangers. Catherine always said he was drawn to trouble like a bear to honey. She was right, of course.

Chapter Five

"Try to remember," Robert said as they walked down a dark street to yet another gathering, "you want to get the men drunk enough so they speak freely, while only *pretending* to be drunk yourself."

Stephen had sipped watered wine like a grandmother all night, but he did not bother to defend himself. He felt restless, despite the late hour.

"Tell me about this Lady Isobel Hume." He kept his voice casual, although he'd been thinking about her all day.

"She is virtuous and unmarried," Robert said. "Not your sort at all."

Stephen laughed. "Come, Robert, a man can be curious, can he not?"

"So long as you do not attempt to satisfy your 'curiosity' with this particular lady."

Some undeserving Frenchman would have that pleasure. For some reason, that galled Stephen to no end.

"Speaking of women," Robert said. "By the saints, Stephen, can you not show some discretion in the women you bed?"

This, just after he'd fended off their last host's buxom and oh-so-willing daughter. "How can you, of all men, lecture me about women?"

"Who better?" Robert said. "I do not suggest you be celibate, God forbid. Only do try to exercise better judgment."

"Did William ask you to speak with me about this?"

Robert's laugh rang out through the empty street. "William would sooner put you in chains as a remedy than have me advise you about women!"

Stephen sighed. "Not that it is your concern, but I am finished with Marie." Of course, Marie did not know that yet.

Marie. Good God, he'd forgotten their liaison tonight. Marie was not a woman easily deterred. When he failed to come to their meeting place, she would seek him out. Even go to his bedchamber—

"St. Wilgefort's beard!" He abandoned Robert in the middle of the dark street and took off running.

Luckily, the men on duty at the gate were drinking companions of his. With a few ribald shouts, they waved him through. He raced across the endless expanse of bailey yard to the Old Palace. Breathing hard, he took the steps to the second floor two at a time and sprinted down the dimly lit corridor to the chamber he shared with Jamie.

If he was too late, William would have his head, for sure.

When he burst into the chamber, two heads popped up from the bed. Marie lay sprawled over Jamie, her gown pushed down below her breasts. But God was with him; the bedclothes were still between Marie and his nephew.

Jamie bolted upright, sending Marie rolling sideways.

With a dramatic sigh, Marie raised herself up on one arm and looked at Stephen. She did not cover herself.

"He is a bit young for you, Marie," Stephen said, keeping his tone light. "You must be twice his age."

A smile twitched at her lips. "I swear, Stephen," she said, widening her eyes, "he gave every sign he was old enough."

He closed his eyes briefly. Would this night ever end? "Time to go, Marie."

She took her time squeezing her breasts back into her tight bodice—a process Jamie followed closely. When she slid down from the high bed, she made sure her gown rode up high on her thighs.

Stephen picked up her cloak from the floor, draped it around her shoulders, and led her to the door.

"The three of us?" she whispered close to his ear.

He gave his head a firm shake. "How does your husband handle you?"

"Not nearly as well as you do," she said as he eased her out the door.

He bolted it behind her, then turned to face his nephew, who sat on the bed looking shamefaced and disheveled. "Stay away from that woman."

"I was asleep—she was on me before I knew it," Jamie fumbled. "She thought I was you, at first. I did not mean to…I…I know she is yours…"

"She is not mine, praise God. Marie has a husband." He sank onto a nearby stool. Wearily, he pulled his boots off and tried to think of the right words. "You are but fifteen—"

"Nearly sixteen," Jamie interrupted. "Surely you'll not tell me I am too young. She would not be my first."

Stephen lifted his eyes heavenward for help that did not come. "Believe me, you are too young to bed this particular woman," he said. "And much too good a man."

He looked at his nephew, trying to see him as the young man he was now, without also seeing the boy who used to toddle after him. Deep blue eyes, dark hair. Too handsome for his own good.

"Many women will want you," he said at last. "That does not mean you must bed them all."

"You do."

Stephen rubbed his temples. "Nay, not all of them."

God in heaven, he was a fool to think Jamie had been unaware. Forget William's wrath, Catherine would skin him alive. How many times had she admonished him that Jamie looked up to him? Lately, he had not believed it possible his nephew still did.

"Aye, there have been a lot of women lately," he admitted, exhaling a long breath. "And I can tell you, there is no lasting satisfaction in meaningless affairs with frivolous women. 'Tis much better to look for what your parents have."

"Then why do you not seek it for yourself?"

Jamie's face was so serious Stephen had to fight not to smile. God, he loved this boy.

"For the right woman," he said, meeting his nephew's eyes, "I would give up all the others without regret." He thought it might even be true.

"So, while a man waits for the perfect woman, he is free to waste time on frivolous ones," Jamie said with a grin. "Then I say, do not hurry, Perfect Woman. Take your time!"

Jamie ducked as Stephen's boot sailed over his head.

"Move over, you lout!" Stephen said, crawling into the bed.

Long after Jamie's breathing grew steady, Stephen lay awake, thinking. When Catherine came into his mind, he smiled. The one perfect woman. He missed her.

With an enormous sense of relief, he realized he'd not imagined taking his sister-in-law to bed in years. Not since he was Jamie's age—and everyone knew what youth of that age were like!

Perhaps he was not as bad as he thought.

His mind drifted to the lady from Northumberland...and to that look she gave him in the first moment they met.

A man might do a lot to see that look again.

Chapter Six

Stephen cursed Sir John Popham as he followed the path along the castle wall to the bailli's residence. With mist hovering over the ground, the bailey yard was eerie at this hour. Did Popham set their appointments earlier each day just to spite him?

He tried to turn his thoughts to the business of the day, but they kept returning to the more interesting subject of Lady Isobel Hume. The more he saw of her, the more intrigued he became. And he saw her often; he made sure of that.

Flirtation seemed not a part of her social repertoire. Unusual, especially for such a pretty woman.

Her smiles rarely reached her eyes. He'd yet to hear her laugh. As with flirting, his efforts there came to naught. He tried to imagine what her laugh would sound like. A tinkling? A light trill?

Aye, he was intrigued. Almost as much as he was attracted. It was not just that she was beautiful, though she was that. He wanted to know her. And her secrets.

Curiosity had always been his weakness.

A peculiar sound interrupted his musings. Peculiar, at least, to be coming from one of the storerooms built against the wall. He went to the low wooden door and put his ear to it.

Whish! Whish! Whish! The sound was unmistakable. Drawing his sword, he eased the door open to take a look.

"Lady Hume!"

She looked as surprised as he was to catch her alone in a storeroom attacking a sack of grain with a sword.

"The poor thing is defenseless," he said, cocking his head toward the sack. Grain was seeping onto the dirt floor from several small tears.

"Close the door!" she hissed. "I cannot be seen here."

And what a sight she was, with her cheeks flushed and strands of dark hair sticking to her face and neck. *God preserve me.* He stepped inside and firmly closed the door behind him.

"I meant for you to remain outside when you closed it."

Though she took a step back as she spoke, she kept a firm hand on her sword. As she should.

With her glossy dark hair in a loose braid over her shoulder, she looked even more beautiful than he imagined. And he'd spent hours imagining it. No man saw a grown woman with her hair uncovered unless he was a close family member. Or a lover. The intimacy of it sent his pulse racing.

Aye, the lady had every reason to feel nervous at finding herself alone with a man in this secluded place.

"That sack cannot provide much of a challenge," he said, trying to put her at ease.

"You make fun of me." There was resentment in her tone, but he was pleased to see her shoulders relax.

"I believe I would serve as a better partner, though I must

warn you"—he paused to glance meaningfully at the sack of grain—"I will not hold still while you poke at me."

Her sudden smile spilled over him like a burst of sunshine.

"But I wonder," she said, raising her sword in his direction, "will you squeal like a pig when I do stick you?"

He laughed out loud. "I am shamed to admit this is my first time matching swords with a woman, so please be kind."

She barely gave him time to take up position before she attacked.

"You have natural skill," he allowed after a few parries and thrusts. "All you need is more practice."

"But you, sir, are astonishing," she said, a little breathless. "Quite the best I've seen."

His chest swelled as if he were a youth of twelve.

"And I thought you excelled only at drinking games."

Ouch. "So you've been watching me. I am flattered."

The deep flush of her cheeks pleased him to no end. He deflected a determined jab to his heart.

He played with her as he did with the younger squires— hard enough to challenge, but not so hard as to discourage. When she pulled her skirt out of the way with her free hand, though, he missed his footing and very nearly dropped his sword.

She stepped back, her brows furrowed.

"Showing your ankles was a clever move," he said, giving her a low bow. "A trick I've not seen before."

"It was not my intention to rely on anything other than my skill." Her tone was as stiff as her spine. "I would not be so dishonorable as to stoop to tricks."

Good Lord. "If your opponent is both stronger and more skilled than you are," he said, keeping his voice even, "then you must use what advantages you do have."

Sword arm extended, he motioned with his other hand for

her to come forward. He suppressed a smile when she took up her sword again and came toward him.

"Then, once you have an opening, you must use it," he said. "Never give up your moment, as you just did. Do not hesitate. Your opponent may not give you a second chance."

"You do not care how you win, sir, so long as you do?" Her tone was scathing.

He sighed inwardly. How naive could she be?

"Use whatever rules you like when you are playing, Isobel. But if a man less honorable should find you alone as I did today, you will wish you knew how to fight without the rules."

She narrowed her eyes at him but did not speak.

"It would be preferable, of course, if you did not wander about alone. You forget you are in dangerous country here."

"'Tis not your place to lecture me."

Someone should. "Now, do you want to continue playing at sword fighting?" he asked, deliberately baiting her. "Or do you want to learn how to protect yourself from someone who intends you harm?"

Green eyes sparking with fire, she raised her sword and said, "Teach me."

Oh, what he would love to teach her! God help him, she was breathtaking like this.

"You should carry a short blade, as well," he instructed as he fended off her attack.

"Why? You think you can knock my sword from my hand?"

"I can." He saw a half-empty sack on the floor behind her. "But I will not have to. You will drop it."

She fought better angry, a good quality in a fighter.

Still, he was better. Much better. He forced her to step

back, and back, and back again. Once more, and her heel caught on the sack. She threw her hands up, sending the sword clattering against the wall as she tumbled backward.

The next moment, she was lying back on her elbows, her hair loose about her shoulders, skirts askew, chest heaving.

He could not move, could not even breathe.

She looked like a goddess. A wanton Venus, sprawled on the dirt floor at his feet. Then she threw her head back and laughed. Not a light trill, but a full-throated, joyful laugh that made his heart soar.

What he would not do to hear her laugh again!

"I'm afraid you have the advantage of me," she said, her eyes dancing. She reached her hand up for him to help her to her feet.

He took it and sank to his knees beside her. "Not true, Isobel," he said in a harsh whisper. "'Tis I who am at your mercy."

His eyes fixed on her lips, full and parted. Well beyond thought now, he gave in to the inexorable pull toward them. The moment their lips touched, fire seared through him.

He tried to hang on to the thin thread of caution tugging at his conscience. But she was kissing him back, mouth open, her tongue seeking his. His ears roared as she put her arms around his neck and pulled him down.

He cushioned the back of her head with his hand before it touched the dirt floor. Leaning over her, he gave himself wholly to kissing her. He splayed his hands into her hair and rained kisses along her jaw and down her throat, then returned to her mouth again.

The sweet taste of her, the smell of her, filled his senses. He was mindless of anything except her mouth, her face, her hair, his burning need to touch her.

He ran his hand down her side to the swell of her hip.

When she moaned, he knew he had to feel her beneath him. Beneath him, pressed against him. Skin to skin.

Slowly, he lowered his body until he felt the soft fullness of her breasts against his chest. Sweet heaven! Oh, God, the little sounds she was making. He let himself sink down farther and groaned aloud as his swollen shaft pressed against her hip.

There was a reason he must not do what he wanted to do, but he could not recall it. And did not want to try.

He buried his face in hair that smelled of summer flowers and honey. "Isobel, I want you so much."

The breath went out of him in a whoosh as he cupped the rounded softness of her breast in his hand. It fit perfectly. And felt so wondrously good he had to squeeze his eyes shut.

He froze the instant he felt the prick of cold steel against his neck. All the reasons they should not be rolling around the floor of an empty storeroom came flooding back to him.

"You are right," she said so close to his ear that he could feel her breath, "'tis wise to carry a short blade."

"Forgive me." He breathed in the smell of her skin one more time. Then he made himself get up.

As soon as he set her on her feet, she began to vigorously brush off her clothes. She was quite obviously embarrassed, but did she regret the kisses? He wished she would speak.

"Isobel?" He stepped close and touched her arm, but she would not look at him. "I cannot say I am sorry for kissing you"—*kissing* seemed hardly to cover it, but he thought it best to leave it at that—"but I do apologize if I have upset you."

"The blame is not all yours," she said, face flushed and eyes cast down, "though I might like to pretend otherwise."

Ah, an honest woman. And a fair one, too.

"You know I am soon to become betrothed."

"I did forget it for a time," he said, hoping in vain to draw a smile from her.

"It was very wrong of me," she said, lifting her chin. "It shall not happen again."

"If it will never happen again," he said, "then let me have a last kiss before we part."

He thought his outrageous request would cause her to either laugh or shout at him. When she did neither, he put his hand against her soft cheek. He leaned down until his lips touched hers. This time, he kept the kiss soft and chaste. He would not upset her again.

But when she leaned into him, he was lost again in deep, mindless kisses. When they finally broke apart, they stared at each other, breathless.

"I must leave now!" she said, backing away.

He caught her arm. "These things happen between men and women," he told her—though it had never happened quite like this to him before. "Please, Isobel, you must not feel badly or blame yourself."

The huge eyes she turned on him told him his words had done nothing to reassure her.

"Come, you will want to put this on," he said, picking up the simple headdress he saw lying on the ground.

She snatched it from his hands, slammed it on her head, and began shoving hair into it.

"'Tis a shame to cover such lovely hair." Unable to keep his hands from her, he helped push loose strands under the headdress. He let his fingers graze her skin as he worked. And tried not to sigh aloud.

"Let me go first to be sure no one is near," he told her. "Watch for my signal."

He felt her close behind him as he eased the door open. "I

am happy to practice with you whenever you like," he said as he looked out into the yard. "Sword fighting or kissing."

He spun around and gave her a quick, hard kiss, looking straight into her open eyes.

* * *

Isobel touched her fingers to her lips as she watched him go. Her breasts ached, and her whole body still thrummed with sensation.

What happened to her? She was stunned by her body's response to his touch and by how it addled her mind. Judgment—indeed, all thought—left her the moment his lips touched hers.

Thank God, the shock of his hand on her breast finally brought her to her senses. She could not fool herself—she knew what path they'd been racing down. And, God help her, she'd been right beside him, matching him step for step.

Out in the yard, Stephen waved for her to follow. As if this were a game! She slipped out the door with her head down and walked as fast as she could in the opposite direction.

So, this must be what it is like to have an affair. Sneaking about, taking pains to be sure no one sees you coming from a place you should not be with someone you should not be with. She swallowed hard. Stephen was so practical about it all. Retrieving her headdress, tucking her hair in, keeping watch for her. So practical. And practiced.

She picked up her pace. 'Twas no comfort to know she was one of many women foolish enough to fall for Stephen Carleton's charms. No comfort at all to know others had fallen further. Fallen? Nay, jumped.

She put her hand to her chest. At least he had listened when she told him to stop. Aye, she asked him with the point of her blade on his neck. But they both knew he could have taken it from her easily enough.

Another man might have felt justified in taking her. For she was brazen, opening her mouth to him, pulling him down on top of her. Good heavens, she was a woman possessed! Even when he covered her with his body—good as that felt—she pressed into him, unable to get as close as she wanted.

Her breath quickened as she recalled the feel of his hands moving over her.

Without a speck of doubt, coupling with Stephen Carleton would be an altogether different experience from having Hume sweating and grunting over her. Just his kisses told her that. His kisses! Remembering how their tongues moved against each other, she could almost imagine—

"Isobel."

She jumped at the sound of Carleton's voice beside her. "What are you doing here?" Good God, she'd just imagined the man naked and—oh, she would not think of it more!

"You can slow down. No one saw us leave the storeroom," he said. "Let me escort you back to the keep."

"Leave me. I can find my way alone."

"Isobel, you are going the wrong way."

She looked around and found she was nearing the Porte Saint-Pierre, the main gate into the town. "Thank you," she said in a tight voice and turned on her heel.

"Truly, it is not safe for you to go about without an escort," he said, keeping pace with her. "Promise me you'll not do it again."

Promise? He had the gall to think he could exact promises from her? She kept her eyes fixed on the keep across the bailey yard and marched ahead.

She knew just what sort of man Stephen Carleton was. Did he think she did not notice how women fawned over him? She was not blind. Even when he was so drunk she was sure he could not tell one woman from another, they looked at him as if he were a gift sent by the angels.

These things happen between men and women. It was as good as saying it was nothing at all. Perhaps "these things" happened to Sir Stephen Carleton all the time, but nothing like it had ever happened to her before.

God's mercy, the man must think she was one of those widows who will allow a man liberties simply because he is pleasing to the eye. She would never stoop to being one of his many women. Someone he forgot as soon as he dressed and left the room.

Never. Never. Never.

Carleton attempted to engage her in conversation, but she ignored him. Idle chatter was well beyond her now.

They were passing the Exchequer, nearly to the keep. Escape was within her reach.

"Good morning, Robert," Carleton called out beside her.

She turned to see Robert bounding down the steps. Damnation! Robert's eyebrow went up a bare fraction as he looked from her to Carleton and back again. It took an act of will not to check her clothes again for bits of dirt and straw.

"I was just coming for you, Isobel," he said. "The king wishes you to serve attendance upon him."

The king? Although she saw King Henry every day in the hall, she'd yet to have a private audience with him.

"When shall I come?" *Please, please, not today.*

"He awaits you now."

"Now?" This time, she did look down at herself. Her cloak was clean, but God knew what her gown looked like underneath.

"You haven't time to change," Robert said, interrupting her harried thoughts, "and you look lovely as you are."

She colored, almost certain Robert guessed the cause of her dishevelment. Yet his eyes showed nothing but kind concern as he reached up and gave her headdress a firm tug to the left.

"There, now you are perfect."

Robert, of course, was as practiced as Carleton at helping a lady with her headdress.

"I very much enjoyed our walk," Carleton said and turned so Robert would not see his wink. "I look forward to the next time."

If Robert were not there, she would have kicked him.

"The king wishes to see you alone," Robert said.

"Alone? But I thought you would—"

"Believe me, this will be no more difficult than your meeting with Bishop Beaufort." Robert took her arm and turned her toward the steps. "You do know Beaufort was his tutor?"

No comfort there! She wanted to protest, but she could hardly tell Robert she was not yet recovered from an early-morning fit of madness.

"Best not keep the king waiting," Robert said, his hand at her back.

Above her, a guard held the door open. She took a deep breath and went up the steps to face the lion. Before going through the door, she glanced back just as Carleton turned to leave. She gaped in astonishment as Robert grabbed Carleton's arm and spun him back around. With no trace of his usual bonhomie, Robert poked a finger into Carleton's chest.

"Lady Hume?"

She dragged her gaze from the scene below and nodded to the guard. God help her, but she hoped Stephen Carleton was a good liar. Very likely, he was exceptional.

She had no time to dwell on it. After passing through a second set of doors, she was in the hall where King Henry held court in Normandy. A man in a simple brown cloak stood looking out one of the tall windows that faced the Old Palace. A monk?

She expected to find the hall full of people, with the king on the dais, dressed in his bright gold, red, and blue tunic emblazoned with row upon row of lions and fleurs-de-lis. She glanced up and down the enormous room. Not a soul was here, save for her and this monk.

Her breath caught. This was no monk, but the king himself.

Her hands shook as she sank into her curtsy. Only thirty years old, and he was legend. At thirteen he led men into battle. At sixteen he commanded entire armies. After being crowned at twenty-six, he unified the nobles and brought an end to the years of chaos and rebellion.

He created a common link among the classes by making English the language of his court in England. For the first time since before the Conqueror, royal edicts were in the language of the common people.

All of England lauded Henry for his skill at governing and admired him for his piety. But what they loved him for were his victories. He was their young warrior king. England was strong again and ready to face her enemies.

"You may rise," the king said.

His cheerful countenance reassured her.

"Caen Castle was the favorite residence of my ancestor, William the Conqueror," he said, letting his eyes travel along the beams overhead. "He built it more than three and a half centuries ago, not long before he crossed the channel to conquer England."

"Then I can see why you made the castle your head-quarters, sire," she ventured.

He rewarded her with a smile. "Richard the Lionhearted met here with his barons before going on crusade."

Isobel turned with him to gaze down the length of the hall. She imagined the room crowded with knights preparing to leave for the Holy Land. Men with serious faces and crimson crosses on their chests. The rumble of deep voices, the clang of metal.

"The man I have chosen for you is Philippe de Roche."

The king's words brought her back with a start. Of course, the king had not called her to discuss history. How foolish of her to forget.

"I summoned de Roche here from Rouen," the king said, all trace of his former cheerfulness gone.

She fought the urge to run from the room. How much time did she have? It could never be enough.

"De Roche replies that he will come as soon as the roads are safe to travel," the king said, biting out each word. "And he doubts they will be safe for some weeks."

Whether the king faulted de Roche's excuse as insincere or cowardly she could not tell. Liar or coward, the king was angry. Heaven help her.

"This from a man who rides with a guard of twenty!" The king took a deep breath, then spoke more calmly. "I hope the wait will not be a trial for you."

"Not at all, sire." *Let him stay in Rouen forever.*

"What has Sir Robert told you about Philippe de Roche?"

"Only that he is an important man in Rouen." She willed the king to tell her more. Something to reassure her.

"Tell me, Lady Hume," the king said, "do you know the reason your father turned traitor?"

The king's words hit her like a blow. Her palms went damp with sweat. "I was only a child at the time..."

But the king was giving no reprieve today. He leaned forward, waiting for her answer.

"I believe he sided with the rebels because...because..." She licked her lips. Did he expect her to defend or blame her father?

"Because?" the king prodded.

What should she say? Was any answer safe? She could not think with her head pounding and the king staring at her.

"He did it because he thought the rebels would prevail," she said, giving him the truth, "not because he thought they should."

The king nodded his head vigorously. The right answer, thank God! She swallowed and wiped her palms on her cloak.

"It was a practical decision he made," she said, then hastily added, "though grossly misguided, of course."

"Then you will understand Philippe de Roche, for he is just such a man." The king's voice held such enthusiastic approval Isobel nearly staggered with relief.

"I have cause to suspect that his loyalty, like your father's," he said, cocking his head, "is based upon self-interest alone, rather than honor and duty."

Isobel was reeling from the unexpected turns of the king's conversation. Why speak to her of the reason for men's loyalty?

"If the people of Rouen accept me as their sovereign lord, I shall welcome them to my bosom," he said, crossing his hands over his heart. "But it is my duty to rule Normandy. If they do not open their gates to me, I shall starve them into submission."

Anyone who saw the fire in King Henry's eyes would be foolish not to believe he would do it.

"Philippe de Roche will save the people of Rouen much suffering if he can persuade them to avoid a siege," he said. "But for de Roche to play his part, he must be kept loyal."

She agreed to this marriage as a lesser of evils. Only now did she understand the responsibility that came with her choice.

"Your charge is to bind him to us," the king said, pointing his forefinger at her. "Do not allow de Roche to misjudge where his interest lies."

"I will do my best, sire," she said, though she despaired of knowing how she would accomplish it.

"Still, he may work against us," the king said. "If you discover he does, I must learn of it at once."

Just what did he expect of her? Isobel ran her tongue over her dry lips again. "Do you mean, sire, I should attempt to learn his true loyalty before the wedding?"

"If de Roche changes his allegiance, you shall send word to me," the king said, his eyes boring into her. "Whether it is before or after your marriage."

Chapter Seven

From the corner of her eye, Isobel watched Stephen Carleton laugh and talk with English knights, common soldiers, and local nobles as he wove his way through the crowded hall. People turned to him like iron filings to a lodestone as he passed.

He sidestepped the voluptuous Madame de Lisieux; the woman tracked him like a hound. In another moment, he was tête-à-tête in a corner with another fair-haired woman. From their frequent bursts of laughter, it was plain the two enjoyed each other's company and knew each other well. Very well, indeed.

"Who is that?" she whispered to Robert.

Robert turned to follow her line of vision. "Who? The woman next to Stephen Carleton?"

"That is the one." Isobel took a drink of her wine. "She is quite beautiful." In sooth, the woman was exquisite.

Robert took a handful of sugared nuts from the bowl on the table. "Aye, Claudette is as lovely as her famous cousin."

"She has a famous cousin?"

"Odette de Champdivers, mistress of the king of France."

Isobel shook her head. "I have not heard of her."

"You know King Charles is mad?" he said, eyes twinkling. "Well, Odette has been his mistress for twenty years without his knowing it."

She laughed; she could listen to Robert spin tales all night.

"Odette was first the mistress of the king's brother, Louis d'Orléans. When the queen took the dashing Orléans as her lover, the two of them sent Odette to the king's bed in her stead—dressed in the queen's clothes."

"The king was deceived?"

"Every night for twenty years!" Robert shook his head. "They say he's never been the wiser, and no one will risk the queen's wrath by telling him."

"And Claudette?" Isobel asked, bringing the conversation back to the woman whose hand rested on Carleton's arm.

"Claudette is more clever than her cousin. She's saved her money and kept her independence." Robert gave Isobel a rueful smile. "But I forget myself, speaking so freely with you."

"I am glad you feel you can," she said. "I do not like being treated as a child."

"Then I will tell you," Robert said, turning his gaze to Carleton, "a man may enjoy a courtesan's company in public without also employing her services in private."

How did Robert always guess what she was thinking?

"Still," he said, a smile lifting the corners of his mouth, "Stephen is not a man afraid to play with fire."

Playing with fire. Heaven help her. Each time she saw him, the episode in the storeroom came back to her. She could almost feel his mouth on hers again, his body pressed against her, his hands . . .

God help her, she could think of little else. Was it possible her new husband could make her feel like that? Was it a sin to hope so fervently it might be so?

She reached for her cup and tilted her head back to take a large gulp.

"Stephen's family is anxious to get him settled," Robert said, "before some husband kills him."

She choked, almost spitting wine across the table. Between coughs she asked, "He has affairs with married women?"

"I shock you again," Robert said, patting her back. "A fine chaperone I am proving to be."

It came as no surprise Carleton had affairs. What made her inhale her wine was the sudden image of him actually kissing another woman the way he'd kissed her.

"For a man who wishes to avoid a wedding at all costs," Robert explained, "married women are the safest choice."

"He could abstain."

Robert's burst of laughter caused heads to turn in their direction, including Carleton's. "That would not have occurred to me, but of course you are right." He took her hand and kissed it as he met Carleton's eyes across the room. "I do hope I am there when you suggest it to him."

As if in answer to the challenge, Stephen Carleton left the exquisite Claudette and strode across the room to them. His words of greeting were polite, but the devilish smile he gave her made it impossible for Isobel to utter a single word.

He sat on the other side of Robert and fell into easy conversation with him. "By summer we will control most of Normandy, including your ancestral home."

"It will be strange to return after so many years," Robert said. "And what of you, Stephen? When will you go to Northumberland to reclaim your family lands?"

Isobel could not help herself. She leaned forward and asked, "Your family lost their lands?"

Carleton's eyebrows shot up. "You did not know? My father joined the northern rebels, same as yours."

So he knew about her father. "But your brother is close to the king, is he not?"

"Lucky for me, William fought for the Lancasters," Stephen said, grinning at her. "William is my half brother. Since he was the only relative not tainted, our mother sent me to live with him when I was twelve."

"But your father's lands were confiscated?"

"Of course." He shrugged as if it were no concern to him.

"You've only to ask," Robert said, "and the king will grant them back to you."

King Henry was allowing most of the former rebels, or their families, to buy back their lands. She had paid the price for the return of her family's lands. What price did Stephen pay? What would cause the king to forgive such a debt?

"We have more in common than you knew," Stephen said, raising his cup to her. "We were both born of foolish, traitorous fathers."

Was his father's treachery not a burden to him? What of his mother? Isobel longed to ask...

The person sitting on her other side tugged at her elbow. She turned to find the pleasant, round face of Sir John Popham, a boring man if there ever was one.

"Have you a guess as to how many English merchants will come to Caen to set up shop in the spring?"

When she shook her head, the man began to talk at length about trade. Since all Popham required of her was an occasional nod, she could give most of her attention to the conversation between Robert and Stephen.

"William says he intends to return to England in the spring," she heard Robert say.

"Aye," Stephen said, "he'll not be away from Catherine any longer than he must."

"And who can blame him? Your brother is a lucky man."

Robert was saying this?

"That he is," Stephen agreed, "that he is."

Who was this woman that she had these two philanderers sighing and envying her husband?

Isobel remembered to give Popham another nod and leaned closer to Robert.

"William says you delay because you fear Catherine."

Stephen's laugh rang out. "I do not fear Catherine, I adore her! But she is intent on seeing me married—and you know how she is."

"That woman has an iron will," Robert said, "and she will bend you to it."

The two men laughed again! Despite the disparaging words, there was nothing but affection and admiration in their voices.

"My only hope is that William will get her with child again." Isobel heard the smile in Stephen's voice. "A new baby might divert her."

"Pray for twins," Robert said. "Pray for twins."

The next thing Isobel knew, Carleton was standing behind her. Her breath caught as she tilted her head to look up at him. Why must he be so handsome?

"Popham, you are boring this lady to death," Carleton said. "If you truly must talk all evening of barrels of wine and bales of wool, let us go off to a corner and spare the others."

Isobel was shocked by Carleton's directness, but Popham laughed.

"You are right, of course." Popham stood and said to Isobel, "I don't know what I would do without him."

She had no notion what Popham was talking about.

Without warning, Stephen leaned down to her. His hair brushed her cheek, making her heart race.

She felt his breath in her ear as he whispered, "You owe me for this."

Before she could recover, he took her hand. She looked at the long, strong fingers and remembered them in her hair. On her breast. She swallowed and looked up into Carleton's face. His eyes went dark; he was not even trying to mask that he was thinking the same thoughts as she.

Heat seared through her body as he pressed his lips to her fingers. He held her hand a trifle too long for courtesy, but she did not pull away.

* * *

Robert sat back and watched the pair. Stephen, who was usually so good at maintaining a facade, was no better than Isobel. He had never seen Stephen like this over a woman before.

The two of them were playing with fire, all right. No matter the king's affection, he would not take it lightly if Stephen jeopardized his plans. Stephen would find a cuckolded husband was nothing compared to an angry king.

Robert suspected things had not gone too far—yet. Still, the two were courting disaster. The fools may as well have been shouting it from the rooftops.

Claudette saw it, of course. There was not much that remarkable woman missed. And Marie de Lisieux, who had none of Claudette's subtlety or discretion, was watching the pair like a hawk.

Not for the first time, he wondered which faction Marie was spying for. Tonight, however, a baser motive even than politics drove Marie. 'Twas a wonder Isobel did not feel the scorch of Marie's eyes on her skin.

Praise God, William was no more perceptive than the king in such matters. The situation was far too delicate to bring William into it. A subtle hand was needed, not a storming of the gates.

He might need William's help. But not yet.

Chapter Eight

*I*sobel dropped her embroidery in her lap, annoyed her thoughts had drifted again to that damn Stephen Carleton. Small wonder, really. She had little else to occupy herself.

Where was de Roche? She stared out her narrow window, trying to imagine him riding through the keep's gate with twenty men behind him. Each day he did not come, she was torn between injury and relief.

She'd been a traitor's daughter; she did not want to be a traitor's wife. What would she do if de Roche changed allegiances after they wed? Caught between duty to husband and king, which would she choose? Either choice would be dangerous for her.

Her attention was caught by a lone rider trotting into the inner bailey yard below. There was something familiar about the way he sat his horse...

"Geoffrey!" She let her needlework fall to the floor in a tangle and flew to her door. In her hurry, she nearly tumbled down the stairs, which were built at uneven heights to trip attackers. A moment later, she was out of the keep and running across the yard to her brother.

"I am filthy," Geoffrey warned as she leapt into his arms. He held her close and said against her hair, "I came as quickly as I could."

"Thank God you are safe," she said, her eyes stinging. "I have been so worried."

"You should not fret so over me, Issie, I am a grown man now." He set her on her feet and took her hands. "Is it possible my sister has grown still more beautiful?"

"Would you scold me if I said my husband's death was good for my health?"

"I would," he said, "though I know you suffered with him."

As a man, Geoffrey could never understand how much she suffered. She did not want him to.

"Come," she said, taking his arm, "I will show you the way to the stables. Then I want you to meet Sir Robert, the kind man who has been looking after me."

She paused to lean her head against his shoulder and smile up at him. "I am so very glad you are here."

"He certainly took his time in coming."

The unexpected voice came from behind them. Isobel whirled around to find Stephen Carleton standing a few feet away, hands on hips, looking anything but his usual good-humored self.

"What kept you?" Carleton demanded, his eyes hard on Geoffrey. "Your delay has been a grave insult to this lady."

She'd never seen Carleton angry before. With temper sparking in his eyes, he looked different. Dangerous.

He turned his searing gaze on her. "I did not take you to be such a forgiving woman."

"I am sorry if I have offended you in some way," Geoffrey said, drawing Carleton's attention back to him. "I came as soon as I received the news my sister was here."

"Your sister?" The expression on Carleton's face showed first surprise, then delight.

"I thought you were that unworthy Frenchman of hers," he said, coming over and clapping Geoffrey on the back. "Welcome to Caen! I am Stephen Carleton, a friend of your sister's."

"You thought he was—" She choked on her words as anger, hot and dark, rose in her chest. "You thought I would embrace a man I did not know in the middle of the courtyard!"

"Better in a busy courtyard than a quiet place," Carleton said with a wink. "Luckily, I did not see you embrace him, or your brother would be dusting off his backside—if he could get up at all."

She wanted to slap him. "What concern is it of yours?"

Geoffrey, ever the peacemaker, said in a soothing voice, "He was only being chivalrous, trying to protect you." He took hold of her arm and began pulling her away. "Come, Issie, it was a hard ride, and I've not eaten in hours."

When she glared at Carleton over her shoulder, he blew her a kiss. The man was maddening.

* * *

What madness, Stephen asked himself, had taken hold of him? When he walked through the keep's gate and saw her clinging to a stranger's arm, her face lit by a rare, radiant smile, he stormed across the yard intent on beating the man to a bloody pulp.

Good God, he could hardly credit it.

Nay. He knew damn well what made him do it. Mindless, raging jealousy. He thought the man was de Roche and that Isobel was looking at him the way she looked at Stephen the day they met.

And he simply could not bear it.

He did not want to contemplate what that meant. Regardless, he intended to get to know her brother.

* * *

Isobel drew her cloak close against the early morning chill. "I was afraid you would forget your promise to practice with me before breakfast," she said, squeezing Geoffrey's arm.

"And risk my big sister's wrath?"

They walked in companionable silence, their feet crunching on the frozen ground.

When Geoffrey spoke again, his tone was serious. "Have you been going out alone, Isobel?"

There was only one person who could have told him. "Did that Stephen Carleton say something to you?"

"Aye, Sir Stephen gave me quite a lecture on the risks," he said, "and on my duties as a brother."

"How dare he!"

"There was no mistaking the man's message, but he was quite cordial," Geoffrey said. "He is an engaging fellow. Both he and his nephew seem to be good men."

She snorted her disagreement. "Stephen Carleton lacks all seriousness of purpose."

"He seemed quite serious about wishing to kill me yesterday," Geoffrey said, fighting a smile.

She remembered how dangerous Stephen had looked. Dangerous, and impossibly handsome.

"A vile temper does not improve a frivolous man." She sounded insufferable, but she couldn't stop herself. "He is, by all accounts, an unrepentant adulterer and drunkard. For all your piety, I am surprised you are willing to overlook his sins."

"You should not believe all you hear," Geoffrey said. "And 'tis not your place nor mine to judge. 'Let he who is without sin cast the first stone.'"

She decided not to test her brother's grace by telling him that the man he was defending had lain on top of her and kissed her senseless. That was a secret best not shared.

"What makes you smile, Issie?"

"Nothing." God help her, but she did not regret those kisses nearly as much as she ought. "Let us speak no more of Stephen Carleton."

"But he—"

She held her hand up. "Please, Geoffrey, do not."

When they reached the storeroom, she ducked through the low entrance and removed her cloak. When she turned to find a place to lay it down, she was so startled she screamed.

Stephen Carleton sat perched atop a stack of grain sacks.

"Good day, Lady Hume," he greeted her, as if he were quite used to women shrieking at the sight of him. "You remember my nephew, Jamie Rayburn?"

Noticing the young man now, she gave him a stiff nod.

"I meant to tell you that Sir Stephen kindly offered to practice with us today." Ignoring her glare, Geoffrey added, "We are fortunate, for he is well known for his skill."

"Please just call me Stephen," Carleton said, dropping down to the ground. "Your sister does."

She was going to argue, but this little falsehood was the least of his crimes.

When her brother went to chat with Jamie, Carleton came to stand beside her. "Stop scowling," he said in a low voice. "You are safe with both Jamie and your brother here. I promise, you will enjoy yourself."

She was tense and distracted at first, but after a time she became absorbed in the play. They traded partners frequently, so she had opportunity to practice with each of them. Stephen—despite herself, she did think of him as Stephen now—was by far the best swordsman and teacher.

"I'm starving! 'Tis long past time for breakfast."

Jamie's announcement caught Isobel by surprise. The hour had passed so quickly.

Jamie sheathed his sword and picked up his cloak from the corner. "Shall we meet again tomorrow?"

Geoffrey gave her a sideways glace and waited.

She smiled and nodded. So long as Geoffrey and Jamie came, too, what could be the harm?

Chapter Nine

*A*s Robert helped her into her cloak, Isobel heard the bells of L'Abbaye-aux-Hommes, the great abbey William the Conqueror built west of town, calling the monks to compline. Geoffrey was there tonight, praying with the monks. He would rise with them twice in the night, for matins and for lauds, then again at dawn for prime, before returning to the castle.

"How did you persuade me to go with you to one of your social gatherings in the town tonight?" she said. "I am sure I shall hate it."

"Who knows? An evening with the rich and dissolute may hold surprises," Robert said as he opened the door for her. "What do you say to walking? The night is fine and clear."

She enjoyed the long walk through the Old Town. By the time they crossed the bridge into the New Town, however, her feet were frozen. They were nearly to the far wall of the city before Robert stopped at the gate of an enormous house.

"Did I mention," Robert asked without looking at her, "that our hosts are Lord and Lady de Lisieux?"

"Marie de Lisieux! You know very well I would not have come if you told me."

"Come, you must admit to some curiosity," Robert said, giving her a wink. "I promise it will be entertaining."

As soon as they entered the house, Isobel noted with satisfaction that it was garishly decorated, with costly but unattractive tapestries and too much furniture.

"Hideous, isn't it?" Robert said in her ear. "Wait until you meet the husband."

Isobel had to struggle not to laugh. "You are a wicked man, Robert."

The food at supper was like the furnishings: rich, but tasteless. The bread was not quite fresh, the fruit green, the meats undercooked and laden with a heavy gravy with an unusual gray cast to it. Isobel was as hungry when she got up as when she sat down.

After supper, the guests dispersed into small groups throughout the public rooms of the house. Robert settled with Isobel on a bench at the back of the largest room and proceeded to tell her unseemly tidbits about the people in the room.

"Do keep your voice down!" she admonished him.

Her laughter caught in her throat when she turned and saw a late guest entering the room.

"You did not tell me Stephen was coming."

Robert raised his eyebrows. "You need to be warned?"

"Of course not."

Still, the very last thing she wanted to do was watch Marie de Lisieux drape herself over Stephen all evening. The woman had her hands on him already.

"You seem tense, my dear," Robert said.

"You are mistaken."

Over the weeks, she'd become accustomed to Stephen's company—and to ignoring the attraction between them. Of course, she'd not been foolish enough to risk being alone with him again.

Geoffrey and Jamie met her for sword practice every morning, regular as rain. Stephen came less often—no doubt it was difficult to rise early after a late night of drinking...and God knew what else. Despite her caution, she found herself warming to him each time he joined them. He was a patient teacher and had charm and wit enough for two.

How could a man of such talent fritter his time away with the most degenerate members of the local nobility? It was such a waste! And there was always some woman at hand, tittering at his jokes and giving him meaningful glances.

Robert raised his arm and called out, "Stephen, over here!"

Stephen distracted Marie de Lisieux with a blinding smile as he removed her hand from his shoulder and squeezed past.

Isobel took a deep breath to fortify herself. Was it to annoy her or to tease Marie that he wedged himself between her and Robert on the bench rather than take the chair opposite? He would amuse himself.

"I am glad you are here," Robert told him. "I must leave for a time, and I do not like to leave Isobel alone. You know what these people can be like."

"I am surprised you brought her." Stephen's tone was sharp.

"Stop talking as if I were not here," Isobel snapped. "I am not a child to be passed from nursemaid to nursemaid."

She was so annoyed she could almost forget the heat of Stephen's thigh against hers. Almost.

"Where are you going?" she asked Robert.

He winked one sea-green eye at her. "I'd rather not say."

An assignation. Was he not getting a bit old for that? Of course, men like him—and Stephen—never stopped.

The two men stood and spoke in low voices. As they talked, Isobel noticed the lovely courtesan Claudette walk past the entrance to the room and catch Robert's eye. Robert took his leave then, and Stephen slumped into the chair opposite Isobel and folded his arms across his chest.

To make conversation she said, "Sir John Popham mentioned again how much he values your assistance with the administration of the town." She'd been surprised by Popham's effusive praise. Apparently, Stephen did more with his time than charm women and drink to excess.

Stephen shrugged and scanned the room. Obviously, his work with Popham was not something he wished to discuss with her. He did not, however, have to be rude. What was the matter with him tonight? It was not her fault he was stuck with her.

Despite herself, she felt hurt. She thought they'd become friends, of sorts, over the weeks.

A handsome older woman bedecked in jewels and crimson silk appeared at Stephen's side. When the woman leaned down and whispered in his ear, he squeezed her hand and nodded.

"Do not move," he told Isobel as he got up. "I shan't be long, but there is someone I must speak to."

Speak to? Ha! She watched Stephen saunter out of the room with the woman. Who did these men think they were, telling her to stay put while they cavorted with all manner of women?

She felt awkward sitting by herself. She had little experience with gatherings such as this. Visitors to Hume Castle were few, and her husband rarely took her anywhere else. She was immensely grateful, then, when Monsieur de Lisieux rushed over to join her.

"To abandon such a beautiful lady!" de Lisieux said, throwing his hands up. "Truly, your friends do not deserve you."

The broken veins and blotchy color of his face showed the signs of excessive drink. Who could blame the poor man, married to that wretched Marie?

"Perhaps you will let me show you the house while they are gone?" de Lisieux suggested.

"You are too kind." She took the arm de Lisieux offered and smiled at the thought of Stephen returning to find her gone.

De Lisieux stopped at a side table to pour her a large cup of wine. He filled it so full she had to drink several large gulps for fear of spilling it. As they moved through the crowded rooms, de Lisieux pointed out various features of the house. Isobel made polite noises of appreciation.

Stephen was certainly taking his time.

She had a nodding acquaintance with a number of the guests from their visits to the castle. De Lisieux, of course, knew everyone. Their progress was slow as they stopped to chat with other guests milling about. Along the way, de Lisieux picked up a flagon of wine, and she let him refill her glass from it.

When neither Stephen nor Robert had returned by the time she and de Lisieux circled back to the front of the house, she was angry enough to spit. Where were they? She was more than ready to leave. If she had to "ooh" and "ahh" at one more ugly family portrait, she might scream.

"You must see the new stained-glass window I had put in the solar," de Lisieux said as he led her toward the stairs. "The craftsmanship is exquisite."

Better a window than another portrait. De Lisieux must have refilled her cup, for she had to drink it half down again so she would not spill it on the stairs. At least her host's wine was better than his food. It took the edge off her hunger.

From the top of the stairs, she turned to look at the people milling about below. She did not see Stephen—or the woman in crimson silk.

"The solar is here," de Lisieux said, drawing her away.

Inside the solar, scarlet pillows with heavy gold tassels were strewn haphazardly across the floor. How odd, with guests coming. Was it overly warm in here? She fanned herself with her hand. The servants must have made the brazier too hot.

"Excuse my pride, but is it not lovely?" de Lisieux said, leading her around the pillows to the window.

"Nice, very nice," she murmured, though there was nothing special about the glass, save for its size.

Ha, Stephen would not think to look for her in here. *If* he was looking for her. The swine. She narrowed her eyes, thinking of what he was likely doing with the woman in the crimson silks. She gulped down the rest of her wine. Without turning, she held the cup out for more.

What was de Lisieux saying? Something about tapestries? She'd ceased listening to his drivel some time ago.

"The one in the next room is most unusual," he said, pulling her through another doorway. "You must see it."

Her head began to spin. "I would like to sit, Monsieur de Lisieux." She was embarrassed that his name came out sounding like "Mi-shoe Di-shoe," but he did not appear to notice.

Good heavens, could she be drunk? Hume's drinking so disgusted her, she never overimbibed. How—

"Of course." De Lisieux's voice was solicitous.

Of course, what? She'd forgotten what she asked him.

"But first, look at the design of this beautiful tapestry."

It was difficult to make out the pattern in the dim candle-light of the room, but Isobel dutifully put her nose close to it and moved along the wall, squinting. A grimacing face, a horse's haunch, a woman's breast... Quite suddenly, she saw it as a whole and for what it was. Too shocked to speak, she stared open-mouthed at the obscene mythological scene of satyrs having intimate relations with human women.

With a sinking feeling, she looked over her shoulder. She was, as she feared, in a bedchamber. She had not heard him close the door behind them. But closed it was. How had she gotten herself into this?

"You should not have brought me here," she said and started toward the door.

De Lisieux tightened his grip on her arm, jerking her back.

She swallowed back her rising panic. Surely he would not dare—the house was full of people. And Stephen was here. Somewhere.

"Let me go," she said as calmly as she could. "Sir Stephen is waiting for me."

"Believe me, Carleton is busy elsewhere, my dear."

Before she knew it, de Lisieux was on her. Wet lips against her neck, rough hands pulling at her gown. She screamed against the hand clamped over her mouth. As she struggled to get her hand through the fichu of her gown to reach her hidden blade, she could see it in her mind's eye lying on the chest in her room. Damnation!

She kicked and clawed as he dragged her toward the bed. At last she managed to sink her teeth into his hand. She had only a moment to savor his howl of pain. The slap was so hard her ears rang, and she saw bright pinpricks of stars.

As her knees gave way, de Lisieux released his hold, and she fell hard against the floor. She struggled to her hands and knees and scrambled across the room, frantic to get away. A rhythmic smacking sound behind her caused her to look over her shoulder.

Stephen was here! He had de Lisieux against the side of the high bed, pummeling him. De Lisieux's head flopped like a child's rag doll with each punch.

"Stephen, stop it!" she screamed. "Stop it!"

Stephen shook his head, as though coming out of a daze. He stepped away, letting de Lisieux slide to the floor.

Isobel sank back onto her heels and pressed her hands over her mouth. She was dimly aware of hearing high-pitched whimpers before she realized the sounds were coming from her.

Stephen knelt in front of her and gripped her shoulders. "Did he hurt you?"

She shook her head, unable to speak.

Stephen pulled her hard against him. "Are you sure?" he asked against her hair.

She squeezed her eyes closed and nodded.

Abruptly, Stephen pushed her back to arm's length and fixed scalding eyes on her. "Sweet Lamb of God," he said, his voice shaking, "what were you doing in here with him?"

"Why are you yelling at me?" To her dismay, she was very near to tears. "You've no need to blashpheme." Frustrated, she tried again. "Blaphsheme. Blapsheme."

"You are drunk?" he said, his eyes wide.

"You dare to criticize me"—she slapped her chest at the word "me," to emphasize her outrage—"for too much drink! And 'twas not my fault. Every time I turned my head, de Lisieux poured more wine into my cup and—"

"Come," Stephen said, pulling her to her feet. "I cannot bear to be in this vile man's bedchamber another moment."

As he half carried her out of the room, she glanced at de Lisieux's body slumped on the floor. "Is he . . . ?"

"He isn't dead," Stephen said, his voice hard.

He led her to the window seat in the solar. After barring the outside door, he sat beside her and took her hand.

"I am sorry I got angry with you, but you frightened me half to death." He stared straight ahead, jaw muscles tight, clenching his teeth. Despite his obvious effort to be calm, his voice rose when he spoke again. "What were you thinking, getting drunk and coming to de Lisieux's bedchamber with him?"

"He was showing me the house."

"Good God, Isobel, you are not a girl of fifteen! How can you be so foolish?"

"That is so unfair!" She wiped her nose on her sleeve and sniffed.

His shoulders sagged. "You are right. I should never have left you. I had business to attend to, but that is no excuse."

"'Tis not your fault." Even if it had been, what woman could not forgive Stephen when he turned those liquid brown eyes on her? It would be like kicking a dog.

He gathered her in his arms and rested his chin lightly on the top of her head. Encircled in his arms, her cheek resting against his hard chest, she felt safe. Protected.

"Why were you so vexed when Robert left me with you?"

"Because you and I should not be alone." His chest rose and fell beneath her cheek as he took in a deep breath and let it out. "You see, I am not good at resisting temptation."

She leaned back to look at him. Truly, he had a beautiful face—the wide, expressive mouth, the hard planes of cheek and jaw. She put a hand to it, wanting to feel the rough stubble against her palm.

For a long moment, he looked at her, eyes troubled. Then he whispered, "Sweet, sweet temptation," as he lowered his mouth to hers. This time they kissed not with the wild passion of that other time, but with a slow melting that made her insides feel like warm honey.

When he ended it and tucked her head beneath his chin again, she heard his heart pounding in his chest.

"We should return to the castle now," he said.

"Not yet." She pressed against him to feel the heat of his body through his clothes. "Not yet."

He unwound her arms from around his waist and kissed the top of her head. "'Tis wrong to take advantage of you when you've had a shock and too much to drink..."

She let her head fall back, hoping for another kiss. "But I hardly feel the wine anymore."

"You lie, Isobel," he said with a grin. "You are drunk as a soldier after a night in town. Come, I must take you back before I forget all sense of honor."

* * *

Stephen hoisted Isobel up onto his horse and held her there as he swung up behind her. Good Lord, she was soused. She was going to feel wretched in the morning. When she fell back against him, she felt so soft and yielding he had to pray to Saint Peter to give him strength.

"What about Robert?" she asked without opening her eyes.

"To hell with Robert."

Stephen was going to strangle him. If Robert knew he must leave for one of his clandestine meetings with the king, why in God's name did he take Isobel with him tonight? And to de Lisieux's, of all places! The only explanation was that Robert planned to leave Isobel with Stephen all along.

Now, that was curious.

Of course, Robert did not anticipate that de Lisieux, that horse's arse, would attack Isobel under his very roof. But he did know Stephen would be forced to escort Isobel back to the castle alone and late at night.

Nothing got by Robert. The man had eyes in the back of his head. Despite Stephen's denials, Robert knew damned well something had happened between Stephen and Isobel the morning he saw them just after... well, just after they rolled around on the floor of the storeroom.

Was Robert deliberately putting temptation in his way? For the life of him, Stephen could not figure out why.

He tried to feel virtuous for withstanding the temptation. But what else could he do with Isobel three sheets to the wind? Still, it was not easy with the smell of her hair in his nose and her backside jostling against him with every step of the horse. He was hard as a rock—and desperate for some distraction.

"When I was little, I used to ride like this with my father." Isobel's voice had a plaintive, faraway quality. "He took me everywhere with him."

Stephen checked his conscience; taking advantage of her drunkenness to learn her secrets did not trouble him at all.

He took the opening she gave him. "Was it your father who disappointed you?" he asked softly. "Tell me your story, Isobel; I want to hear it."

She was silent so long he thought she had dozed off. When she finally spoke again, she seemed to have forgotten Stephen's presence altogether.

"Father told me I was to save the family..."

Isobel spoke in fits and starts, as if giving voice to only a part of her thoughts.

As she told her tale, Stephen saw her clear as day: a girl on the brink of womanhood, standing in the tall grass with a wooden sword in her hand and laughter in her eyes. A headstrong girl, used to getting her own way.

Old Hume should have had his member cut off and fed to the pigs for lusting after such a girl. He must have been older than her grandfather.

When her voice faded into silence, Stephen prompted her. "Your father must have had his reasons for agreeing to the marriage."

"Hume gave him the money to buy back our lands," she said.

So Isobel was her family's sacrifice—her virginity sold to satisfy an old man's lust, her happiness traded for land.

Isobel's head rocked softly against Stephen's chest. Since he'd get no more of her tale tonight, he turned his horse toward the castle gates. Isobel barely stirred as he carried her up the back stairs to her chamber in the keep.

Would that useless maid never open the damned door? He rapped a second time and a third. When she finally let him in, she giggled at the sight of Isobel, loose-limbed in his arms.

"Don't you breathe a word of this to anyone," he told the maid as he carried Isobel to the bed. He did not like bullying servants, but he had to ensure the woman's discretion. "If you do, I swear I will have that archer you're so fond of sent to join Gloucester's army."

He looked down at Isobel and felt a surge of tenderness for the girl she once was, the girl whose father broke her heart.

When he brushed his knuckles against her cheek, Isobel smiled in her sleep. How he longed to lie beside her! To enfold her in his arms and drift to sleep with his face in her hair. To awaken to that smile in the morning and make love to her. And then to stay in bed with her the whole day through.

The maid would leave if he told her to...

He let out a deep sigh. She was not his. And could not be.

Chapter Ten

December 1417

*G*eoffrey sent word he could not join them for practice, so it would be just her and Jamie. Stephen had not come once since...Isobel shook her head to clear it of the memory of her night of wanton drunkenness.

She sent her maid back when she reached the storeroom. Though it was not precisely proper to be alone with Jamie, he was still a boy, to her mind.

As soon as she ducked through the low doorway, she realized her mistake. Stephen stood—quite alone—in the center of the room, sword in his hand. He must have come early to practice on his own. Puffs of steam came from his mouth as his breath hit the cold air. His white shirt clung to his skin.

Isobel remained by the door, her feet rooted to the ground.

"Your brother is not coming?" Stephen asked.

She shook her head. "What—what of Jamie?"

"He could not come, either," Stephen said. "Isobel, do

stop looking at me as if I were the Green Knight come to cut off your head. I did not know your brother would not be here. Surely you know by now I would not harm you."

She knew no such thing. He looked dangerous, casually twirling his sword. His gaze took in every inch of her.

"Come, let us begin," he said and went to retrieve her sword from its hiding place. When she hesitated to take it from him, he asked, "Are you afraid that without the others here, you will be unable to keep your hands off me?"

Not once had Stephen said anything to embarrass her about what happened that night at the de Lisieuxs'. Not one word, not one veiled remark. Nothing at all to remind her of her drunkenness. Or her foolishness in following de Lisieux into his bedchamber. Or how she begged Stephen to kiss her.

Truly, she was grateful he waited until now, when they were alone, to tease her. That did not mean she liked it.

"You have quite enough women throwing themselves at you, Stephen Carleton." She took her sword from his outstretched hand, whipped it through the air, and pointed it at his heart. "'Tis my sword, not my hands, that should worry you."

They practiced hard. Once again she was struck by his grace and beauty with a sword. His movements were fluid and effortless as he drew her toward him, letting her attack, but always in control.

"How many women are 'quite enough'? " he asked.

"What?"

"You said 'quite enough' threw themselves at me," he said, all feigned innocence. "I assume you were counting."

Stephen seemed not the least bit winded, which only added to her irritation with him.

"One may as well attempt to count the stars," she said,

attacking once more. "I prefer to devote myself to some useful purpose. Perhaps you should try to do the same."

He stepped into her thrust to block it. For a long moment they stood inches apart, the tension of sword pressed against sword between them.

"To what use would you put me, fair Isobel?" Stephen asked, then waggled his eyebrows at her.

She laughed and stepped back. "You are impossible!"

"You should laugh more often." He wiped his brow on his sleeve. "Come, let us take a rest."

He spread his cloak on the dirt floor where they could rest their backs against sacks of grain piled high against the wall.

"Now," he said, stretching his legs out, "will you tell me the rest of your story sober, or must I ply you with strong wine to get it?"

Isobel closed her eyes. "I hoped I had not truly said all those things to you."

He picked up a loose straw from the floor and twirled it between his thumb and finger. "What of your mother? Did she argue against the marriage?"

"My mother could not be bothered to leave her prayers long enough to speak for me." Hearing the bitterness in her voice, Isobel pressed her lips together.

Stephen touched her arm. "It might help to speak of it."

Would it? She never had anyone she could tell it all to. There was so much she could not share with Geoffrey, even now that he was grown. Why did she feel she could tell Stephen now? She did not understand the reason, but she did.

"It was for her that he did it," she said in a whisper.

Isobel watched bits of dust floating in the air as she tried to recall the laughing mother of her early childhood.

"After we lost our lands, my mother wanted to escape this life. She devoted herself to prayer, morning to night…until she seemed to forget us altogether."

After a time, Stephen asked, "Your father thought regaining your lands and position would restore her?"

"I knew it would not, but he would not hear me." In her frustration, she'd screamed at him that he could increase their lands a hundredfold and still she would not change.

"Did your mother say nothing to you about the marriage?"

The memory always lay just beneath the surface, scraps of it coming to her unexpectedly and catching her unawares. For the first time, she tried to recall the whole of it.

She remembered her heart pounding in her ears as she ran across the field and through the castle gate.

"I found her on her knees in the castle chapel." Chest heaving from running so hard, she stood waiting for her mother to acknowledge her until she could stand it no longer.

"You will let him do this to me?" she asked, her voice coming out high-pitched and shaky.

When her mother's lips continued moving in silent prayer, Isobel clenched her fists to keep from taking her mother by the shoulders and shaking her.

Finally, her mother lifted her head and looked at Isobel. Except for the lack of expression, her face was as lovely as ever beneath the plain headdress.

"I asked your father," her mother said in a quiet voice, "to delay the marriage until your next birthday."

"He would do anything—*anything*—you ask of him," Isobel said, her fingernails digging into her palms, "and all you can ask for me is three months!"

"Your father says Lord Hume will leave you a wealthy widow. That is the most a woman can hope for in this world."

"You could save me from this, Mother!" Isobel's words echoed off the stone walls of the small chapel.

Her mother remained placid, hands folded in her lap.

"Can you not help me this one time?" Isobel pleaded.

Her mother turned her head and her gaze grew unfocused. "I am sorry you must pay for my sins."

What sins did her pious mother imagine she had committed?

"Isobel." Stephen's voice pierced through the veil of her memories. "Take this," he said, pressing a kerchief into her hand.

Only now did she realize tears ran unchecked down her face.

"I should not have pressed you." Stephen rubbed his hand up and down her back, soothing her as if she were a child.

But she was determined to finish it now. "Do you want to hear the last words my mother said to me in this world?"

"Only if you want to tell me."

"She said, 'We women are born to suffer.' Then she went back to her prayers."

Isobel remembered swallowing back the sobs that threatened to overtake her and turning her back on her mother. Her breath came in hiccups as she marched, stiff-legged, across the bailey yard. With each step, she willed herself to harden her heart.

"I did not have a choice, of course," Isobel said to Stephen. "But I told myself I would do it for my brother—and not for that useless, pathetic woman who was my mother."

Stephen enfolded her in his arms. After a time he asked, "The marriage was very hard?"

She nodded against his chest. He tightened his hold; his arms felt good around her.

"You did not forgive your father."

"I refused even to see him." In that, at least, her husband had indulged her. The only time she saw her father during the years of her marriage was at her mother's funeral.

She should not let Stephen comfort her like this. But after the intimate story she shared with him, it seemed ridiculous to fret over his being too familiar. Even his smell—horses and leather and just Stephen—comforted her.

"You deserve to be happy," he said.

"What if de Roche is horrid?" she blurted out. "He does not want me or this marriage, or he would have come by now."

Why, after holding self-pity at bay for so long, should she suddenly give way to it now?

"The fool does not know the prize that awaits him," Stephen said in a soft voice. "Once he meets you, he will regret every moment he wasted."

She sighed and rested her head against his chest again. "My father told me not to believe in fairy tales."

Stephen brushed a loose strand of hair from her face and kissed her forehead. "There is nothing wrong in hoping for something rare."

She felt his breath in her hair as he held her.

Unleashed emotion swirled inside her. She heard the change in his breathing and felt the tension grow between them. She waited, expectant.

She nuzzled her head against his shoulder, hoping he would kiss her hair again. When he did, she sighed and lifted her face to him. His eyes locked on hers, but he made no move to kiss her. She slid her hands up his chest and rested them on the back of his neck.

He shook his head. "This is not wise, Isobel."

Neither was it fair that she might spend the rest of her days married to a man whose kiss, whose every touch, was hateful to her. "'Tis just a kiss, Stephen."

"I do not think just a kiss is possible between us."

Since the day her childhood came to a crashing end, she'd done what she should and what she must. She was sick to death of it.

She pulled Stephen to her and pressed her mouth to his. The kiss was at once all heat and passion, tongues moving, bodies rubbing, hands searching. When his hand covered her breast, she let her head fall back and closed her eyes. She felt the softness of his lips, the heat of his breath on her skin, as he moved down her throat and back up again.

"What makes me want you so badly?" he breathed against her ear. "Is it that I know I cannot have you?"

But he could have her.

She had no will to stop him. Nay, she would not let him stop. When she ran her tongue across his bottom lip and slipped her hands under his shirt, he understood the invitation. He leaned her back onto the floor. She loved the feel of his hands in her hair, the urgency of his kisses.

She raked her fingers down his back, reveling in the feel of tight muscles beneath the cloth. When she reached his buttocks, he groaned and pressed his hips hard against her. He held her face and covered her with kisses: her mouth, her cheeks, her forehead, her eyelids, her temples.

All she wanted was for him to keep on kissing her, touching her. She deserved this. She needed this. They rolled and kissed beneath the curtain of her hair. And then rolled again. His tongue was in her ear. The unexpected sensation drove away the last bit of guilt nagging at the edge of her mind.

Her every muscle tensed as he made his way, sucking and kissing, down the side of her throat and along the edge of her gown. She arched her back, wanting without knowing what. When his mouth found her breast through the cloth, she had her answer.

She felt drunk, mindless. When he moved toward her other breast, she jerked her bodice down. A groan came from deep within him. As he caressed and kissed her bare breasts, sensations ripped through her. She entwined her fingers in his hair and wrapped her legs around his waist. She cried out as he sucked on her breast, pulling sensations all the way from her toes.

Then his mouth was on hers in deep, frantic kisses. She held on as he moved against her, her arms and legs wrapped around him like a vise.

Abruptly, he pulled away. He hovered over her on his hands and knees, looking down at her with eyes dark and wild. He was breathing as hard as she was.

"I am sorry," he said. "We cannot do this."

She clung to him even as he pulled her to her feet. Of their own accord, her arms went round his waist. She moaned at the feel of the rough cloth of his shirt against her sensitive breasts.

Dropping her hands to the tight muscles of his buttocks, she pulled his hips against her. She felt the hardness of his member. His ragged breathing told her he could not hold out against her.

Suddenly, his mouth was on hers again, hot, hungry, demanding. Her knees grew weak under the assault of sensations pounding through her. His hands were on her breasts, her hips, her thighs. Squeezing, stroking, kneading.

When her feet left the ground, she wrapped her legs around him. Without lifting his mouth from hers, he carried her backward until she felt the wall against her back. Deep, deep kisses. She was dizzy with them, drunk with them. And still she wanted more.

As he ran his hands under her skirts, along the bare skin of her thighs, an aching need grew inside her. She felt his desperation rise with hers as they moved their hands frantically over each other.

He reached between them and touched her center. The jolt of sensation made her cry out. Even through the cloth, the place he rubbed was so sensitive it was almost more than she could stand.

And yet she was pleading, "Please, please, please."

His breathing was harsh against her ear. "I must be inside you."

His raw need for her caused a responsive spasm deep inside her. He was tugging at her skirts. *Please, Stephen. Please. Please!* She grabbed a fistful of cloth caught between them and jerked at it, trying to help him. In frustration, she bit his shoulder.

She opened her eyes as the door to the storeroom flew open and crashed against the wall. A huge man entered.

She was too startled to move. But with the lightning reflexes of a fighter, Stephen turned, retrieved his sword from the ground, and pulled the knife from his belt. All the while, he kept his body between her and the intruder.

Almost at once, Stephen relaxed his stance and let the point of his sword drop to the ground.

"Hello, William."

How Stephen managed that flat, even tone she could not imagine.

Lord FitzAlan swung the door closed and moved inside the room. Though he had not yet said a word, he fairly vibrated with anger. He seemed to fill the small space to bursting.

"Get your armor, Stephen. The army leaves within the hour. Lady Hume, I will escort you to your chamber."

Over his shoulder Stephen said in a low voice, "Are you covered?"

Belatedly, she jerked her bodice up and began straightening her gown. Never in her life had she been so embarrassed.

Stephen placed her headdress in her shaking hands, wrapped her cape about her shoulders, and pulled her hood up.

He lifted her chin with his finger, forcing her to meet his eyes. "I hate that you feel shamed," he said in a soft voice.

"Stephen, the men are gathering."

The commanding voice behind them made Isobel jump, but Stephen showed no sign he heard it.

"'Tis lucky William came when he did," he whispered, touching her cheek. He broke into a devilish smile that squeezed her heart. "But I wish to God he hadn't. How I want you, Isobel!"

Before she could catch her breath, he kissed her cheek and was gone.

FitzAlan gave her a curt nod and held out his arm. Without glancing to the left or right, he led her out into the bright sunshine, a man sure of himself and his virtue.

Humiliation, loss, and longing warred inside her as she walked beside him. The keep seemed miles away.

"Keep your head up," FitzAlan ordered.

She did as she was told. FitzAlan did not break the silence again until they passed Saint George's chapel.

"I apologize for my brother's behavior," he said, looking straight ahead. "'Tis not like him to force his attentions."

She made herself say it: "He did not force his attentions on me."

FitzAlan gave a slight nod, still not looking at her. "The king has other plans for you, Lady Hume. But if things went...too far...with my brother, Stephen will marry you."

"They did not proceed 'too far,'" she bit out, surprised at her sudden anger. It did nothing to soothe her temper to know FitzAlan's suspicions were reasonable, given what he saw. "And I would not force Sir Stephen to marry me—or have you force him—if they had."

The corner of FitzAlan's mouth lifted briefly in what looked suspiciously like a smile. It was the first she saw the slightest resemblance between the two brothers—and she did not like it.

"My brother would do as honor required, regardless of my wishes," FitzAlan said. "Or yours, Lady Hume."

It sounded like a warning.

* * *

"By all the saints, Stephen, are you possessed?" William thundered at him as soon as they had ridden out of the city gates.

The main force was a quarter mile ahead. William, however, rode at a pace that signaled he was in no hurry to catch up.

"Possessed or mad," Stephen replied. There was no other explanation.

"Do you not have enough women?" William shouted. "This one you cannot have without marriage. And the king has already chosen a husband for her!"

"I did nothing that might require marriage." A brief moment more, and he very likely would have. Sweet Jesus! He'd been swept in a raging lust that left no room for thought of consequences.

"She said the same," William said, his voice calmer.

"You should not have embarrassed her by asking," Stephen snapped. "I wish you would not meddle in my affairs."

"I am inadequate to the task," William said, "but Catherine and our mother would be displeased if I did not make some attempt to guide your love life in their stead."

Stephen was not amused. He kept his silence for a good long time. But, as always, it was impossible to outlast William.

"We march to Falaise?" he asked. He'd known for some time the king would break tradition and campaign through the winter, but no one knew where Henry would attack first.

"Aye," William said. "The king decided last night."

"The people here believe the city walls of Falaise are impregnable," Stephen said. "The city will hold out."

"Aye, it will be a long siege," William agreed.

The prospect of spending weeks camped out-of-doors in midwinter, bored silly, dampened Stephen's spirits further.

"Perhaps we shall be gone long enough for you to get back what little sense you once had," William said. "But I shall put my hope in her new husband taking her away before our return."

Isobel, gone from Caen? Stephen needed to see her at least once more. Backing her against a wall and very nearly ravishing her was hardly a proper farewell. Proper farewell or no, sweat broke out on his forehead thinking about it.

When he could still smell her hair, her skin, how could he imagine her gone? Or worse, with her new husband. He could imagine that. His jaw began to ache from clenching it.

Yet the Frenchman seemed in no hurry to claim her. Perhaps she would still be there when he returned. Perhaps the fool would never come...

"De Roche will come," William said, interrupting his thoughts. "Henry has him by the balls."

Chapter Eleven

January 1418

*I*sobel controlled her thoughts during the day. But her dreams betrayed her. Some nights, she dreamed of Stephen telling her stories and woke up smiling. Other times, she awoke hot and breathless with the memory of his lips on her mouth, his hands moving over her body.

Last night she had one of those dreams that drove her from her bed. She stared out her window into the darkness and imagined herself in a river, the dark water running over her, until the desire to have him touch her lessened enough for her to sleep again. This morning, wisps of the dream still floated in her head. A vague longing and a heaviness in her heart remained.

Looking out her window in the harsh light of day, she lectured herself on how lucky she was Stephen was gone from Caen. She prayed she would recover from her madness before he returned. For it was madness. Madness to risk angering the king. Madness to risk being sent home to England in disgrace. And where would she have to go but to her father's household?

Humiliated, dependent, wholly subject to her father's will. Her father would not even permit her to escape to a nunnery. He would deem it a waste of an asset, however reduced in value. After sullying her reputation and earning the king's ill will, what sort of marriage would her father broker for her this time?

It was past bearing.

Her father's treason brought them enough dishonor; she could not add to her family's shame.

For her to risk so much—ach, and for such a man! It was beyond foolishness. Even if she were a wealthy widow who could choose a man to please herself, she would be wise to stay away from the likes of Stephen Carleton.

She did not hope for a man she could love. Indeed, love would give a man far too much power over her. All she wanted was a man she could respect. A man devoted to honor and duty. Not someone who frittered his talents away on frivolous pursuits—especially the pursuit of beautiful women.

Ha! Stephen did not pursue women—he drew them like flies to a dead fish. She blew out her breath in a huff. Aye, she was just one more fly buzzing, no better than the rest.

What if FitzAlan had come to the storeroom a short time later? She put her hand to her chest. No matter what she told FitzAlan, she and Stephen would have been forced to wed. Stephen seemed no more sensible of the consequences at the time than she. But marriage was like the plague to him. Why, he went so far as to delay claiming his family lands to avoid it. How he would resent her! He would grow to hate her.

And there would always be those other women, buzzing about. She knew infidelity was commonplace among men of her class. Why, then, did imagining Stephen being led off discreetly by one lady or another leave her seething?

What was she doing, wasting her time thinking of Stephen and getting upset? She snapped up her sewing from the table and set to work.

She was diligently stitching when Robert knocked on her chamber door.

"Where is your maid?" he asked when she let him in.

She shrugged. "I do not know half the time."

"We shall deal with her later," he said, taking both her hands in his. "Isobel, he is here."

Stephen was back! The smile froze on her face. Robert would not seek her out to tell her Stephen Carleton had returned to Caen. Nay, Robert did not know—could not know—she waited every day, every hour, for Stephen's return. Foolish, foolish woman that she was.

If not Stephen, then who? Her spirits plummeted further as the answer came to her. "De Roche?"

Robert pressed his lips into a line and nodded. "The king has just come from Falaise to meet with him. You are to join them in the Exchequer hall."

She dropped her eyes to hide her rising panic and pretended to fuss with her gown. When Robert lifted her chin with his finger, she saw sadness in his face.

"Is—is he so terrible?" she asked.

Robert squeezed her hand and said, "'Tis only that I let myself forget you would eventually leave my care."

Tears stung at her eyes. "How I shall miss you!" she said, surprised by the strength of her feelings. "Surely it will take a good deal of time to settle the marriage contract. And then we must wait for the banns to be posted."

He touched her cheek. "If the king wishes it to be done quickly, it shall be."

"But suppose I do not like him? What if he is a hateful man?" The words tumbled out of her in a rush. "What if he is a traitor? Would the king still make me—"

"Hush, hush," Robert said, enfolding her in his arms. "Let us meet the man first."

She rested her head against his chest, crushing the velvet of his beautiful tunic, but he didn't seem to mind. Having Robert hold her like this reminded her of how her father used to comfort her when she was a little girl. Her stomach tightened with unexpected longing for the father of her childhood.

"I am glad you will be with me," she whispered.

Robert leaned back and held her at arm's length. "Your new husband cannot help but adore you," he said, his eyes crinkling at the corners. "I predict your new life will be one of love and grand adventure."

A short time later, they were ushered into the Great Hall of the Exchequer. Isobel clutched Robert's arm as he led her to the far end of the room, where King Henry sat on a raised chair. No one would mistake the king for a monk today. For this occasion, he wore an ermine-trimmed robe over a tunic emblazoned with his royal herald, the lion and fleur-de-lis, in gold, red, and blue.

They halted a few paces behind a man with whom the king was speaking. As they waited for the king to acknowledge them, Robert squeezed her fingers resting on his arm. When she raised an eyebrow at him, Robert tilted his head toward the man and nodded.

This, then, was the man who would be her husband for the rest of her days. Even from the back, she could tell he was young and strongly built. He was well dressed, from his colorful silk brocade tunic and matching leggings down to his magnificent high black boots. Beneath the elaborate liripipe hat, his hair was almost black. He wore it long, fastened with a bloodred ribbon.

She leaned to the side and craned her neck, trying to catch a glimpse of his face. Warts. Boils. Pox. Blackened teeth. She tried to prepare herself. It simply was not possible that he could be wealthy, well connected, young, *and* handsome.

The king's next words jarred her from her observations.

"We are pleased, Lord de Roche," the king said, sounding anything but pleased, "that you have seen fit to heed our summons. At last."

"I apologize for my delay, sire."

De Roche did not sound any more contrite than the king sounded pleased. This did not bode well.

"I assure you, I spent the time on your behalf," de Roche continued. "I've devoted myself to persuading the men of Rouen of the wisdom of recognizing you as our sovereign lord."

"They should not need so much persuasion." The king gave him a hard look and added, "You must tell your compatriots not to try my patience—or God's."

"Of course, sire."

De Roche's complacent reply did not sound as though he took the king's warning as seriously as Isobel thought he should.

"I assume," the king said, the sharp edge still in his tone, "you are prepared to enter into a marriage contract?"

Isobel dropped into a low curtsy as the king shifted his gaze to her.

"Lady Hume," the king said, signaling for her to rise. "May I present Lord Philippe de Roche."

When the man turned, Isobel drew in a sharp breath. God's

mercy! He was a vision of masculine beauty. An Adonis— an Adonis with a mustache and trim goatee that matched his dark hair. She snapped her mouth shut and forced herself to drop her eyes.

"'Tis good to meet you at last," de Roche said in a deep, rumbling voice as he stepped closer to greet her.

Blushing fiercely, she risked another glance as she held her hand out to him. Cool gray eyes swept over her from head to toe before fixing on her face.

"An English rose," he said as he bent over her hand.

A nervous ripple ran through her as she felt the warmth of his breath and the tickle of his mustache on the back of her hand. Oh, my.

"You are more beautiful than I had hoped," he said in a low voice meant for her ears alone. "And I assure you, Lady Hume, my hopes were high."

Though it was midwinter, she suddenly felt so warm she wished she had a fan. This handsome man was looking at her with the intensity of a hungry wolf. A good sign, surely, in a future husband. Aye, she was flattered. And pleased. A little breathless, too.

She managed to murmur a greeting of some sort.

"Since Lady Hume's father cannot be here to negotiate the marriage contract..."

At the sound of the king's voice, Isobel dragged her gaze away from de Roche's face.

"...that responsibility falls to her brother. Since he is young, however, I have asked Sir Robert to assist him."

The king stood. "Now I have other matters to attend to."

Despite the king's unmistakable signal the interview was at an end, de Roche spoke again.

"My king, I am grateful for the opportunity to serve you. I do so out of deep concern for the welfare of the people of Rouen—and, indeed, all of Normandy. Neither French faction is capable of bringing us peace and prosperity. I praise God you have come to save us."

"'Tis God's will that I do," the king said.

Heads bobbed as the king swept out of the hall.

Isobel cast a nervous glance at de Roche. Neither the king's irritation nor meeting his future wife appeared to have ruffled him. A confident man, to be sure. A bit arrogant, perhaps.

His unequivocal profession of loyalty to King Henry relieved her. Though his speech lacked subtlety, he sounded sincere. She prayed he was.

Isobel took the arm de Roche held out to her. As they made their way down the length of the huge hall together, she listened to the rhythmic tapping of their feet on the stone floor. She was keenly aware that this was the first of many times she would walk at this man's side.

How many times would she do this in her lifetime? A thousand? Ten thousand? How many times would she do it before de Roche did not feel a stranger to her?

How many times before Stephen did not cross her mind as she did it?

Chapter Twelve

February 1418

Stephen huddled further under his blanket and cursed himself. He had no one but himself to blame that he was here freezing his buttocks off. The midwinter siege was every bit as miserable as he had thought it would be. 'Twas the coldest winter in memory. So cold, in fact, that the king ordered huts built so his army would not freeze to death before the city succumbed.

Worse than the icy rain outside his hut was the foul smell of the men crowded within. Few washed, and most still wore the clothes they arrived in more than two months ago. If he was not sure to be a frozen corpse by morning, Stephen would sleep outside to get away from the stench.

Yet he chose to be here. In weekly missives, Sir John Popham begged the king to send Stephen back to Caen. The king, however, acceded to Stephen's request to remain until the city surrendered.

Each time Stephen thought of leaving, the slaughter at Caen came back to him: the women's screams, the old men hacked to death, the blood of innocents splattered on his boots.

Nay, he could not leave. He must stay and do what he could to prevent a recurrence of that horror when Falaise fell.

How he longed for the siege to be over! The tedium nearly drove him mad. The day-and-night bombardment against the city walls gave him a constant headache. Weeks of abstinence made him more irritable still. Under such conditions, the camp women did a lively trade. But Stephen was never one to use whores. Even if he were fool enough to risk the pox, just the sight of those sorry women depressed him.

With so much time on his hands, little wonder his thoughts were so often on Isobel. But why no other women? Even his dreams were all of her. He would lie on his cot and try to imagine other women, but their features always faded into hers. Serious green eyes were the only ones he saw.

He missed her.

What was that? He sat up on his cot and listened to the strange quiet. The bombardment had stopped. Tossing his blanket aside, he drew his cloak on and left the hut.

He found William warming his hands at one of the fires that were kept burning day and night.

"We've smashed a breach in the walls," William said by way of greeting. "The town has agreed to surrender at first light."

"Will the king speak to the men?"

William knew what he was asking. "The king will remind them he will tolerate no rape or murder," William said. "Still, there are always some who will do it."

An hour after dawn, the king led his army through the city's open gates. Stephen was relieved the soldiers appeared to take the king's warning to heart, for they remained orderly. Perhaps the men were too cheerful at the prospect of sleeping in the warm houses of the town to commit mayhem. The soldiers did comb the city for valuables, the legitimate spoils of war. Though "the lion's share" went to the crown, the finders got a percentage of the value.

As he and William continued patrolling the streets without incident, Stephen began to relax. Men were helping themselves to drink, waving swords, and bashing in doors, but there was no real harm in that. He and William turned their horses down a quiet street of well-kept houses and shops.

Stephen heard a muffled sound; he could not tell if the yowl was dog or human.

William pulled his horse up beside Stephen's. "What was that?" he asked, cocking his head.

When the high-pitched cry came again, they bolted from their horses. William kicked open the door to the house, and Stephen rushed in. The room was empty. Hearing the clomp of boots overhead, Stephen crept up the stairs with William hard on his heels.

As soon as his head was above the floorboards, he signaled to William that there were three men. The men had their backs to him. Their attention was on the prey they had cornered, a boy and girl of eleven or twelve who looked so remarkably alike they had to be twins. The boy stood in front of his sister, holding a sword a foot too long for him.

"Halt!" William's voice filled the room.

The men, rough-looking foot soldiers, spun around with their short blades ready in their hands.

"Did you not hear your king's command?" William shouted.

The men showed no inclination to slink away or beg forgiveness.

"Since the king's punishment for rape is death," Stephen said, "you should be grateful Lord FitzAlan and I have come in time to save your miserable lives."

He used his brother's name deliberately. Upon hearing it, the three men exchanged nervous glances.

"Still, it seems to me the mere intent to commit the offense is deserving of some punishment," Stephen said. "We should at least give them a serious beating, should we not?"

From the sidelong glance William gave him, his brother did not think the beating strictly necessary, but he said, "Let us be quick about it, then."

Stephen called out to the twins to stand back as the first man charged him. Stepping to the side, he knocked the knife from the man's hand, grabbed him by the collar, and threw him against the window. He heard the satisfying crunch of the wooden shutter breaking as the man fell through it.

He turned around in time to see William send the other two men sailing down the stairs.

"Damn, you always outdo me," he said. "Could you not have left the third one to me?"

Before the words were out of his mouth, two streaks of blond hair shot past him. He caught the two children and held them, one under each arm. As they kicked and bit at him, he shouted at them in French that he would not harm them.

He looked up to find William watching him, a glint of amusement in his eyes.

"Damn you, take one before I drop them!"

William took the boy, held him firmly by the shoulders, and leaned down until the two were eye to eye. "We do not mean you harm, son," he said. "Where are your parents?"

From what Stephen saw in the boy's eyes before he dropped his gaze, he could guess the answer.

"Is there someone else looking after you?" William asked.

"I look after my sister."

"And I look after him," the girl spoke for the first time, her voice equally defiant.

William straightened and sighed.

They had been speaking to the children in Norman French, the language the English nobility shared with Normandy, but they switched to English now so the children would not understand them.

"Have you taken a good look at this girl?" Stephen said. "She is far too pretty to be safe here with only a boy to protect her."

"The boy is almost as pretty as his sister," William said, shaking his head. "Come, Stephen, do not give me that look. Do you think those men did not intend to have him after the girl?"

His brother had lived with armies years longer than he had, so Stephen did not doubt him. Still, he was profoundly shocked.

"What do you suggest we do with them?" William asked.

"We could take the boy to a church or monastery."

"You think a boy with those delicate looks is safe with priests?"

Stephen clamped his mouth shut as he absorbed this latest remark. "I will take them with me to Caen," he said after a moment's reflection. "The boy can serve as my page."

"And the girl?" William said, raising an eyebrow. "You cannot keep her. People will think the worst."

Stephen scowled at the notion anyone could think him so depraved. The girl was, what, eleven?

"I suppose we can find someone to take her in as a kitchen maid," William said, sounding dubious.

"I know a lady who needs a new maid," Stephen said, brightening at the thought. "And she will be kind to the girl."

It was only when the girl turned her startling blue eyes up at him that Stephen realized she'd stopped squirming long ago.

"Who is this lady?" she asked in accented English.

Stephen laughed. "So you speak English, you rascal?"

"But of course." The girl did not add "you fool," but it was implied in her tone. "What is the lady's name, *s'il vous plaît?*"

"Lady Isobel Hume," he said, grinning down at her.

He heard William curse under his breath, but he ignored it.

Chapter Thirteen

February 1418

*I*sobel felt like Job. After her years of suffering, God was rewarding her. De Roche was young and handsome. Respectful, attentive. A man of honor, bent on doing good in the world.

He was solicitous of her, sharing a trencher with her at every meal, taking afternoon walks with her when the weather permitted. When it was too wet for strolling, as it was today, he sat with her by the keep's great hearth and talked with her while she sewed.

De Roche was a serious man, and he talked of serious matters.

She stifled a yawn as he spoke yet again of his responsibility as a man of rank and fortune to help bring peace and prosperity to Normandy. She agreed wholeheartedly. His determination was admirable. Still, she found the repetition, well, a trifle tedious.

Damn that Stephen Carleton! If not for him, she would not even notice de Roche's lack of humor.

She had every reason to be content. She would be content.

'Twas true, de Roche never made her laugh. But duty weighed heavily upon him. He had an important role to play in the service of his country; it would gratify her to support him.

"Now, King Henry—there is a man born to lead armies," de Roche was saying. "A man born to command."

De Roche sang the king's praises so often her mind began to wander.

When would he kiss her?

Would his kiss make her feel the way Stephen's did? She stared at de Roche's mouth as he talked. Wondering. Longing to find out. Perhaps, once de Roche kissed her, she could stop thinking about Stephen.

A full month since his arrival, and de Roche had not kissed her once. He often looked at her as if he wanted to. On more than one occasion, she thought he tried to separate her from her guardian. Robert, however, took his duty more seriously than before, for he was there at every turn.

The thought niggled at her that de Roche could have found a way around Robert if he wanted to badly enough.

Stephen would have.

A sudden clamor of voices from outside drew her attention toward the hall's entrance. As she watched, a man burst through the door and shouted, "The army returns! Falaise has fallen! Falaise has fallen!"

They were back. Praise God! A laugh of relief caught in her throat when she turned and saw de Roche's face. The man had gone pale as death.

"Have you taken ill?" she asked. "What is—"

"I must see what has happened," he cut her off. Without a backward glance, he left her and rushed out of the hall.

The hall was soon flooded with soldiers. After the quiet of the last weeks, it felt chaotic and much too crowded. Servants scurried about, setting up the tables and carrying great jugs of ale and wine and platters piled high with roasted meats.

Isobel stood, craning her neck. Despite herself, she searched the room for a glint of auburn hair. Hearing her name above the din, she swung around to see Geoffrey making his way toward her through the throng.

When had her little brother grown into this barrel-chested man, so like their father? He reached her in three long strides and lifted her into a bear hug.

"You look in such good health!" she said, standing back to drink him in. His skin was as tan as in high summer. Perhaps he was not ill suited to a soldier's life, after all.

"You must tell me of your adventures," she said, pulling him down to sit beside her on the bench.

"I had time to write a great many poems during the siege."

To her dismay, he pulled a roll of parchment from the pouch at his belt and began at once to recite aloud.

Geoffrey was not a bad poet. But why must he write these dreary poems of martyred saints? After two or three, she caught herself searching the room again.

"You are usually better at pretending an interest in my poetry," Geoffrey chided with his usual good nature.

"Of course I want to hear them," she lied.

"Issie, who are you looking for?"

"De Roche," she lied again. "I want to introduce you."

"He is in Caen? Why did you not tell me at once!" Geoffrey leaned forward, face earnest, and took her hands. "Is he a good man? Can you be happy with him?"

She bit her lip, trying to think what she could tell her brother that would be truthful. De Roche was so much more than she had dared hope for. But sometimes . . . well, it mattered naught. And after Hume, she should be happy married to a toad.

"De Roche is a fine man of serious purpose," she said at last. When the worry did not leave Geoffrey's face, she gave him a bright smile. "He is also the handsomest man I've ever seen."

De Roche was pleasing to the eye, but it was a third lie, nonetheless.

"Now go and eat," she said, giving Geoffrey a gentle shove. "You must be as hungry as the rest."

She let her shoulders slump as she watched Geoffrey's broad back disappear through the crowd. For the sin of lying to her brother, she could at least claim good intent. For her sinful thoughts of Stephen, she had no excuse.

She could not even claim repentance.

* * *

Stephen kept the reins to the twins' horse wrapped around his fist as they rode through the streets of Caen. With their striking fair hair and near identical faces, the two children would draw glances anywhere. The sight of them astride a single horse in the midst of a line of armored knights caused the townspeople to stop and gape open-mouthed.

Stephen was taking no chances with this wily pair. After an all-too-brief pretense at docility, they tried to escape. Repeatedly. He would gladly let them go if he thought they would be safe. But no family member came looking for them before he left Falaise. If there was anyone in the whole of Normandy willing to take responsibility for them, the twins were not telling. They refused even to give him their names.

Once inside the castle gates, Stephen parted from the

other men and rode straight for the keep, twins in tow. He needed to get this girl off his hands. He smiled to himself, pleased to have a good excuse to seek out Isobel at once.

Now he just had to figure out how to look for Isobel without losing one of these troublemakers. He swung off his horse and grabbed the girl as her feet touched the ground. Once he had her, the boy came easily.

"You're hurting me!" the girl whined as he dragged the pair up the steps of the keep.

"If you would quit pulling, it would not hurt," he said evenly. "Now, I want you to pretend that you are a very good girl so Lady Hume will agree to take you. Believe me, she is much nicer than I am."

The girl gave a loud snort to let him know what she thought of his request. A little wistfully, he thought of his gaggle of nieces and nephews. They could be a handful, but he never had this much trouble with them.

He paused inside the entrance of the busy hall, a twin on either side, and searched the crowd for Isobel. He found her almost at once, across the room near the hearth. When she looked up and met his eyes, his throat went dry.

Her face glowed, as though she were truly pleased to see him. Suddenly, he had a vision of her as she was the last time he saw her. Hair loose and tangled, lips swollen from his kisses. He strode across the room, seeing nothing and no one but her.

A sharp tug on his hand saved him from sweeping Isobel into his arms in full view of everyone in the hall. He looked down, surprised to see he still held the twins. Recalled to his purpose, he turned his attention back to Isobel.

And at once forgot what he meant to say. How could she have grown still lovelier? The green velvet gown made her eyes a deep forest green.

"I am glad for your safe return, Sir Stephen."

His stomach tightened at Isobel's formal greeting. *Sir Stephen.* So that was how it was.

"And who is this lovely girl?" Isobel asked, touching the child's arm.

To his astonishment, the devil girl gave a graceful curtsy and looked up at Isobel with a beatific smile.

"My name is Linnet. I know you are Lady Hume because Sir Stephen told me Lady Hume is as kind as she is beautiful."

Isobel gave a musical laugh that made Stephen's heart do an odd leap in his chest. Though he doubted the girl—*Linnet*—could keep up this pretense of good behavior, he winked at her to show he appreciated the effort.

It seemed unkind to mention the children's circumstances in front of them. Without thinking, he leaned close to Isobel to whisper in her ear. The smell of her skin sent him reeling.

When he remembered to speak, he said, "They are orphans in need of protection. I will take the boy as my page, but the girl..." He lost track of what he was saying. It was so very tempting to run his tongue along that delicate earlobe, to place a kiss in the hollow just below it.

Isobel jerked her head away before he could say—or do—more.

"Of course I will take her," she said, looking at him with wide, serious eyes.

She turned to the girl and took her hand. "This is fortunate, indeed! My maid asked leave to marry one of the king's archers. I would be so grateful if you would agree to take her place."

As Linnet looked over Isobel's fine clothes, her smile brightened. "I would fix your hair and help you dress in pretty gowns?"

Isobel nodded.

"And I could read you all the love poems men send you," Linnet said, her eyes glowing. "I am sure you have many!"

Many love poems? Or many men sending them? Either way, Stephen did not like it.

"You can read?" Isobel asked, surprise showing in her voice.

"Of course." Linnet gestured toward her brother. "As does François."

Stephen watched with sympathy as the boy melted under the warmth of Isobel's smile. He felt his own insides go soft when she said, "You are fortunate to serve a knight as skilled as Sir Stephen. Pay attention and you will learn much from him."

François gave her a solemn nod.

How had Isobel done it? Already she had these two little hellions in the palm of her hand.

Stephen heard a man clear his throat beside him and turned to find cold gray eyes upon him. The dark-haired man they belonged to inserted himself between Stephen and Isobel and tucked Isobel's hand into the crook of his arm.

So, this must be Isobel's delinquent Frenchman.

Stephen let his eyes drift slowly over the man. He knew just how he would take him. Years of practice taught him that. William had decided that a boy with a sharp wit and a big mouth had better learn how to handle himself in a brawl as well as on a battlefield. Each day, his brother assigned a different man to fight him. The lessons did not stop until Stephen learned to assess a man's strengths and weaknesses at a glance.

The man before him now was cocky, overconfident. He had a powerful build—the kind that would turn to fat as he grew older, Stephen thought cheerfully. Strong, but not too quick. Stephen would first grab him by the—

These happy contemplations were interrupted by Isobel. "Sir Stephen Carleton, may I present Lord Philippe de Roche."

Stephen waited, deliberately letting the silence fall between them. If he'd been a cat, his tail would have twitched.

"He is from Rouen," Isobel added, her voice tense.

Stephen knew damn well where the man was from. Since Isobel had not called him her betrothed, perhaps she was not yet irrevocably tied to this man with ice in his eyes. The man's too-perfect features made him look soulless.

Aye, a broken nose would add character to his face.

"You take advantage of my intended's soft heart," de Roche said to Stephen, then turned to Isobel. "You need not take some unknown girl this man has picked up off the streets."

Isobel put her arm about the girl's shoulders. "But where shall I find another maid who can read poetry to me?"

Stephen wanted to kiss her.

The muscles of de Roche's jaw tightened, but he patted Isobel's hand. "Keep her if it pleases you, my dear."

The endearment reminded Stephen what this man would be to her. Her husband. Her bedmate. His chest began to ache.

"Come, I will show you my chamber," Isobel said to Linnet.

Isobel nodded her good-bye to François, but the smile left her face when she turned to take her leave of Stephen. As she looked at him with those wide, serious eyes, the ache inside him grew until he thought his chest might burst with it.

She seemed to startle when de Roche tugged at her arm. With a quick curtsy, she turned away.

He and François were still watching when Linnet turned to give them a sly wink over her shoulder. Linnet was an ally now, thanks to de Roche. As twelve-year-old girls went, she was not a bad ally to have.

Ally in what? Stephen took a deep breath and shook his head. What would he do if he won the prize? He wanted to take Isobel from de Roche, have her leave on his arm instead. And he most definitely wanted her in his bed. Badly. But since he did not want a wife, this was a battle he had no business trying to win.

He felt a light touch on his arm and turned to find Claudette at his side.

"What a foolish man you are!" she said in a low voice. "Stop staring after her. Do you want everyone to know?" She took his arm and firmly turned him toward François. "Since it is better to have them think you lose your head over every pretty woman, try to look at me as this boy does."

When he looked down and saw the slack-jawed expression on the boy's face, he laughed and tousled François's hair. The poor boy was having quite the day.

"Do you want the king to banish you to the wilds of Ireland?" Claudette said between her teeth. She smiled and batted her eyes at him. "You do Lady Hume no favors by drawing attention to her."

Realizing, belatedly, that Claudette was right, he picked up her hand and kissed it. He let his gaze linger on her.

"Thank you," he whispered. "You are a wise woman."

"Of course you missed me," she said in a voice just loud enough to be overheard, "but you will make me vain with such compliments!"

"I do not deserve you, Claudette."

"You do not," she agreed and began walking him out of the hall. Dropping her voice again, she said, "There is that dreadful Marie de Lisieux, lying in wait for you near the door."

"I suppose I should cast lustful glances her way," he whispered back to tease her.

"I know how difficult that is for you, Stephen."

He gave Marie a broad wink and swiveled his head as they passed.

Claudette gave him a hard pinch for his efforts. "I did not say you must stare at her bosom."

He laughed with genuine amusement this time. "Marie would think something was amiss if I did not."

"Just looking at her makes my back ache," Claudette said, lifting one delicate eyebrow in disdain. "No matter what the fashion, men will always like big breasts."

"Not every woman can have your perfect proportions," he told her, as he knew she expected him to. "But, in sooth, I do not think I have ever seen a pair I did not like."

"Men are so simple." She heaved a sigh of feigned weariness that made him laugh again.

When they were safely out the door, she turned and wagged a finger in his face. "Now let us be serious. You must promise me you will use that clever head of yours and not get into a cockfight over Lady Hume."

He opened his mouth to object, but she held her hand up.

"You best remember," she warned, "the king has bet upon the other cock."

Chapter Fourteen

𝒯hank God for the girl. If Linnet were not annoying de Roche with ceaseless chatter, he might notice how Isobel's hands shook. Isobel tried to make herself listen to what Linnet was saying but could not.

How could Stephen return just when she had put all thought of him behind her? That was not quite true. Not nearly true. But having him in Caen where she would see him every day made it so much worse.

She heard Linnet mention Stephen's name and almost missed the step. "What was that you said?"

"That my brother and I were very wicked to Sir Stephen."

How easy it was to be wicked with Stephen!

When she saw him coming through the crowd toward her, his smile like a swath of sunlight, her heart leapt in her chest. He looked so pleased to see her, too. For a moment, she thought he would sweep her into his arms.

She half hoped he would.

Perhaps more than half.

But then, Stephen could play her for a fool without even knowing it. As she left the hall, she turned to see whom Marie de Lisieux was watching so intently. It was Stephen, of course. He was already laughing and whispering with that breathtaking courtesan. While Isobel was shaken to her soul at seeing him again, he forgot her the moment she was out of sight.

He would be making his way around the room now, adoring woman to adoring woman. Making each and every one of them believe she was special.

Not that Isobel cared what he did.

She would think of her future. De Roche was a handsome man, every bit as attractive as Stephen Carleton. Surely she would find his kisses just as exciting. She would. Her mind was set on it. And for once, Robert was not here to interfere.

They were at her chamber door before she realized she had not spoken a word to de Roche since they left the hall.

"Wait inside," she whispered to the girl, giving her a gentle push inside.

She lifted de Roche's hand to cup her cheek and looked steadily into his eyes. Seeing how quickly the irritation in his eyes shifted to lust, she smiled, pleased with herself. It had been easy, after all. She would get her kiss now.

When he kissed her cheek, she was disappointed. Nay, annoyed. But then he began to work his way down her neck. She closed her eyes and tried to concentrate on the soft lips and warm breath against her skin. Instead, she found herself thinking of his heavy-handedness in trying to get her to change her mind about taking Linnet. And his utter lack of feeling for the poor girl's circumstances.

That Stephen had taken responsibility for the two orphans

surprised her. And yet...it did not. Wastrel, womanizer, drunkard that he was, Stephen did have a kind heart.

She'd forgotten de Roche when, suddenly, she was slammed against the door, the latch poking painfully into her back. De Roche's mouth was on hers, bruising her. With his tongue down her throat, choking her, she could not breathe. Panic surged through her as she tried in vain to push him away.

She fell backward with a shriek as the door opened behind her. De Roche caught her and leveled furious gray eyes at the cause of the interruption.

"M'lady, do you want these cleaned?" Linnet stood implacably in the doorway, holding a pair of boots in one hand. Not at all the humble maidservant.

"Thank you for escorting me," Isobel said before de Roche could shout at the girl. She straightened and held her hand out.

"Until tonight then," he said in a tight voice.

The gaze he fixed on her as he brought her hand to his lips held both anger and desire. She fought the urge to jerk her hand away when she felt his tongue on her skin.

As she watched him go, she wiped her hand against her skirts.

* * *

Claudette's serene expression gave nothing away, but Robert saw the glint of annoyance in her crystal blue eyes as she crossed the room toward him.

"Thank you," he said into her ear as he helped her into the seat beside him. "A woman's touch was needed."

"Stephen does need a woman's touch," she hissed. "That is precisely the problem."

She smiled and waved delicate fingers at an acquaintance passing by. "I tried to reason with him, but reason does not work on a man who is thinking with his—"

"With his heart?"

Instead of laughing, she gave a faint sigh. "Let us hope not."

Robert handed her the bowl of sugared fruit he'd taken from the table. "I must see what is taking de Roche so long to escort Isobel to her chamber."

"No need," Claudette said, glancing toward the entrance. "The snake has returned." Claudette had disliked de Roche from the moment she laid eyes on him.

From the way de Roche stormed across the room, Isobel had fended for herself well enough. De Roche went at once to join a small group in the corner, which included Marie de Lisieux.

"You know they are lovers?" Claudette said.

"'Tis a shame," he said, popping a sugared fruit into his mouth, "that murdering him would cause political complications."

She laughed this time—a lovely tinkling sound that always drew men's attention.

How he would love to catch de Roche in some treachery against the king. He drummed his fingers on his knee. "Tell me, do you think de Roche both clever and brave enough to play two sides at once?"

She turned to him and raised one perfectly shaped eyebrow. "Surely vanity and overconfidence would serve, as well?"

Claudette was right, of course. She always was about men.

"Tonight, however," she said, "he is too absorbed with looking down the front of Marie's gown to be conspiring about aught else."

Robert took a long swallow of his wine. Damn, it was too much to hope he could catch de Roche in some treachery in time.

How else could he save Isobel from this marriage? He narrowed his eyes, considering. All he had to do was stir the pot a bit. But the risks were high. High for all of them.

He chuckled to himself. What was life without a little danger?

Chapter Fifteen

"You are a handsome devil," Stephen murmured, "the fastest of them all, a matchless wonder."

Lightning nickered his agreement.

"I think he likes me now," François said, brushing the horse with long, firm strokes, just as Stephen had taught him. "He only tried to kick me twice today."

Stephen rubbed Lightning's nose and fed him another carrot.

Sighing, he rested his head against the horse's. "I know she is to be wed. And truly, I have tried to stay away. But she will think me rude if I do not see her."

Lightning munched the carrot, unpersuaded.

It was not just good intentions that kept Stephen away. He hated to see her with de Roche. He did not want Isobel to suffer with a second husband who disgusted her, but did this Frenchman have to be so handsome?

Stephen thought of how Isobel's breath caught when he

touched her. How her head fell back as he kissed her throat. Oh, God, how she pulled him down on top of her.

Would she do the same with de Roche?

Lightning jerked his head up as quick, light steps approached.

"Linnet, do not run or make sudden moves around a horse like Lightning," Stephen said as he patted the horse's neck to reassure him.

As soon as Stephen stepped around the horse, Linnet jumped into his arms and kissed him on both cheeks. "Thank you, thank you!" she squealed. "I love Lady Hume. She is as kind and beautiful as you said."

Her brother emerged from the horse's other side, and she ran to embrace and kiss him, too.

Stephen stepped between her and the horse and hauled her back to a safe distance. "Does Lady Hume know where you are?"

"She'll not mind that I come to visit my brother."

So, she had not told Isobel. "If I catch you going about alone again, I shall whip you until you beg for mercy."

Linnet rolled her eyes. "How silly you are! Maids do not require escorts."

All the same, he would speak to Isobel about it.

"I brought you a treat from the kitchen," Linnet said, reaching into the cloth bag slung over her shoulder. "Sir Robert told me these are your favorites."

The smell of the warm apple tarts diverted him from his lecture, just as she intended.

He grabbed François by the shoulder and pointed to the bucket of clean water. "The tarts will taste better after you wash the smell of horse from your hands."

The three of them sat on a pile of clean straw in the corner to eat their tarts.

"I like Sir Robert," Linnet said between bites and licking her fingers, "but who is this...this de Roche?" She wrinkled her nose as though smelling dung.

Stephen liked the girl better all the time. "De Roche is the man your mistress is going to marry. He is from Rouen."

Through a mouth stuffed full of tart, François mumbled his own speculation that de Roche came from hell. These children were wise beyond their years.

Linnet furrowed her brows in a pretty frown. "I cannot go to Rouen and leave François. When is this marriage to take place?"

"I do not know." Stephen suppressed a sigh. "Let us not worry about that yet."

"We cannot wait until it is too late," Linnet objected.

"Perhaps you could marry her instead?" François said.

Stephen laughed and shook his head. "You want me to marry to please the two of you?"

"She is very pretty," François said, "and I know how much you like her." The boy leaned forward, mouth hanging open like a half-wit, in what Stephen took as an imitation of himself.

Linnet threw her head back and hooted with laughter.

Stephen rubbed his temples. What had he done to deserve these two demons? "I do wish Lady Hume a better husband, but de Roche is the man King Henry has chosen for her."

Linnet dismissed the king's wishes with a very French lift of her narrow shoulder.

"Come," Stephen said to her. "I shall take you back now."

He expected an argument, but Linnet jumped to her feet. After bidding adieu to François and Lightning—who withstood her exuberance with uncharacteristic calm—she was ready to go.

When they reached Isobel's chamber in the keep, Linnet

pushed the door open and ran inside. Stephen followed, intent on speaking to Isobel about Linnet.

As he closed the door, he saw Isobel. She was standing before the basin on the table against the wall, as if about to wash her face. Her long, dark hair was in tangles, and she wore just her shift.

The sight left Stephen dry-mouthed. When she turned and met his eyes, heat scorched between them like a fire.

He'd seen countless women rise from bed wearing less, but none stirred him as she did, covered neck to ankle in a plain white shift. The thought came to him, unbidden and unwelcome: He could see her like this every morning and never tire of it.

He remembered the silky feel of her hair in his hands. His fingers itched to touch it, but his feet were fixed like stone weights to the floor.

His eyes traveled down the lovely curve of her neck. He longed to run his tongue along the delicate collarbone just above the edge of her shift. Then, shameless man that he was, he let his gaze drop precipitously to her breasts. They were round and full, the tips pressed against the cloth.

He could not get enough air.

Still, he followed the folds of the white cloth down, pondering the sweet mysteries underneath. He was a drowning man. Down, down, down he went, until he reached slim ankles and bare feet. He wanted to hold her delicate foot in his hand and kiss each toe. And then move up her leg.

He dragged his gaze back up, savoring every inch in reverse. When he reached her face again, he thought his heart would stop. Her eyes held that same look of longing he remembered from the first time they met.

Blood pounded in his ears. He wanted her so badly he could taste the salt of her skin. With this fire sparking between them, the first time would be hot and fast. But then he would take her behind those bed curtains and spend the rest of the day making slow love to her. He would run his tongue over every—

"Lady Hume, you must put this on!"

The voice penetrated his reverie. Vaguely, he realized he'd been hearing Linnet's voice for some time. Whatever was the child doing here?

"Lady Hume!" The girl was tugging on Isobel's arm. "Isobel!"

This time, Isobel heard her. Before Stephen could cry out in protest, Isobel snatched the robe from Linnet's hand and whipped it around her shoulders. She looked so beautiful with her cheeks flushed and her hair swept over one shoulder, Stephen could almost forgive Linnet the robe. Almost.

But the girl had to go. Now.

Linnet had to leave so Stephen could gather Isobel in his arms and take her behind those bed curtains—

Just what had Isobel been doing behind those bed curtains? Tousled and in her night shift in the middle of the afternoon?

Was there a man behind those curtains? De Roche? Nay, she would not. She could not. Jealousy settled in his belly like a corrosive poison.

"Are you ill?" he asked, keeping his voice calm with considerable effort. "Is that why you are abed at this hour?"

"I haven't slept well lately. After Linnet left, I decided to rest awhile," she said, pushing her hair back from her face. "But why are you here, Stephen?"

"I was returning Linnet."

"From where?" she asked. "She only went to the kitchen."

"You were here alone, asleep, with your door unbarred?" Stephen could not control his temper with so much emotion roiling inside him. "And you should not let the girl wander all over the castle on her own. For God's sake, Isobel, the place is filled with soldiers."

Isobel took Linnet's hand and spoke to her in a soft voice. "Sir Stephen is right; you must be careful where you go alone. Most of the castle is safe, but avoid the places where soldiers congregate and other women are unlikely to be about."

He was relieved Isobel was giving the girl sensible direction, though it was not as restrictive as he would like.

"An isolated area," Isobel continued, "is even more dangerous."

"Such as the storerooms along the outer wall," he could not help putting in.

With her practice partners gone to Falaise, had Isobel taken to going alone to the storeroom? He took her arm to pull her aside and ask. As soon as he felt the heat of her skin through the thin fabric, lust blazed through him again.

Whatever he meant to tell her was gone from his head. All he could think to say was that he wanted to see her naked.

Isobel jerked her arm away as if his touch burned her, too. "Of course, the most dangerous place to be caught with a man is a bedchamber," she said between clenched teeth. "Stephen, you must leave."

Ludicrous as it was, he felt pleased that she was calling him just "Stephen" again. He loved to hear her say his name.

He bowed and left, baffled by his loss of control. If Linnet had not been there, he would have had Isobel on the bed before a word passed between them. Nay, they never would have made it to the bed. It would be on the floor, or against the wall—

The saints preserve him, he was light-headed from breathing so hard. He'd be better off lost to drink than lost in lust to a woman he could not have.

That was not quite the truth of it. Isobel was a woman he *should* not have. She may not know it, but he *could* have her. He did not mistake the look in her eyes. That made her all the more dangerous.

He truly must stay away from her now. God help them both if he could not.

Chapter Sixteen

March 1418

Stephen managed to avoid Isobel for a full week, though sometimes it seemed as if all the world conspired against him. How Robert found him here in the armory he could not guess.

"You must ask someone else," Stephen said without looking up from the blade he was sharpening. "I am busy."

"There is no time," Robert said. "All I ask is that you go tell Isobel I've been called away so she does not sit waiting for me all afternoon."

"She can wait."

Robert glanced at the men hammering metal at the far end of the armory and lowered his voice. "The king needs me to come at once, and I cannot just leave her there."

"I see I shall have to tell you the truth," Stephen said and slammed the blade down on the bench beside him. "'Tis for her own protection I cannot go. The lady is not safe with me."

Robert's mouth twitched with amusement, which annoyed Stephen more than he thought possible.

"Surely I can trust you not to attack Isobel in broad daylight in a common area of the castle?" Robert said, widening his eyes in mock horror. He leaned down and whispered, "The king wishes me to listen behind the secret door *while he meets with de Roche*."

That did it. Stephen wiped his blade and returned it to his belt. When he looked up, Robert was halfway out the door.

"You will find her," Robert called over his shoulder, "in the small garden behind the Old Palace."

The small garden! With tall hedges on three sides and a wall on the fourth, that garden was made for liaisons. Stephen should know. He opened his mouth to call Robert back, but his friend was long gone.

Damn, damn, damn. So much for good intentions.

A smile tugged at the corners of his mouth. Stephen fought it, but he could not prevent it from spreading into a grin.

A man could fight fate only so long.

Isobel. He could hardly wait to see her.

* * *

A rat scrabbled along the secret passageway behind Robert. God's beard, it was filthy back here! Three hundred and fifty years of royal spies and lovers traipsing through it, and he doubted it had ever seen a broom.

Robert pressed his ear to the hole again.

"I have persuaded my cousin Georges de la Trémoille to do all he can to keep Burgundy on your side."

Robert remembered the beady-eyed Georges from

boyhood—a pompous ass if there ever was one, but a wily one. If Georges was taking the English side, it was for his own reasons.

De Roche droned on about various members of the Burgundy faction, all of whom he claimed he could influence. Not a word passed de Roche's lips that Robert could use against him. Damn the man.

At long last, the king dismissed de Roche and his guards.

"You were right to suggest I use common soldiers as guards today," the king said as Robert stepped through the hidden panel. "De Roche assumed they could not understand French and spoke freely."

The soldiers could not, in fact, follow the conversation. That was Robert's job.

"He told you nothing we did not know," Robert pointed out as he brushed a cobweb from his tunic. "He is a slippery one. We cannot know on which side he will land."

The king slapped his fist against his palm. "Then it is time to force his hand with the betrothal."

Robert did not believe it would be so easy to flush de Roche out. He would wait to share this insight, however, until the king was ready to hear it.

"At the pace you and de Roche are negotiating this marriage contract," the king fumed, "I may as well have asked the lawyers to do it."

Robert was rather proud of how long he'd managed to drag it out. He had to stifle a smile—until he caught the steely glint in the king's eye.

"I will have this betrothal settled," the king said, pointing his finger at Robert, "within a sennight."

Seven days. That did not give him much time to thwart the king's plans. Rather, it did not give Stephen much time.

He hoped matters were progressing in the garden.

* * *

Isobel let her head rest against the wall behind her. It felt heavenly to be alone in this peaceful garden, knowing de Roche would not come looking for her. God bless King Henry for giving him a private audience today! It took constant vigilance to avoid being caught alone with de Roche again.

Stephen, on the other hand, she'd barely glimpsed since she sent him from her chamber. How close she had been to succumbing to temptation that day! She should have been insulted by the way Stephen's gaze moved so blatantly over her body. Instead, his hunger seduced her, made her insides go hot and liquid. Without a single touch, she was his.

Or would have been, but for Linnet. God would punish her for being such a sinful woman.

Stephen had avoided her ever since. When she did chance to see him, he was always occupied. Talking with merchants from the town. Drinking with local noblemen. And there was always a woman nearby—touching his arm, laughing at his jokes, following him with her eyes. It was as if Stephen wanted to show her she did not matter.

Sometimes, though, she felt his eyes upon her. But when she turned to look, his gaze was elsewhere.

"Isobel."

She looked up, and there he was, so handsome he took her breath away.

"Robert could not come, so he sent me to fetch you."

"Will you not sit for a while?" she asked, patting the bench beside her. "With the sun out, it almost feels like summer in this sheltered garden."

He pressed his lips together and shook his head.

"Are you angry with me?" She was embarrassed by the

quaver in her voice, but she pressed ahead. "You almost run when you see me, as if you cannot bear the sight of me."

To her astonishment, Stephen threw his head back and laughed. He had a wonderful, infectious laugh. It filled the small garden and lightened her heart.

He dropped down beside her. Smiling his most wicked smile, he leaned too close and asked, "You will pretend you do not know why I keep my distance?"

She swallowed and shook her head. "I do not know."

"You lie, Isobel, but I will tell you all the same."

She could not breathe with him this near.

"I stay away because whenever I see you"—he kept his eyes fixed on hers as he ran his finger slowly up her forearm—"all I want to do is drag you off to bed, and keep you there for a week."

A week. Oh, my. Her mouth went dry, and she wet her lips with her tongue. Her stomach tightened at the desire she saw burning in his eyes.

"I cannot be in a room with you," he said, his voice thick and husky, "without imagining what it would be like to take your clothes off. To feel your bare skin, warm and soft beneath my hands, against my chest. To smell your hair, to taste—"

He stopped abruptly and closed his eyes.

Isobel tried to slow her breathing, but there was nothing she could do about her racing pulse.

He rested his forehead against hers and whispered, "Tell me, what is this between us?"

She had no answer, at least none that she would give him.

She felt weak and liquid as he took her face in his hands. *Kiss me. Please. Just once more.*

When he pulled away, she felt bereft, wanting.

Stephen fell back against the wall and rocked his head

from side to side. "This is more dangerous for you than for me. 'Tis why I tried to stay away." He rubbed his hands over his face and muttered into them, "What am I to do with her?"

Kiss me, kiss me, kiss me. She clenched her fists to keep from saying it aloud.

He dropped his hands and asked, "Do you want to marry him?"

She blinked at him, startled by the question.

"Now that you've spent time with de Roche," he persisted, "are you content to be his wife?"

"It does not matter what I wish," she said, though he should not need to be told. She straightened her spine. "I must do my best to be content with the fate God gives me."

"That is no answer," Stephen said.

And not fair to her future husband, either. She felt a wave of guilt for her disloyalty.

"Truly, the king has chosen well for me," she said. "Philippe de Roche is far above me in both wealth and position. The match exceeds every reasonable hope I could have."

For a certainty, de Roche would make a better husband than her last. She shuddered to think what sort of man her father would have given her to this time. God forgive her for not being as grateful as she ought. For wanting more.

Stephen took her hand and squeezed it. "You deserve to be happy this time."

She did not bother telling him that what a woman deserved had very little to do with what she got, at least in this life.

Chapter Seventeen

The noisy clatter and conversation in the Exchequer hall came to an abrupt halt. Isobel barely had time to scramble to her feet before the king and his commanders left their places at the high table and filed out of the hall.

As she sat back down, Isobel risked a sideways glance down the length of the table. No woman sat next to Stephen tonight.

And it could snow in July, too.

What did Stephen mean, asking her those questions this afternoon? One moment he was teasing her, the next acting tormented.

"Isobel?"

She started at the sound of de Roche's voice beside her.

"I had to say your name three times," de Roche said. "Who were you looking at?"

"My brother," she said, relieved to have an excuse ready. "I worry he spends so much time at L'Abbaye-aux-Hommes."

That much was true. What was troubling Geoffrey that

caused him to keep vigil with the monks so often? And now he was desperate to tell her about a holy relic at some other abbey. What did he say the relic was? A saint's finger joint? She had promised to meet him later. Heaven help her, he'd probably written a poem about the shriveled finger.

"You can have no objection to your brother's devotion," de Roche said, interrupting her thoughts again.

Isobel did not mistake his pronouncement for an invitation to explain her concern. De Roche never asked her questions of a personal nature about her family. She was relieved, and yet... How different he was from Stephen. Stephen would not be content until he wheedled every dark family secret from her.

This time she was jarred from her thoughts by something warm and heavy on her leg.

"For once, your vigilant guardian has left us." De Roche was looking straight ahead, but his lips were curved up at the corners.

She glanced up and down the table. Both Robert and Stephen had disappeared. Off in search of amusement in the town, no doubt.

She grasped de Roche's hand to halt its progress up her thigh.

"You are tired, my dear," de Roche said. "Shall I see you to your chamber?" Without waiting for her answer, he gripped her elbow and hoisted her to her feet.

"I began to wonder if Sir Robert would ever leave your side," de Roche said in her ear as he whisked her out of the hall. "The man protects you as if you were an innocent virgin."

She felt uneasy and a little breathless as he marched her purposefully down the steps of the Exchequer and along the path to the keep. The night air was cold. Through the thickness of her cloak, she could feel de Roche's heat.

Could he not say something to soothe her?

He maintained both his silence and his brisk pace all the way to the keep. By the time they reached the corridor outside her chamber, her heart was slamming in her chest. His teeth gleamed in the rushlight as he spun her toward him. She tensed as de Roche ran his fingers down her throat.

When he reached the sensitive skin along the top of her bodice, she grabbed his wrist. "Someone will see us!"

"No one is here." He dipped a finger into the valley between her breasts. "Besides, we are nearly betrothed."

This man would be her husband. Soon she would share his bed as often as he wished her to. It seemed silly to protest this small familiarity.

The old hope returned. The hope that her new husband could make her feel the way Stephen did when he kissed her. That he could give her that feeling of being swept away, as if nothing else mattered so long as he touched her.

Was it possible? She needed to know.

"Kiss me," she said, lifting her face to him. This time, it would be different.

This kiss was different. Softer. Not frightening, like the first time. And not disgusting, like Hume's. Her mind was cold and clear as she waited for the thrill to seize her. And waited. The kiss felt...pleasant. But no more than that.

She could come up with no explanation. De Roche was handsome, young, healthy. True, the heavy scent he wore gave her a bit of a headache. But his lips were soft and warm. The tickle of his mustache did not bother her.

De Roche ran his hands up and down her sides. Her body began to respond to his caresses. But where was the mindless passion? What she felt was a dim candle to the roaring fire that burned through her when Stephen touched her.

She would try harder. Determined, she moved her hands

to the nape of his neck and kissed him back. She opened her mouth to him and slid her tongue over his the way she remembered had brought moans from Stephen.

Before she knew it, she was crushed against him. She felt trapped, unable to move. She was so startled by the suddenness of the assault that it took her a moment to realize de Roche's hand was like an iron band around her wrist.

She made frantic little cries against his mouth as he forced her hand downward. He was so strong! She felt the hardness of his cock against her palm. Up and down, up and down, he rubbed her hand against it.

She bit his lip and tasted blood. Though he tore his mouth away, he did not release her hand. His breath was coming in horrid gasps against her ear. She was flooded with the memory of Hume's putrid smell gagging her in the darkness.

With a surge of strength, she wrenched her other arm free and swung at him. He caught her hand midair. They stood inches apart, staring at each other. Both were breathing hard, but she was choking back tears.

"Stop, please." Her voice was small, barely a whisper.

His eyes were black with rage. "After the way you kissed me, you will pretend you do not want me in your bed tonight?"

"I meant only a kiss," she stammered, feeling confused and ashamed.

"Ah, you mean to tease me." His voice was all the more menacing for its softness. "That is not a nice game to play."

Looking straight into her eyes, he cupped her breasts with his hands. She was too shocked and too frightened to move.

"Once I take you to bed," he said as he rubbed his thumbs in slow circles over her nipples through the cloth, "you will want to learn the kind of games that will keep me there."

* * *

There was a time when Stephen would have been pleased to be included in the king's meeting with his commanders. But not tonight. Although King Henry placed considerable importance on the just administration of his new territories, the other men looked bored as Stephen gave his report. And why not? Stephen was bored himself.

In sooth, he was not so much bored as anxious to leave. The moment the king released him, he made his escape. He pretended not to see William's signal to wait for him. As he ran along the dark path to the keep, he asked himself why he was going to find Isobel.

What would he say when he found her? He had no idea.

This was lunacy, even for him. If he wanted to forget all honor and seduce her, he could have done that already. He recalled the moment when he knew she was his for the asking—and almost forgot to breathe.

What she did to him! He felt better about himself when he was around her. More interesting. More clever. Certainly more virtuous! He wanted to protect her, to drive the sadness from her eyes.

He would not let himself think what that meant now.

He entered the keep and raced up the back stairs, two at a time. As he climbed, he thought of the last time he came here. When she leapt from the bed in her shift. His heart beat so hard now he thought it might burst from his chest.

He ran down the corridor and made the last turn.

And stopped dead in his tracks.

Despite the dim light, he could not fool himself into believing the woman was anyone other than Isobel. He'd spent too many hours studying that profile. And that foolish goatee could belong to none other than de Roche.

When Isobel slid her hands behind de Roche's neck and pulled him into a deep kiss, she may as well have reached into Stephen's chest and ripped his heart out. How could she? How could she do this?

Then he saw her hand, covered by de Roche's, reaching down. Sweet Jesus, he did not want to see this. Not this. When she began stroking de Roche's crotch, Stephen leaned against the wall and squeezed his eyes shut. And still he could hear the little sounds she was making. He had to get out of here. Now.

And yet he looked again. He could not help himself.

The lovers stood apart now, eyes locked. Stephen watched, transfixed, as de Roche covered her breasts with his hands and rubbed his thumbs over the tips. It was such a blatant show of sexual ownership that Stephen could stand no more.

He turned and fled without a sound.

* * *

Stephen drank with a purpose. Though his lips and even his fingertips felt numb, sweet oblivion escaped him. The drink had yet to loosen the knot of jealousy in his stomach. Nor had it dulled the loss that weighed down every muscle.

The woman was heavy on his lap—he had no idea who she was and how she got there. He wanted her gone, but it would take too much effort to make her move. The overpowering smell of cloying perfume, sweat, and sex turned his stomach. Even with his eyes closed, he could not pretend she was Isobel.

Quite suddenly, the weight was off his lap. He heard a sharp exchange of female voices, but he did not feel curious enough to open his eyes.

"You must be far gone to let that one near you! She'd give you the pox for sure, you fool."

"Claudette?" He opened his eyes to find her looking down at him, her hands on her hips. "It is you."

He was so glad to see her he leaned against her and put his arms around her waist. Though he was vaguely aware he should not have his face buried between her breasts, it felt comforting to be surrounded by all that softness.

Someone was pulling on his shoulders, and he heard a familiar voice behind him. Reluctantly, he released Claudette and fell back. All this movement was making his head spin.

"Jamie? What are you doing in this den of sin?" he asked. "William will have a fit."

"He is the one who sent me."

"William sent a fifteen-year-old to play nursemaid to me?" Stephen's voice sounded distant to his own ears.

"Aye, that is just what he did," Jamie said with a grin, "except that I am almost sixteen."

William sent Jamie with Claudette? More proof the world made no sense. No sense at all.

"How could she prefer de Roche?" he asked.

Jamie gave him a puzzled look, but Claudette—dear, dear Claudette—understood.

"She would be a fool to prefer him," she said and touched his cheek.

"But I saw her." The words came out of his mouth of their own accord; he could not stop them. "She was kissing him. And touching him, for God's sake. And—"

"Of course she was. She has to marry the man," Claudette interrupted. "Women must be practical."

Practical? Did women truly think that way?

"Kissing me was not practical."

"It certainly was not," Claudette agreed. "Not for either of you."

The next thing he knew he was in a carriage, bouncing over cobblestones, his head banging against the side.

Cold air woke him, and he got his feet under him. Snatches of conversation came to him, as if from a long way away: Jamie saying he could manage alone; the guards' loud jibes; his own voice suggesting they find Isobel.

When next he opened his eyes, he saw his feet dragging along the floor. Then some kind soul hoisted him onto the bed. He was sinking, sinking, sinking.

Jamie's voice brought him back from the land of the dead. "What did Claudette mean about women being 'practical'?"

"She means...a woman will bed a man"—he sighed because of the effort it took to respond, but Jamie shook his shoulder again—"because it makes sense to her...though she has no true feeling for him. They are all heartless, heartless."

"A virtuous woman would not do that."

"Virtuous ones are the worst!" God in heaven, even Catherine took a stranger to her bed.

Had he said that last part aloud? Nay, he'd never tell.

"You are drunk. She would never do that. No one could be a more devoted wife."

"Shhhe would neber do that to William. Nebber, nebber, nebber." But even Catherine...even she was practical once. Took a stranger to bed. A stranger.

"What did you say?" The voice seemed to be coming from inside his head. But it was damned persistent.

"Who was it? What happened?"

Stephen wanted the questions to stop so he could sleep.

"He could not get her with child. Her other husband. That cursed first one. So shhhe let someone else do the job. Thasss how she got ssweet little Jamie. Big sssecret. Shhh."

Chapter Eighteen

Stephen awoke with a bad feeling that had nothing to do with his hangover. A very bad feeling. Beneath the pounding headache, lurching stomach, and dry mouth, something more sinister lurked. He had the uneasy feeling he'd crossed a line. Committed some grave, unpardonable wrong.

Had he gone to bed with someone he shouldn't have? He turned his head, careful not to move too quickly, and let his breath out. If that was what he'd done, at least she was gone.

But he did not think that was it.

He crawled out of bed, poured cold water from the pitcher into the basin, and splashed his face.

What was it? He tried to piece together what happened after... The image of de Roche with his hands on Isobel was all too clear. His rising pulse caused his head to throb violently. He leaned over the basin and poured the rest of the pitcher over his head.

First he went to the public house nearest the castle gate.

Then to the one near the old church. Sometime later, he ended up in the seamiest part of town. He remembered the smell of cloying perfume. Then Claudette appearing like an angel of mercy. And Jamie.

A carriage ride. Jamie dragging him to bed. Someone asking endless questions. About women being practical...

He squeezed his eyes shut. God help him, had he said those things about Catherine aloud? And to Jamie? He could not have. He had wheedled the secret out of an old servant years ago and never told a living soul. Never would.

He turned and looked about the empty bedchamber. Where was Jamie now? Trying not to panic, he threw on his clothes, grabbed his cloak and sword, and tore out of the room.

He had to find Jamie. God help him if he'd told Catherine's secret to her son last night. If he had, he would have to explain it to Jamie, try to make him understand.

And then he would have to tell William what he'd done.

* * *

Isobel looked everywhere for her brother. When she could not find him, she began to worry. Last night he said he had something important to tell her. Why did she not make him tell her at once? Of course, she did not expect de Roche to take her off so suddenly. And then, after what happened—she would not think of that now—she forgot completely about her brother.

Linnet's fair hair whipped about her face as they raced across the bailey yard. "We have not tried the stables yet," she shouted against the wind. "If his horse is there, you will know he has not gone far."

"You are a bright one," Isobel said, forcing a smile. She could not say why she was so worried.

Halfway to the stables, they saw François running toward them.

"Lady Hume, I've been looking for you," he called out as he drew near. He was as breathless as she. "Your brother asked me to give you a message."

"A message? What is it?"

François screwed his face up as if he were concentrating to be sure he got it right. "He and Jamie Rayburn have gone to an abbey two hours' ride from here to see a holy relic."

"You saw Geoffrey leave?" she said, fighting to sound calm. "With Jamie?"

"At first he was going to go alone," François said. "I told him it was too dangerous with all the brigands and renegades roaming the countryside. But he said, 'God will protect me.' I swear, that is just what he said."

Good Lord, she would kill him for taking such a risk! Even this child knew it was foolish to travel alone here.

"Then Jamie came tearing into the stable in such a state," the boy said, his eyes wide. "Your brother pulled him into a corner where I could not hear. Next thing I know, your brother gives me this message—and they ride off!"

"How long ago was this?"

François shrugged. "An hour? I looked a long time for you."

She must find someone quickly to ride after them and bring them back. By now, people would be gathered in the hall for breakfast. She ran headlong for the keep, the twins dogging her steps.

"Jamie is a good fighter," François called out in a valiant attempt to reassure her.

She would find de Roche. He came to Caen with a large contingent of armed men. Surely he could gather enough of them quickly to go after Geoffrey and Jamie.

She barely slowed to a walk as she entered the keep. "Wait here," she told the twins as she went through the great arched doorway to the keep's hall. She spotted de Roche at once and made straight for him.

"Philippe, help me!" she called out when she was close enough to be heard. She ignored the disapproval on his face; he would understand as soon as he heard what happened.

He held up his hand. With a laugh, he said to the man next to him, "My bride is anxious to see me."

"Geoffrey has gone off!" she cried. "You must go after him and bring him back."

"Calm yourself, my dear. Tell me you have not been running. You are quite out of breath."

"My brother is gone," she said between gasps. "You must go at once, or he'll come to harm, I know it."

"If you will excuse us," he said to the man. He took her arm in a bruising grip and led her to a corner.

"You should have asked to speak to me in private," he said, his eyes flaring with anger. "How dare you approach me in public making demands, telling me I must do this, I must do that!"

"I am sorry, but my brother—"

"Your brother is a grown man. He can make his own decisions and live with the consequences."

"But can you not go after him? He does not understand—"

"Good God, Isobel, do you think I have nothing better to do than chase after your foolish brother?"

"Do you?" As far as she could tell, he had nothing to do in Caen but negotiate the marriage contract with Robert—and that was going so slowly he could not be giving much time to it.

"I do not need to explain myself to you," he said. "Your brother is bound to think better of his actions and return. I suggest you go to your chamber and wait for him."

What sort of man was he? How could he refuse to help her? She had no time to argue. He would not be moved, in any case.

She rose up on her tiptoes to look over his shoulder for someone else she could ask. When she saw Lord FitzAlan, she shouted his name and waved her arms.

"Stop that at once," de Roche said. "You are making a spectacle of yourself."

FitzAlan was already striding toward her. Praise God! And that was Stephen, right behind him.

"Lord FitzAlan, Sir Stephen," de Roche greeted them as they approached.

FitzAlan ignored him. "What is it, Lady Hume? You seem distressed."

"François says my brother and Jamie have ridden out of the city alone," she said, trying to keep her voice under control.

Stephen gripped her arm. "Does François know their destination, or in what direction they rode?"

"To an abbey, two hours east." A fragment from one of Geoffrey's poems came to her. Something about a finger of a martyred saint and... "L'Abbaye de Saint Michele, could that be it?"

"I'll meet you at the stables," FitzAlan said to Stephen. "I must leave word for the king that I've gone."

"We shall find them," Stephen said and gave her arm a quick squeeze as they turned to go.

"Wait," she called after them. "I will come with you."

"Don't be foolish—" de Roche began, but FitzAlan cut him off.

"Keep her here," FitzAlan commanded, pointing his outstretched arm at de Roche.

Then they were gone.

Dropping her eyes on the floor, Isobel said, "I will wait in my chamber, as you suggested." She dipped a quick curtsy and left before he could say a word.

Linnet caught up with her on the stairs. As soon as they reached her chamber, Isobel opened her trunk and took out the clothes she had been mending for Geoffrey.

"Cut six inches from the sleeves and leggings, and help me change," she ordered Linnet. "Quickly now."

She brushed aside Linnet's objections. The voice in the back of her head told her what she was doing was foolish; she ignored that, as well.

Geoffrey was all she had in the world.

She could not sit here and wait. From the time Geoffrey was little, she was the one who protected him—from their father's criticisms, their mother's indifference, his own blindness to the world around him.

"If someone comes for me, tell them I am asleep," she said as she strapped on her sword. "Say I am unwell, a headache."

Thank goodness her cloak was a plain one. She told Linnet to fetch it as she pushed her hair under a cap. After giving Linnet a hurried kiss on the cheek, she pulled the hood over her head and ran out the door.

She got to the stables just as Stephen and FitzAlan were riding out. She ducked her head as they galloped past, then turned to see that they were headed toward the eastern gate, Porte des Champs.

When she found François inside, he was no more keen on her plan than his sister. Still, she made him help saddle her horse and swore him to secrecy. He looked so uneasy that she forgot her disguise and touched his cheek.

"I shall catch up to them in no time," she assured him. "They will keep me safe."

"Take good care, m'lady," François said. "They are going to be very angry."

She almost laughed—François was far more concerned about what Stephen and FitzAlan would do to her than the brigands and renegades.

Porte des Champs took her directly into the fields east of the castle. Far ahead, she could see two riders. She held her horse back, not wanting to close the distance too soon. Her plan was to wait to reveal herself until they were midway to the abbey, when they would find it easier to take her to the abbey than bring her all the way back to Caen.

Before long, she dismissed her fear of being discovered too soon. She was a good rider, but at each rise, the two men seemed farther and farther ahead. She lost sight of them altogether in the dips between.

When she crested the next hill, she could not see them at all. A surge of fear went through her as she realized how alone and vulnerable she was. She darted looks side to side and behind her. Should she go back? Heart pounding, she craned her neck and searched the empty horizon.

Suddenly, two riders burst out of the trees on either side of her. Her shrieks filled the air as they charged toward her. At the last moment, the two riders pulled their horses up. Their horses reared, hooves high in the air. Her horse shied away from them, nearly unseating her in its fright.

When Isobel saw who the riders were, she thought she might faint with relief. She pressed her hand to her thundering heart. "Praise God it is you! I thought you were brigands!"

"Isobel?" Stephen said, his eyes wide. "Isobel!"

She wanted to throw her arms around them both. The men were not nearly as glad to see her. In sooth, they looked as if they'd like to murder her.

"Are you possessed?" Stephen shouted at her. "Did you think we would not notice someone following us? If your screams were not so...so...so *female,* we might have run you through!"

He sounded as though he wished they had.

"You were a fool to come," FitzAlan said. "And that de Roche is a bigger fool for not making certain you did not."

"But I am here," she said quickly. "Geoffrey and Jamie cannot be far ahead now. We must keep going."

When she saw the look that passed between them, she knew she would get her way. But they were not happy about it.

"We shall take you to the abbey, and leave you there," FitzAlan said. "In chains, if need be."

With that, he turned his horse and galloped off.

"Stay close to me," Stephen ordered. "We'll ride behind until his temper cools."

They spurred their horses forward and rode side by side.

Stephen could not let it go just yet. "Truly, Isobel, that was foolish in more ways than I can name."

"Anyone seeing me will think I am a man," she said, though she was feeling worse and worse by the moment. "Surely 'tis safer to travel as three armed men than two."

"Safer, with you?" he said, turning and raising an eyebrow. "Your being dressed like that serves only to distract me. Why, I can see the shape of your leg all the way up to—"

"Be serious, Stephen."

She looked ahead, embarrassed. At least the anger was gone from Stephen's voice. Judging from the stiffness of FitzAlan's back, he would not forgive her so easily.

Stephen seemed to read her thoughts. "I've not seen a woman other than his wife provoke William this much before."

"He gets angry with her often? The poor woman."

"Poor Catherine?" Stephen laughed. "Believe me, she has the great commander wrapped around her little finger."

He was quiet a moment. "There is nothing he would not do for her," he said, his voice wistful. "Or she for him."

Who would have guessed the stern commander harbored a great love? Inexplicably, the thought made Isobel's eyes sting.

"Do not fret over William's displeasure," Stephen said. "He is so angry with me, he can have little left for you."

"What happened?"

"It is because of me," he said, staring straight ahead, "that Jamie ran off."

She averted her gaze from the naked pain on Stephen's face and tried to think of something she could say to comfort him.

"William!" Stephen roared.

She jerked her head up. Time stopped as she tried to make sense of the scene before her: FitzAlan slumped over his horse, a rain of arrows falling all about him. Was FitzAlan injured? How was it possible?

Stephen's shouts brought her to her senses.

"To the wood, Isobel! Now!" He pointed in the direction he wanted her to go and then shot forward on his horse.

She turned her horse into the field and galloped across it toward the wood beyond. When she risked a glance over her shoulder, her heart went to her throat.

Stephen had put himself between his wounded brother and the stand of trees from which the arrows were coming. As she watched, he leaned over, caught the reins of FitzAlan's horse, and took off again. Praise God!

Before she entered the wood, she looked for him again. Stephen was galloping, with FitzAlan in tow, in a wide arc that would bring them into the same wood, but farther up.

She entered the wood and rode, as fast as she dared, to meet them.

At last she saw movement ahead through the trees. When she came upon the two horses, panic surged through her. Their saddles were empty. Then she saw Stephen beside a fallen log, hunched over his brother.

She leapt down from her horse and knelt beside him.

"What can I do?" She gripped Stephen's arm and peered down at FitzAlan.

Oh, my God. FitzAlan was drenched in blood. An arrow stuck out of his neck above his chain mail shirt.

"We should have taken the time to don full armor," Stephen said as he worked the arrow out of FitzAlan's neck. "Find something to bind the wound. Quickly."

Isobel removed the food bundle she had stowed inside her shirt. She let the bread and cheese fall to the ground, shook out the cloth, and folded it tightly.

"I am ready."

Stephen pulled the arrow free, and she pressed the cloth against the spurting wound.

God help them, FitzAlan was insensible and pale as death.

Stephen kept pressure on the wound while she cut a long strip from the bottom of her cloak. Then, working together, they wound the strip over the cloth covering the wound, around his back, and under his arm. Stephen tied the binding tight across his brother's chest.

As soon as it was done, Stephen gripped Isobel's arms and looked into her face. "Those men are still out there. I must divert them before they come into the wood."

"You are going back?" *Sweet Jesus, no. Please no.*

"I will come back for you as soon as I can." He pulled the sword and short blade from FitzAlan's belt and handed them to her. "But you must be ready should one of them get by me."

Oh God oh God oh God.

"You can do this, Isobel," he said, his eyes fixed on hers. "If a man does come, he will believe he sees a helpless woman. That is your advantage."

She looked down and saw that her hair fell loose about her shoulders. Where was her cap? It must have fallen...

Stephen took hold of her chin and turned her back to face him. "Use his ignorance against him. Use your sword. Kill him, Isobel. Kill him."

Could she do it? Could she? His eyes drilled into hers until she nodded.

He took her face in his hands and kissed her hard. "Give him no second chances."

As Stephen's horse crashed through the underbrush, she gazed down upon the man entrusted to her care. King Henry's famous commander. Beloved of Catherine. 'Twas her fault he lay here grievously injured. She had distracted them from the real danger.

She took a deep breath and went to retrieve a blanket and flask from the horses. After wrapping the blanket around FitzAlan, she shooed the horses away so they would not give away their hiding place. Then she gathered armfuls of leaves and piled them around FitzAlan.

When she was satisfied FitzAlan was well hidden, she settled down beside him behind the fallen log. The smell of decaying wood and leaves filled her nostrils as she dribbled ale from the flask into his mouth. He swallowed without waking.

She alternated between checking FitzAlan and peeking over the top of the log. Though Stephen could not have been gone long, each moment seemed a day. She would not let herself think of what she would do if he did not return.

God, please keep him safe. Keep him safe.

She heard a twig snap. Gripping the sword in one hand and the short blade in the other, she inched up until she could see over the top of the log. Nothing.

She held her breath and listened.

There it was again.

She turned toward the sound, searching.

And then she saw him. A man, twenty yards off and coming straight toward her. She set down the sword to wipe the sweat from her hand.

Mary, Mother of God. She prayed under her breath that the man's presence did not mean Stephen was dead.

The man was coming closer. She had to think, to make her plan. He wore no armor, so she had a chance. She heard Stephen's voice in her head, saying, *Isobel, you can do this.*

She waited until he was ten feet from her.

She stood abruptly, keeping her hands behind her. "Sir! Please help me!"

The man's eyes went wide. "Now, here's a bonus," he said, relaxing his sword arm and breaking into a wide grin. "I was not told there would be a woman."

From his accent and his rough clothing, she could tell he was a French commoner. "English soldiers took me from my home," she called out, pretending to cry. "You must help me, please!"

The man came toward her slowly, as if she were a horse easily spooked. What if he was not one of the attackers? What if he was just some peasant who meant to help her? He had a sword, but—

The man raked his eyes over her, and she knew with utter certainty he meant her harm. And when he was finished with her, he would murder FitzAlan.

She stood very still and waited. One more step. One more

step. When he was just on the other side of the log, not four feet from her, he lunged for her.

The shock of resistance as the point of her sword entered his body made her arm shake. She clenched her teeth and pressed forward with all her weight. For a long, dreadful moment, he swayed on his feet, staring at her with eyes wide with surprise. Then he fell backward, ripping her sword from her hands.

She jumped over the log and stood over him, her heart thundering in her chest. The sword. She had to have it back.

Fighting back nausea, she took hold of the hilt with both hands and tugged. It would not give! Her hands felt cold and clammy. Sweat trickled down her back. She had to have it back.

She put her foot on the man's chest and pulled with her weight behind it. At last the sword gave way with a wet sucking sound. She fell back a step but kept her hold on it.

The blade was dripping with the man's blood. She could not take her eyes from it.

At the sound of a loud grunt behind her, she whipped around and saw FitzAlan. He had one arm over the log, trying to support himself. A chill ran through her as she realized his eyes were not on her. They were fixed on something behind her.

FitzAlan's free arm moved in a blur and something whizzed past her ear. When she turned back to look the other way, she saw a second man not five feet from her. FitzAlan's knife was in his chest.

She was behind the log before she knew she'd moved.

"My vision is not good," FitzAlan said in a rasping voice. The poor man's face was wet with sweat, and the bandage on his neck was soaked in blood. "But I think there are one or two more of them in the wood."

One or two more?

She swallowed hard. "I shall be ready this time."

"Good girl."

Isobel grabbed FitzAlan's sleeve to break his fall as he slid to the ground.

Chapter Nineteen

*I*sobel kept watch as before. FitzAlan's color was not good. Not good at all. She leaned down and put her ear to his chest again. *Thump thump, thump thump.* The strength of his heartbeat reassured her. *Thump thump, thump thump.*

She heard a rustle and opened her eyes to see a man leading a horse through the trees. There was no use hiding. The log did not block them from this side, and the man had already seen them. She got to her feet and stood in front of FitzAlan.

The man halted several feet away, giving her time to notice the glint of silver on his horse's saddle and his fine clothing. This one was a nobleman. A French nobleman.

"Lord FitzAlan, the English king's great commander, reduced to having a woman champion." He shook his head and gave her a bemused smile. "It is quite splendid of you, dear lady. But hopeless, nonetheless."

So this was no random attack! These men knew their quarry. Somehow they must have learned FitzAlan rode out without his men today. But how was that possible? Who could have told them? And gotten the word to them so quickly?

The man took a step forward, and she shouted, "Halt!"

"I will not hurt you," the man said, his voice calm. "'Tis FitzAlan I've come for."

"What will you do with him?"

"Take him for ransom." He took another step forward. "FitzAlan is quite a prize, you know."

Isobel did not believe him for a moment. These men had sought to kill FitzAlan from the start.

"Halt," she cried again as the man took yet another step forward. She kept her sword pointed at him.

"I may have to take you with me; otherwise, no one will believe me," he said, sounding amused. "I'll wager your husband will pay a hefty sum to have you back."

A cold calm settled over her as she accepted she would have to fight him. She felt a wave of gratitude toward Stephen. Every day he practiced with her had made her better. But would she be good enough? She looked the man over, to judge him as Stephen had taught her.

Nothing about him reassured her. He was taller and stronger than she was. What worried her more was that he walked with an easy grace that suggested he would be quick and light on his feet. Damn, damn, damn.

What did Stephen tell her? Find her advantage and use it. Too bad she had no skirt to lift to show her ankles.

She remembered Stephen's reaction to her leggings and unfastened her cloak with one hand. When she shrugged it off, the man dropped the point of his sword and gaped open-mouthed at her legs. Before she could overcome her surprise at how well it worked, he brought his gaze back up to meet her eyes.

"I'd wager your husband finds you a handful." His tone was still amused, but the glint in his eyes had her backing up. "I would love to be there when you explain to him how you happen to be traveling alone with FitzAlan and his brother...dressed as a man."

Her heel hit FitzAlan's prone form. She could step back no farther. With the man just two or three feet beyond the reach of her sword, she could wait no longer to begin her farce. She made a clumsy swing at him with her sword.

This time, she did not miss her moment.

When the man threw his head back, roaring with laughter, she lunged forward with her sword aimed straight at his heart. At the last instant, he jumped back and saved himself.

"You are full of surprises!" He was smiling, but he had his sword at the ready now.

She had no more tricks. There was nothing for it but to fight as best she could. He came at her hard and fast. The first attack she fended off. Then the second, and the third. But he was quick and strong, and more skilled than she.

"I see 'tis true that chivalry is dead among the French nobility," she jeered. "You are the worst kind of coward, to attack a man so gravely injured and a defenseless woman."

"You are hardly defenseless, my dear." He was circling, waiting for her to give him an opening. "I must ask, who was your teacher?"

She did have one advantage left, after all. From the way he was fighting, he was trying only to disarm her. She fought with no such constraint; she would kill him if he gave her half a chance.

As they moved forward and back, swords clanging, he showed no concern he might lose. In sooth, the man appeared to be enjoying himself. He spun in a circle, returning in time to block her thrust. Good heavens, the fool was showing off!

The next time he spun about, she was ready. She lunged at once, putting all her weight behind it. Somehow he managed to duck below her sword, and she fell crashing forward. The air went out of her as he caught her around the waist.

"You tried to kill me!" the man said.

He hit her wrist with the side of his hand. The sharp pain made her hand go numb, and she dropped her sword.

"For that, I shall make you watch FitzAlan die," he said. "He must mean a good deal to you, for you to risk your life for him."

She kicked and screamed and bit as he dragged her with one arm back to where FitzAlan lay unmoving beside the log. Holding her against his side with one arm, he raised his sword arm over FitzAlan. The bandage around FitzAlan's neck looked like a bloody target.

"No, no!" she screamed.

He raised his sword higher. Desperate to stop him, she wrenched sideways, caught his raised arm, and clung to it.

The man threw her to the ground. Her head hit something hard, stunning her. When her vision cleared, she saw him raising his sword again. She scrambled across the rough ground on hands and knees and flung herself on top of FitzAlan.

The man above her was shouting a string of curses at her, but Isobel was screaming back. Suddenly, he jerked her to her knees by her hair. She looked up at the man's face, mottled with rage, and braced herself to be backhanded across the face.

As he swung his arm back to strike her, she heard a roar. The man turned, his arm frozen in midair. From the corner of her eye, she saw a blur of movement through the trees.

Thunk!

She stared at the hilt of a blade protruding from the man's left eye socket. Blood gushed from it, splattering on her. Even when his grip on her hair loosened and he fell to the ground, her mind could not yet grasp what had happened. She felt herself sway just before strong arms caught her.

Then Stephen was holding her against him. He was squeezing the breath out of her, but she did not care. As he covered her face with kisses, she sucked in gasps of air that came out as choked sobs. He murmured into her hair words she did not try to understand. But his voice comforted her.

She could not say how long he held her. It might have been an eternity, but it would never be enough.

Once her heart stopped pounding so violently in her chest and her sobbing subsided, a dense wave of exhaustion rolled over her. The leaf-strewn floor of the forest swirled beneath her.

"Thank you," she whispered and closed her eyes.

* * *

Stephen entered the wood riding at a pace that risked his horse, cursing himself for taking so long. Damn, there had been just too many of them. He charged into them, slashing his sword from side to side. He killed two in the first foray, but the next two took more time. While he fought them, the others scattered.

A few rode off across the fields, but he thought he saw at least two go into the wood. That was why he was riding like a madman through the trees.

He rode straight for the log where he'd left Isobel and William. When he saw them, his heart stopped in his chest. Isobel's body lay over William's. A man stood over them, holding a sword. God, no! They were dead! He was too late!

Over the sound of his horse crashing through the trees, he heard Isobel's screams as the son of Satan lifted her up by the hair.

Stephen was very good with a knife—he'd learned from William, after all—but could he risk throwing it with Isobel so close? When the man drew his arm back to strike her, a yell of rage and madness ripped from Stephen's throat. As he thundered down on them, he threw the blade through the trees.

Then, in one motion, he leapt off his horse and pulled Isobel into his arms. Nothing in his life would ever feel as good as holding her against him at this moment.

He wanted to weep with relief. God in heaven, what a woman! Fighting like a she-wolf, screaming curses at the man. Jesus help him, she used her body to shield William!

When her knees gave way, he carried her to the log and held her while he scanned the woods. There could be one or two more in the wood. When he spotted two bodies lying on the ground, he blew his breath out with a whoosh. Thank God.

He turned to check on William. *Oh, God,* but William was pale. Moving quickly, he pulled the flask from inside his shirt and held it to Isobel's mouth until she drank. As soon as she was able to sit on her own, he dropped to his knees beside his brother.

William's pulse was strong, but he'd lost a lot of blood. If they got him somewhere safe—and soon—he could be saved. As he replaced the bloodied bandage with a strip of cloth from his shirt, he looked up at Isobel. She was almost as pale as William.

"We must go quickly," he said. "Where are the horses?"

His question seemed to startle her out of her daze. She got up at once, saying, "I shall get them."

As he cradled William's head to pour ale down his throat, William opened his eyes.

"Bit slow, weren't you?" William said in a weak whisper.

Good God, William was teasing him.

"I shall have to tie you to your horse," he said.

William attempted to nod and winced with pain.

Stephen looked up to see Isobel coming through the trees, leading the horses.

"Ready?" he said to William. "One, two, three."

William gasped as Stephen lifted him onto the log.

At Stephen's nod, Isobel brought William's horse around and held him steady.

"One, two, three," he said again to warn William and then hoisted him up onto the horse.

William got his feet in the stirrups before slumping forward over his horse's neck.

Just as well he is not awake for this.

As he tied his brother to the saddle, he looked over his shoulder at Isobel. She was mounted and awaiting his signal, her face serious and intent.

"The abbey is not far," he said, keeping his voice calm. "I don't want to frighten you, but we must get there with all possible haste. The monks will know what to do for William."

He did not tell her his other reason for haste. If this was not a random attack—and he suspected it was not—those men would not give up easily and move on to other prey. They could be part of a larger force, as well.

Stephen rode in front, leading William's horse. Twice Isobel called out that William was sliding off, and he had to stop. He told Isobel to stay mounted and kept his eyes on the horizon as he retied the ropes.

When the abbey finally came into view, he gave a silent prayer of thanks. Surely God was with them this day.

As they approached, the gates opened and Jamie and Geoffrey came running out. Jamie went at once to William.

"How badly is he injured?" Jamie had his knife out, ready to cut the ropes.

"Best to keep him on the horse until we are inside," Stephen said as he tossed the reins to Jamie.

Jamie swung up behind his father. Leaning protectively over William, he spurred the horse through the gates, across a narrow bridge, and up the short slope of the outer courtyard to the church. With monks trailing him now, he turned his horse and rode along the side of the church and through an arched doorway.

Stephen ducked his head as he followed Jamie through the arch. With a twinge of uneasiness, he realized they were in the monks' cloister. God might forgive them for bringing horses into this quiet place, but the monks would not.

"The infirmary is there," Jamie said, pointing to a doorway off the opposite side of the small courtyard.

Together they cut the ropes and lifted William down. Jamie blanched when William's head lolled back, revealing the bloody bandage around his neck.

Stephen met his nephew's frightened eyes. "There is no one stronger. He will make it." Stephen needed to believe it, too.

"With God's help."

Stephen turned to see who had spoken. It was an ancient monk with a bent back and pure white tonsured hair. The monk waved them through the low doorway Jamie had pointed to and followed them inside. As they laid William down on a cot in the corner, he moaned. He did not waken, but he was alive.

"Bring me the lamp," the monk said as he lowered himself onto a stool beside the cot.

While Jamie fetched a lamp from across the room, the old monk pressed his ear against William's chest.

"The heart is strong, and he is able to draw air," the monk said as he straightened. "Remove the bandage."

Stephen knelt beside the cot. As soon as he cut off the blood-soaked bandage, the old monk cleaned the wound from a basin of water he seemed to pull from the air. The monk snapped his fingers at Jamie and pointed to several pots on a shelf. Faster than seemed possible, he mixed a smelly paste.

"Does he have other injuries?" the monk asked as he spread the paste with flat, bent-back thumbs over the oozing wound.

"Just this one," Stephen said, "where he took an arrow."

"Has he wakened since?"

"Once, briefly, more than an hour ago."

"He awoke a second time," Isobel said behind him.

Until he heard her voice, Stephen did not realize she had followed them inside. He was grateful for her presence. It comforted him to have her near.

"There was a man I did not see," she said, a quaver in her voice. "Lord FitzAlan threw a dagger into his heart."

Stephen reached for her hand and squeezed it, then kissed her icy fingers. "'Tis so like William, to wake just when needed to save the day. He is the best man I know."

Stephen heard a choking sound behind him and got to his feet to put an arm around Jamie.

"'Tis my fault he is hurt," Jamie said in a cracked voice.

"Nay, the blame is mine, not yours," Stephen said, feeling the full weight of his misdeeds. "I am so sorry."

The old monk's ears were still sharp. "'Tis God's will this

man was struck," he said without turning. "And with God's help, he will survive."

He turned on his stool and craned his neck to look up at them. "You are all big fellows, are you not? It will take time for this one to get his strength back, but he will heal."

"He will recover?" Jamie asked.

"He is not out of danger. But aye, I believe he will." The monk made a shooing motion toward Stephen and Isobel. "Take the woman and leave the lad with me. I need only one pair of helping hands."

Stephen nodded but said, "I need a word with my nephew first." Best to get this over with.

"I know what I told you upset you," he said when he had Jamie in the far corner of the room. "It all happened a long time ago, when your mother was not much older than you are now. 'Tis not my place to tell you the whole of it, but neither is it yours to judge her. She did what she had to do to survive."

Jamie kept his gaze on the floor and his lips pressed tight together, but he was listening.

"William has been father to you since you were a child of three," he said. "You've always known you do not share his blood, but you are the son of his heart."

Jamie nodded and wiped his nose on his sleeve. "He is the best of fathers."

"And your mother?"

"I wish she were here," Jamie whispered. "The rest doesn't seem important anymore."

Stephen gave Jamie's shoulder a squeeze and led him back to the cot where William lay. Under the old monk's ministrations, William's color was already much improved. He appeared to be resting comfortably.

"Your father is in good hands," Stephen said. "He will be fine, I am sure of it."

This time when the old monk shooed them, Stephen thanked him for his care and left with Isobel. Outside in the cloister, they found Geoffrey waiting. The tall, distinguished-looking man with him could only be the abbot.

"We are grateful for your hospitality," Stephen said after Geoffrey introduced them.

The abbot took Stephen's arm and led him a few steps down the walkway. "We welcome travelers, of course, but these are troubled times," he said in a low voice and shook his head. "And we are a small abbey. It is...difficult...for us to accommodate...female guests...comfortably."

Stephen suspected the abbot was concerned not so much with Isobel's comfort as with the brethren's peace. Having a beautiful woman—dressed in leggings, no less—within the confines of the small abbey was a disruption the abbot did not want.

"We shan't stay long," Stephen assured him. "I intend to ride back to Caen under cover of darkness tonight and return on the morrow with a large contingent of soldiers."

The abbot's eyes widened in alarm. "We have but two small guest rooms—" he began in a querulous voice.

"If it is safe to move my brother," Stephen interrupted, "we shall all depart by midday tomorrow."

The abbot heaved a sigh of relief. "One of our brothers grew up in the next village. He can lead you the first part of the way in the dark."

The abbot wanted them gone.

"I will have food brought to you in the guest quarters," the abbot said.

"You are too kind," Stephen said. "Perhaps after we eat I could take Lady Hume outside for a walk?"

"A walk would be just the thing to soothe her," the abbot said, brightening at the prospect of having Isobel removed for the afternoon. "There is a lovely path that goes along the river and up to our orchard. The land is within the precinct walls, so it is quite safe."

Stephen ate with Geoffrey and Isobel at the small table in the woman's tiny guest room. As they ate, he questioned Isobel about what happened after he left her and William in the wood.

His stomach tightened as she told him. How close he'd come to losing them both! It took his breath away to think about it. He hoped Isobel did not realize the men would have raped her first; he wished he did not know it himself.

The image of her sprawled over William's body, when he thought them both dead, was burned into his memory forever. He took her hand, not caring what her brother might think.

"A walk would help take our minds off all that has happened," he said. "The abbot told me there is a path we can follow along the river."

"If we are to leave tomorrow," Geoffrey said, getting to his feet, "I would like to spend the remaining hours praying before the abbey's holy relic."

Isobel gave him a faint smile. "'Tis why you came."

"But please take Isobel," Geoffrey urged him. "It will do her good."

Isobel's brother was naive to the point of foolishness. Stephen knew damn well what would happen if they went out alone this afternoon. After their brush with death, neither of them was likely to exercise caution this time.

Stephen got to his feet as Geoffrey went to the door.

"I shall pray for Lord FitzAlan's recovery," Geoffrey said.

"Thank you," Stephen said. Looking down at Isobel, he added, "We are all in need of your prayers today."

As Geoffrey's footsteps echoed on the stone floor outside the room, Stephen held his hands out to Isobel. He knew what he wanted now. If she was willing, he would have her.

Isobel met his eyes, making no pretense she did not understand. She took his hands.

Chapter Twenty

*I*sobel saw the naked hunger in Stephen's eyes. If she were going to refuse him, she must do it now. She took his hands. Today she did not care what was right or wrong, wise or foolhardy. This one time, she would take the man she wanted, not the man she must. She would allow herself this gift and not think about what came after.

There was no falseness between them. No pretense as to what they intended to do. Without a word passing between them, Stephen took the woolen blankets from the cot and folded them beneath his cloak.

They followed the stone walkway past the kitchen. Beyond the kitchen garden, they found the gate that led to the river path. Thankfully, it was neither the season for harvesting apples from the orchard nor the time of day for hauling in the fish lines for the monks' dinner. There was no sign of another living soul on the river path.

Once they were hidden from view by the trees, Stephen

put his arm about her shoulders. She sighed and leaned into him. It felt right, walking with him like this.

After the harrowing events of the morning, the chirping birds and gurgle of the river soothed her. The sun was out, and the air had none of the blister of March she was used to in Northumberland. Spring came early here. The trees were budding, and crocuses poked their bright heads out of the ground. An unexpected peace settled over her.

Neither spoke until they came to a fork in the path.

"Do we continue along the river, or go to the orchard?" Stephen asked, waving his arm first in one direction, then the other.

Stephen's lopsided smile made him look so handsome that, on impulse, she reached up to touch his face. As soon as her fingers grazed his stubbled cheek, his smile left him. His eyes darkened, sending a rush of desire through her that almost curled her toes.

"Come," he said and pulled her by the hand up the orchard path.

They moved with a sense of urgency now. As the trail went uphill, they left the scrub trees that grew near the river. They entered a field that would soon be planted with wheat or rye. Beyond the field was the apple orchard. An old croft stood between the two, its wooden door hanging at an angle.

"This is such a pretty spot," she said, looking around her. "What would make a tenant abandon this croft?"

"Likely he had to," Stephen said as he heaved the door open, "when his lord gave the land to the abbey."

As Isobel stepped over the threshold, she saw that the croft had not been abandoned so very long ago. The sun poured in through gaping holes in the thatched roof, but the walls had not yet begun to crumble. There were piles of leaves in the corners where the wind had blown them.

Her heart rose to her throat as she watched Stephen clear debris from the earthen floor with his boot and spread one of the blankets. Knowing it would happen now, she was suddenly gripped by nerves.

Stephen turned and took her hands. "Are you sure you want this?" he asked in a quiet voice. "We can still go back."

"I want to stay." How like him to make her say it. With Stephen, she could never pretend to herself she was seduced against her will.

She saw his Adam's apple rise and fall as he swallowed. He pushed a stray strand of hair from her face, following it with his eyes. "I do not want you to have regrets."

"I shall have none."

When this did not seem sufficient to reassure him, she said, "If I died today . . ." She ran her tongue over her dry lips and tried again. "What I would regret is never knowing how it feels to bed a man I want to touch me."

She could never have been so bold to say this to another man. Somehow, she knew Stephen would neither judge her nor make her feel bad for it.

When he still made no move toward her, she rose on her tiptoes and touched her lips to his. His lips felt so soft and warm, the kiss unbearably sweet. She had expected lust, not this tenderness that welled up in her chest until she felt she might burst with it.

When she dropped back onto her heels, he held her face in his hands and ran a thumb along her cheek. "You need only tell me if you change your mind."

Did he not want this as much as she did?

"But I hope to God you won't," he said before the uneasy feeling could take hold. Then he scooped her up in his arms and held her across his chest.

Their eyes were locked as he dropped to his knees and

lay her down on the makeshift pallet. As his mouth met hers, she felt as though she were still sinking back. The kiss was warm and deep, their tongues moving against each other.

When he broke away, she would have complained— except that the kisses he ran along the side of her face felt so good. A deep sigh escaped her, and she gave herself over to following the course of his lips. He pressed kisses along her jaw and behind her ear. As he moved down her neck, he unfastened her cloak and pushed it off her shoulders.

"I love this spot, right here," he said and ran his tongue along the hollow above her collarbone.

She forgot she wore her brother's clothes until she felt the warmth of Stephen's breath through the cloth at her throat. Wanting to feel his mouth against her skin, she began tugging at the tunic and shirt that were in the way.

"Let me," he said, taking hold of her hands. "Please."

Grinning, he rose to his knees, unfastened his cloak, and tossed it in the corner. He lifted her tunic and began to pull her shirt out of her leggings ever so slowly. The smooth linen fabric moved against her skin, followed by a rush of cool air.

She would never have guessed that his lips, his tongue, his loose hair, would feel so good against the bare skin of her belly. As he inched his way slowly upward, exposing more skin as he went, she felt a tightening in her womb.

Oh, my. She shivered with the sensations racing through her body. When he abruptly stopped and pulled her shirt back over her stomach, she opened her eyes wide.

Stephen was on his hands and knees above her, a frown of concern on his face. "You are cold."

"Nay, I am not," she said.

The brocade of his tunic felt rough under her fingers as she took hold of it and pulled him down. Despite the deep, lingering kiss she gave him, he held his body away from hers.

"I want to feel you against me," she whispered.

"Oh, Isobel," he said, sliding down beside her and burying his face in her neck, "you will undo me."

He held her tight against him so that she could feel his warmth from her head to her toes. She pressed her face against him, blocking out the faint smell of rotting apples from the orchard and the heavier smell of mildewed thatch. She wanted to breathe in only his scent. Horse and healthy sweat and wool and leather. And just Stephen.

When he kissed her this time, he did not hold back. The passion exploded between them. She wrapped her arms around him and pressed against him until a blade of grass could not have fit between them. And still, she was not close enough.

When he rolled on top of her, he felt so good that she tore her mouth away to tell him. Before she could form the words, he slid down her body, kissing her through the cloth until, again, he found bare skin. His mouth felt as good on her belly as the first time.

As he moved upward, she breathed, "Don't stop this time."

He moved so slowly that her breasts were aching for his touch long before he got to them. Hardly aware of what she was doing, she ran her own hands over them. She heard Stephen groan and felt his large, warm hands cover hers.

"Jesus, Isobel," he whispered, "you cannot expect me to go slowly when you do that."

"Must you go slowly?"

He gave a half-strangled sound and lifted one of her hands to press his mouth against her palm. When he ran his tongue in a circle over it, she felt her nipple harden through the fabric beneath her other hand. She drew in a sharp breath as he ran his thumb along the underside of her breast.

"Mmmmm," came from her throat as he dragged his tongue along the line his thumb had just traveled. She arched her back, lifting her breasts to him.

"Aye," she breathed as his other hand slid under her shirt, and "aye," again, when it finally covered her breast.

The rough skin of his thumb over her nipple sent ripples of sensation down to the depths of her belly.

She meant to offer another word of encouragement. But then he rolled her nipple between his finger and thumb, and the sounds that came from her lips would not shape themselves into words. She felt the warm wetness of his mouth on her other nipple and was lost in a swirl of sensation.

How did he know how she wanted to be touched before she knew it herself? The more he touched her, the greater was her need. Never, never did she imagine it would be like this.

He pulled her up to a sitting position, and they leaned against each other, both breathing hard.

"Stephen, that felt..." She tried, but she could not find words to describe it.

"Can we take this off?" he asked, fingering the bottom edge of her tunic.

"You first," she surprised herself by saying.

He rewarded her with a wide grin that lit up his eyes. Before she knew it, he whipped off his tunic and shirt together in one quick movement and sat before her bare-chested.

She drew in a long breath as she ran her eyes over the hard muscles of his chest. How many other women had looked at him like this and found him so beautiful it made them ache? She would not let herself think of those other women now. Today he was hers and no other's.

She reached out and ran possessive hands over his chest, feeling the roughness of hair over the sinewy muscle and warm skin. This close, she could see that black hairs were interspersed with the curly auburn hair on his chest. She followed the hair down to his flat belly.

Would it feel as good to him as it had to her to kiss him there? When she dropped her head to try, he gripped her shoulders and pulled her up onto his chest. She feared she'd done something wrong—until he smashed his mouth against hers.

"Your clothes now. All of them, off," he gasped against her ear. "I need to feel you naked against me."

She lifted her arms without a word and let him pull shirt and tunic over her head.

"My God, you are beautiful."

A small voice in the back of her head asked how a man who'd seen so many women's breasts could manage to sound awed. When he lifted his gaze to her face, though, he looked as though he meant it. Whatever he might think later, right now he wanted no one but her. It was enough.

When Stephen gathered her into his arms again, she understood. Skin to skin, it had to be. His chest felt so good against her bare breasts she had to close her eyes to bear it. The kiss he gave her was at once so gentle and so full of longing she felt as if he were squeezing her heart in his hands.

Stephen, Stephen, Stephen. No other man could kiss like this, she was sure.

A surge of lust ran through her that had her rubbing herself against him like a cat. Without lifting his mouth from hers, he rolled her until she felt the scratch of the wool blanket beneath her back. She ran her hands over him, reveling in the feel of skin and tight muscle beneath her fingers.

He kissed her throat, then moved down to suckle first one

breast and then the other. Sensations tore through her until she was arching against him and begging for she knew not what.

When he began to ease down the top of her leggings, she felt a moment of panic. 'Twas a serious sin she was about to commit. At least she broke no vow, in this brief respite between marriages.

It was *possible* Stephen could get her with child. But how likely from just one time? Not once did she conceive in all her years of marriage. Surely the risk was small. In any case, she would be married soon enough.

Stephen ran his tongue along her abdomen, wiping all such thoughts and fears from her mind. If she never felt this reckless joy and passion again, she would have it now.

She lifted her hips to help him slide the leggings down. As he pulled off first one leg, then the other, he paused to kiss her thigh, her knee, her calf. He sucked her toe into his mouth as he ran his hand slowly up the inside of her leg. A shiver ran through her.

He had her completely naked now. She watched his chest rise and fall as he raked his eyes over her. His slow perusal sent her pulse beating so hard she thought he must hear it.

When she shivered again, he lay down beside her and spread the other blanket over them.

"Are you warm enough, sweetheart?" he asked and kissed her shoulder.

She nodded and tried to concentrate on the feel of his callused hand running up and down her side. And not on how easily "sweetheart" and "love" rolled off his tongue.

"What is it, Isobel?"

So much was right, she did not want to ruin it. She rested her hand on his shoulder and met his troubled brown eyes.

"I did not know it would feel as good as this," she said and felt the taut muscles relax beneath her fingers.

He nuzzled her neck and playfully bit her earlobe. But that was not what she wanted now. She moved his hand from her side to her breast and turned in to him to give him an open-mouthed kiss. His playfulness vanished.

With a fierceness that matched her own, he kissed her back. He gripped her hip, and she liked the strong, possessive feel of his hand there. When he slid his other hand up the inside of her thigh, her whole body tensed with anticipation. Surely it would not be long before they committed the final act of sin.

The thought of having him inside her sent a spasm through her even before his fingers reached her center. Once he touched her, his fingers moved in ways that did magical things to her.

"What are you doing?" she asked, a little breathless.

"If you do not know, then your husband truly was a swine," he murmured. "Do you wish me to stop?" From the humor in his tone, she could tell he was confident of her answer.

"But...but...," she tried to speak but could not hold her thought long enough. "I never...this feels so...so...so very..."

She rubbed the back of her hand against his hard stomach. When she brushed against the rough cloth of his leggings, she grabbed his forearm to stop his hand. "Will you not take your leggings off, as well?"

"What is it you want, Isobel?" His voice was soft, but she heard the tension in it.

"I—I—" She fell silent, embarrassed by what she'd been about to say.

"You must feel free to tell me anything, love," he said, touching her cheek. "Especially when we are in bed."

If she were going to have only this one time with him, she wanted it just right. She could not have explained why, but she could not bear the thought of him just pulling it out of his leggings to take her.

Though it made her cheeks flush hot, she told him. "I want you as naked as I when we are joined."

"I can bring you pleasure, sweetheart, without putting my cock inside you."

The crude directness of his words startled her. 'Twas hard to think past "bring you pleasure" and "cock inside you."

"If we are to avoid the risk of getting you with child, 'tis best I leave my leggings on." He ran a finger along the side of her face and said, "Believe me, it will be harder for us to stop in time if they are off."

She looked into those melting brown eyes and heard herself ask, "Must we stop?"

He coughed, then said in a choked whisper, "I want you to be sure. This is a serious choice we make here."

From what she heard about him, it was a choice he made all the time. She felt her heart constrict. "Do you not want to?"

His eyes flashed, and he broke into a wolfish grin. "Oh, aye, without a doubt I do," he said. "In sooth, I can think of nothing but being inside you."

His words sent a jolt of desire through her.

"'Tis all I can do," he said, tracing her bottom lip with his finger, "to keep myself from employing every argument I have to convince you."

In a voice just above a whisper, she asked, "What arguments would you make?"

"Not the kind you hear with your ears." He gave her another of those devilish grins that nearly stopped her heart.

He kissed her senseless then. When he guided her hand to the fastening of his leggings, she felt a lurch of awareness as her fingers touched the hardness of his shaft through the cloth. She rubbed her palm down its length, reveling in the moan he made. She sucked on his tongue as she rubbed up and down, pulling new sounds from deep in his throat.

"You will have me spilling my seed like a youth," he said, grabbing her wrist.

She smiled, pleased at the desperation in his voice. "You said you would take your leggings off."

He sat bolt upright. After a couple of quick movements under the blanket, he raised his arm aloft with the leggings and threw them across the room. This time when he took her into his arms and kissed her, he was fully naked against her.

And heaven above, he felt good!

The feel of his shaft pushing against her belly sent a thrill through her, right to her core. She bit his shoulder as she ran her hands down the small of his back and over the firm, rounded muscles of his buttocks. He slipped his hand between her legs. As his fingers went round and round, he swallowed her moans in deep liquid kisses.

His breath was hot in her ear. "How does this feel?"

"I—I..." *What did he ask?* She could concentrate on nothing but what he was doing to her with his hand. "Don't stop. Please."

"I won't," he said in a husky voice, "not until you cry my name in your pleasure."

She did not understand what this feeling was welling up inside her.

"Trust me."

She did trust him. She did.

He lowered himself to pull the tip of her breast into his mouth, his hand never stopping. Tension grew and grew in her. She could feel it in him, too. In the tautness of his muscles, the pulsing shaft against her thigh, the heat vibrating off his skin. As he sucked her breast harder, she pressed herself against his hand, her body wanting still more from him.

When she thought she could bear no more, her body spasmed in wave after wave of pleasure that shook her to her very soul.

Oh God oh God oh God.

After, her limbs felt weak and limp. Stephen's head rested against her chest; his heart beat wildly against her stomach. With an effort, she lifted one hand and ran her fingers through his hair. She felt a small squeeze inside her when she felt his hard shaft against her leg.

Just when his head began to feel heavy on her chest, he turned with her so that they were on their sides, face to face.

"I never felt that before," she told him.

He took her face in his hands and gave her a kiss that was slow and deep. When he hooked his leg around her, she ran her hand over the taut muscle of thigh and buttock. All the while, they kissed, tongues sliding against each other.

She wanted to touch him. When she reached down and ran her finger along the length of his shaft, he drew in a sharp breath.

"Could you?" he asked in a tight voice. He wrapped her hand around it and moved their hands together to show her what he wanted.

Even she realized where this was going. She stopped her hand. "You said you wanted to be inside me."

He drew back to peer into her face. "You have given yourself to no man but your husband." He paused, then asked, "Why choose me, Isobel? Why me?"

Why did the reason matter to him?

"I've come this far in my sin. I want to know all of it," she said. That was part of it, but far from all.

Was that disappointment in his eyes? Hurt? What did he want her to say? That she knew no other man could make her feel this way?

"You are the only one I would have." Her pride would let her confess only this much. "The only one I want."

Feeling uncertain, she kissed his cheek and guided his hand to where he had touched her before. She wondered uneasily if he would jerk his hand away when he felt how wet she was. Instead, he groaned with what sounded like almost painful pleasure.

Soon she was lost in his kisses, his touches, the burning heat between them. She hardly noticed when he rolled her onto her back. When she felt the tip of his shaft against her opening, all she could think was *at last, at last, at last.* She may have whimpered the words aloud.

They both gasped when he pushed into her. She wrapped her arms and legs tight around him. She clung to him as he moved against her, slowly at first and then faster.

"Sorry. I cannot...last too long...this time," he gasped, "I...can...not."

He was ramming into her, harder and faster with each thrust. *Harder, harder, harder,* she egged him on. A burst of pleasure hit her, even stronger than the one before, and she cried out.

He was trying to pull away from her, but she held on to him with all her strength, refusing to let him go. And then he was moving inside her again and she was weeping and calling his name, over and over. He cried out with her, and she felt his seed empty inside her.

When he finally lay still in her arms, she held him to her, saying his name again and again and kissing his face and hair.

"Jesus," he said without lifting his head. He rolled to the

side, pulling her with him, and tucked her head under his chin. In a fading voice, he said, "Isobel, my love, my ..."

She heard his breathing grow steady. Could he possibly have fallen asleep? Nothing short of a wild boar could have gotten her to move, but she was too awash in emotions to sleep. A hundred questions spun through her head as she tried to fathom what had happened between them, and to her.

She leaned back, taking advantage of his dozing to study him in repose. In the shaft of sunlight that fell upon his hair, she saw that what looked auburn from afar was in fact a hundred shades of red and gold.

His face was near perfect, to her mind. She liked his straight dark brows, his strong jaw and cheekbones, the blade nose, the glint of bristles from a day's growth of beard. His generous mouth. Even at rest, the corners seemed to tip up.

She felt an overwhelming tenderness toward him. Was it merely gratitude for the unexpected pleasures he gave her? Was it something else? Something more?

She brushed a lock of hair away from his face and sighed. What did it matter? She recalled her mother's last words to her: *We women are born to suffer.*

Aye, she would suffer for this.

But she would not regret it.

* * *

Stephen kept his eyes closed, not wanting to waken and find it was all a dream. A smile spread across his face. Nay, that could not have been a dream. He'd always known Isobel had a passionate nature beneath that sober exterior, but God in heaven, he was a lucky man.

Aye, he must admit to one disappointment. He was not so foolish as to expect her to profess abounding love. But she did not even admit to a particular fondness for him. Did she simply desire him? Surely that alone would not be enough for a woman like Isobel to cross the line and commit herself.

Even at the end, he tried to pull out to preserve at least some possibility she could change her mind and avoid the marriage. God knew how hard that was! Surely she understood why he did it. Her answer was unmistakable: she wrapped her legs around him like a visc.

It had been heaven.

Other men could give her pleasure, so that could not be the only reason she chose him. Since the only other man she'd been with was that ancient husband of hers, it was possible she did not know that. Well, she would never know it now. No man but he would touch her again. He'd cut de Roche's hands off if he tried.

Strong mutual desire was not a bad start to marriage; it was more than many had. She enjoyed his company. Still, he hoped she saw more in him than a charming jester who could please her in bed. He wanted her to think better of him than that. Nay, he wanted to *be* a better man than that for her.

He opened his eyes. The sight of her was like a sharp stab to his heart. She looked unspeakably lovely, with her tousled dark hair, smooth pale skin, and serious green eyes.

"Did I sleep long?" he asked.

A softness came into her eyes, and a hint of a smile lifted the corners of her mouth. She shook her head a fraction.

"I am a lout to let you get chilled," he said, gathering her into his arms. "Good Lord, you are covered in gooseflesh!"

He rubbed her back and arms until she laughed and begged him to stop. As he held her to him, he glanced up through the holes in the roof to judge the light.

She must have heard his sigh, for she asked, "What is it?"

"We must return to the abbey in another hour," he said.

"The monks have their supper early. If we are not back before then, someone is bound to notice we are still gone."

She shrugged one fine-boned shoulder.

"Surely you do not want to be the cause of even more sinful thoughts among these poor monks?" he chided her with a smile. "You'll have them doing penance for months."

When she laughed at his joke, he had to kiss her. And just like that, he was hard again. From the way her eyes widened when he leaned back to look at her, she'd noticed. Her lips curved upward. A very good sign.

"You need do no more than look at me, and I want you." He breathed in the summery smell of wildflowers in her hair and felt her nipples harden against his chest.

This time, he intended to take her slowly. He did not know when they might have opportunity to sneak away again, so he wanted to be sure she would not soon forget. As he kissed her, he wondered vaguely if the king would truly banish him to Ireland for this. If so, their next time together might be on a boat.

"Do you get seasick?" he asked between nips at her earlobe.

"Mmmm?" she asked, but when he stuck his tongue in her ear and pressed his shaft against her thigh, he knew she forgot his question.

When she reached down and took him in her hand, he forgot it, too.

He was a man who knew how to please a woman; usually he went about it with deliberation. This was different. With her, he went on instinct and emotion. From touch to touch to touch, he followed her sighs. He sought to make every inch of her his own.

There was no need for caution this time. When he finally entered her, he thrust all the way into her. She welcomed him, moved with him. This time, he made it last.

"You are mine," he told her as he moved inside her. "Only mine."

She was his. Now and forever.

After, he was flooded with such tenderness toward her that he could find no words to tell her. He could not speak at all, except to whisper into her hair, "Isobel, my love, my love."

As they walked hand in hand back to the abbey, he felt relaxed, happy. Surprising, how content he felt at the prospect of being bound for life. "Forsaking all others" gave him no twinges of regret. Truth be told, he was relieved to have done with that part of his life. Isobel was all he wanted.

Stephen began to make his plan. To win the king's blessing, he must have all his ducks in a row. It would be wise to have William with him when he approached the king. A shame Catherine was not here to play on her childhood friendship with King Henry. But Robert would speak for him, too.

The king would insist on questioning Isobel. That could not be helped, but he would prepare her.

All would be well. He would see to it.

Chapter Twenty-one

*I*sobel lay on the hard cot in the small, windowless guest room. The long night stretched out before her. At midnight, Stephen left for Caen, promising to return with twenty armed men two hours after first light.

She did not see him alone after they returned from the orchard. When they went to check on FitzAlan, they could hear him arguing with the old monk from outside the infirmary door. Reassured, Isabel left Stephen to spend the remaining hours at his brother's bedside.

She was so exhausted she felt light-headed. But how could she sleep when the rough blanket still smelled of him? She held it to her nose and drew in a deep breath. She wanted to remember every moment of their afternoon together.

Every touch, every look, every word. The way her stomach fluttered as she watched him spread the blanket. The solicitude and longing warring in his eyes when he asked if she was certain. From that first soft kiss, there was no chance of her changing her mind. She brushed her fingers over her lips now, remembering it.

Though vivid, her memory after that was a jumble of sensations and emotion. She'd had no notion being with a man could be like that. It was a wonder couples who had that kind of passion between them ever left their beds.

Perhaps it was rare for it to be so perfect.

Regardless of what others might have, all she had was one afternoon. One afternoon of her life! She balled her hands into fists and pounded the thin mat beneath her.

After her burst of frustration, the bleakness of her future settled over her like a heavy weight. Tears trickled down the sides of her face and into her hair. Perhaps tomorrow she could be hopeful about her life with de Roche, but not tonight. Not when the smell of Stephen was on her blanket and her skin still burned with the memory of his touch.

Would it have been better not to have gone with him? Better not to know what it was like? He could not have been kinder or more passionate. He gave her such pleasure she thought she might die from it. And happily so.

Nay, she could not wish she had not done it. She was a sinful woman. And an unrepentant one.

Stephen made her feel as if she were special to him. Perhaps that was his secret, the reason women were so drawn to him. He made each one believe it. For once, she felt sympathy for Marie de Lisieux. She understood why Marie could not let him go, even when it was plain to all he was done with her.

Isobel had too much pride for that. And she had her duty. Even if she had a choice—which she did not—she was bound by her promise to the king. She was not like her father. She would not abandon loyalty and honor with every change in the wind.

Soon she would make her pledge to de Roche. A sacred pledge.

Just for a moment, she let herself imagine joining hands with Stephen instead.

Unbidden, a childhood memory came to her. A memory of her father gazing at her mother, his expression one of pain and unbearable longing. Her mother never cared for him. Isobel had always known it, as a child knows without understanding. Her father loved his wife with a hopeless, helpless passion. She met it with cordial indifference. After their lands were lost, that indifference shifted to complete unawareness.

It must have killed him.

For the first time, Isobel saw her father with an adult's insight. The great wrongs he committed were desperate acts. He sacrificed both his honor and his daughter in the vain hope that wealth and position might finally gain him his wife's love.

How much more unhappy she would be, wed to Stephen! Unlike her mother, who devoted herself to God, Stephen would share his affections with woman after woman after woman. Surely that would be worse.

Stephen was a man who gave in to temptation readily. And temptation fell into Stephen's lap at every turn. If he were her husband, how would she bear sharing him with other women? She could not. She could not do it.

How ridiculous she was! Lying here on this cot, furious with Stephen over imagined slights in an imagined future. He was not her husband; he made no pledge to her. Though he showed her warm affection, he spoke only of the moment.

He never even said he loved her. Not once.

In any case, her future was set. Locked in place and bolted shut. In the morning, Stephen would take her back to Caen. To de Roche.

She rolled onto her side and held herself in a tight ball. And wept for all that she wanted and could not have.

Isobel awoke to the sounds of voices and hurried footsteps outside her door. A moment later, her brother knocked and stepped in, fully dressed and sword in hand.

"A dozen armed men are riding hard this way," Geoffrey said in a rush. "They are not English soldiers."

She bolted upright, heart racing, and saw Jamie in the doorway behind her brother. She was on her feet and strapping on her sword by the time Jamie was in the room.

"I fear it could be the men who attacked you yesterday," Jamie said, "and that they've come to take my father."

Geoffrey got her cloak for her from the peg behind the door, and they raced out behind Jamie.

As they ran across the cloister, Isobel grabbed Geoffrey's arm. "Surely they would not take FitzAlan by force from a holy place?"

The grim set of Geoffrey's jaw told her that was just what he thought they would do. And worse.

"You cannot believe the abbot would give him up?"

Geoffrey nodded and charged ahead of her through the archway and along the path. When she reached the front of the church, she saw the abbot and several monks gathered below by the open canal that ran inside the perimeter wall. On the other side of a narrow bridge that crossed the canal, two lay brothers were lifting the heavy bar that held the gate.

"Do not open the gate to them!" Geoffrey shouted.

The abbot glared over his shoulder at them as he signaled for the men to continue.

"Get FitzAlan into the church," Geoffrey called back to her as he raced down the hill after Jamie.

Isobel saw the sense in it at once. Even godless men would hesitate to take a man from the sanctuary. She hurried back toward the infirmary, wondering how she would get FitzAlan into the church. As she rounded the corner, she nearly collided with two monks carrying FitzAlan on a litter.

The old monk hobbled beside the litter, admonishing the two men to make haste. Praise God the old monk saw the danger! She took his arm and helped him the last few steps.

He shook her off the moment they were inside the church. "Cover your hair, woman!"

Though it seemed unlikely God would care at such a moment, she swallowed back her panic and yanked her hood over her head.

"How does your patient fare?" she asked.

"He would not stay abed," the monk complained, shaking his head. "So I gave him a sleeping draught."

Hearing a burst of shouting, she turned to see monks were pouring into the church. Holding her hood in place, she pushed past them to the front steps of the church. What she saw below sent her heart to her mouth.

On the other side of the bridge, crowded between the canal and the front gate, were at least a dozen armed men. Geoffrey and Jamie stood on this side, swords drawn, looking like the men of ancient Thermopylae holding off the Persian hordes. Behind them lay the abbot. A four-foot shaft stuck up from the center of his chest.

Fearing she would see her brother and Jamie meet the same fate, she clasped her hands together and began praying aloud. "Mary, Mother of God—"

A voice rolled out like thunder across the grounds: "You violate this holy ground at your peril!"

At first Isobel did not recognize the voice as her brother's. But it was.

"God has put his strength into our swords," Geoffrey shouted. "We are the instruments of His wrath!"

Isobel could swear she felt the ground shake. The men on the other side of the bridge must have felt it, too, for they stopped dead in their tracks. At the back of the group, the only man in full armor jerked his helmet off and shouted at them. The men still hesitated, exchanging nervous glances. Only when their leader called them by name did the first two men start across the bridge.

To Isobel's amazement, Geoffrey and Jamie cut the two down so quickly her eyes could not follow their swords. She flicked her eyes back to the leader. His black hair whipped about his face as he hurled curses at his men.

This time, three men came across the bridge.

Geoffrey's sword flew as if the wrath of God truly did move his arm. Never had Isobel seen her brother fight like this—nor had she suspected he could. He dispatched two more rapidly than she thought possible. While Jamie fought the third, Geoffrey came behind the man, lifted him by the collar, and threw him into the canal. Splashing and crying out in terror, the man scrambled up the other side to safety.

"God has seen into your hearts!" her brother shouted. "He knows you intend to murder these holy men. Turn and go, or he will strike you down where you stand!"

Her brother was acting like God's own raging angel. Despite their leader's angry shouts, the men turned as one and fled past him out the gates.

The black-haired man held his horse in place. Without hurry, he swept his eyes over the abbey grounds and up the rise to where Isobel stood alone before the church. A chill of fear went up her spine as their eyes met and held across the distance. He could not harm her now. And yet she could not breathe until he turned his horse and rode out the gate.

Isobel ran down the hill so fast she nearly fell head over heels. When her brother saw her coming, he opened his arms and caught her in midair.

"You were magnificent!" she said, burying her face into his neck. When he set her down she asked, "How did you ever think to say those things to them?"

"I spoke the truth," her brother said. "God's truth."

She was taken aback. Everyone spoke to God in prayer. Few, however, claimed God spoke to them—at least not with such clarity. She did not quite know what to make of it.

Geoffrey smiled, showing he both understood and forgave her doubting nature. With all the righteous fire gone from him, he was her sweet brother once again. They walked arm in arm up the hill to the church.

Jamie caught up to them, his eyes shining. "We did well, did we not?"

"Aye," Isobel said. "Your father will be proud of you."

"Those men may get their courage back." Jamie squinted at the early morning sun, still low on the horizon. "'Tis less than an hour since daybreak. I hope to God Stephen returns before they do."

"I shall pray he does," Geoffrey said.

"You do that," Jamie said, slapping Geoffrey on the back. "He seems to hear your prayers."

The three of them went into the church and huddled around FitzAlan. He was awake, his color much improved. When he looked at Jamie, the fierceness of the love in his eyes caused Isobel to suck in her breath. Isobel looked away; it felt intrusive to observe that moment between them.

The sanctuary felt crowded with all the monks gathered inside. With Jamie hovering over FitzAlan and the old monk close at hand, there was no need for her ministrations. Geoffrey was on his knees in one of the alcoves. Having no occupation herself, she told Jamie she would act as lookout.

She climbed the narrow stairs that led to the small gallery overlooking the nave. From there, she had to duck her head to go up the even narrower set of stairs above. She pushed a wooden door and found it opened onto a perch at the peak of the church roof. When she stepped out onto it, her stomach filled with butterflies and her palms grew sweaty. She looked at the slats for climbing the spire above her and nearly swooned.

The perch was high enough.

From here, she had a bird's-eye view of the fields and woods on all sides of the abbey. Her eyes followed the winding river and the path that led up to the orchard. She sighed, remembering the sound of birds and Stephen's arm about her. Squinting, she picked out the abandoned croft. If only she could go back with Stephen one more time. Just once more.

That was pure foolishness! No matter how many times, she would always want more.

A fine lookout she was. Annoyed with herself, she turned her back on the croft and scanned the horizon to the west.

What was that? In a copse of wood she thought she saw the gleam of metal. She watched until she made out the shapes of horses and men, tiny as ants, through the trees.

Their attackers had not fled far. Would they go on their way, or return for a second attack? It was impossible to tell. She decided not to panic the others until she knew.

She grew cold and stiff as she watched and waited. Surely it was a good sign they took so long. She imagined the black-haired leader ranting at his men down there under the trees. *Please, God, let the men resist him until Stephen returns.*

She risked taking her eyes off the wood to glance to the

northwest, in the direction of Caen. Two hours after dawn he would come. How long had she been watching? An hour? Surely Stephen would come soon.

She saw first one rider, then another leave the cover of the wood. "God, no, please, no."

They rode straight toward the abbey. She waited, muscles taut, to count them. Four, five, six. Their line strung out, the space between increasing with each horse that left the wood. She read reluctance in their slow trot. Still, they came. Ten, eleven, twelve.

She must warn the men below.

She cast one last look in the direction from which Stephen would come, willing him to be there.

God be praised! Stephen was coming!

The riders cresting the faraway hill were no more than dots on the horizon. They were twice the distance from the abbey as the others, but they swept down the hill, moving fast.

Isobel flew down the narrow stairs.

"He comes! He comes!" she shouted as she ran across the sanctuary to Jamie and FitzAlan.

"The men who attacked us are returning," she said when she reached them. "But Stephen rides hard behind them."

FitzAlan pulled himself up on one elbow with a grimace, then commenced to fire questions at her. "What is the distance between them? How many men in each?"

Feeling like one of his soldiers, she gave him her report. She was rewarded with a nod of approval.

"Stephen will chase them off," FitzAlan said, "but we'd better get to the gate on the chance he needs help."

Despite Jamie's efforts to hold him down, the fool man tried to heave himself up.

"Lord FitzAlan, lie down at once!" she said, standing over him, hands on her hips. "I shall not forgive you if you reopen that wound and bleed to death after all we've been through."

"Geoffrey and I can hold the gate until Stephen comes," Jamie said, his voice quiet and sure.

FitzAlan and Jamie locked eyes. Then FitzAlan gave his son a tight nod.

As Jamie ran past her, he squeezed her arm in thanks.

"Take me outside where I can see," FitzAlan shouted at some monks hovering nearby.

Four of them rushed to do his bidding. At his insistence, they carried his pallet out the door and propped him up against the wall. The monks almost knocked Isobel over in their haste to get back inside the church.

She sat down beside FitzAlan. From their high spot, she could see over the abbey's wall to the first rise beyond.

Looking out, she said, "There is fresh blood on your bandage."

"I've fought in worse shape."

FitzAlan's sword lay beside him on the pallet; his hand was on the hilt. If the need arose, FitzAlan would find the strength to charge down the hill, sword swinging. She had no doubt of it.

If it came to that, she would go with him.

Over the chanting of the monks' prayers inside the church, she heard the faint sounds of shouts and galloping horses. She jumped to her feet. As the sounds grew louder, she rose on her tiptoes, straining to see. A group of riders broke over the hill. A moment later they streaked past, riding along the wall of the abbey and into the woods on the other side.

Then a second, larger group came thundering over the hill. As they rode in front of the abbey, the lead rider broke away and waved the others on. It was Stephen; she knew it before he rode through the gate. He pulled off his helmet and looked up the hill, his eyes searching, until he found her.

Now that the danger was past, she felt tears welling up. She remembered how Stephen comforted her after the killing in the wood. How she longed for that now! To feel his arms so tight around her she could not breathe. To hear him mutter soothing, senseless words into her hair. She clenched her fists until the nails dug into her palms, to keep from running to him.

Stephen tossed his reins to Jamie. With a lightness that belied his long journey and heavy armor, he trotted up the hill. Afore God, he was a beautiful man, with the sun glinting off his armor and shining on his hair.

But he was coming straight for her. Panic seized her as she saw the intention in his eyes. Surely he knew better than to embrace her here, in front of everyone? Did he not care if they all knew?

As he came near, she took a quick step back and said in a voice much too loud, "Your brother is able to sit up, as you can see, Sir Stephen!"

Had she truly said that? After he rode through the night and back again to save them?

"Thank you. Thank you so very much." Her words fell awkwardly from her lips, showing her for the idiot that she was.

Stephen raised an eyebrow, but he came no closer.

Now that she knew he was not going to do anything foolish, she wanted to say something more to acknowledge his feat. "I—I saw you coming from the church roof."

He leaned his head back and squinted up at the church, a smile playing at the corners of his mouth. "Watching for me, were you, now?"

Isobel glanced down at FitzAlan. Could the man not save

her from further embarrassment and offer some word of greeting?

When she noticed the sheen of sweat on FitzAlan's brow, she dropped to her knees beside him. *Where is the old monk?* She looked about but did not see him.

"How are you, William?" Stephen's voice above her was soft, worried.

FitzAlan was saved from answering by the arrival of Jamie and Geoffrey.

"Better late than never," Jamie said, slapping Stephen on the back.

Stephen gave Jamie a puzzled look. "Late?"

"These same men attacked us at dawn," Jamie said. "Geoffrey and I sent them running like scared rabbits."

"This was God's doing, not ours," Geoffrey said.

Stephen looked from one to the other. The light left his eyes as he realized they were not having a joke on him.

"Forgive me, I came as fast as I could."

"You came when you were needed," Jamie said. "We could not have held them a second time."

Stephen did not look any happier.

"One of the men lived long enough to confess," Jamie said. "They meant to sack the abbey, murder all the monks, and blame the English army."

FitzAlan dozed off before Jamie was done giving Stephen a full account.

"He is bleeding through the bandage again," Isobel said, looking up at Stephen.

Stephen sent Jamie and Geoffrey to fetch the old monk and knelt beside her. "How bad is he?"

"He has lost too much blood," she said. "He is weaker than he would have us know."

Chapter Twenty-two

Stephen's men gave up the pursuit and returned shortly. Their mission was to return FitzAlan to Caen as quickly as possible. Within an hour, the horses were watered and fed, the men had eaten, and FitzAlan's wound was freshly bound.

Isobel found Stephen supervising four men loading Fitz-Alan's litter onto a cart. To her relief, FitzAlan was awake and complaining loudly that he could "damn well ride." Still, the pallor of his skin made her anxious.

When she touched Stephen's arm, he turned and fixed worried eyes on her. He looked tired. She wondered if he'd had time to sleep at all.

"Thank you for the gown," she said. "'Twas very kind of you to bring it."

With all he had to do in his short time in Caen in the night, how had he thought to retrieve a gown for her? He saved her a good deal of embarrassment. Monks might try to avert their eyes, but soldiers were another matter. It would have been a long ride back with all the men staring at her legs.

Stephen acknowledged her thanks with a nod. "I want you to ride in the cart with William," he said in a low voice. "He will not fight you as he would Jamie or me."

"Of course."

Her breath caught as Stephen placed his hands on her waist. When he hesitated, she sensed he wanted to pull her against him as much as she wanted him to do it. Then her feet left the ground, and she was beside FitzAlan in the cart.

The journey back to Caen took forever. Though FitzAlan did not complain of the pain, he flinched each time a bump in the road jarred his wound. She tried to get him to rest.

The usually taciturn man, however, was set on passing the time talking with her. Since it seemed to distract him, she gave in. He plied her with questions until she told him every detail of what happened the day before, after he was hit with the arrow.

FitzAlan closed his eyes, a smile on his face. "There is no man I'd rather have at my back in a fight than Stephen."

"Aye," she said, "he was a wonder to see."

FitzAlan opened his eyes a slit. "My brother has the heart of a hero, always has," he rasped. "He only wants for opportunity to show it."

She wondered why it was so important to FitzAlan she understand this. Speaking cost him considerable effort.

"A man could not do better for a brother or a friend," he said, ignoring her attempts to shush him.

Despite the pain he was in, she did not think these were the ramblings of an addled mind. FitzAlan's speech seemed to be directed to some purpose, but what?

She thought he was finally drifting off to sleep, when he spoke again. "He will make some woman a fine husband one day."

As she wiped his brow, she muttered under her breath, "If a woman does not mind sharing."

His ears were sharper than she credited. When his bark of laughter turned into a groan of pain, she regretted her remark.

As she leaned over him to check his bandage, he opened his eyes again. They were honest eyes, the color of golden amber.

"'Tis only the follies of a young man," he said between harsh breaths. "Stephen needs—"

"Lord FitzAlan, please, you must lie still." His wound was bleeding again, and she was truly worried. "We shall speak no more now. You must be quiet and rest."

He closed his eyes, a faint smile on his lips. "Catherine... she would like you. I promised... Catherine... I would come home..."

'Twas true, then. The great commander did love his wife. Isobel could hear it in his voice. This was not the offhand affection most men felt for their wives. This Catherine was the joy of his life. The reason he wanted to go home again.

Tears stung at the back of Isobel's eyes. Perhaps it was all the emotions of the last two days hitting her now. It seemed a lifetime since she left Caen, so much had happened. She was so tired! And worried half to death about FitzAlan.

"Isobel." It was Stephen's voice.

She wiped her eyes and turned around to where he'd drawn his horse next to the cart.

"Are we near Caen yet?" she asked, her voice breaking. "I fear he grows worse, and there is little I can do for him here."

Stephen's face was grave as he looked at his brother. "Another hour, perhaps. We cannot go faster with the cart."

Isobel sensed the tension beneath the calm of his voice.

"Take Jamie and a few others ahead," Stephen called out to the nearest man. "Get a physician and have a room prepared at the castle for Lord FitzAlan."

She understood Stephen's purpose. He did not want Jamie to see how grave FitzAlan's condition was before they had him safely inside the city walls.

Stephen rode beside the cart for the remainder of the journey, but they spoke little. When at last they reached the city, the king's own physician was waiting at the gate. The elegantly dressed man waved at the driver not to stop and leapt into the moving cart.

"To the keep!" the physician called out as he began to examine his patient.

Jamie was waiting at the steps to the keep. Before she knew it, he and Stephen lifted FitzAlan's litter and carried him inside the keep. The physician trotted behind in their wake.

Quite suddenly, Isobel found herself alone, relieved of responsibility. She leaned back and let out a long breath. Now that the ordeal was over, she felt so weary! She could not convince herself to rise and get out of the cart.

"Lady Hume."

She opened her eyes to see King Henry and Robert standing beside the cart. It was the king who had spoken.

"Thank you for caring for my good friend," King Henry said, holding his hand out to her.

She glanced at her blood-encrusted nails. When she hesitated, the king flustered her completely by lifting her bodily from the cart. It was easy to forget the king was a strong and athletic young man.

"Thank God you are safe," Robert said, greeting her with a kiss on each cheek. The lines on his handsome face had deepened since she saw him last. "Until Stephen returned last night, I could only guess what happened to you."

Her heart constricted as she realized she was the reason he looked so haggard. "I am sorry I worried you."

"That little Linnet, I wanted to strangle her," Robert said. "I could not squeeze a word out of her."

Despite his words, Robert sounded impressed.

"I can see you are weary from your ordeal," the king said and held his arm out for her to walk with him. "But as soon as you are rested, you must tell us everything that happened."

"As you wish, sire." What would the king want to know from her that Jamie or Stephen could not tell him?

"Women often notice things that men do not," the king said.

"Try to recall every detail you can about the men who attacked you—horses, clothes, weapons. An unusual piece of jewelry. Anything that might reveal who these fiends are."

"I shall do my best, Your Highness."

"We must learn who these men are," he said, biting off each word. "These cowards who would lie in wait to murder my commander and commit sacrilege *in my name*."

She could feel his rage vibrating through her fingers resting on his arm.

"I shall have their heads on pikes." More calmly, he said, "You shall tell Robert everything you can remember. Later, I may wish to question you again myself."

Exhausted as she was, she could not help noticing the king and Robert were on friendlier terms than she thought. 'Twas odd, too, that the king relied upon Robert to help discover the identity of the attackers.

Just what role did Robert play for the king?

Perhaps she underestimated Robert, just as she had Stephen. There was more to both men than met the eye.

Chapter Twenty-three

*I*sobel awoke weighed down by guilt. There seemed no end to the consequences of her rash decision. FitzAlan was injured, Robert's feelings were hurt, Linnet was barely speaking to her. She hardly knew where to start making amends.

Since Linnet was close at hand, she would begin with her.

Just as Isobel opened the bed curtain, Linnet came through the door with a rush of cold air and a tray laden with food. The smell of warm bread made Isobel's stomach growl. She'd slept through supper last night.

"Thank you, Linnet, that was thoughtful of you."

Linnet kept her eyes on the tray and did not speak. Isobel sighed and wrapped her robe around herself. Motioning Linnet to join her, she sat down at the small table.

"You must have been frightened when I did not return by nightfall," she began. "I am sorry for that."

Linnet lifted eyes swimming with unshed tears. "You did not need to go," she said, accusation sharp in her voice. "Sir Stephen and Lord FitzAlan would have brought them back."

"I was too afraid for my brother to think clearly."

Linnet pressed her lips together. After a long moment, she nodded. "For François, I would do the same."

Linnet forgot her annoyance as Isobel related the story of the first attack.

Eyes wide, Linnet said, "'Tis something to see Sir Stephen and Lord FitzAlan fight, is it not?"

"I forgot you saw them fight in Falaise—"

Someone pounded on the door so hard it shook, startling them both to their feet.

The door swung open and de Roche stood in the doorway, his eyes black with fury. "What kind of fool woman has this English king saddled me with?"

Linnet flew to Isobel's side and clutched her hand.

De Roche slammed the door, causing them both to jump again.

"Foolish *and* disobedient," he said. "Did I not tell you to wait in your chamber for your brother's return?"

He strode across the room. When he stood not a foot from her, he asked again. "Did I not tell you?"

As a girl, Isobel had played with the boys. She knew about bullies. Cowering emboldened them.

"Aye, you did," she said in a clear, unapologetic voice. Anger welled up in her, fast and hard. She opened her mouth to call him a coward for not going after her brother himself.

Just in time, she remembered de Roche would be her husband and bit her tongue. No man could forgive being called a coward, especially if the words were just. If she were to have any hope of a cordial relationship with her husband, she must not say it.

De Roche stared at her tight-lipped. Then, quite suddenly, the anger left his face. She let her shoulders relax. The awful moment was past, thank heaven.

"I begin to see the appeal of a spirited woman," de Roche said, letting his gaze slide over her.

He pushed Linnet away and slammed Isobel against him. His mouth was hungry on hers, his hips ground against her, his erect shaft pressed against her belly. Beside them, Linnet was shouting and pulling on Isobel's arm.

De Roche released her just as suddenly.

"Perhaps you are worth the trouble, after all," he said, smiling. He gave her cheek a hard pinch, then turned and left.

As soon as the door closed behind him, Linnet drew her to the bench under the arrow-slit window. Linnet sat close beside her and held her hand. Isobel could not stop shaking.

"Must you marry him?" Linnet asked in a small voice.

"Aye, 'tis the king's command," Isobel said as calmly as she could. "You mustn't judge him by one angry moment. He had cause to be displeased with me, and he was over it quick enough."

Isobel cursed her dead husband under her breath. Must she suffer for the rest of her life for Hume's foolishness? She should be mistress of her own home, living in peace in Northumberland.

"Help me dress," she said, patting Linnet's hand. "I must see how Lord FitzAlan fares."

A short time later, she stood outside the door to Fitz-Alan's sickroom. She lifted her hand to knock, hoping and dreading she would find Stephen within. The door was ajar. She could hear voices.

One of them was Stephen's.

After a deep breath, she rapped lightly. The people inside

were talking so loudly, no one seemed to hear her. When they broke into laughter, a flood of relief ran through her. FitzAlan must be out of danger. Smiling, she poked her head through the door to ask permission to enter.

She froze as she took in the scene before her. On a stool beside FitzAlan's bed sat a breathtakingly beautiful woman. The woman leaned over the injured man, holding his hand in both of hers. Lady Catherine FitzAlan. The woman was fair, where Jamie was dark, and she looked far too young to be his mother. Still, Isobel had no doubt that was who the lady was.

The three men in the room leaned toward her like sunflowers toward the sun. The usually stern FitzAlan was beaming up at her like a boy in his first puppy love. Jamie stood behind, a hand resting on her shoulder. Completing the circle, Stephen sat beside her, a hand on her other shoulder.

It was not Stephen's hand on the woman's shoulder that made it impossible for Isobel to breathe—though that did not help. It was what she saw in his face as he gazed at the woman.

Bits of what she had overheard Stephen say about his brother's wife spun through her head. *But I adore Catherine. There is no woman like her.* Worse still, she remembered the wistful tone of his voice when he spoke of her.

Suddenly, it all made sense. Why Stephen avoided a betrothal. Why he wasted time with worthless women like Marie de Lisieux. She swallowed against the pain rising in her chest.

Stephen was in love with his brother's wife.

Though Lady Catherine had to be several years older than Stephen, she was yet a great beauty. Isobel's heart might hurt less if she could believe physical beauty was all that drew him. But when Stephen spoke of her, it was not of her beauty.

Nay, he loved this woman for herself.

Lady FitzAlan must have felt Isobel's stare, for she turned and looked at Isobel with eyes as blue as Jamie's.

"Come in," she called out. She rose to her feet and held her hands out to Isobel, saying, "You must be Lady Hume."

Caught like a rat in a trap. Isobel stepped into the room and took the woman's hands, for she could do naught else.

"I am Catherine," the woman said, kissing Isobel's cheeks. "Forgive my familiarity, but I've just heard how you saved my husband's life. God bless you!"

She startled Isobel further by pulling her into a full embrace. Isobel could not recall the last time she was embraced by another woman. She had no sisters, no close aunts or female cousins. It must have been when she was a small child, before her mother lost her warmth and laughter.

Isobel let herself be enveloped in the softness and breathed in Lady FitzAlan's light, feminine scent. Much as she might want to, she could not hate this woman now.

Lady FitzAlan pulled her into the room and made her sit on the stool Stephen gave up for her. Though Isobel felt Stephen's eyes on her, she could not look at him.

She sat mute, stunned by her discovery. *He loves her. He has always loved her.* The words went round and round in her head. She struggled to follow the lively talk in the room but could not.

She tried again to listen, determined to leave at the first break in the conversation. Lady FitzAlan was speaking of a premonition so strong that she sent her children to her mother-in-law. Then she paid the owner of a fishing vessel an exorbitant amount of gold to carry her across the channel between winter storms.

"'Twas foolish to risk yourself," FitzAlan said. He had not once taken his eyes from his wife since Isobel sat down.

"'Tis good she came," Stephen said behind her. "Catherine is the best medicine."

Isobel could not bear to hear his voice.

When Stephen started to say something about the Fitz-Alans moving into a house in the town, she got to her feet. She had to get out. This very moment.

Murmuring a feeble excuse—she hardly knew what she said—she went out the door before anyone could stop her.

Clamping a hand over her mouth to keep from sobbing aloud, she hiked up her skirts and ran down the corridor. She did not get far before Stephen caught her arm.

"Isobel, we must talk," he said, spinning her around. "I am sorry you are upset with me for not speaking to the king yet. I could not leave my brother, and then Catherine came. But I will do it today, now, if the king will see me."

"The king?" What was he saying?

"If the king insists on questioning you separately," he said, "I shall ask Catherine to go with you."

"Why must you speak to the king?" She had to hear him say it to be sure.

"Because of de Ro—" A look of distaste passed over his face, and he began again. "Because the king made other plans for you, 'tis best to obtain his permission before we marry."

"I know you feel honor-bound to do this," she said, "but I will not let you."

He was chivalrous enough not to show relief. But perhaps he did not yet believe she meant it.

"Do not fret," he said, giving her arm a squeeze. "The king will blame me, not you. I'll not lie to you, he will be angry. Quite angry, for a time. But all will be well in the end, I promise."

"You shall not speak to the king about me."

Stephen drew his brows together. "Isobel, surely you know we *must* marry."

He did not call her "love" now.

"I know no such thing," she answered, her voice tight. "If bedding a woman meant you must wed her, then you would have a great many wives by now."

As soon as the words were out of her mouth, the easy, familiar Stephen was gone. The man glaring at her was the other Stephen—the dangerous one who would ride into shooting arrows or throw a blade into a man's eye.

"We shall marry as soon as—"

Stephen stopped at the sound of someone calling his name. Isobel turned to see François running toward them down the corridor.

"Stephen," François said between gasps of breath, "Madame de Champdivers says you must come at once. She has something you want."

Isobel's blood turned to ice. She would be a fool to risk all and marry this man. Between his hopeless love for his brother's wife and his constant affairs, there would be no end to her suffering. He would crush her heart worse than her father had.

"I shall find you when I return, and we shall talk," Stephen said, his tone as hard as granite. "And then I shall go to the king."

She jerked her arm away and glared at him.

"We shall do what is right here, Isobel."

Chapter Twenty-four

$\mathcal{I}$ thought you would never come," Linnet scolded Stephen as she let him and François into Isobel's chamber. "You must save her from that horrid man."

Stephen sighed. At least the twins were on his side. Isobel had been so angry when he tried to apologize for not yet speaking to the king. Damn, he should have stayed and talked with her instead of going on that wild-goose chase.

Claudette had sent François to fetch him after over-hearing de Roche and Marie de Lisieux having a furious argument. As Claudette passed by a window in the Old Palace—Stephen did not ask Claudette what she was doing there—she noticed de Roche and Marie in the garden below. Claudette caught only a few words of the argument, but she heard Marie say both Stephen's name and "abbey."

Stephen tried telling Claudette that, by now, everyone in the castle knew of the attack. But Claudette was certain Marie knew something. And she was equally certain that Stephen was the only one who could worm it out of her.

When he finally tracked Marie down, she was pleased to see him. Too pleased. He did not believe Marie was involved in planning the attack, but she did know something. He was not willing, however, to go to bed with her to find out what. After all, he was almost a married man.

Whether his wife-to-be knew it or not.

Where in the hell was Isobel? It was late; they had no more time to waste. His head was throbbing long before he heard voices outside the door.

The twins ran to meet Isobel at the door.

"François, 'tis nice to see you," Isobel said as she came in. She sounded tired.

"I must go with François," Linnet said as she and her brother scurried past Isobel.

"Linnet!" Isobel called as the door closed behind them. Isobel collapsed onto a stool and buried her face in her hands.

Stephen felt himself softening toward her, but he fought it. He must be firm with her.

When he stepped into the circle of light from the lamp on the table next to her, she looked up, startled. She looked so lovely he could not speak.

"Did you get what you wanted from Madame de Champ-divers?" Isobel snapped her mouth closed, as if the words had slipped out before she could stop them.

Was it possible she was jealous? Of Claudette?

Ridiculous as it was, could that be the reason for her reluctance? The thought cheered him. Much better she be jealous than indifferent.

"Claudette is a friend, nothing more."

Isobel made a dismissive snort and looked away.

"We must go talk with William and Catherine about how best to approach the king. 'Tis late, and my brother needs his rest, so we mustn't tarry." He held out his hand to her.

She rose without taking it and stood toe to toe with him. "I will not," she said flatly.

He sucked in a breath to calm himself before speaking. "We must accept the consequences of our actions. I'd prefer you entered into this marriage gladly. Regardless, I will try to be a good husband to you. I hope, in time, I can make you happy."

"I will deny anything happened between us."

He was stunned. "But why?"

She clamped her lips together and refused to answer.

"You cannot wish to have de Roche as your husband."

It was bad enough that she was less than enthusiastic about marrying him. But surely she could not prefer that smarmy Frenchman over him?

"I made a promise to the king," she said, crossing her arms, "and I will make good on it."

"And what of our promise to each other?" he asked. "We made a promise by what we did in the old croft at the abbey."

"From what I hear, Stephen Carleton, you give such 'promises' to women all the time."

"Those women were different."

"How?" she demanded, giving him a hard look.

Why did he need to explain this to her? "Those women took me to their beds for pleasure only. It was understood between us. I misled none of them. Most were not even free to marry."

"Then I am no diffcrent," she said. "I took you for pleasure, and I am not free to marry."

Her words were like a knife to his heart. Had she really used him like that? Had he been so mistaken in believing what happened between them meant as much to her as it did to him?

At least he knew how to play it now. This was a game he was good at. He would take his own advice. In a fight for your life, you must use the advantage you have, not the one you wished you had.

He pulled her roughly against him and slowly, deliberately, ran his thumb over her full bottom lip.

"De Roche would disappoint you."

She looked up at him with wide green eyes and blinked once, twice. Already, her breathing changed.

"I want you naked." He held her gaze and let her see how much he meant it. He did want her that way, he just wanted her heart more.

Her lips parted, and her gaze dropped to his mouth. "I...I..." She tried to speak, but her words drifted off as he ran his finger along the side of her neck and down her throat.

When he reached the top of her gown, her breath hitched. He could almost hear her thoughts, they were so plain on her face. She was telling herself she should back away, but she wanted his touch too much to listen.

He would make sure of it.

He brushed his finger ever so slowly along the delicate skin at the edge of her bodice, across the rise and fall of her breasts. Like warm beeswax, she melted against him.

"You want to be kissed?" He tried to hang on to his cool calculation, but it was hard with her looking at him like that.

When she rose onto her tiptoes to meet him, his heart leapt in his chest. What kind of fool was he? Who was seducing whom? Who would be vanquished? He feared it would be him again.

Stephen never suffered from a lack of courage. Truth be told, he threw himself into danger with nary a thought. But his knees trembled as he leaned down to take this gamble.

As soon as his lips touched hers, there was fire. As there was every time they kissed. He let it envelop him, lap all around him, as he sank into her. He wanted to touch all the places he loved: her face, the enticing curve of her back, the long line of her thigh. Her hair, he had to have his hands in it. Without lifting his mouth from hers, he began pulling the pins that held her headdress.

"Let me," she gasped, breaking the kiss.

While her hands were busy with pins and coils, he moved down her body. He pressed his lips to the soft skin above her bodice, then dropped to his knees to kiss her breasts through the cloth of her gown. When her hair fell over his hands, he sighed with pleasure and rested his head against her.

But he could not afford to let her catch her breath and reconsider. He rose to his feet and spun her around to unfasten her gown.

"We should not . . . ," she began, but her voice trailed off as he reached around and cupped her breasts. Soft and full, they fit perfectly in his hands. She leaned her head back against his shoulder, making little sighs and moans.

He kissed her neck, then whispered into her ear, "I want to feel your skin against mine again."

This time, she made no pretense of objecting. As soon as he unfastened her gown, she pushed it off her shoulders and let it fall in a pool at her feet. As she turned around to face him, he pulled his tunic and shirt over his head. He drew in a sharp breath when she put her arms around his waist and he felt her breasts against his chest.

She looked up at him, eyes dark and serious. "I know it is wrong, but I cannot help myself."

"There is no wrong in it, if we are to marry."

"I would rather sin than suffer every day—" Her voice broke in a sob.

He could not begin to understand her. What could she mean? "We would have joy between us, can you not see that?"

She shook her head violently from side to side. With the passion broken, he could feel her slipping away from him. Before she could change her mind, he lifted her in his arms and carried her to the bed.

This was no time for fighting fair.

He began by kissing her senseless.

When she slipped a hand under the top of his leggings, he grabbed her wrist. Holding both her hands over her head, he nipped at her ear and ran his tongue along her collarbone. By the time he reached her breasts, she was squirming and arching her back.

Slowly, he circled her nipples with his tongue. Round and round, then flicking with his tongue until she slammed her fist against the bed.

Good. He ran his fingers up the inside of her thigh, inch by inch, as he continued teasing her nipple with his tongue. When he reached her center, she was hot and wet and he wanted her so badly he nearly forgot his purpose.

With renewed determination to control himself, he drew her breast into his mouth and pleasured her with his hand. Every sigh and moan made him want her more.

When he stopped to run his hand along the inside of her thigh again, she opened her eyes.

"Good things come to her who waits," he said, grinning down at her. He set to teasing her, moving his fingers in circles ever closer to her center until he brushed it with each turn with a feather touch.

The saints preserve him, she had beautiful breasts! He kissed the one closest to him. She made a little high-pitched sound when he took the nipple between his teeth. As he increased the pressure between her legs, her breathing grew ragged.

"Stephen, don't stop," she said, her voice urgent as she tried to pull him down to her.

When she cried out, he wrapped his arms around her and buried his head in her neck. He felt overpowered by emotions so strong he did not know what to do with them.

He squeezed his eyes shut as she ran her fingers along the side of his face. He was tight as a bowstring. When she turned in to him to kiss him, the tips of her breasts touched his chest. This was the way to ruin. He let himself enjoy a painfully languid kiss before he broke away.

"On your stomach," he told her and sat up.

Giving him an uncertain look, she turned. He gathered her mass of dark hair and swept it to the side. As he kissed her neck, her lips curved up. He leaned back and let his eyes travel down the graceful line of her spine. To let her know how much he wanted her, he rubbed his cock against her buttocks.

In truth, that was just for him.

It did get her attention. She looked at him over her shoulder, eyes wide and lips parted. She looked so beautiful he had to fight the urge to part her legs and enter her right then.

Whoa! He shook his head.

He gave her buttocks little bites that made her laugh, even while they aroused her. Then he turned her over to kiss her breasts again. How did she smell so good?

He played with her nipples as he worked his way down. He paused to stick his tongue in her belly button. As he moved lower, he felt her tense. He rose up to kiss her for a long while, his hand between her legs.

"You will like this, I promise," he said next to her ear before he moved back down to show her.

She did. Her release was so exciting he thought he would have his own against the bedclothes. Sweet Jesus, she was going to kill him.

Sometime later, he once again had her on the edge, just where he wanted her. She was clinging to him like warm honey. He hovered over her, teasing her—and torturing himself. It took all his strength of mind not to plunge into her.

"Now." She wrapped her legs more tightly around him, her voice was urgent. "I want you inside me. Now."

"Say you will marry me first."

She made an indecipherable sound.

"You must say it, Isobel," he insisted. "I will not again risk giving you a child unless I have your word."

"I cannot!" she half moaned, half cried. "Do not make me, Stephen. Please. Please. Do not make me."

Even in the midst of passion, she would not give in to him.

A man can take only so much. When she lifted her hips to him, he let his shaft slide over her. He closed his eyes and moved against her, again and again, until he spurted his seed over her belly.

He rolled off her and lay on his back, arms crossed over his face. He'd never felt worse in his life. The humiliation alone might kill him. But it was nothing to this aching hole in his chest where his heart had been. He wanted to crawl off into a corner like a wounded animal. But he could not move with this heavy sadness lying over him like a great weight.

Though they did not touch, he felt the heat of her body next to him and heard each shallow breath she took. There was one demand he had to make. Though she won all else, he was determined to have his way in this one thing. He gathered his strength and what little pride he had left, and said it.

"I will not allow another man to raise my child."

He let the silence linger to give her time to absorb this before he told her how it would be.

"'Tis unlikely," she said in a bare whisper. "I have never conceived. I—I may not be able to."

He was resolved in this, and he would have her know it. Fixing his eyes on the ceiling, he let the coldness he felt show in his voice.

"You will find a way to delay your marriage to de Roche until you know for certain," he said. "If you are with child, I will give you two choices. You can marry me, or you can have the child in secret and give it to me to raise."

He got up from the bed. As he pulled on his clothes, his hurt and disappointment turned into something cold and hard within his chest. The silence was thick between them as he sat and methodically put on one boot and then the other.

He was not going to slink out of Isobel's bedchamber half dressed. He was not that kind of man anymore. He had tried to do the right thing. He still wanted to.

Gritting his teeth, he strapped on his belt and sword. Only then did he look at her. She was sitting with the bedclothes clutched to her chest, her hollow eyes fixed on him.

"Understand me. I will not allow you to pass my child off as de Roche's," he told her. "I would kill him with my bare hands before I let that unworthy piece of shit have a child of mine."

She nodded.

It was enough. He turned and left her.

Chapter Twenty-five

Stephen waved aside the guards' cautions and rode out the gate. Brigands and renegades be damned.

Lightning liked galloping in the dark. Stephen gave the horse his head, though it risked both their necks. The cold helped clear Stephen's mind. When Lightning slowed to a walk, he looked up at the star-filled sky and tried to draw hope from it.

After he left Isobel, he was in such a tangle he awakened Catherine for advice. She showed no surprise at his intention to marry Isobel. Good God, was he so obvious?

Catherine demanded he tell her all. He was not about to confess he'd just tried to seduce Isobel into agreeing to the marriage. Tried *and failed.* As it turned out, all Catherine wished to know was what he *said* to Isobel.

"You told her you 'must' marry?" Catherine said in her most exasperated tone. "Not that you *wanted* to marry her? That you love her? That you cannot live without her? For God's sake, Stephen, what were you thinking!"

Obviously, he had not broached the subject in the best possible way. He should have mentioned how much he cared for her. But how could Isobel not know it?

Those ugly remarks she made about other women were insulting. He'd not gone to bed with another woman since he met her, for God's sake. And it was not as if he had no offers.

The simple truth was he did not want any woman but Isobel. He'd told her he was done with other women...or had he? Surely his determination to marry her said as much?

Stephen and Lightning rode through most of the night. He did not turn around until he was sure he could speak with Isobel without getting angry again—no matter what foolishness she might say. A storm rolled in with the dawn, soaking him to the skin before he reached the castle gate.

He rode straight for the keep, hoping to find the king at breakfast in the hall. This time, he meant to talk with the king first. Then, when he spoke with Isobel, he could assure her the king was willing to release her from her promise.

The king would not like it, but he would approve the marriage. Being a pious man, what else could he do when Stephen told him what they'd done?

* * *

Last night, Linnet had found Isobel naked and weeping on the floor. The girl wrapped her in blankets and frantically pressed her with questions. Distraught as she was, Isobel made the mistake of telling her Stephen wanted to marry her.

Linnet was still furious with her this morning for her "utter, utter foolishness" in refusing him.

Was she being foolish?

What should she have said to Stephen? That she loved him

so much her heart ached every moment of every day? That this, more than anything, frightened her? That she wished with all her heart he loved her back?

Yet even that would not be enough. She wanted the impossible. Unless he loved her *always,* being his wife would cause her too much pain.

Isobel felt ill from so much weeping. If she could, she would remain in bed for days with the curtains closed. The king, however, sent a message summoning her to join him for breakfast. Vaguely, she recalled he wished to know about the attackers. She tried to turn her mind to it. But misery engulfed her, leaving her thoughts disjointed and scattered.

Linnet maintained her stony silence while helping Isobel dress. For spite, the girl chose the green velvet gown Isobel wore on the day of Stephen's return from Falaise. Blinking back tears, she ran her fingers over the soft fabric.

When Robert came to escort her, she forced a smile. Taking his arm, she said, "You look well today."

"I should. Somehow I managed to sleep all of yesterday." He frowned at her. "But I can see you have not recovered from your ordeal. You look pale, my dear."

"I am sorry I caused you such worry," she said. "It was thoughtless of me not to leave you a message."

Robert laughed. "A message would not have helped, unless you had the good sense to lie to me."

"Has the king summoned me to ask about the attackers?"

"I can think of no other reason," Robert said with a shrug. "I was supposed to question you yesterday, so he must have grown impatient."

When they entered the hall, Isobel took a quick look up and down the tables. Stephen was not here, praise God. She needed time to think. Now, that was odd—de Roche was in the honored place next to the king. Her brother was seated at the far end of the high table, looking anxious.

After the king acknowledged her and Robert, he gestured for them to sit beside de Roche. Isobel sat without meeting de Roche's eyes. After his volatile and offensive behavior of late, the prospect of sharing a trencher with him made her queasy.

Isobel could not think of a single word to say to him. She was relieved when the king rose to speak.

"This is a happy occasion," the king said, holding his arms out. "Today we celebrate the symbolic joining of England and Normandy…"

Isobel barely heard a word the king said. She was startled to attention, though, when Robert leapt to his feet beside her.

"But, my good sire, I must beg you to put off this betrothal a little longer," Robert said, his voice tense. "We have not yet completed negotiation of the terms of the marriage contract."

"Since you proved unable to accomplish this simple task, I took it upon myself to assist her brother," the king said. "The three of us met an hour ago. Agreement was easily reached."

"With your good guidance, I'm sure it was readily done," Robert said in a clipped voice.

"Lord de Roche has been exceedingly generous," the king answered in an even tone. "I assure you, Lady Hume can have nothing to complain of."

Isobel felt as if she were watching events unfold from a great distance. Surely this was not happening. Not now.

She was vaguely aware of Robert cursing under his breath as he sat down. With his hand on her arm he whispered, "I had no notion the king meant to do this today."

"Lord de Roche wishes to have the marriage ceremony take place in his home city of Rouen," the king announced. "The banns will be posted there."

"Merde!" Robert hissed beside her.

Isobel kept her eyes fixed on the untouched food in front of her while the king talked on and on. She flinched each time she heard the word "betrothal" but took in nothing else.

God help her. It was too late.

When the king finished speaking, de Roche stood and took his turn. His words flowed like thick honey of the bonding of two great kingdoms, God's will, the king's destiny.

Isobel started at the sudden weight of a hand on her shoulder and looked up into hard gray eyes.

"'Tis time to sign the marriage contract and pledge our troth," de Roche said.

To the sound of halfhearted clapping, he pulled her to her feet. Geoffrey walked to her from the far end of the table.

"I am sorry to surprise you," he whispered as he laid the marriage contract before her. "The king would brook no delay."

She took the quill and signed without reading it.

De Roche signed with a flourish, then took her hand. His deep voice filled the room as he made his formal promise to her.

All eyes in the hall turned to her. Panic seized her. She could not do this. Not now. Not yet. Not ever. She took a step back, her eyes on the door.

King Henry stood before her, blocking her way. She opened her mouth to tell him—

Tell him what? That she could not do this now? Surely the king would demand a reason.

I must wait until I know if I am with child. I have committed the sin of fornication, with a man other than the one I agreed to wed.

She could not tell him that. Not before all these witnesses.

The king cleared his throat. When she looked into his magnetic hazel eyes, Isobel felt the full force of his will for the first time. Before her was the king who united England, the commander men followed gladly into war. His every aspect exuded utter certainty that he knew what was right.

King Henry was relentless in pursuing the destiny God set out for him. Every day, he did his duty with all of his being. With his steady gaze, he was telling her that today he expected her to do hers.

The king prompted her, telling her what she should say. She did as he bade her. She repeated back the simple words of the promise to marry.

It was done.

A gush of wind went through the hall, causing the lamps and candles to flicker. Isobel turned and saw a dark figure at the entrance, rain dripping from his cloak. Her heart caught in her throat. Even before he threw his hood back and pushed the wet hair from his face, she knew it was him.

"Sir Stephen," the king called out, a smile lighting his face. "Come, we will make room for you here."

Stephen strode up to the high table and made his bow to the king. But when he lifted his head, his dark eyes were fixed on Isobel.

"You are just in time to hear the good news," the king said, gesturing toward Isobel and de Roche. "Lord de Roche and Lady Isobel Hume are betrothed. They leave today for Rouen."

Isobel felt faint under Stephen's gaze. Though his face was expressionless, she saw the muscles in his jaw working. How angry he must be with her! Only hours since he demanded she delay this marriage, and already she had bound herself. Only hours since she lay naked with him, and she stood beside the man who would be her husband. She wanted to cry out that it was not her fault—the king gave her no choice.

But none of it mattered. What was done was done.

"I wish you every happiness," Stephen said between his teeth. Without another word, he turned on his heel.

Isobel watched the dark drops of rainwater fall from his cape and hit the gray stone floor as he walked across it. Long after he was gone, she heard the echo of his boots in the silent hall.

Isobel sat on the bench in her bedchamber, staring blindly out the window slit as Linnet packed her chest. Glancing down, she saw she was dressed in her traveling clothes. She had no memory of changing.

Now and then, Linnet asked a question about the packing. Isobel could not muster the strength to answer. When she saw Linnet carry her sword to the chest, though, she forced herself to speak.

"I shall have to give that up." Her voice came out as a croak. "My new husband will not approve."

Linnet glared at her over the top of the chest as she laid the sword inside it. Then she stalked over to Isobel.

"We shall wear our daggers." Linnet flipped up the skirt of Isobel's gown and strapped a dagger to her calf.

"But we'll be traveling with twenty of de Roche's men—"

"I stole an extra for each of us." Linnet slapped a second dagger into Isobel's hand. "Find a place to hide it on you."

It was easier to slip the dagger through the fichu of her gown and fasten it to the belt underneath than to argue.

"You need not come with me," Isobel said, though the thought of losing the girl, too, brought her to the brink of tears again. "You will want to stay with François."

"We are both coming," Linnet said. "Sir Robert said you will have need of us."

Isobel took Linnet's hand and squeezed it, unable to find words to tell her how grateful she was.

Linnet jerked her hand away, still furious with her for letting this happen. Isobel leaned her head back against the stone wall and let the tears slide down the sides of her face. She could not seem to stop weeping. Perhaps if she were not so very, very tired.

Linnet brought a cold, wet cloth for her face. As Isobel took slow, deep breaths through the cloth, she told herself that if she could survive eight years married to Hume, she could survive anything. Even this. She drew in one last deep breath and set the cloth aside.

"Thank you, Linnet." She rose to her feet, dry-eyed at last. "I am ready."

It was still raining, so they made their good-byes inside the keep. Somehow, she managed to make the expected nods and murmurs as she moved from group to group with de Roche.

She faltered only twice.

The first was when she saw Lady Catherine FitzAlan. Isobel could not help thinking Stephen would not be happy, either, in love with his brother's wife. Though Lady Catherine had been kindness itself when they met, she offered no good wishes now. The blue eyes fixed on her, as if asking a burning question.

Isobel faltered again when she bade farewell to her brother and Robert. How she would miss them! All that kept her from breaking down was Robert's promise to visit her soon.

"Do not tell de Roche, but I go in secret to Paris now," Robert said in a low voice when de Roche turned to speak to someone else. "I shall come see you upon my return."

She felt certain Robert knew what was between her and Stephen, though they never spoke of it. When he embraced her for the last time, she could not help whispering in his ear, "He did not come. He did not come."

"You will be happy yet, Isobel, I know it."

Despite Robert's effort to hide his worry behind a smile, she saw it in his eyes as he waved good-bye to her.

They had two days' ride before them, and de Roche was anxious to be gone. With a twin on either side of her, Isobel urged her horse forward with the rest of their party.

As they crossed the bailey yard, she turned for a last look at the storeroom along the wall where she spent so many happy hours practicing. Where she and Stephen first kissed.

A movement on top of the wall drew her eye upward. A dark, hooded figure stood against the gray sky, black cape flapping in the wind.

Stephen had come to see her off, after all.

Though she could not make out his face, she felt his eyes burning into her long after she rode out the gate.

God help her, she loved him. Her life was in ruins.

Chapter Twenty-six

*E*ven with an escort of twenty men, the road to Rouen was dangerous. They rode hard, rarely stopping, except to camp a few hours overnight on the bank of the Seine. Isobel was past exhaustion by the time she saw the towers and church spires of Rouen on the horizon at dusk on the second day.

A formidable city. The city walls went on forever and had more towers than she could count. Weary as she was, she could not help wondering how King Henry hoped to take it.

The others must be tired, as well. The entire party slowed to a sluggish pace now that Rouen was within sight. By the time they passed through the city's massive gates, it was full dark.

De Roche dropped back to ride beside her. "Follow close behind me," he told her. "The house is not far now."

Isobel fought to stay awake as she followed de Roche's horse through the narrow, winding streets. Every few yards, she turned to check on the twins, who rode, heads bobbing, just behind her.

At last they came to a halt before the gate of a massive, walled house. De Roche helped her down. Her legs, stiff from riding all day, gave way as he set her to the ground.

Strong arms lifted her. The man's smell was wrong, but she could not summon the strength to open her eyes. She heard hushed voices around her. Then there was nothing but the lulling, rocking motion of being carried upstairs.

Isobel sat straight up, heart racing, not knowing where she was. When she saw Linnet amid the tangle of bedclothes beside her, she put her hand to her chest. Thank God. She took a deep breath to calm herself. But then the events of the last days came back to her.

Slowly, she lay back down on the bed.

Memories of Stephen ran through her head. Stephen, speaking in a cold voice of what she must and must not do. Strapping on his belt and sword, too angry to look at her. His face when he understood what she had done. The echo of his boots as he left the hall.

And the last time she would ever see him: A dark figure on the wall, cape flapping in the wind.

God give her strength.

She wept silently, trying not to waken Linnet, but her sobs shook the bed. She forced herself to take slow, deep breaths. Nothing was to be gained by more weeping. Blinking back her tears, she sat up and pushed the heavy bed curtain aside.

It was late, judging by the light. Though she was grateful de Roche had saved her from meeting his mother last night, she must not delay making the acquaintance of her mother-in-law any longer. The woman would think badly of her.

Isobel stood on the cold floor, hugging herself, and looked

about the bedchamber. It was a dark and austere room, the only furniture the bed, a bench, and a table with pitcher and basin. What light there was came from the adjoining room.

Isobel stepped through the doorway into a cozy solar. It had a coal brazier for warmth and was comfortably furnished with a small table, a chair, and two stools. The best feature was the large double window that bathed the room in late morning light. Beneath it was a window seat with colorful cushions.

Isobel stepped up onto the window seat to look out. Her rooms, she saw, were on the third floor overlooking an interior courtyard. A single tree filled the courtyard, its branches rising higher than her window. A row of small brown birds perched on the slender branch closest to her, heads twitching back and forth as they chattered.

At the sound of a light knock, Isobel hopped down just as a pretty maid opened the door.

"The lord awaits you in the hall, m'lady," the maid said, bobbing a curtsy. "I am to help you dress."

Isobel decided to let Linnet sleep. A short time later, she followed the young woman down two sets of stairs and through several rooms to the hall. There, she found de Roche sitting alone at a long table set before the hall's huge hearth.

He rose and greeted her with a kiss on each cheek. "Your rooms are satisfactory?" he asked as he helped her sit.

"They are lovely, thank you, especially the solar."

Several trays were on the table, piled high with food. De Roche pushed his trencher toward her and nodded for her to help herself. All this food for just the two of them? The rest of the household must have long since broken their fast.

She nibbled at a piece of bread. "I am sorry I missed your mother. When shall I meet her?"

"My mother is not here just now." De Roche stabbed a

slab of ham with the point of his knife and stuffed it into his mouth.

Not here? His mother must already be out visiting friends in the town.

"I'm afraid you shall not see much of me for the next week or two," de Roche said, chewing.

He surveyed the tray of steaming bread, picked a thick slice, and dipped it in the bowl of honey. Dribbles of sticky honey ran down his chin and fingers, reminding her disturbingly of Hume.

Between bites of the bread and licks at the honey running down his hand he said, "I will be busy persuading the men of the town to take King Henry's side in this fight."

This, at least, was good news.

"I'm glad you will speak for our king," she said. "You can assure them he is a just ruler who cares for all his people."

De Roche snorted. "That is hardly an argument that will persuade the men who matter."

"I do not understand the resistance to King Henry," she said. "There can be no sincere dispute as to his right to rule Normandy." His right to rule all of France was not so clear, so she did not mention it.

De Roche patted her hand. "Do not trouble yourself with such matters."

"But I want to be your helpmate in all things," she protested.

"Leave the politics to me," he said. "Your other duties will more than fill your time."

At his signal, one of the servants brought a small bowl of water for him to rinse his fingers. De Roche kept his eyes on her as he wiped his wet fingers on the cloth the servant held out to him. Uncomfortable at the intensity of his gaze, Isobel set down the slice of bread.

"Come," de Roche said, rising from the table. "I shall show you the house. I have an hour to spare before I must leave."

The smell of ham and warm bread wafted up her nose. Stomach rumbling, she stood and took his arm. He was an important man with duties to attend to; she would not keep him waiting.

De Roche walked her past several rooms without giving her a chance to look in. There must be some part of the house that he was particularly proud of, a set of rooms he wished to show her first.

"Shall I meet your mother at supper, then?" she asked as he hurried her past yet another room.

"Hardly. She is in Paris."

"Paris? Your mother is in Paris?"

"'Tis safer for her there, while Normandy is unsettled."

Surely de Roche would not bring her to stay in his house without a female family member present.

"If your mother is not in the house, who is?" When he made no immediate response, she said, "You know I cannot stay here with no one to serve as chaperone."

"It is a huge house," he said, putting his arm around her waist and guiding her forward. "And with all the servants, you cannot say we are alone."

How could he put her in this position? It was all she could do not to shout at him. Not that it would do any good now. After one night under his roof, the damage was done. People would think what they would.

"Come, I want to show you the new wing of the house, where I have my rooms." He opened a heavy wood door and motioned for her to precede him.

She folded her arms and turned to face him. "You should have told me your mother would not be here."

"We are betrothed," he said, leaning down until his breath was hot against her ear. "As good as wed."

Before she could get the words out to object, he hoisted her up and carried her through the timber-framed doorway.

"Put me down! Please!"

De Roche carried her through a large, richly furnished solar and into an adjoining room. Centered against the wall of this second room was an oversized bed with a dark wood frame and heavy burgundy curtains tied back with gold cords.

This was quite obviously de Roche's bedchamber. And his bed.

He set her on her feet and walked her backward until she felt the high bed behind her. She arched back against it to keep from touching him; his sickly sweet scent filled her nose.

Reaching past her, he patted the bed behind her. "Your most important duty is here."

Her heart thundered in her chest. She did not want this. When she turned her head away from his kiss, he ran his mouth down her throat. Then suddenly, he was all over her—hands squeezing her breasts, knee pushing between her legs, mouth sucking on her neck.

"Stop, you are hurting me!" she cried as she tried in vain to push him away.

He was pulling at her gown, yanking it up.

"You must let me speak!" she shouted at him.

He leaned back, breathing hard. "I beg you, be brief."

"I am not well."

He smiled. "Oddly enough, I feel feverish, myself."

"I'm having my courses." The lie tumbled out of her mouth before she thought it. Blushing, she added, "They began this morning."

"I see." De Roche stepped back and straightened his tunic. "Well, then, we can wait a few days."

"Aye," she said in a voice just above a whisper, "we should wait."

Hume had followed the church's admonition to abstain from relations during her monthly bleeding. She'd used the excuse as often as she dared. From the expression of distaste on de Roche's face, she suspected this reprieve was due to a perverse squeamishness rather than a desire to avoid sin.

De Roche marched her back to her rooms, not bothering to hide his displeasure. As if she could help having her courses! She lied, but he did not know that.

Well, she was angry with him, too. And she had good cause! Displeasing him, however, would not serve her well in the long run. The man could make her life a misery in a thousand ways, if he chose.

So why did she lie to put him off? If she carried a child, then bedding de Roche now was the safest and wisest course. The only sensible course. If her husband suspected the child was not his... She closed her eyes. Nothing could be worse.

Still, she could not make herself do it. She could not yet take that final step. A betrothal plus consummation made a marriage, regardless of the formalities.

She would honor Stephen's demand, as best she could. Though she was not able to delay the betrothal, she would forestall completion of the marriage until she knew if there was a child. Stephen's child.

'Twas foolish, for Stephen could not save her now. Even if he wanted to, he could not.

Chapter Twenty-seven

As if being punished for her lie, Isobel awoke the next morning with a damp stickiness between her legs.

Nay, it could not be! She closed her eyes and tried to pretend she did not know. But it could mean nothing else. She rolled to her side and hugged her knees to her chest.

There was no baby.

Only now could she admit to herself how much she had wanted it. If she were with child, there would be no way for Stephen to know of it, no way for her to get word to him. Still, she harbored the hope that somehow he would know. And come for her.

It made no difference that he would have married her for the child's sake. Nor that she would make a pathetic wife, always hoping to make him love her. In her secret heart of hearts, she wanted to be forced to take her chances with him.

Regardless of all else, she wanted this baby. Stephen's child. A part of him she could love and keep.

Linnet stirred on the bed beside her, bringing her sharply back to the present. There could be no escape from her betrothal now. Her life was here in Normandy. With de Roche.

Isobel was lost in such despair that days and nights blurred together. She did not stir from her rooms, refused to dress, and ate only what Linnet forced down her.

Although she told herself she must gather herself and face her future, she simply could not do it. It took all her strength to drag herself from her bed to sit in her solar. She spent most of her time there, gazing out the window at the tree in the courtyard. It was in blossom now.

She ignored the tug on her arm. When it persisted, she turned her gaze from the tree to find Linnet at her side.

"I've been trying to tell you!" Linnet's voice was urgent, upset.

Isobel tried to make an effort, for the girl's sake. "What is it?"

"I told them all you have a raging fever, but it has been a week and de Roche is asking for you."

How could Linnet believe she cared about this?

"Listen to me!" Linnet put her hands on her hips and stamped her foot. "I swear, I shall slap you if you do not quit looking at that damnable tree. François and I need your help."

Before Isobel could drift off again, Linnet lifted a cup of wine to her mouth and held it there until she drank. She felt the wine hit her stomach and travel down her limbs. With so little in her stomach, she felt light-headed when Linnet hauled her up from her chair.

Could the girl not leave her in peace? She looked longingly

over her shoulder at her tree. The sharp slap on her cheek
startled her.

"Linnet!"

"I warned you," Linnet said without the slightest show of
remorse. "Now you shall eat the food I brought you, and then
you shall wash and dress. Did you not promise the king you
would keep watch on de Roche? I tell you, he is up to something. We must find out what it is before it is too late."

Too late? It was already too late, for her. But Linnet was
right. She was neglecting her duty. If de Roche was changing
loyalties, she must try to turn him back. She was so bone
weary, though, she did not know how she would do it.

"I will get dressed and do my duty," she told Linnet. Bleak
as her future looked, she did not want to add traitor's wife to
her list of burdens.

As if by some signal, there was a knock on her door
the moment she was dressed. She heard whispers, and then
François appeared before her. He must have grown half a
foot since Stephen first brought him from Falaise. Overnight,
he'd gone from boy to youth on the brink of manhood.

"'Tis good to see you up and about, Lady Hume," he said
in a new, deep voice. "Are you feeling better?"

"I am, thank you." She did feel a bit better for having eaten.
"Linnet tells me you have some news I should hear?"

"'Tis about Lord de Roche," François said. "Linnet and
I believe he is plotting against King Henry. Late at night,
he meets with men in the small parlor, where none of the
servants can overhear them."

"This means nothing," Isobel protested.

"But we heard them from the bushes outside the window,"
Linnet said.

Good heavens, what had the two of them been up to?
Isobel felt a surge of guilt for her neglect.

"We did not hear much," François admitted, "but they kept mentioning King Henry and—"

"—Burgundy and the Dauphin," Linnet finished for him.

"So they speak of politics? In these times, men talk of little else. I am sure de Roche is only doing what he pledged to do. He is persuading these men to support King Henry."

The twins shook their heads in unison.

"De Roche sounded as if he wanted to spit each time he said the king's name," François said, as if that settled the matter.

Though there was no reason for the late night meetings to make Isobel suspicious, the twins' certainty made her uneasy. Had de Roche changed loyalties? To find out, she would have to join him in the hall and learn whom he entertained as guests.

The thought of seeing him caused her palms to sweat and her throat to go dry. There was no point, however, in delaying the inevitable.

She stood. "I shall go speak with him now."

"There is something else you must know," François said.

Was there no end to this? Isobel nearly snapped at him before she noticed his gaze was on the floor and he was shuffling his feet.

"What is it?" she asked, touching his arm.

François's voice was so low she had to lean forward to hear him. "No one in the city knows of your betrothal."

"That cannot be," she said. "By now, the banns must have been read in church at least once."

François shook his head, then looked sideways toward the door, as if longing to escape.

To what end did de Roche delay? News traveled slowly between the English- and French-held parts of Normandy, but it did travel. He could not hide her forever.

Isobel found de Roche sitting behind a table scattered with parchments in his private parlor. When he saw her in the doorway, he leapt to his feet and crossed the room.

"I'm glad to see you are well!" he said, taking her hand and kissing her cheek. He seemed genuinely pleased to see her. "You look lovely, if a little thin. Come, you must sit."

He put his arm around her and guided her to the chair closest to the brazier. His solicitude made her feel guilty for letting the twins' wild speculations run away with her.

"I am sorry to interrupt you," she said.

"I am glad to see you before I leave. 'Tis a shame I must go just as you are better, but I cannot delay visiting my mother any longer." Roche shifted his gaze and pulled on his ear. "I cannot have her hearing of our betrothal secondhand. You see, she rather dotes on me."

So this was the reason for his delay in having the banns read! No excuse was adequate, to be sure. Still, she was relieved his motive was no more sinister than consideration for his mother.

"You are a good son," Isobel said, pleased to learn it was true. "But should I not go with you?"

"Don't be foolish! You've just risen from your sickbed," he said. "I would not have you risk the roads again, in any case."

They were interrupted then by one of his men-at-arms. "Lord de Roche," the man said from the doorway, "the men are ready and await you outside."

"I shall join you shortly," de Roche said, dismissing the man with a nod.

Isobel sighed with relief; she could delay the unpleasant task of questioning him about politics a little longer.

"I can escort you to your chamber before I leave," de Roche said, rising to his feet.

At the door he stopped abruptly, as if he had forgotten something, and went back into the room. His back was to her, but Isobel saw him take one of the parchments from the table and lock it in the drawer.

He took her straight to her rooms, his brisk steps conveying he was in a hurry now. Outside the open door of her solar, he kissed her hand and bade her an abrupt adieu.

When he turned to leave, something inside the room caught his attention. A wave of unease passed through Isobel as she followed the direction of his gaze. What caught de Roche's attention—and held it still—was Linnet.

The girl sat on the window seat, head bowed over her needlework, sunlight shining on her fair hair. How had Isobel failed to notice? Linnet, like her brother, was growing up. Her emerging shape was a trifle too apparent in the too-small gown.

Isobel drew in a sharp breath when Linnet looked up and fixed her deep blue eyes on them. Heaven help the child. A girl so alone in the world should not be this lovely.

As Linnet's mistress and lady of the house, Isobel could protect her from most men. But not from de Roche. If he was dishonorable enough to take advantage of a dependent, Isobel was powerless to stop him.

Well, perhaps not completely powerless.

"Philippe," she said, pointedly using his Christian name.

He dragged his gaze away from Linnet to look at her. Forcing a smile to her lips, she took a half step closer and rested her palm against his chest.

She had his attention now.

Coy did not come easily to her. She tilted her head and looked up at him from under her lashes. "Must you go?"

De Roche wrapped his hand around hers and brought it slowly to his lips. "I fear I must," he said, regret tugging at his voice. "I can delay no longer."

Isobel took a deep breath and let it out on the single word "Alas."

Roche ran his tongue over his lips as his gaze dropped to her breasts. For a long moment, she feared her act had worked too well. When he gave his head a shake and stepped back from her, she sent a silent prayer of thanks to every saint she could think of.

"I shall return in a week," he said, raking his eyes over her one last time.

As Isobel watched him disappear down the stairs, she thought about what was in his eyes when he looked at Linnet. Not just lust, but possession. De Roche felt he had a right to take her. Isobel was not naive; she knew how it happened. The lord might give the serving girl a few trinkets or coins, but he would not allow her to refuse him.

Isobel would delay the inevitable no more. She would not protest that the banns must be read thrice.

When de Roche returned, she would go to his bed.

She was not vain enough to believe she could divert de Roche forever. Eventually, she had to get the girl out of his house. But she could buy time. When Robert came to visit, he could take Linnet away with him. How long before Robert's promised visit? A few weeks? She could distract de Roche that long, if she tried.

Isobel could not save herself. But by the saints, she would save Linnet.

Chapter Twenty-eight

April 1418

*R*ouen was a prize second only to Paris. From La Char-treuse de Notre Dame de la Rose, the Carthusian monastery set on a hill to the east of the city, Stephen could see over Rouen's walls and watch the bustle of this prosperous city of 70,000 souls.

The city's defenses had been strengthened since English forces last tried to take it, some thirty years ago. Stephen scanned the long line of the wall, with its sixty towers. To lay siege here, King Henry would have to bring an army large enough to encircle the city and guard all six gates. He would also have to block supplies from reaching the city from both the south and the north via the Seine, which flowed beside the city.

Besieging Rouen would be an arduous task. All the same, the city would fall. Stephen did not hold out much hope he could convince the men of Rouen of that truth, though.

As the king's envoy, he was tasked with putting a single question to them: Would Rouen submit willingly, or would its people be starved into submission?

Stephen wondered again why the king chose him for this mission. He sensed his brother's hand in it. Perhaps it was Robert's. Stephen had plenty of time to contemplate that puzzle on the two-day ride to Rouen. Instead, all he thought of was Isobel—and what he was going to do about her when he got here.

It had been two weeks. Two weeks since she lay naked beneath him. Two weeks since she refused him.

Two weeks since she made her pledge to another.

For the thousandth time, he asked himself why she did it. How could she? How could she do it right after she agreed not to? She did it so soon after he left her bed, his smell must have been on her skin as she made her pledge to de Roche.

Somehow the king had suspected Stephen's intentions toward Isobel, or so Robert believed. The king was not the only one to guess. Apparently, Robert, William, and Catherine had planned to speak to the king on Stephen's behalf that very day. King Henry acted swiftly, before his friends could approach him.

Robert insisted the king surprised Isobel, as well. But still, it was she who spoke the promise of marriage. Stephen's only comfort was that Isobel did not look the happy bride that morning, with her eyes swollen and her skin as pale as death.

A betrothal between a man and woman of consenting age was very nearly irreversible. But surely pregnancy by another man was a valid ground for breaking it. Time was short. Her marriage to de Roche could be completed in a week or so.

If Isobel was with child, it would be a simple matter. Stephen would carry her off and deal with the consequences later. If she did not agree to marry him at once, he would wear her down by the time the child was born.

What would he do if she did not yet know if she carried his child? Or worse, if she were certain she did not? He would not let himself think of that.

"Stephen!"

He turned to see Jamie and Geoffrey hurrying toward him.

"The city has replied to the message you sent today," Jamie said, holding out the rolled parchment.

Stephen scanned the long and flowery missive.

"The city will graciously welcome King Henry's envoy on the morrow," he summarized for Jamie and Geoffrey. "But they 'invite' my escort of English knights to remain here at the monastery while I conduct my business in the city."

"You cannot agree to go alone," Jamie protested. "At least take Geoffrey and me with you."

"They will not permit it," he told them. "And there is no need, since they have guaranteed my safety."

"Their guarantee!" Jamie scoffed. "These Frenchmen murder even sworn allies and close relations."

"If they mean to violate their guarantee," Stephen said, "one or two men could not save me."

He would ride into Rouen alone on the morrow. Within a day or two, he would know the city's fate. And his own.

* * *

Linnet rushed into the solar and slammed the door behind her. "De Roche has returned!"

Isobel's stomach clutched; her reprieve was over.

"The servants are all abuzz, because no sooner was he in the house than he left again," Linnet said, her cheeks pink with excitement. "You'll not believe it! 'Tis even worse than we thought!"

"Slow down, Linnet. What will I not believe?"

"François overheard the men talking while he helped with the horses," Linnet said. "De Roche was in Troyes, not Paris!"

Isobel tried to make sense of this news. "Troyes? Is that not where the Duke of Burgundy and the French queen are?"

Linnet nodded her head vigorously up and down. "Proof that de Roche betrays the king!"

Word had reached the city that Burgundy had captured the queen and set up a sham government in Troyes. Everyone expected Burgundy to break his alliance with King Henry any day now.

"François heard the men say Burgundy parlays with the Armagnacs, proposing terms to join forces against King Henry."

"What was François doing—hiding in the straw? I wish he would not take such risks! Where is he now?"

"He followed de Roche, of course," Linnet said. "I told him to."

"Do you wish to get your brother killed?"

For the hundredth time, she wondered about the twins' background. They refused to tell her anything except that they were orphaned. One thing was certain. Linnet was not raised to be anyone's servant. She was every bit as willful as Isobel was at that age.

They sat up past midnight sewing—or pretending to sew—while they waited for François. Just before Isobel heard a light tap on the door, Linnet tossed her sewing aside and ran to open it.

"Where did de Roche go?" Linnet asked François as soon as she closed the door. "Did you see whom he met?"

"I followed him to a house where Armagnac supporters were meeting."

"You should not do everything your sister tells you," Isobel scolded. "These are powerful men with much at stake. That makes them dangerous."

"De Roche never saw me," François said with a cocky grin.

Why was de Roche meeting with Armagnacs? Was he in league with both factions against the king? Aloud she said, "'Tis possible de Roche attempts to persuade them of the rightness of King Henry's cause."

Linnet gave an unbecoming snort.

"He was never loyal to the king," François said.

King Henry was not beloved here as he was in England, so she sometimes wondered at the reason for the twins' fervent loyalty. But this, like their parentage, was not something they shared with her.

"The king must be warned," Linnet insisted.

"Of what would we warn the king?" Isobel asked, trying to reason with them. "Even if we knew something worth the telling, how would I get a message to the king?"

"There is a way," François said, beaming at her. "King Henry has sent an envoy to Rouen."

"The king's envoy is in the city?"

François shook his head. "He is outside the city, awaiting permission to enter. The garrison commander and the city leaders spent the whole day arguing over what to do with him."

"How do you learn these things?" Isobel asked. "You mustn't go everywhere about the city as you do."

"Someone must bring us news, and you will not let me go," Linnet said. "Now, how shall we get a message to the envoy?"

"But we have no proof de Roche acts against the king," Isobel argued. "You expect me to betray him on so little?"

Linnet lifted her chin. "If we find the proof, will you do it?"

Isobel looked from one pair of bright blue eyes to another.

Would she betray her king, or de Roche? Before she could answer that, she must learn the truth. But how?

In bed. Aye, that would be the best time to ask him. Tonight, after their first time together.

Chapter Twenty-nine

*I*n the morning, Stephen dressed in the clothes he brought to play the part of king's envoy. Elaborate liripipe hat, knee-length velvet tunic, jeweled rings and brooch. Even particolored hose, God help him. As he fastened a heavy gold belt around his hips, he heard a low whistle. He looked up to see Jamie grinning at him from the doorway.

"'Tis certain they'll notice you, Uncle."

"Only doing my duty," Stephen said with a wink. "Now, you be sure to get out of here fast if there's trouble."

"Trouble?" Jamie asked. "You mean when the ladies start to fight over you?"

Stephen laughed and put his hand on Jamie's shoulder.

"The worst they will do is hold me for ransom," he said in a hushed voice as they walked outside together. "If I do not return or send word before nightfall tomorrow, ride hard for Caen. Wait no longer, or they may come to the monastery and take you, as well."

"I shall do what needs be done," Jamie said.

"I know it. You always make me proud."

Stephen did not think the good citizens of Rouen would throw him over the wall and set him afire. But they might. So he embraced his nephew, not caring if he embarrassed him before the other men. Ready now, he mounted Lightning and rode down to the city's main gate.

He arrived just as the bells of the city churches rang for Sext, the agreed-upon hour. An escort of two dozen knights met him at the gate and accompanied him the short distance to the Palais de Justice. At the Palais, he was received with all the tedious protocol due the English king's representative.

It was better than throwing his lifeless body over the wall. But they could always do that later.

After the welcome, he was taken to a room in the Palais and left there "to rest from his journey." Since the ride from the monastery was no more than half a mile, this meant the important men of the city were not yet agreed on what to do with him.

News of the arrival of King Henry's envoy would have spread to every corner of the city by now. If de Roche was still the king's man, he should find a way to have a private word with Stephen. Stephen did not expect him.

Since de Roche was a man of influence here, Stephen needed to settle the king's business before his own. De Roche must not suspect Isobel was leaving with Stephen before the city gave its formal reply. Better still if de Roche did not learn of her departure until they were a good half day's ride away.

There was little Stephen could do now but pace. After an hour or two, a servant appeared at his door to advise him there would be a reception in his honor that evening.

De Roche was bound to attend with the other local notables. Which meant Isobel would be there, too. Stephen had to find a way to speak to her alone so they could make their plan.

* * *

Isobel stood at the top of the stairs, dressed in her green silk gown with silver trim and matching slippers and headdress. She smoothed the skirt one last time. Then, with trepidation in her heart, she went down the stairs.

Last night she'd been so sure de Roche would come to her that she sent Linnet to sleep with the kitchen maids. She lay awake for hours listening for the scrape of the door. Near dawn, she heard voices below. When the house grew silent again, she finally drifted off to sleep.

This morning, Linnet woke her with the news that de Roche had already left the house "to commit more treachery." François came later to tell them the city was rife with rumor that the envoy was locked up or murdered in the Palais.

All day she was tense, waiting for de Roche's return. Finally, an hour ago, de Roche sent a servant to tell her to dress for a grand reception at the Palais. That must mean the envoy was at the Palais—but alive and well.

The reception would be her best—perhaps her only—opportunity to give a message to the king's envoy. If de Roche was involved in some treachery against King Henry, she must try to learn what it was before they arrived at the Palais.

De Roche was waiting for her in the front entry. His eyes widened when he saw her.

"I would much rather stay home with you this evening," he said as he took her arm. "But the reception is for King Henry's envoy, and he will expect to see you."

"Who is the envoy?" she asked. "Do I know him?"

He shrugged. "I did not hear the name. Come, the carriage is waiting. We are late."

She had so little time! What would be the best approach? Flattery? Pouting? She was off playing with swords when the other girls learned these useful skills.

"'Tis a shame," she said once they were settled in the carriage, "you could not even come to greet me after being gone a week."

De Roche's teeth flashed in the dim light. "You missed me."

She looked up at him through her lashes and nodded. In sooth, his almost constant absence was all that gave her hope of surviving this marriage.

She turned her head away and gave a sniff. "I hope you had good reason to neglect me."

He put his hand on her thigh. "I told you the men here are hardheaded," he said, leaning closer. "It takes much effort to persuade them to the right course."

He began kissing her neck. When his hand went to her breast, she panicked and blurted out, "Are you with the Armagnacs now?"

De Roche sat back abruptly. In a voice so cold it sent a shiver through her, he said, "What is it that you think you know, Isobel?"

"Nothing, I know nothing," she said in a rush. "'Tis only that I worry about you. These are such dangerous times."

He remained silent, examining her with narrowed eyes.

"You cannot think the Dauphin would ever make a proper king!" Though a part of her knew she should be quiet, the arguments spewed out of her mouth of their own accord. "By all accounts, the Dauphin is a weak and unworthy youth. And after all the queen's affairs, many doubt he is the mad king's true heir."

God help her, what made her say it! 'Twas too late now for pretense.

"If you are planning to break with King Henry, I beg you not to do it," she pleaded, "for your sake, as well as mine and our future children."

"Which one of the servants is telling you these lies?" he demanded. "I promise you, he will regret his loose tongue."

"Please, Philippe, you must tell me if you have changed loyalties."

"I must tell you nothing." His voice was tight with barely controlled rage. "There is but one thing a man must do with his wife. In that you have thwarted me, but not for long."

"I fear for your safety if you cross King Henry," she tried again. "He will prevail in the end."

"Do you intend to tell tales on your husband tonight?" Bits of his spittle hit her face as he spoke. "Do I have a spy in my own home?"

"Nay!" Her voice was high-pitched, panicked. "I would never be disloyal. I want to make a good wife."

"Then you are unwise to displease me." He grabbed her wrist. "I warn you, Isobel, do not leave my side tonight."

Chapter Thirty

Stephen stood before the crowd of well-dressed merchants and nobles in the great hall of the Palais. The reception was to begin with his formal speech pleading King Henry's case. The king had drafted it himself, taking only a few of Stephen's suggestions.

As Stephen unrolled the parchment, he scanned the room again. De Roche and Isobel were late.

"King Henry comes not as your conqueror, to take plunder and lay waste to the land, but as your rightful sovereign lord," he read in a loud voice. "To all who pledge loyalty to him, he will welcome you to his bosom with great joy and generosity.

"But be warned! If you defy him, he will crush you without mercy. He shall claim what is rightfully his. The victor of Agincourt is rolling across Normandy, and none can stop him. God is with him. He will prevail."

Stephen took a deep breath, glad to have the formal speech over. From Henry's mouth to their ears: "Crush without mercy." He hoped the people listening in the hall tonight knew King Henry meant every word.

For the next two hours, Stephen stood at one end of the hall as the city notables took turns coming to pay their respects.

Where is Isobel?

He made himself pay attention to the useless platitudes of each person, listening for hints of what lay beneath. So far, they seemed an overconfident lot. It mystified him how they could believe their city walls could withstand English cannon when the famed "impregnable" walls of Falaise could not.

He heard them boasting to each other. "Burgundy will come to our defense." "The Armagnacs will never let the great city of Rouen fall." What made these men think either faction would bring their armies to save Rouen? For months, both stood by as city after city in Normandy fell.

Stephen saw the uneasy expressions on the faces of their wives. If only the decision were in the pragmatic hands of the women, instead of these strutting cocks.

Where was Isobel? The crowd was thinning out, and she and de Roche still had not arrived.

And then he saw her. Politics, war, his official duties—all flew out of his head as Isobel and de Roche came into the hall through a side entrance. Stephen forced his gaze to drift past them. Eventually, de Roche would have to come to him.

De Roche did not delay but came straight to him. And then Isobel stood before him—so close he could have touched her if he reached out his arm. After so long away from her, it took all his will not to sweep her into his arms. He could almost taste her.

How was it possible she was so beautiful? Her skin was pale, though, and she looked thin.

"Have you been ill?" he asked her.

"I am well now, thank you. And you, Sir Stephen?"

Her voice. He wanted to listen to it and nothing else. But de Roche was blathering something to him, like a gnat buzzing about his head.

"What?" he snapped. He let his eyes burn over de Roche, letting the man see that Stephen thought he was a worthless sack of horseshit. "The king will be displeased to hear you've made little progress with the city leaders. Your failure will bring the people of Rouen to grief."

De Roche's face flushed a deep red. When he opened his mouth to speak, Stephen cut him off.

"Lady Hume, you are much missed in Caen," he said as he took her hand and lifted it to his lips. Her fingers were trembling and icy cold. "The king sends his warmest greetings."

Keeping his eyes on hers, he said, "I hope Lord de Roche will permit me to speak with you in private before I leave the city, for I have news of your brother." Switching to English, he added, "And a question to ask."

She sent a furtive glance at de Roche, who was staring fixedly at the wall above Stephen's head. Then she gave her head an almost imperceptible shake. That tiny movement hit Stephen like a heavy blow, knocking the wind out of him and sending him back a step.

"Of course you may speak with her, if time allows," de Roche said, unaware that Isobel had already given Stephen the only answer that mattered.

There was no child. Stephen watched in a daze as de Roche took Isobel's arm and led her away.

No child, no child. He'd been so certain.

Somehow he managed to gather himself and pretend the world was not crashing around his ears. He did his duty by his king. But it was the longest evening of his life.

When the reception finally ended, he retired to his room and collapsed upon the bed. He stared at the ceiling. To see her and not touch her. To talk with her and not be able to say the things he needed to say to her. It had nearly killed him.

He was so sure she was with child. Because he needed her to be. It shamed him that he wanted to use the child to force her hand, to make her wed him instead of de Roche. In time, she would have seen it was for the best...

He heaved a sigh. What would he do now?

He could not leave without telling her what was in his heart. If she wanted him, he would find a way. How, he did not know. But he would.

There was a rap on his door. Please, God, make them go away! When the knocking persisted, he rolled off the bed. He opened the door and found himself looking into a pair of blue eyes beneath a head of shaggy blond hair.

"François!" He pulled the boy into the room and closed the door behind him. "'Tis good to see you! I swear you've grown still more since you left Caen. How is your sister?"

"Truth be told, she is a constant worry to me."

"Nothing new in that," Stephen said, slapping the lad on the back. "You are just the man I need. Where is Isobel staying? I need to speak with her."

François flushed and dropped his gaze to the floor. Unease rolled through Stephen.

In a low voice the boy said, "She stays in de Roche's house."

Blindly, Stephen found his way to the nearest chair and fell into it. Isobel was living in the man's house? He had not expected this. How could she agree to it? A betrothal was difficult enough to break, but a betrothal plus consummation made a marriage.

"'Tis a very large house," François said, stretching his

arms wide and speaking in a quick, nervous voice. "Her rooms are in a separate wing, and Linnet stays with her."

"But he must have family there, some married woman responsible for guarding Isobel's virtue."

When the boy dropped his eyes again, Stephen was suddenly so angry he wanted to punch his fist into the stone wall. Good God, it could not be worse.

"What was she thinking, agreeing to this...this... arrangement?" he said, throwing his hands up. Was she *trying* to torture him?

Had she done it? Had Isobel slept with the man? This time he did slam his fist against the wall. God's beard, that hurt!

François's eyes went wide as Stephen shook his hand out and muttered curses.

"I need to speak to Isobel alone. When is the best time to find de Roche gone?"

"He is often out late," Francois said with a shrug. "He rarely shows himself in the hall before the midday meal."

"And Isobel," Stephen asked between clenched teeth, "does she rise late, as well?"

"Nay, the lady is always up early."

He was a lost man, that he would take heart from so little. Though it seemed a lost cause now, he would go see her. He had to.

"Tell me what you know of de Roche's activities," he said to change the subject.

"He's always meeting in secret," François said. "Sometimes with Armagnac sympathizers, other times with the Burgundy men."

"What is he up to?" Stephen asked.

François shrugged again. "Lady Hume says we have no proof, but Linnet and I believe he is involved in some treachery against King Henry."

Isobel, married to a man like her father, whose oath of loyalty meant nothing. A man of no honor.

* * *

Isobel squeezed her eyes shut, grateful for the darkness of the carriage. Her hands would not stop shaking. Stephen. How it tore her heart to see him! She was grateful de Roche dragged her from the Palais without introducing her to anyone.

"There was a rumor in Caen about you and this Carleton." De Roche's voice was low, menacing. "I did not believe it at the time, but now I wonder."

De Roche grabbed her chin and jerked her face toward him.

"Were you bedding him, while you played the virtuous lady with me? Were you, Isobel?"

"You insult me grievously and with no cause," she said, forcing herself to speak in a steady voice. "I have gone to bed with no man, save for Hume."

He released her chin and sat back. "In sooth, I could not imagine you risking marriage to me for a dalliance with that wastrel. I vow I do not know what women see in him."

That he is ten times the man you are.

At least her anger kept her from weeping now.

De Roche did not speak again until the carriage came to a halt before the front gate of his house. "I must return to the Palais for more discussions," he said, sounding distracted.

Discussions over the city's response to King Henry. Which side would de Roche argue? She hardly cared anymore, so long as he was away from her. Her foot was on the carriage step when de Roche's voice stopped her.

"Leave your door unbarred tonight."

She took a candle from the sleepy-eyed servant who opened the front door and assured him she could find her way to her rooms alone. As she walked past de Roche's private parlor, she recalled talking with him there. She stopped in place. In her mind's eye, she saw the scattered papers on the table...de Roche returning to lock something in the drawer...

The locked drawer. If he had something to hide, it would be there. Perhaps she could find a clue as to his true allegiance. She had a right to know something that affected her future so significantly.

Should she look now? De Roche was gone, the servants abed. Heart pounding, she stood still and listened. No sound of anyone moving about. She eased the parlor door open and slipped inside.

She felt her way through the dark room to the window on the courtyard. Looking out, she saw no light in any of the rooms save for her solar, where Linnet waited up for her.

It was safe, then, to light the lamp.

She lit the lamp on the table with her candle, then tried the drawer. Locked. As she looked about for something to use to pry it open, a small vase on the corner of the table caught her eye. Would de Roche be so obvious? She turned the vase over onto her hand. She smiled as the key fell onto her palm. The man was wholly lacking in subtlety.

The key made a satisfying click as she turned it in the lock. Aha! A single sheet of parchment lay in the drawer. When she began to read it, her sense of satisfaction drained from her.

She sat down on the chair and smoothed the parchment with shaking hands to read it again.

Cousin,

All is arranged. We are assured the pious H will insist on hearing Mass on such an occasion. Thus the great H will die on his knees. I shall be there to see it.

The complicity of others comes at a high cost. Have your share of the gold ready when I arrive.

T

Murder. That was what de Roche's cousin intended for "H." Who was this "H"? She sucked in her breath. King Henry, of course! He was both "great" and "pious," to be sure. And it was well known he had Masses said on every possible occasion.

And the cousin "T"? That could only be de Roche's wily and powerful cousin Georges de la Trémoille.

But what was the "occasion" at which they intended to murder the king? She had a vague recollection of Robert complaining of how dull Caen would be with the king spending all of Lent in fasting and prayer. But at Easter, there was to be a grand event at which scores of men would be knighted.

Mass was a central part of the knighting ceremony.

A number of nobles who followed Burgundy—Henry's supposed ally—would be invited to this important event. Trémoille could easily attend.

A shudder ran through Isobel at the thought of King Henry murdered on his knees in church. The greatest king England had seen in generations, struck down by a coward's blade. If it was his fate to die young, such a king should fall in glory on the battlefield.

She had to get word of this conspiracy to Stephen so he could warn the king. But how? Carefully, she put the letter back as she found it, locked the drawer, and returned the key to the vase. She blew out the lamp and sat in the dark, trying to think how she would do it.

Stephen had asked de Roche's permission to visit her. If he did come, she could tell him then. She bit her lip in frustration—de Roche would never allow her to meet with Stephen alone. If she could find François, she could send a message with him...

But François was already in danger. De Roche raged about finding the servant who told her of his secret meetings. She must get both the twins to safety. But how?

She could think of no way to accomplish all that she must. A feeling of hopelessness took hold of her. She buried her head in her arms on the table and let herself weep. For her king. For the twins. For the misery of her life. For Stephen. How she longed to see him, to hear his laugh, to have his arms around her one more time.

How long had she been weeping when she heard voices?

She wiped her face on her sleeves and got to her feet. What had she been thinking, remaining in Roche's parlor? As she started toward the door, she heard the voices again. She went to the window and listened.

A scream reverberated through the courtyard. Isobel's blood froze in her veins. Linnet.

Isobel was out the door and running for the stairs. *Please, God, let me not be too late.* De Roche was the only one who would enter Isobel's rooms at night without permission.

The memory of Hume taking her the first time came to her sharp and clear as she raced up the stairs. There was nothing Isobel would not do to save Linnet from that. Nothing she would not do to save the girl from being forced to lose her innocence to a man she loathed.

Her heart was beating wildly in her chest as she reached the top of the stairs and flung open the solar door.

De Roche had Linnet pinned against the wall, holding her wrists over her head with one hand.

"Stop it, stop it!" Isobel screamed.

Linnet looked at Isobel with wide, terrified eyes. There was a studied casualness to de Roche's expression as he turned to her.

"A man must make do when he cannot find his bride." He

spoke with a cold calm that was more frightening than if he had raised his voice. "Where were you, Isobel?"

"I...I was just in the courtyard," Isobel stammered. "Let her go, Philippe. Please, I beg you, let her go."

"Waiting for the banns, the formalities...it all seems...so...unnecessary to me," de Roche said. "Does it not to you, my sweet?"

"Let Linnet go, and I will do whatever you want."

"Whatever I want." His white teeth gleamed in the candlelight. "That is just what I hoped you would say."

The moment he released Linnet, the girl ran to Isobel and threw her arms around her waist.

De Roche took out a handkerchief and wiped the blood from the scratches on his cheek. "I should have the girl whipped."

"No, Philippe."

"You will find," he said, wiping his hands on the handkerchief, "I can be as agreeable as you are."

Isobel pushed Linnet's hair back and kissed the girl's forehead. "Go now."

"I'll not leave you," Linnet whimpered against her.

"I shall be fine," Isobel said in a firm voice. She led Linnet to the door and removed the girl's arms from around her waist. As she pushed Linnet out the door, she whispered, "Go to your brother and do not return until morning."

The bar made a *thunk* as Isobel slammed it into place. She closed her eyes and rested her forehead against the door. Nothing could save her now. She would be the wife of this dark and treacherous man until the day she died.

She would, however, get Linnet out of Rouen. She gathered herself and turned around to face her husband.

De Roche was already unfastening his belt.

Chapter Thirty-one

When the knocking continued, Isobel spun around.

"Linnet, stop this!" she called out loudly enough to be heard through the door. "You must go away now."

A male voice answered, "Is Lord de Roche with you, m'lady?"

De Roche fastened his belt as he stomped to the door. After pushing Isobel aside, he slid the bar and jerked the door open. An elderly servant stood on the other side, rubbing his bony hands together and blinking nervously.

"What is it?" de Roche demanded.

In a high, quavering voice, the servant said, "The visitor you were expecting on the morrow, m'lord…he…he has just arrived and…and he is asking for you."

Isobel was startled by the sudden change in de Roche. The angry impatience was gone, replaced by a palpable fear.

De Roche turned hard gray eyes on her. "Do not leave your rooms tonight."

Without another word, he followed the servant out.

Isobel lay awake most the night, dreading the moment of de Roche's return. She must have eventually drifted off, for she was in a deep sleep when Linnet returned in the morning.

Linnet looked sharply about the rooms with narrowed eyes. "Where is he?"

"De Roche had a visitor shortly after you left," Isobel said. "He did not return."

The tightness in Linnet's face eased. "François did not come back, either."

"Come, I do not know how long we have," Isobel said as she led Linnet to the window bench. "I must tell you my plan."

As Isobel expected, Linnet objected to the plan at first.

"We must save the king," Isobel told her. "I shall have your promise that you will play your part, for there is no other way."

They spent the rest of the morning holding hands and talking quietly of small, unimportant things. Nothing could be gained by talking more about the difficulties ahead.

Isobel prayed de Roche would not come to her bedchamber before Stephen's visit. She did not want to have the memory of de Roche touching her when she saw Stephen for the last time. But what if Stephen did not come today? What if he did not come at all?

It was midafternoon when a servant came to tell Isobel that Sir Stephen Carleton was waiting in the hall to see her. De Roche, too, would be told of Stephen's arrival. If she could get to the parlor first, she might have a moment alone with Stephen.

"Hurry, please," she urged Linnet. Isobel tried to help with the headdress, but her hands were shaking so violently that Linnet slapped them away.

Isobel stared, unseeing, into the polished brass mirror as Linnet worked. She was so caught up in planning how to get the news of the murder plot to Stephen that she'd given no thought as to why Stephen wanted to see her. What reason could he have? Any news of Geoffrey he could have told her at the reception.

Could he be here to ask if she carried his child? She closed her eyes and swallowed. She'd been so sure Stephen understood her silent message.

"If I do not get to speak with Stephen alone, Linnet, tell him"—she said it with her eyes still closed—"tell him...there is no child."

It hit her again. There was no child.

Isobel opened her eyes. In the mirror's reflection, she saw her fist clutched against her chest and slowly lowered it to her lap. Did she hope Stephen cared? That he would suffer as she was suffering? Nay, she would not wish this pain on him.

Linnet touched her shoulder. "I've finished."

Isobel met Linnet's eyes in the mirror. "Wait outside the door until I call you."

Linnet nodded.

"Trust me." Isobel stood and took the shawl Linnet held for her. Taking a deep breath, she hurried out the door.

She was within a few steps of the entrance to the hall when a voice behind her stopped her.

"I was just looking for you, my dear," de Roche said, taking her arm in a firm grip. "We should welcome our guest together."

She would not have even a moment alone with Stephen. Before she could prepare herself, de Roche led her in.

Her heart stopped at the sight of Stephen. Last night, he looked like an impossibly handsome prince, bedecked in jewels and gold trim. Today he was in the sort of clothes he regularly wore. Their very familiarity made her ache to run her fingers along his collar, down his sleeve.

The usual humor and mischief were missing from his expression, however. His face was drawn, the laughter gone from his deep brown eyes. How could she have found fault with the easy, lighthearted Stephen of before? The man who made her laugh. She missed him now more than she could say.

It was evident Stephen's purpose in coming was to speak to her alone. It was equally clear de Roche would not permit it. After straining to make small talk for a few minutes, Stephen rose to his feet.

"I leave the city today," Stephen said, "so I must bid you adieu now, Lady Hume."

"Wait!"

She said it more loudly than she intended. Both men looked at her expectantly. De Roche's eyes were narrow, suspicious; Stephen's hand was on the hilt of his sword.

"Sir Stephen, I must ask you to take back the two servants you loaned to me," she said in as cool a voice as she could manage. She lifted her chin. "My new husband has more than enough servants to meet my needs."

Stephen furrowed his brow. "You are welcome to keep Linnet and François all the same. I am sure they are a comfort to you in your new surroundings."

"My husband provides for my comfort," she said. "I do not wish to have the girl here. She is headstrong and difficult. Her behavior is an embarrassment to me."

Stephen visibly stiffened. The shocked disapproval on his face almost made her falter.

She kept her expression hard and called out, "Linnet!"

On cue, Linnet came quietly into the room. The girl played her part to perfection. She stood, eyes cast down, tears rolling down her cheeks.

"You and your brother are leaving with me," Stephen said. Lips pressed together, he grabbed Linnet by the wrist and charged out. At the door, he turned to cast a scorching look at Isobel that nearly knocked her from her feet.

The hall was silent, save for the muffled sound of retreating footsteps. De Roche stood, mouth agape, staring after them. It happened so quickly he had no time to object—or to speak at all.

She had done it.

She had saved Linnet and François. They were in Stephen's hands now, and he would protect them. And she had uncovered the plot to murder King Henry. The twins would tell Stephen, and he would warn the king. It was enough.

* * *

After collecting François, Stephen strode ahead, barely aware of the twins trailing at his heels. Every now and then, Linnet's sobs penetrated his stormy thoughts, and he was angry all over again.

How could she dismiss Linnet so coldly? Little Linnet, who was wholly devoted to her. What she said about Linnet was surely true, but Isobel was always patient and tolerant with the girl before. What happened to her? Was it possible for a woman to change so much in so short a time?

Her new husband provides all the "comfort" she needs! Comfort, indeed. That remark was meant to cut him to the quick. It had.

He did not notice until he reached the Palais that François and Linnet had fallen behind.

"Sorry, we could not keep up," François said as they caught up to him on the steps. It was not François, whose legs were nearly as long as Stephen's, who could not keep up.

Stephen's blood was still pounding in his ears. He took a deep breath in an attempt to calm himself. "I apologize, Linnet. Come, we shall go to my room now."

Linnet blew her nose loudly and half coughed, half sobbed. Stephen narrowed his eyes at her—something was not quite right here. Deciding not to press her at the entrance, where anyone could be watching, he led the way to his room.

The servant assigned to watch him was frantic. "Where did you go, sir? You should have told me—"

"Be gone until morning," Stephen said as he shoved the man out of the room, "or I shall tell them how easy it was to slip by you."

As soon as he slammed the door, Linnet threw her arms up and danced around the room. "Was I not wonderful? You did not guess! François, you should have seen his face! And de Roche's!"

He clenched his fists to keep from strangling the girl.

"How could you believe Isobel would throw me out?" Linnet asked, rolling her eyes at him.

"Tell me the reason for this farce," he demanded.

In the blink of an eye, Linnet's face changed from delighted self-congratulation to anguish. "Isobel sent me away so I could tell you that de Roche and his cousin are plotting to kill King Henry."

What? His head was spinning. "How does she know this?"

"By spying on de Roche, of course," Linnet said.

Stephen sat down and closed his eyes. Alone, without a friend in this city, Isobel was spying on de Roche while living in his house? He shook his head. "What can she be thinking?"

"She is only doing her duty," Linnet said.

"Is Isobel quite certain of this plot?"

Linnet nodded. "Aye, she found a letter from his cousin in a locked drawer."

God help her, she was taking chances!

"The cousin writes that all is set to murder the king in church upon some grand occasion."

Murder the king! He stopped to think. "I wonder if they mean to do it at the knighting at Easter..."

"That is what Isobel believes," Linnet said. "And she says the cousin is Georges de la Trémoille, because the letter is signed 'T.'"

Stephen nodded, his thoughts on Isobel. "But why did Isobel devise that ruse to send you away? Surely she could have found another way to get a message to me."

Linnet's fair skin went red, and she would not meet his eyes. Stephen turned and raised an eyebrow at François.

Blushing as fiercely as his sister, François stepped next to him and whispered, "As we were walking here, Linnet told me de Roche was...that he was...after her. She thinks Lady Hume used the message as an excuse to get her away from him."

God's blood. Stephen wanted to kill the man with his bare hands.

François straightened and said, "She is right to trust you to protect my sister."

But who would protect Isobel when de Roche discovered the games she was playing? What could Stephen do now that she was living with the man? Nothing! Nothing at all. She was de Roche's wife now, beyond his reach.

He must go quickly to warn the king. Easter was still two weeks away, but men would begin arriving sooner. The conspirators could be in Caen any day, ready to act. He swallowed hard at the thought of leaving Isobel, of perhaps never seeing her again. Still, he had to go. He could not let his king be murdered.

But how could he leave her?

His thoughts were interrupted by a knock at the door.

It was one of the Palais guards. "This young woman says you arranged a...meeting...with her." The man waggled his eyebrows and jerked his thumb behind him.

Before Stephen could protest, a stunning woman with smoky dark eyes emerged from behind the guard. In a voice rich with unspoken promises, she said, "Claudette sent me."

Stephen winked at the guard. "Claudette knows the best."

He put his arm around the woman and let his hand slip down to squeeze her nicely rounded bottom as he pulled her inside. With another wink and a grin, he tossed a gold coin to the guard and kicked the door closed.

He moved his hand to the woman's arm and guided her to a seat. With languid ease, the woman sank into the chair.

Linnet was scowling at him furiously.

"My name is Sybille," the woman said in her sultry voice.

"You are a friend of Claudette's?"

The woman nodded. "I've just come from Paris, where I saw her. She asked me to carry some news to you. Something she thought you should know."

An hour later, Stephen walked her to the door.

"Thank you, Sybille," he said. "I hope coming here has not put you at risk."

The woman shrugged her shoulders and gave him an unconcerned smile. "The guards know me. I have visited important guests at the Palais before."

Stephen reached into the pouch at his belt, wondering how much a woman like this cost.

Sybille put her hand over his and shook her head. "I owe Claudette a favor."

She ran her tongue over her top lip and leaned forward until her breasts were a hair's breadth from his chest. She smelled divine.

"Since it is a very big favor I owe her, I could…"

"I appreciate the offer, and you are breathtaking," he said, putting his hand to his heart, "but I cannot."

She gave a soft laugh. "You made me lose my wager with Claudette."

With a saucy wink at François that made the boy blush crimson to his ears, Sybille went out the door, hips swaying.

Stephen sat down to think. What the courtesan told him changed everything.

Chapter Thirty-two

Stephen donned his showy clothes—the heavy gold belt, particolored hose, and all the rest—for his grand departure. He had no choice but to leave the city. A dozen heavily armed men waited outside to make sure he did.

Guy le Bouteiller, the garrison commander, rode beside Stephen to the gate. Stephen liked le Bouteiller and was glad for the opportunity to have a few words with him.

"I am flattered," Stephen said, glancing at the column of men armed to the teeth, "but how much trouble do you think these two children and I could cause on our way to the gate?"

"'Tis not what you would do that concerns me," le Bouteiller said, returning the smile. "Let's just say there are men in Rouen who might wish to answer the king of England by returning his envoy without his head."

"I tell you," Stephen said, "an honorable man like you would be happier serving King Henry."

Le Bouteiller did not dispute the point.

Before they parted at the gate Stephen said, "The men of this city make a grave mistake by spurning his peaceful offer."

"Return in a few months," le Bouteiller said in a low voice. "Much could change by then."

"The city should take the generous terms he offers now," Stephen said, not bothering to keep his own voice down. "Next time, King Henry will come himself, and he will bring his army."

With that last warning, Stephen turned his horse. He signaled to the twins to follow and galloped out the city gates.

* * *

Isobel felt Linnet's absence so keenly in her rooms that she simply had to get out for a little while. She slipped down the stairs, intent on reaching the courtyard unseen. Perhaps everything would not seem so very hopeless in the sunshine.

Seeing Stephen again—and then having him leave her in anger—left her ragged and shaken. Losing the twins at the same time was more than God should ask of her. The gaping hole in her heart would never heal.

After Stephen and Linnet left, de Roche had taken her hand and told her all was settled. As if it still mattered to her. It gave her no comfort to know de Roche was prepared to go through the formalities to finalize their marriage now.

She stepped lightly as she passed the door to de Roche's private parlor. Just when she thought she was safe, the parlor door creaked open behind her.

She closed her eyes and stood perfectly still, wishing him away. Did God hate her so much that he would even deny her an hour of solace in the courtyard? Now she would have to listen to de Roche lecture her about not following his command to wait in her rooms for him.

She had a vision of her life constantly alternating between terror and tedium. Pride had led her to this. She would have been better off in her father's care than under the thumb of this tyrant.

He cleared his throat behind her. Slowly, she turned to face him. If she could have drawn breath, she would have screamed. It could not be! The man standing before her was not de Roche, but the black-haired man who had led the attack on the abbey.

She knew she was not mistaken. The distance from gate to church had not been far in the small abbey; the piercing eyes and hawkish face were chiseled in her memory.

With the slightest inclination of his head he said, "I seemed to have startled you, madam."

He did not know her.

"I—I expected Lord de Roche," she said.

His black eyes seemed to go through her. Panic closed her throat as she waited for him to recognize her. Then she remembered: She wore her brother's clothes that day at the abbey. He had no cause to guess the finely dressed lady before him was the same person.

"My name is LeFevre," he said.

She forced herself to offer her hand to the monk killer. When he touched his lips to it, she swallowed the bile that rose in the back of her throat.

"And you, madam, are ... ?"

"Lady Hume," she said. "Lord de Roche's betrothed."

His eyes widened. "Philippe's betrothed?" He paused, as if expecting her to contradict him, then said, "I shall chastise Philippe for not sharing his good news with me."

She could not remain in his presence a moment longer.

Aware she was making an awkward departure, she gave him a stiff nod and turned back the way she had come. The courtyard would not do now. She wanted a barred door between her and the black-haired man. With his eyes burning into her back, she fought not to break into a run before she turned the corner.

She sat on her window seat, shaking and holding her arms across her belly until she was calm enough to think. LeFevre. LeFevre. Where had she heard the name before?

Then it came to her. One day she overheard Robert and Stephen speaking in low voices about men associated with the Dauphin and the Armagnacs. They mentioned several names before they noticed her and abruptly changed topics.

LeFevre had been one of the names.

So it was the Armagnacs who were behind the attack on FitzAlan and the abbey. What was she doing, sitting here? King Henry was adamant about how important it was for him to have this information. Somehow she had to get to the Palais and tell Stephen before he left the city.

She was reaching for her cloak when she heard angry voices echoing through the courtyard. One of the voices was de Roche's. Whoever was arguing with him could not be a servant, because both of them were shouting.

Damn him! She could not risk attempting to leave the house with de Roche just below. When the shouting faded, she stood on her window seat and leaned out the window. Had they moved into another part of the house? Or were they simply speaking too quietly for her to hear? She would have to take her chances.

No sooner did her feet hit the floor than the solar door banged open with a crash. De Roche filled her doorway.

"My Lord," Isobel said, dipping her head. How would she get to the Palais with him barring her way?

De Roche stood glaring at her with hard, angry eyes. "I thought you would wish to know," he said, his voice slow, taunting, "Carleton has left the city."

Though she tried to cover her reaction, she felt herself pale. *He has left me, he has left me, he has left me,* ran through her head like a chant. She wanted to sink to her knees and cover her face in her hands.

"I must say, Carleton looked rather grim during his visit to our fair city." De Roche walked around the solar, picking up things and setting them down again, as though what he said held little interest to him. "Still, I don't believe it will take him long to forget you."

He made a tutting sound with his tongue. "No time at all. In fact, I'm told he looked considerably more cheerful when he rode out the gates this afternoon. But then, he'd just spent an hour with the highest-priced courtesan in the city." He gave a loud sigh. "Sybille would cheer any man."

A courtesan? Without thinking, she parroted the words Robert once told her: "A man may enjoy a courtesan's company in public without employing her services in private."

Roche laughed aloud, appearing to be genuinely amused. "But he did 'enjoy her company' in private. The hour they spent together was in his bedchamber at the Palais."

"Since Sir Stephen is neither married nor betrothed," she said through her teeth, "he is free to do as he pleases."

De Roche laughed again. "You are mistaken if you think betrothal or marriage will cause a man to forgo other pleasures."

A courtesan. Stephen went to a courtesan right after leaving her.

De Roche cupped her cheek, forcing her attention back to him. "My betrothal will not stop me from taking you."

His words made no sense.

He ran his hands down her arms and encircled her wrists. "You look puzzled, Isobel."

The heat in his eyes told her what he wanted from her. With Linnet safely away, she could try to put him off.

"The banns have not yet been read thrice," she said.

He forced her back until her heels struck the wall. Holding her wrists against the wall on either side of her head, he leaned down until his nose nearly touched hers.

"The banns? The banns?" She felt the moisture of his breath on her face as he spat the words out. "Did you believe I would marry a woman so beneath me?"

He released her and spun away. "Me, a de Roche! I am blood relation to the greatest families of France! My wealth is ten times that of your father's."

Isobel rubbed her wrists as he stormed up and down the room, ranting. She was good and truly frightened now.

"Marriage to you would bring me no titles, no land. A pittance of a dowry. And yet your king thought I should be grateful—" He was so angry he choked on the word. "Grateful, because you are an *English* noblewoman."

He stopped his pacing. A cold stillness settled over him that frightened her more than his ranting. As he started toward her, a shiver ran up her spine.

"I shall make your father pay a ransom three times the paltry sum he offered as dowry," he said, jabbing the point of his forefinger against her chest. "And while I wait for him to pay it, I shall make you my whore."

"But we are betrothed!" Her voice shook, despite her effort to keep it steady. "I cannot be your... your..."

"My English whore."

Why was he talking ransom and saying such horrid things to her? "You know very well that if you take me to bed, I will be your wife in the eyes of both the church and the law."

"That would be true," he said, speaking slowly, "if I did not already have a wife."

"A wife? You have a wife?" She shook her head from side to side, unable to take it in. "You cannot. It is not possible."

"I assure you, it is. I made a very advantageous match with a young lady whose family is close to the Dauphin. Since her father was not entirely…supportive…of the marriage, we wed in secret shortly before I came to Caen."

"Then why did you come to Caen?"

"What better way to persuade King Henry of my loyalty than to agree to a marriage alliance?" de Roche said with a shrug. "I never intended to go through with it."

She was too shocked to speak.

"Your friend Robert was no more anxious to settle the marriage contract than I, so it was easy to put Henry off." He took a deep breath and shook his head. "I needed but a few weeks more."

"But you made a formal pledge to me," she said. "Before witnesses. Before the king."

"I admit Henry surprised me," he said. "He cornered me before I had a chance to slip out of Caen. I had no choice but to go through the sham betrothal."

How could any man be so wholly lacking in honor? And she, what had she done?

"Is that not bigamy?" Was it? Was she guilty of the sin, as well? "And what of the other lady? I cannot think she or her family will be pleased with the news of a second betrothal."

"I went to a good deal of trouble to ensure they would not learn of it," he said. "'Tis a shame you told my cousin."

"Your cousin?"

"Aye, you met Thomás today, downstairs." He shook his

finger at her. "My cousin is a dangerous man. You should have stayed in your rooms as I told you."

"Thomás? You mean LeFevre? LeFevre is your cousin?" She sucked in her breath. Was Thomás the "T" in the letter? Had she warned the king of the wrong man?

"So many questions, Isobel. Fortunately, it is as much in Thomás's interest as mine to keep the secret." He tilted his head and said, "Still, he is quite angry with me. You see, it is his young half sister who is my wife."

She was reeling from all the revelations. One thought rose above all the others clamoring in her head. If de Roche was married and her betrothal false, *she was not bound to him.*

Roche lifted her chin with his forefinger. "No matter what Thomás says, I shan't give you up soon."

She slapped his face, hard.

He regarded her with icy gray eyes as he touched the red mark she left on his cheek. "Your king has quaint notions of chivalry. Since he told me he would send an envoy—and I could not yet risk offending him—I had to take care with you before."

He took her wrists and held them in an iron grasp in one hand. Then, his expression cool, he swung his other arm and backhanded her so violently that her ears rang.

"But now?" he said. "Now there is nothing to keep me from doing whatever I want with you."

He kissed her hard, bruising her lips and grinding his hips against her. Still stunned from the slap, she did not fight him. When he released her, she fell back against the wall. She focused on the hair's breadth between them and pressed herself against the wall.

"I shall not be able to return to you until late." He rubbed the back of his fingers against her stinging cheek. "I suggest you spend the time thinking of ways to please me."

He gave her cheek a pinch that made her eyes sting before finally turning to go out the door. She heard the key scrape in the lock as she sank to the floor.

How long did she lie there, clutching her knees and shaking so hard her teeth chattered? The room grew pitch-black, and still she could not make herself get up.

How would she bear it? How could she live until her father sent the ransom? Would her father pay it? Or would he leave her here forever? If she went home, it would be in shame—perhaps with de Roche's child in her belly. The blemish on her virtue would be no less for not being her fault.

She pounded her fists on the floor. How could she have mistaken de Roche's stern nature for honorable character? His arrogance for seriousness of purpose? The man was an oath breaker of the worst kind. And he was related by blood—and by marriage—to that monk killer. She could hardly breathe thinking of LeFevre being under the same roof.

As she lay on the floor in the darkness, bits of what de Roche told her floated through her head. Then the bits began to fit together.

Did de Roche know of his cousin's attack on the abbey? God preserve her! Was de Roche the traitor who sent men to ambush FitzAlan that day? Isobel covered her face and rocked her head back and forth against the floor. If he did it, then de Roche was the vilest of men. As vile as his cousin.

A memory came to her of Linnet, eyes bright with anger, slapping a dagger in her hand. Isobel sat up. She would have de Roche's blood before she let him touch her again!

Her thoughts returned to LeFevre as she hurried to light the lamps. If Thomás LeFevre was the "T" who signed the letter, then he was the cousin involved in the plot to murder the king, not Trémoille. Would Trémoille's head be on a pike because of her false accusation?

She stood stock still. If she had the wrong man, she could have everything else wrong, as well. She thought the murder was planned for the knighting ceremony only because of Trémoille. Armagnacs, however, would choose some other occasion—and the king would have no warning.

To have any hope of saving the king, she must first save herself. Somehow she had to escape from the house and steal a horse. Once she got out of the house, she would figure out how to get to Caen.

After trying the locked door, she jumped onto the window seat and leaned out the window. She might just be able to reach the top branches of the tree and climb down. If she did not break her neck, she could escape through the house from the courtyard.

She needed her weapons. She ran to her chest and tossed gowns and slippers to the floor until she found her daggers. Then, through the layers at the very bottom, her fingers touched the scabbard of her sword.

When she leaned down to strap a dagger to her calf, she caught sight of dull brown in the midst of the colorful silks and velvets heaped on the floor. Her brother's tunic! She would be far less conspicuous traveling as a man than as a silk-clad noblewoman.

She slid her sword into the narrow space between the mattress and the frame of her bed for safekeeping while she changed. It was out of sight but within easy reach, should de Roche return before she was ready.

The blade of her dagger served as lady's maid. One long stroke and she stood naked, the cold sweat of fear on her skin. Moving swiftly, she donned her brother's shirt, hose, tunic. Then she rammed her feet into her boots and hooked one dagger into her belt. As she slid the other dagger into her boot, she heard voices outside the door.

There was no time! Heart in her throat, she dashed into the solar and leapt onto the window seat. She heard the muffled rattle of keys as she heaved herself up onto the window ledge. She had one leg dangling outside before she realized she'd left her sword behind. Damn, damn, damn!

She heard the soft *click, click* of the key turning the lock. Heart thundering, she swung her other leg over the ledge. She peered through the darkness, trying desperately to judge the distance to the nearest branch. It looked much farther than before.

The door scraped against the floor.

"God's blood!"

De Roche's voice rang out behind her as she pushed off, flinging her arms out. She grasped at leaves and branches as she fell crashing through the tree. For a moment she hung, suspended in the air, clinging by the fingers of one hand to a spindly branch. It snapped, and she fell again.

"Ooof!" The breath was knocked out of her as she landed on her stomach on a thick lower branch.

De Roche was shouting above her for help. Since most the servants were abed, she still might have time to escape. Circling her arms around the branch, she slid over the side, hoping to hang down and drop safely. Her palms stung from being scraped. Before she was ready, her hands let go.

Arms and legs flailing, she fell the last few feet to the ground. She tasted blood and dirt. Squeezing her eyes shut against the throbbing pain in her ribs, she dragged herself up to her hands and knees. The next thing she knew, her feet were dangling in the air.

"I cannot breathe," she squeaked to the man holding her up by the collar.

"Lady Hume?" the man said, surprise in his voice. "I thought you were an intruder."

A cold chill of fear swept through her. The man holding her was Thomás LeFevre.

He set her down so that her feet rested on the ground, but he did not release his hold.

"Send the servants back to bed and wait there," he called up to de Roche. "I shall bring you what fell out of the window."

Turning back to her, he said, "I take it you were as displeased as I to learn of my cousin's duplicity."

He must think she jumped because she learned of de Roche's prior marriage. Thank God, neither man had reason to suspect she knew about the murder plot!

Isobel tried to clear her head. Though shaken and bruised, she was not seriously injured. She must try to get away before LeFevre took her upstairs. However poor her chances, they were better with one man than two. She must choose her moment carefully.

LeFevre stood behind her, calm but alert, his hands resting on her shoulders as if he were a friend or lover. It was odd, both of them waiting and listening. The sounds of voices and people moving about the house gradually subsided. One by one, the rooms on the courtyard went dark, save for her solar.

LeFevre clamped a hand over her mouth and pulled her roughly to the doorway. Isobel grabbed the doorframe with both hands and tried to scream. Barely breaking his stride, he jerked her hands free. She struggled against him, kicking and biting as he dragged her relentlessly up the stairs.

When they reached her solar, LeFevre kicked the door open. He hauled her across the room and shoved her into the bedchamber. She fell sprawling across the floor. When she looked behind her, alarm pulsed through her. Both LeFevre and de Roche were staring at her.

"I've never seen a woman clad in men's leggings before," de Roche said, examining her from head to toe. "I shall have to ask you to wear them for me again."

She could not defend herself against both of them. But if she waited until the last minute to pull her knife, she might succeed in killing the first who tried to touch her.

De Roche took a step toward her. Fine. It would be he who felt her blade. He deserved to die at her hand.

"Wait!" LeFevre put his arm out to stop de Roche.

That was not lust in LeFevre's eyes. Still, his penetrating gaze frightened her even more than de Roche's.

"Pull your hood up and push your hair into it," LeFevre ordered her. "Do it now, or I shall do it for you."

If he took hold of her, she could lose her chance to pull her knife. She did as she was told.

LeFevre narrowed his eyes. Then his expression cleared, as if he found the answer to a question that had been puzzling him.

"She was with FitzAlan at the abbey," LeFevre said.

"What?" de Roche said. "How could she?"

"She was there, dressed as she is now," LeFevre said in a flat tone. "And she saw me."

De Roche started to speak again, but LeFevre cut him off. "You recognized me from the first, when we met outside the parlor," LeFevre said to Isobel. "It was a mistake for me to dismiss the fear I saw in your eyes."

"What shall we do?" de Roche asked, the edge of panic in his voice. "We cannot have our involvement in the abbey attack known. The Dauphin would distance himself from us without a second thought."

LeFevre's black eyes never left Isobel's face.

"We shall have to kill her, of course."

Chapter Thirty-three

"When do we sneak back to get Isobel?" Linnet asked.

Stephen sat with the twins and Jamie at a simple wooden table in the abbey guesthouse. While the other men were preparing to ride, he was giving Jamie a brief recounting of events and advising him of his plan.

"*You* are not going, Linnet." He wished he did not have to take François, either, but he needed the boy's help to get into de Roche's house. Damn, damn, damn.

Ignoring Linnet's glower, he told Jamie, "I shall go back into the city after dark."

"How many of us do you want to go with you?" Jamie asked.

"François and I will go alone. I need you to lead the men back to Caen."

When Jamie started to object, Stephen held up his hand. "This is a command, Jamie. The king must be warned of the murder plot without delay. He needs to know of the Burgundians' treachery. I shall follow as soon as I am able."

How he would manage to get to Caen with Isobel and François he did not know. He would worry about that after he got Isobel out of de Roche's house.

Jamie seemed resigned. Within a quarter hour, he had the men mounted and ready. Linnet was another story. Lips pressed tightly together, she refused even to bid Stephen and François good-bye before riding off with the men.

Stephen changed into his regular clothes and wiped mud onto his and François's boots to give the illusion of long travel. At dark, they mounted and headed toward the city. A cold wind picked up with nightfall, giving them excuse to draw their hoods low and wrap their capes close about them as they approached the gates.

If the men at the gate thought the merchant on the fine horse unwise to travel outside of the city accompanied by a single servant, they did not bother telling him.

"Once you get me inside the house, come back and wait for me near the gate," Stephen told François. "We need to make a plan for you in case I do not return."

Stephen ran a hand over his face and tried to think. Damn, damn, damn. "I wish I knew one soul in this wretched city I could trust," he muttered half aloud.

"What about Madame... er, Sybille?"

Stephen rolled his eyes heavenward. Lord above, was this wise? The courtesan had something else in mind when she whispered her address in Stephen's ear. Nonetheless, he had it.

"If I do not return by dawn, her house is on Rue St. Romain next to the small church," he said. "Sybille can get a message to Robert, and he will figure out how to get you back to Caen."

They took a circuitous route to the narrow lane that abutted the back of de Roche's house and stables. Then Stephen hid in the shadows with the horses while François called out at the gate.

"'Bout time you showed your face, boy."

The gruff greeting was followed by the creak of the gate. Luck was with them—the man had not been informed François was no longer in de Roche's service. Stephen eased his grip on his sword.

"You been gadding about the town again when you're s'posed to be working?" the gruff voice continued.

"Of course!" François said. "How else would I have stories to tell you? I've brought you a flask of wine, as well."

The man's laugh rang out in the darkness. "Come in, then, you rascal." Their voices faded as the gate clanked closed.

François was in.

Stephen paced up and down the dark lane, wondering how long he would have to wait. François said the man would be well into his cups by this hour. The waiting seemed endless.

Would he find Isobel alone? God, please, he did not want to find her in bed with de Roche.

Killing de Roche would be satisfying, to be sure. But not in front of Isobel. She would suffer shock enough when he told her the news Sybille brought. After hearing whispers in Paris of de Roche's secret marriage, Claudette confirmed it with de Roche's mother, of all people. Stephen knew he would have to tell Isobel to convince her to leave with him.

When the gate creaked again, every muscle of Stephen's body tensed. The outline of a figure appeared, leaning out the gate.

"Stephen," François called out softly into the darkness. When Stephen joined him at the gate, François said, "'Tis safe. He's drunk as a bishop. He'll not wake 'til morning."

"Good work." Stephen squeezed François's shoulder as he slipped through the gate. "Let us hurry."

"The door into the house from the stable yard is not locked," François said in a hushed voice as they trotted across the yard. "But Isobel's rooms are at the top of the house. I can show you from the courtyard."

Stephen touched the rope wound around his waist. It would be safest to bring her down from the window; the less time the two of them spent walking through the house, the better.

"No talking inside," Stephen warned when they reached the door. "As soon as you show me which window is hers, leave for the city gate."

Stephen barely heard the soft click and swish of the door. François had a talent for this. Once inside, François led Stephen down a short corridor and around a corner. He stopped in front of a large window and eased a shutter open to reveal a square courtyard of perhaps fifteen feet across. An overgrown tree filled the small space.

He heard a shout from the lit window above as something fell crashing through the tree.

"Get out, now!" he said to François. When the boy did not move, Stephen took hold of the back of his cloak and turned him around. "Go!" he said, giving François a shove in his back.

Dear God, those were Isobel's screams echoing off the walls of the courtyard!

Stephen spun around. He was halfway out the window before he saw the man standing in the shadows. Another man was leaning out of the window above, bellowing his head off. It was all Stephen could do to make himself wait.

When the man in the courtyard pulled Isobel roughly to her feet, Stephen clenched his jaw so hard his teeth ached. He decided he would kill this man before he left the house tonight.

"Send the servants back to bed and wait there," the man called up. "I shall bring you what fell out of the window."

Good. Better to have the servants abed when he and Isobel made their escape.

When the man in the window turned his head to bark orders at someone behind him, Stephen recognized de Roche's ridiculous pointed goatee. But who was the man in the courtyard? Not a servant. The voice was cultured, used to command. He thought he'd heard it before, but where?

The man was experienced; he did not lose patience and move too soon. Instead, the devil's spawn waited until the rooms went dark and the voices stilled before dragging Isobel into the house. At least Isobel was not badly injured from the fall. She was scratching and kicking like a madwoman.

What a woman! Jumping out the window!

She must have learned about de Roche's wife.

Stephen followed them up two sets of stairs. With Isobel struggling at every step, the man did not once look behind him. At the top, the man kicked a door open and carried Isobel inside.

The door closed behind them. Damn.

Stephen padded up the last steps and pressed his ear to the door. The two men were talking. He could not make out the words, but something in their tone had the hair on the back of his neck standing up.

Stephen drew his sword from its scabbard. Though de Roche was a skilled swordsman, he was not as good as he thought he was. His arrogance would lead him to make a mistake.

The other man worried Stephen more. If he had a choice, Stephen would take him first. Having made his plan, such as it was, Stephen eased the door open with his boot.

Nothing happened. He nudged it a few inches wider.

Now he could see the room—a small solar—was empty. The voices were coming from the adjoining room.

Stephen stepped lightly across the room and pressed himself against the wall next to the open door. He could hear more clearly now. De Roche was saying something about an attack on an abbey. An abbey? Could de Roche—

As the other man spoke, Stephen's speculations came to a jarring halt. His words turned Stephen's blood to ice.

"We shall have to kill her, of course."

Stephen stormed through the door.

In that first instant, he saw where each person in the room stood in relation to him and to each other. Isobel was farthest away, her back to the bed. Though her face was scratched, the fire in her eyes told him she had her wits about her. Thank God. De Roche was two steps from Isobel.

Fortune placed the other man closest to Stephen. A black-haired man.

"Stephen," Isobel called out, "he is the one who attacked the abbey."

"You blasphemous pig, murdering unarmed holy men," Stephen spat out as their swords clanked together. "I shall send you to the devil!"

Stephen thrust his sword toward the man's heart. At the last instant, the man leapt to the side. He was right to worry more about this one than de Roche. Still, he would take the man.

From the corner of his eye, he saw de Roche take a step forward to join the fight. The fool had his back to Isobel. She was already reaching for her dagger. Stephen wanted to shout at her not to take the risk, but his warning would draw de Roche's attention to her.

Stephen whirled around to parry behind his back. While the wild stunt did keep both men's eyes on him, the black-haired man's sword nearly caught him. Stephen felt the blade slash the back of his tunic as he spun out of the way.

De Roche screamed and threw his arms up, arching his back. Eyes bulging and mouth agape, he looked caught between shock, outrage, and agony. God's blood, Stephen hoped it was a death blow. If not, the man would turn on Isobel with a vengeance.

Damn, he needed to finish this monk killer and help her. But the man was good. Too good. De Roche's scream reverberating in the small room did not distract him.

The man did not even flinch.

Their swords flew in a blur of movement as they parried and thrust back and forth. Stephen worked his way closer to Isobel. When de Roche turned and staggered toward Isobel, Stephen gave de Roche a kick that sent him sprawling at her feet.

"Isobel, here!" He tossed his short blade onto the bed and shouted at her, "Kill him now! While he is down!"

Stephen dropped to the floor. As he rolled, he felt the wind from the blade passing over his head. It would do Isobel no good to kill de Roche if he let this son of Satan get the better of him. She stood no chance against a man as skilled as this.

With Stephen on the floor, his opponent committed fully to his thrust, believing it to be the final one. Stephen sprang to his feet, sword forward. Before his opponent could recover and withdraw, Stephen slashed the man's sword arm.

The man did not spare a glance at the blood soaking his sleeve. The wound was not fatal, but his eyes held a fury that might serve, as well. Rage could cloud a man's judgment and make him rash.

Not so with Stephen. His anger was hard and cold. It sharpened his senses and focused his mind.

He pressed the worthless scum, attacking again and again and again, until he pushed him into a corner. His opponent had no room to maneuver, no means to escape Stephen's sword. Stephen saw his opening. Right through to the heart, in one swift thrust. Just as he was poised to deliver the piercing blow, Isobel cried out behind him.

Stephen fell a half step back and took a quick look over his shoulder. Sweet Lamb of God! Isobel's chest was covered in blood! The breath went out of him.

De Roche was sliding down her body to the floor, leaving a swath of blood. Isobel stood, a bloodied knife raised in her hand. The blood was de Roche's. Not hers, praise God! The realization took no more than an instant.

But it was time enough for his opponent to knock the sword from his hand.

Stephen backed up slowly, one step at a time. For a certainty, he could not save himself. What he must do is live long enough after the first blow to take the man with him.

"You cannot save her," the man said with a thin smile, guessing Stephen's intent. "No man is that good."

The man inched forward, backing Stephen closer to the bed and Isobel.

"'Tis a pity I cannot spare her, since she saved me the trouble of killing de Roche," the man said. "I came to regret helping him wed my half sister."

"Odd that bigamy should offend you when murder does not."

"What are a few monks more or less?" the man said, lifting an eyebrow. "I have but one sister, and I would not have her shamed."

Stephen decided how he would do it. He would deflect the sword from his heart with his left arm and grab the dagger from the man's belt with his right. By the time the man brought his sword back, Stephen would be plunging the dagger up under the man's breastbone.

Neither would live, but Isobel would get away.

Stephen took another step back from the point of the man's sword. He felt Isobel just behind him. It was time.

"Your hand," she whispered.

Cautiously, he brought one arm to his side. When her hand brushed his, he felt a rush of gratitude. One last touch before he died. He sucked in his breath and prepared to make his move.

Chapter Thirty-four

With LeFevre's attention riveted on Stephen, Isobel side-stepped to the foot of the bed as quickly as she dared. One half step. Then another. And another.

LeFevre closed in slowly, as if approaching a cornered animal that might prove dangerous and unpredictable. The end of the deadly dance was near, and both men knew it.

Isobel slipped her arm under the folds of the half-fallen bed curtain. She reached back between the mattress and the bed frame until she felt it. Cold steel, welcome and familiar.

The mattress held the scabbard in place as she slid the blade free. Under cover of the fallen curtain, she brought the sword to her side. Stephen was so close now she could feel his heat, feel the tension running through him.

And then she knew, as clearly as if he said it aloud. Stephen was about to sacrifice himself to save her.

"Your hand," she whispered.

When the side of his hand brushed hers, she pressed the hilt of the sword against it.

Stephen moved so fast then, she did not even see him strike. But LeFevre was falling, mouth open in surprise, the telltale spot of blood over his heart. His head made a dull thud as it hit the floor.

Stephen whirled around and crushed her against him.

Like a rushing river, the terror she had held at bay flooded through her. She buried her face in his shoulder.

"I thought you were gone," she whispered.

His arms tightened around her. "I could not leave you."

She drew in a deep breath. His familiar smell comforted her. Wrapped in the strength of his arms, she felt safe for the first time since leaving Caen. Safe. She was safe at last.

Much too soon, he pulled away.

Stephen's face was strained, but he gave her a small smile. "You must be brave a little longer. Someone may have heard us. We must be gone."

She straightened and nodded. This was no time for weakness. When she felt the chill of wetness and looked down, she faltered. Her shirtfront was soaked with de Roche's blood.

"I will give you a clean shirt when we are out." Using the torn curtain, Stephen wiped the blood from her face and neck. Then he kissed her forehead and squeezed her hand.

"I have horses waiting outside," Stephen said and handed her sword to her.

"That is—was—de Roche's cousin, Thomás LeFevre," she said, pointing to the other body on the floor. "The letter was from him, not Trémoille."

Stephen wiped his dagger clean of de Roche's blood and stuck it in his belt.

"We must warn the king," she said as he led her into the solar. "Others may go forward with the plot. They are Armagnacs, so it will not happen at the Easter knighting, as I believed."

By this time, Stephen had unwound a rope from his waist and fastened one end of it to the bench under the window. He handed her the other dagger, cleaned of blood.

"We'll talk later," he said and lifted her onto the bench.

Isobel held on to Stephen as he instructed. Hand over hand, he took her down the rope. As soon as her feet touched the ground, he took her hand and led her from the courtyard into the house. It was pitch-black inside.

Relief flooded through her as she stepped out the door to the stable yard. They made it! She saw the outline of horses in the shadows by the gate.

Wait, was there a rider on one of the horses? She tightened her grip on Stephen's hand. He cursed under his breath but did not slow his pace.

When they reached the horses, he said in a harsh whisper, "I told you to wait at the city gates!"

"I heard the shouts and thought you would need me."

François! She wanted to weep for joy at hearing the boy's voice. Before she could run to him, Stephen lifted her onto a horse. In another moment, the three of them were out the gate and trotting down a narrow lane away from the house.

"We must stop at the house on Rue St. Romain," Stephen said to François. "'Tis on the way."

She saw the gleam of François's teeth in the dark and wondered what on earth could make him smile tonight. And why Stephen would take the risk of stopping somewhere.

They rode down back streets, with François leading and Stephen at the rear keeping watch to see that no one followed.

When they drew their horses up before the door of an elegant house, François piped up, "Let me get her for you."

Stephen said, "Stay here and keep quiet."

Stephen spoke in undertones to the servant who answered

the door. A short time later, a woman appeared. Her long, fair hair fell loose over a red silk robe. As she drew Stephen inside, her husky laugh drifted through the night air.

"Who is that?" Isobel whispered to François.

"A friend of Madame Champdivers."

A "friend" of Marie's! Despite all his other lies, had de Roche spoken the truth about Stephen and the beautiful courtesan? What hold did the woman have on Stephen that he would come here now, in the midst of their escape?

"She is very, very beautiful," François said with a sigh.

The door opened again, casting a wedge of light on the narrow street. As Stephen kissed the woman's cheek, Isobel saw her press a pouch into his hand. Without a word of explanation, he mounted his horse and signaled for François to lead.

Isobel should have expected the city gates to be barred at this late hour. Still, her bowels turned liquid when the guards came out of the gatehouse, weapons drawn.

"My good fellows!" Stephen called out. He held a hand up in a calming gesture as he dismounted.

After a brief exchange, Stephen held up the pouch the woman had given him and swept his arm toward the other men circled about them. Then he shook the pouch into the outstretched hand of one of the guards. Glittering coins overflowed the man's palm and spilled onto the ground.

When the guard grabbed Stephen's shoulder, Isobel broke out in a cold sweat.

What? Were they laughing? The guard pounded Stephen on the back as if they were old friends sharing a merry joke. Soon the other guards were snickering and snorting, as well.

Stephen's voice grew louder and she caught a few words. "...then the Englishman said, 'Why do you think we raise so many sheep? For wool?'"

Good heavens, Stephen was telling them jokes! Obscene jokes, from the sound of it. After another round of laughter, Stephen remounted his horse, and the men opened the gate just wide enough for them to ride through single file. They departed the city amid calls of "baa baa" and a spate of good-natured obscenities.

Stephen turned and waved as they headed down the dark road.

"How did you do that?" Isobel asked.

"Night-guard duty is dull work, and the men are always grateful for a few jokes," Stephen said. "But it was the coins that opened the gate. The guards' job is to keep attackers out of the city; they can see no harm in taking a little silver to let someone out."

Isobel suspected Stephen had not been nearly as confident the guards would let them pass as he pretended.

"They will be repeating those awful jokes for hours," he said. "With luck, that will divert them until we are well away."

"When those guards came out, I imagined your head on a pike," she said. "And I would wager you did, as well."

"Aye," he said. "And you imprisoned, guarded by an ugly hunchback who gives you lewd looks."

François burst into laughter, but Isobel was thoughtful.

"We will camp in those woods for the rest of the night," Stephen said, pointing into the darkness ahead.

"Where is Linnet?" Isobel asked, guilt-stricken that she did not think of the girl sooner.

"I sent her back to Caen with the men who came with me."

Until this moment, she'd given no thought to the journey back to Caen. They had a long and dangerous road to travel.

But Stephen was here. He would keep them safe.

Chapter Thirty-five

St. Winifred's beard, that was close at the gate! Isobel thought he was joking when he said he imagined her held captive by a hunchback. The image was so real he'd almost forgotten the end of that absurd sheep joke.

Because their lives depended upon it, he carried off the facade of easy bonhomie. But the sweat ran down his back.

And now? He rubbed his hand over his face and cursed himself. Riding through the countryside with no other men-at-arms was an open invitation to the worst kind of trouble.

He felt better as they neared the wood. At least they would be safe here for the night. In the morning, he would watch the road for a large party they might join. It would be a long night for him, keeping watch alone. He might have to tell himself stupid sheep jokes to stay awake.

What was that? It sounded like the snort of a horse coming from the wood. He put out his arm, signaling for the other two to stop. Praise God, they had the sense not to speak.

His head hurt from the strain of listening so hard. What

was that? A rustle of leaves? A footfall? He drew his sword soundlessly and urgcd his horse forward.

"Stephen? Is that you?" came out of the darkness.

His nephew should be halfway to Caen by now. And yet it was his voice coming from the high grass just off the road.

"Jamie?"

Jamie rose up from the grass, as beautiful to Stephen as Venus rising from the water.

Jamie shouted over his shoulder, "'Tis my uncle!"

Several shadowy figures came out of the trees, calling greetings. The tightness around Stephen's heart eased, and he laughed.

"I see you ignored my orders," he said as he dismounted. He put his arm around his nephew's shoulders. "Thank God you did!"

"In sooth, I never intended to follow them," Jamie said. "If you did not come by morning, I was going to ride into Rouen and get you."

"François! Isobel! Stephen!"

Stephen heard Linnet's shouts as she ran toward them, her fair hair shining in the darkness.

The ride back to Caen was a nightmare. Every hour, Stephen had to weigh the exhaustion of his charges and horses against the need to reach Caen before the king departed for Chartres.

The Armagnac men who controlled the often-mad French king had proposed a secret meeting between the two monarchs at Chartres in just a few days' time. King Henry agreed, since such a meeting could lead to a negotiated end to the conflict. To keep the meeting secret, King Henry would leave his army behind and travel to Chartres with only a small escort.

If the Armagnacs intended to murder King Henry, the rendezvous in Chartres provided them with the perfect opportunity.

Stephen had allowed his group only two or three hours' rest in the wood outside Rouen. This morning, they rose early and rode hard all day. He called a halt tonight only when darkness made riding too dangerous for the horses.

He found Isobel sitting before the crackling fire with Linnet's head in her lap. She looked up as he approached and gave him a weary smile.

"I hate to wake her to finish her supper," she said.

"I'll see she gets an extra portion in the morning." He knelt to lift the girl. "You should sleep, as well. We'll break camp at first light."

It hurt him to see how drawn Isobel's face was.

"I have never been so tired," she said, pushing her hair from her face. "Still, I cannot sleep just yet."

Linnet's arms and legs hung limp against him as he carried her to the blanket she would share with Isobel. When he returned, Isobel was gone. He looked across the fire to where Geoffrey, Jamie, and François were rolling out their blankets.

"She went to the stream to wash," Geoffrey said.

"Watch over Linnet," Stephen ordered, irritated that they let Isobel go alone.

By moonlight, he followed the bank of the stream away from the camp. All day he had wanted to speak with her. But the ride was too strenuous for serious talk, and he had to keep constant watch. Now that he finally had his chance, he was uncertain how to broach the subject with her.

He heard a splash of water and spotted a dark shape squatting at the edge of the stream. He hurried to her and helped her to her feet.

"Isobel, you will freeze to death!" He wrapped his cloak about her and held her until she stopped shivering.

He leaned back to look at her face, but the moonlight was not bright enough to read her expression. Surely she knew what he wanted to say? He took her hands and waited, hoping she might say something to encourage him.

Finally, he simply told her what he wanted: "As soon as we arrive, I want to ask the king's permission for us to marry."

He heard her sharp intake of breath.

"We must act quickly, before the king decides upon another husband for you." He was determined not to let the king outflank him again.

"I thought you understood," she said in a halting voice. "I do not carry your child."

Her words were like a knife to his heart. "You see that as the only reason for us to marry?" Hurt rang in his voice, but he could not help it.

When she did not deny it, he swallowed his pride. "But you still need a husband; de Roche may have given you a child." He kept his voice soft, though the thought of the villain's hands on her wrenched his guts.

"You need not rescue me from that, as well." Her voice was high, tense. "I am in no danger of having his child."

Stephen sagged with relief. God be praised, the vile bastard had not taken her.

Still, the conversation was not going as he had hoped.

"I wish to have you as my wife," he said, belatedly recalling Catherine's advice, "because I love you."

"If that be true," she snapped, "I am sorry for it."

His hopes were like dust in his mouth. Fighting to keep calm, he asked, "Do you not care for me at all?"

"Not care?" Isobel raked her hands through her tangled hair. "If only I did not care! If only I did not love you!"

All the tension and tiredness fell from him. He felt light, happy. All would be well. Isobel loved him!

But when he tried to pull her into his arms, she threw her hands up.

"'Tis because I love you I could not bear the betrayals," she said, backing away.

"How can you think I will betray you?" he said, reaching out to her. "I love you."

"Do you think I do not know about all your women?" she said, her voice rising. "I was there. I saw you every day in Caen."

"I will honor my marriage vows," he said, an edge to his voice. Did she not see how she insulted him?

"One day in Rouen, and you have courtesans giving you money, doing you favors!"

"I can explain about the women—"

"If it is not women, it will be something else." When he tried to speak again, she covered her ears and shouted, "Have I not suffered enough?"

He grabbed one of her hands and pressed it to his heart. "For you, I will be the best man I can be. I want to make you proud of me, to be proud of myself. I will be a good husband, a good father. Isobel, please. Trust me."

"I cannot, I cannot!" She jerked her hand away and ran from him into the darkness.

When he started after her, Geoffrey stepped out of nowhere to block his way.

"Let her go," Geoffrey said with his hand pressed against Stephen's chest.

"But I must tell her—"

"Not now," Geoffrey said, holding his ground. "Not tonight. Can you not see how weary she is?"

But he needed to tell her about the spying so she would understand about the women. "She is upset, I—"

"For heaven's sake, Stephen, she still has the last man's blood on her!"

Stephen shuddered as he recalled the moment he turned and saw her chest drenched in blood.

"She was trying to wash it off," Geoffrey said.

Stephen knew what it was like to be covered in that much blood. Though he gave her a clean shirt and a bucket of water last night, nothing short of a full scrubbing in a steaming hot bath could get the blood out of all the cracks and crevices.

Geoffrey took Stephen's arm and turned him around. "You must give her time to recover."

"You are right, of course," Stephen said, feeling wretched. Less than a day after she escaped rape and murder by her last betrothed, he was pressing her to marry.

"I see more than my sister gives me credit for," Geoffrey said. "Sit down and I will try to help you."

Stephen slumped down beside Geoffrey in the tall, wet grass by the stream. "Does she not believe I love her?" he asked, desperation rising in his throat.

"You concern yourself with the wrong question." Geoffrey picked up a stone and tossed it into the water. "What Isobel wants to know is, can she trust you? Will you be there when she needs you? Or will you sacrifice her for something you want more?"

Stephen stared at the dark, moving water. He heard the splash of another stone and watched the ripples in the reflected moonlight.

"I was too young to remember our mother before our family's fall from grace," Geoffrey said. "But it was different for Isobel. Both she and our father felt abandoned."

"Isobel told me something of it."

"That loss made their bond closer still," Geoffrey said. "They enjoyed each other's company and liked to do the same things—sword fight, ride fast. She became both companion and the kind of son he wished he had. 'Tis lucky Isobel has a good heart, for our father could not tell her 'nay.' He adored her."

"And still," Stephen said, "he traded her happiness for a chance to have his lands back."

"It devastated her," Geoffrey said, shaking his head. "I worry for her soul, for she has yet to forgive him."

"So, no matter that I love her, she believes I will betray her, too?"

"'Tis worse than that," Geoffrey said.

"Worse?"

"Aye. She loves you."

"How can that be worse?" It was the one thing that gave Stephen hope.

"That is why she is so determined not to marry you," Geoffrey said, patting Stephen's shoulder. "She knows the more she cares, the more you can hurt her."

"Isobel would not throw happiness away for lack of courage," Stephen argued. "Would she?"

"She has courage to spare," Geoffrey said, getting to his feet. "The problem is, she has an equal measure of stubbornness."

Damn! Stephen leaned back on his hands and gazed up at the moon. Somehow he must find a way to convince her she could trust him. But how?

"I suggest you pray," Geoffrey said, above him.

He heard Geoffrey walking through the brush in the direction of their camp.

"Pray without ceasing," Geoffrey called out from the darkness. "That is your best course."

Chapter Thirty-six

*C*aen Castle was a glorious sight, the distinctive stone of its high walls pink in the light of sunset. At long last! When Stephen finally led his bedraggled group through the gates, one of the king's guards was there waiting for him.

"The king had us watching for you from the towers," the man told him. "You must come at once."

When they reached the Exchequer, Stephen helped Isobel dismount. She was so exhausted, she fell into his arms.

"I cannot see the king like this," Isobel pleaded.

Poor Isobel, she still wore men's clothes. Despite her attempts at washing, she was as filthy as the rest of them.

"I'm sorry, but the king will want to hear of the plot from your own mouth," Stephen told her. "He'll tolerate no delay."

She had dark circles under her eyes and looked so weary he was tempted to carry her. Instead, he fastened her cloak for her and pulled her hood low over her face.

"Now no one will see what you wear," he said, "except the king, and he will not notice."

They were ushered into the king's private parlor behind the great hall. To Stephen's relief, the king was unattended save for Robert, William, and Catherine.

"God be praised you are safe," the king said before Stephen could exchange greetings with the others. "Once we learned de Roche was involved in the attack on the abbey, we feared for you both."

"How did you learn of de Roche's role?" Stephen asked.

The king smiled at Catherine. "Your sister-in-law got it out of Marie de Lisieux."

Catherine smiled back. "I could not let the men risk their virtue by questioning her, could I?"

Stephen gave them a brief recounting of the events in Rouen. The king seemed more intrigued than disturbed by the news of the murder plot. After peppering Stephen with questions, he turned to Isobel.

Stephen was worried. She was swaying on her feet, and the king had to ask her repeatedly to speak up. After she recited the critical letter from "T," the king narrowed his eyes and stared off into the distance.

"The Dauphin is behind it," the king said, rubbing his chin. "He has the most to lose, and this is just the sort of cowardly act he would favor."

"He would not act without key Armagnacs behind him," William said.

"Perhaps not," the king said. "But I doubt King Charles—or that depraved queen of his—had any part in this scheme."

"That would make for awkward relations when you wed their daughter," Robert put in.

The king broke into laughter. "Too true!"

The king's expression grew serious as he turned his

attention back to Stephen and Isobel. "I am most grateful for this service and wish to reward you."

Stephen bowed. "'Tis an honor to serve you."

"Lady Hume," the king said, "I owe you a husband."

Damn! Could Henry not give him even a day to get matters settled with Isobel?

Stephen caught Robert's wink and looked to his brother. William's nod confirmed it. They had already spoken to the king on his behalf. Isobel was his.

"I apologize for my first choice of husband," the king said, "but I believe you will be happy with my next."

The king's eyebrows shot up as Isobel fell to the floor at his feet.

"Please, I beg you, sire," Isobel said. "Do not make me do it. If you are grateful for my service, release me from my promise."

The king glared at William and Robert. "You told me she would be pleased."

Robert motioned to the king, urging him to continue.

"Please, do not make me," Isobel wailed and pounded her fist on the floor. "Can I not be left alone!"

"Lady Hume is past exhaustion," Stephen said, ignoring William's signal to be quiet. "Please, sire, can this wait until tomorrow, when she is rested?"

The king gave Stephen a curt nod.

"Thank you, sire," Stephen said.

He made a quick bow and helped Isobel to her feet. As he half carried her out of the hall, he tried to speak to her. She made no response to his entreaties.

William caught up with them at the bottom of the steps. "Lady Hume," he said in a gentle voice as he took her arm. "My wife and I want you to stay with us at our house in the town."

Catherine appeared behind them and pushed Stephen aside to take Isobel's other arm. Without a word to him, husband and wife walked away with the now-placid Isobel between them.

William turned to give Stephen an exasperated look over his shoulder. As if the scene inside had been his fault! Stephen clenched his fists in frustration.

He felt a hard thump on his back and turned to find Robert standing beside him on the steps.

"That did not go as well as we had hoped," Robert said. "Did you not realize the king has chosen you to be her husband?"

"I guessed as much." Stephen sank to the bottom step and rested his head on his arms. It was all too much. He was bone weary. "But I could not take her like that."

"Come, come," Robert said, settling down next to him. "Isobel thought the king was marrying her off to another scum like Hume or de Roche. Who could blame her for objecting?"

"She does not want to marry me."

"Isobel will come around, once she realizes how much she cares for you."

"She says she loves me," Stephen said without lifting his head from his arms. "It does not help my cause."

Chapter Thirty-seven

*I*sobel could not breathe! De Roche's hands were around her throat, squeezing with a ferocious strength as he leaned her backward over the bed.

"You! You!" he croaked, his eyes bulging.

Panic surged through her, giving her the strength to do what she should have done before. With one sweep of her arm, she brought the double-edged blade across his throat.

For one horrifying moment, de Roche hovered above her, gushing blood like a fountain. Blood splattered her face, soaked her shirt, and ran in rivulets down the sides of her neck. Then de Roche collapsed against her, trapping her against the bed. He was so heavy! Gagging convulsively, she fought to push him off.

Isobel sat up in bed, her heart racing.

A dream. This time, it was a dream.

Gingerly, she touched her fingertips to her chest to be sure. The cloth was dry. She looked down and let her breath out when she saw the clean white shift.

De Roche and LeFevre were dead. She was safe.

She heard a door scrape, and her hand flew to her throat.

"Lady Hume?" a cheerful voice called out. "Are you awake?"

Isobel pulled the bed curtain back as a plump older woman entered the room carrying a steaming tray.

"Feeling better today?" the maid asked over her shoulder as she set the tray on a table near the door.

"I am, thank you," Isobel answered. "Did I sleep long?"

"A full night and day, m'lady," the maid said with a laugh. As she came toward the bed, she pinched her brows together. "Tsk, tsk, those are nasty bruises."

Isobel dropped her hand from her throat.

"Such a tired lamb! You gave me quite a turn, you did, falling fast asleep in the tub."

"You scrubbed the blood from my fingers," Isobel said, remembering.

She was so grateful she could have kissed the woman. For two days, every time she looked down at her hands on the reins, she saw de Roche's blood crusted under her nails. She couldn't get it off, washing in the dark with no soap.

How could Stephen and the king speak to her of marriage when she still had de Roche's blood on her boots and leggings and matted in her hair?

"I would have let you rest longer," the maid said, "but your brother has come to take you to the king."

"To the king?" It felt as if she had just left him.

She closed her eyes. Damn that old fool Hume! If he'd not been taken in by Bartholomew Graham's lies, none of this would have happened. She would never have met de Roche, she would not have had to kill anyone, and she would not have bruises on her throat. She would be living peacefully in Northumberland, running her household.

What would be her fate now? That a marriage alliance had failed to ensure de Roche's loyalty would not deter the king from trying again. Which French nobleman did King Henry wish to bind to him now?

Or would it be Stephen? Could he convince the king? If he did, what would she do?

She would agree. Of course, she would.

How long would it be before he broke her heart? A few weeks? Six months? A year? Regardless, she would rather be unhappy with him than be with another man. If God were kind, she would have children to comfort her.

An hour later, she entered the Exchequer hall. Her heart dropped to her feet when she saw that Stephen was not there.

She stood before the king, once again waiting to hear her fate. Geoffrey and Robert stood on either side of her.

Where was Stephen? If he wished to claim her, surely he would be here. Perhaps he had already spoken to the king, and it was all settled.

"I hope you have recovered sufficiently to discuss your future," the king said, kindly enough.

Isobel flushed, recalling how she had flung herself at his feet, begging. She as much as told the king he owed her a debt of service—and how he should repay it. She never would have done it if she had not been utterly exhausted.

"I leave Caen at dawn and want to settle this matter before I leave," the king said, unrolling a parchment in his hands.

She turned her head to see if Stephen had come in.

"I have a letter from my uncle, Bishop Beaufort."

Bishop Beaufort! Had he not caused her enough grief?

"He spoke to your father about increasing your dowry."

Why? What were they planning now? How many times must she suffer the choices of men who held power over her? She was sick to death of the decisions they made on her behalf.

"The bishop prevailed upon your father to increase your dowry to a handsome sum."

She could imagine Bishop Beaufort "prevailing upon" her recalcitrant father. If she were not so tense, she might be amused.

"Your Highness, if I may?" her brother said. When the king nodded, Geoffrey said, "Our father will increase her dowry further when he learns I am joining the Cistercian order."

Isobel tried to smile at her brother. Though it was an unlikely choice for an only son, she was happy for him.

"I admire the Cistercians' devotion to poverty, prayer, and arduous labor," the king said. "Your father should be proud."

Ha! The king might hear their father's shouts all the way from Northumberland when he heard the news.

"'Tis a shame the dowry won't be needed now," the king said, shaking his head. "I am releasing you from your promise to marry a man of my choosing."

"Your Highness?" Isobel was too stunned to be sure she heard him correctly.

"If you will not take a husband, you must have an income," the king said. "So I'm granting you the Hume property, as well."

She blinked at him. "But the Hume lands belong to Bartholomew Graham now."

"Graham was caught consorting with Scottish rebels," the king said. "So the bishop confiscated the lands for the crown."

She stared at him. Was it possible?

"I intended to give the property to your new husband as a wedding gift," the king said, frowning.

Isobel felt dizzy. The Hume lands were hers, at long last.

It was what she'd waited for all these years. Never again would she suffer the humiliation of being sold like cattle for land or political need. She could run her own household, dependent on no man.

Quite suddenly, she was struck by the loneliness of the life before her. The life she had prayed for since she was a girl of thirteen.

"Surely this is the best of news," Geoffrey said as he led her out of the hall.

"Aye, the best," she murmured.

She could not remember if she thanked the king. Or made the proper curtsy before leaving his presence.

"You look pale," Robert said on her other side. "Are you unwell?"

She turned to look at him. "Do you think the twins would go to England with me?"

Robert made a face and shook his head. "'Tis best they stay here. Sooner or later, a relative is bound to turn up and claim them. Until then, I'll look after them."

She was unaware they had left the castle grounds until they stood before the door to FitzAlan's house.

"I would like to be alone now," she said.

"But the FitzAlans are waiting to hear your news," Robert said.

"They have been so kind," Geoffrey added, "surely you can visit with them for a little while?"

She nodded, knowing her brother was right.

"The family is expecting you," the servant at the door told them. "They are in the solar."

"Thank you," Robert said. "We can find our own way."

"The king has released me to escort you home to Northumberland," Geoffrey said as they went up the stairs. "You will need to say your good-byes to the FitzAlans soon."

Isobel felt the prick of tears at the back of her eyes. She'd become fond of the FitzAlans, especially Jamie.

"You've visitors!" Robert called out as they reached the top of the stairs. He stepped aside to let Isobel enter the solar first.

She stopped dead at the threshold. Leaning against the wall opposite, arms folded across his chest, was Stephen Carleton. Long and lean and perfect. When he turned and met her eyes, the breath went out of her.

The sad, sweet smile he gave her as he came to greet her made her insides go soft. When he touched his lips to the back of her hand, she had to close her eyes against the wave of emotion that washed through her.

"We must let Robert and Geoffrey come in," he said in a soft voice.

She moved on stiff legs as he drew her away from the doorway. The warmth of his hand on her arm was so comforting, she longed to rest her head against his shoulder.

She stood mute as Robert and Geoffrey told the others of her good fortune. No one showed surprise at the news.

"So, you shall be a wealthy landowner in your own right," Lord FitzAlan said with false heartiness. Despite his words of congratulation, the look he gave her was full of sympathy.

"You will return to England soon?" Lady Catherine's voice, unlike her husband's, was cold, and her eyes were angry.

"Aye, we will," Geoffrey answered for her.

"We go home ourselves," FitzAlan said. "Perhaps we can travel together as far as London."

"I am leaving, as well," Stephen said beside her.

The tightness that had been around Isobel's heart like a vise eased a bit. She would not have to say good-bye to Stephen until they reached London, and that would take at least a week.

"You travel to England?" Robert's tone was casual, as if this were a matter of little concern. "To Northumberland to claim the Carleton lands?"

Northumberland! Why, they would journey together for two or three weeks. If Stephen remained in Northumberland, she might even see him at gatherings from time to time.

"I stay to fight with the king," Stephen said. "I am taking command of William's men."

Isobel's stomach gave a lurch.

"I must bid you all adieu now," Stephen said. "We march at dawn."

March? At dawn? Isobel felt herself sway on her feet.

As Stephen left her side, she felt a rush of cold where his hand had rested on her arm.

Stephen and FitzAlan slapped each other's backs.

"I know you will watch over Jamie for us," FitzAlan said and pulled Stephen into a fierce bear hug.

Jamie was leaving, as well? Would she have no chance to bid him good-bye?

Lady Catherine fell into Stephen's arms, weeping openly. "Promise me you will come back. Promise."

"Give my love to the children," Stephen said and kissed her cheek.

After saying his farewells to Robert and Geoffrey, Stephen returned to stand in front of Isobel. His eyes were soft as he took her hands.

"Isobel, I wish you every happiness."

"You have a command, as you wanted," she said, her voice cracking.

"I told you what I want." He attempted a smile, but his heart was not in it.

He gave her hands a final squeeze and was gone.

* * *

Isobel flung the water jug against the wall. It bounced instead of smashing to bits, giving her no satisfaction at all.

Now that she finally had what she wanted, why was she not happy?

She paced the small bedchamber until her legs ached. Finally, she crawled onto the bed and lay on her back. The bed curtains encased her like a tomb. Tears of frustration slid down the sides of her face and into her hair, making her head itch.

If not for Stephen, she would be content. Nay, she would be overjoyed! He had taken that away from her.

What did he mean, telling her he wanted her and then leaving? She pounded her fists against the bed. And then she cried in earnest until her head ached and her throat was parched.

The door opened with no warning knock. A moment later, someone jerked the bed curtain back with a snap and thrust a candle in her face.

"How can you be so foolish!"

Lady Catherine. Could the woman not leave her to her misery? Isobel locked her arms over her eyes.

The mattress sank as Lady Catherine sat on the bed.

"Please go," Isobel groaned.

"If it were only you who suffered, I might." Catherine's voice was sharp. "Have you no sense of what you are doing to Stephen? I fear he will not survive the first battle."

Isobel sat up. "But he is a skilled fighter."

Ridiculous as it was, her confidence in Stephen's abilities was such it did not occur to her until now he might be killed.

"'Tis a dangerous thing," Catherine said, "to send a man off to war when he does not care if he lives or dies."

Isobel felt as though a fist squeezed her heart. "You do not truly think—"

"I do," Catherine said.

"Then he must not go," Isobel said, wriggling out from under the bedclothes.

When she tried to squeeze past, Catherine caught her arm and held it. "Stephen will not take you if you only wish to save him. He told me he tried to force your hand before, and he will not do it again."

"Then you know he only wanted to wed me because he thought I might carry his child."

Catherine blew out a long breath. "Of course, Stephen would do the honorable thing. But are you such an idiot you cannot see he loves you?"

Isobel shook her head violently from side to side, though she did believe Stephen loved her now.

"Stephen is such a good man, kindhearted and thoughtful," Catherine said, her voice growing softer. "You could not ask for a better father for your children. 'Tis a rare man who is so good with little ones."

Isobel's heart ached, because all that Catherine said was true.

"I can see you love him, too," Catherine said.

"Of course I love him! He could not make me so very wretched if I did not." Isobel looked hard at Catherine, willing her to understand. "I promised myself I would never let another man have the power to hurt me as much as my father did."

"It is too late for that." Catherine brushed the hair back from Isobel's face. "Come, tell me what it is you fear."

"That he will fail me when I need him most," Isobel blurted out. She drew in a shaky breath and then added in a whisper, "That he will abandon me, as both my parents did."

"I see I shall have to tell you," Catherine said, shaking her head, "though Stephen made me swear not to."

Isobel leaned forward. "Tell me what?"

"You know Stephen has been spying for the king?"

Spying? Stephen spied for the king?

"The king is exceedingly grateful for the service," Catherine said. "He offered the Hume lands to Stephen—and he wanted Stephen to take them."

How naive she was! Hume Castle was a border castle; of course, the king would want a strong man to hold it.

"The king decided to throw you into the bargain, as men will do, when we told him Stephen wished to wed you."

"The king chose Stephen for my husband?"

Catherine nodded. "But Stephen asked the king to free you from your promise and to give the Hume lands to you."

"Why? Why would Stephen do this? He said he wants to marry me."

"Because he wants your happiness more," Catherine said, gripping Isobel's arms. "Stephen wants you to choose him freely—or not at all."

Stephen sacrificed his own gain, his own happiness, so that she might have hers.

He had the heart of Galahad, strong and true. Time and again, he proved it. In his devotion to his family, his kindness toward the twin orphans, his willingness to risk his life for those he loved . . . including her.

Honor would always mean more to him than position or power. His loyalty ran deep. It did not waver.

He would not fail her.

"How near dawn is it?" Alarm had Isobel leaping from the bed. With impatient hands, she jerked at her gown. Thank heaven she had not bothered to take it off!

"I waited as long as I dared," Catherine said as she knelt to help Isobel into her slippers. "'Tis yet an hour before dawn. Robert is waiting downstairs to take you to the castle."

"Robert is waiting?"

"Robert always had faith in you," Catherine said. "Now give me your other foot so we can get you on your way."

As Isobel raced down the stairs, she called back, "The angels should sing your praises, Lady Catherine!"

Robert caught her in his arms. "I knew you would choose happiness in the end, but did you have to take so long?"

Horses were saddled and ready outside the door. Robert flung her on one, and they rode hard through the empty streets. When they reached the castle gates, the guards waved them through.

Isobel slid off her horse at the steps of the Old Palace.

"Stephen is in his old chamber," Robert said, taking her hand as they ran down the corridor.

They skidded to a stop before Stephen's door.

"Tell Stephen not to worry about the men," Robert said, gasping for breath. "William is sending orders to put someone else in command."

After the headlong rush to get here, Isobel stood staring at the closed door. What would she say to Stephen? Would he still want her after what she put him through? Could he forgive her?

"Don't make the poor man wait any longer!" Robert opened the door and pushed her inside.

The door closed behind her with a loud thump.

Stephen sat at the small table beneath the arrow-slit window. From the state of his clothes, he had not been to bed. A single candle glowed on the table, its holder resting in a pool of melted wax.

With a rush of regret, she realized it was an hours candle. Stephen must have used it to count the hours until his departure—and the hours remaining for her to come to him. Only a stub remained.

He rose to his feet and put his hand on the back of the chair, as if to steady himself. Though he did not take his eyes from her, neither did he come to her. His handsome face was etched with lines of tension and fatigue.

"Why are you here, Isobel?"

To think she might never have heard this voice she loved so well again. A sob caught in her throat when she attempted to speak. Still, he waited.

She swallowed and tried again. "I've loved you for a long time, but I was afraid to trust your love for me. I feared you would betray and abandon me."

"I would never do that," Stephen said. Still, he made no move toward her.

"I understand that now."

"Isobel, tell me why you are here."

She took a single step forward. "I come because I choose you, Stephen Carleton, to be my husband." She took another step. "I choose you because you brought joy and love back into my life, and I do not want to lose them again."

With each step she took, her voice grew stronger.

"I want to sleep beside you each night and wake to see your face each morning. I want to meet your mother."

His eyes crinkled at the corners.

"I want to know the nieces and nephews you speak of with such fondness. I want to go home with you to Northumberland. I want us to raise our children there."

She took the last step and stood before him. "I do not want to waste more time or spend another day apart."

"I love my mother, but I think we should wed before you meet her," Stephen said, his face lit by the smile she loved so well. "I can't risk having her scare you off."

In the next instant, she was in his arms.

"I tried to keep my hope," he said into her hair, holding her tightly. "But it was hard."

He lifted her off her feet and twirled her in his arms. With his eyes warm on hers he said, "Every day of my life, I will thank God you chose me."

He kissed her then. A soft, warm kiss that made the world swirl around her. She pressed against him, glorying in the joy and comfort of having his arms around her again.

Stephen was hers. Always and forever.

She leaned back and fiddled with the collar of his tunic. "'Tis hard to see why we should wait for the ceremony, since we've already..." She let her voice trail off, having no doubt he understood what she was proposing.

"I'll take no chances with you," Stephen said, laughing. "We shall make our pledges before witnesses tomorrow, but I shall hear your pledge to me now—*before* we do aught else."

* * *

Stephen had attended numerous betrothals over the years, but he'd never paid the slightest attention. Still, he was fairly certain all he had to get right was the essential promise to make it binding.

"Lady Isobel Hume, I pledge you my troth and take you as my wife."

Isobel raised an eyebrow—in appreciation, he believed, of his admirable simplicity.

"Sir Stephen Carleton," she said in turn, "I pledge you my troth and take you as my husband."

"Now I have you!" With immense satisfaction, he pulled her into his arms.

He felt awash in his love for her. He smiled, thinking of hardheaded little girls with bouncy dark curls and serious green eyes. And, God forbid, wooden swords in their pudgy little hands. Girls like that would need brothers to keep them out of trouble.

Isobel pursed her lips and tapped her finger against her cheek. "Is there not something more we must do to make the promise binding? Something that makes it...irrevocable?"

Irrevocable.

"I believe," he said, his voice turning husky as he leaned down to touch his lips to hers, "'tis consummation after the promise that does it."

They kissed for a long, tender moment. When she opened her mouth to him and pressed against him, his desire grew into an urgent, pulsing need. He lifted her in his arms to carry her to the bed.

"Come, wife, we are to bed." He smiled—he'd waited a long time to say that.

He awoke hours later, suffused with contentment. Nothing and no one would ever take Isobel from him now. With her at his side, he was ready to take his place in the world. He would claim his lands, serve his king, be a husband and father.

His life was full of golden promise.

Epilogue

Northumberland, England
1422

"Ouch!" Isobel sucked on her finger and set her needlework aside.

He should be here by now, should he not? She paced up and down the empty hall, glancing toward the entrance at each turn.

Where was he?

Sunlight fell across her face as she passed one of the long windows, reminding her how much she loved this house. She and Stephen built it on the Carleton lands. It held only good memories for her.

Only this last remnant of discontent from her old life remained. Both Stephen and Robert urged her to put it to rest.

When she turned again, he was standing at the entrance.

"Father!" Her heart constricted. When had he become an old man? She gestured toward the table set up near the hearth. "I have sweet wine and cakes for you."

"You remember my sweet tooth." He pulled a handkerchief from inside his tunic and blew his nose.

After pouring him a cup of wine, she took a cake for herself from the platter between them. There were so many unspoken words between them, she did not know where to start.

"I am grateful to your husband," he said, "for bringing the children to visit me from time to time."

Isobel's cake caught in her throat.

"Sir Stephen is well respected on both sides of the border," he said. "He seems an honorable man."

The word "honorable" hung between them like an accusation.

"His eyes shine when he speaks of you," her father said, his voice cracking. "I need to know you are happy, Issie. Tell me you are."

Her happiness mattered to him. She nodded. When she could speak, she asked, "Why did you do it?"

Even after all this time, she wanted to know.

He ran his hands through his white hair. "We lost everything. Everything. I was responsible for the three of you. Geoffrey was so young, and your mother...she was never strong like you. You were the only one who could restore the family. I could think of no other way."

He took a deep breath and shook his head. "I did not believe Hume would live through the winter."

Isobel folded her hands on the table and fixed her gaze on them. "I know men marry off their daughters for such reasons all the time," she said, keeping her voice steady. "But you did not raise me like other girls. You made me believe I was special."

"You were special from the day you were born," he said, wrapping his big, warm hands over hers. "God knows I've made more than my share of mistakes, but the one thing I did right was to claim you as my own."

Isobel's eyes flew to his face. Could he know the truth?

"Your mother gave birth six months after we were wed." He gave Isobel a bittersweet smile and shrugged. "I can count as well as the next man, but what was I to do? Send her away?"

He never considered it, Isobel was certain.

"She seemed happy enough in those first years," he said. "But when our lands were taken, she saw it as God's punishment for her sins. I thought if I could get them back, she..." He sighed and shook his head over long-ago regrets.

"His name is Robert," Isobel said in a quiet voice. "I met him in Normandy."

His eyebrows shot up, but he knew whom she meant.

"He would not have made her happy, either," she said.

After a quarter century of traveling and philandering, Robert finally settled down. Thank God he found Claudette.

"He is a good friend now. But when I was a child, he would not have been as good a father to me as you were."

As soon as she said the words, she knew them to be true. For the first thirteen years of her life, he was the best possible father she could have had.

He was looking at her with such hope, such love, she felt the bands of anger around her heart give way. She leaned down and pressed a kiss against his rough knuckles. When she looked up, tears were running down the crevices of his weathered cheeks.

A squeal of laughter tore her attention from her father to the arched entrance of the hall.

"They escaped their nursemaid again," Stephen called out as he came through the doorway carrying one child under his arm and holding the other by the hand.

"I found the little one outside eating dirt," he said, tilting his head toward the giggling boy under his arm. "His big sister told him to do it."

Their daughter, Kate, gave Stephen a mischievous grin so like Stephen's that Isobel felt her heart swell. Lord help her, that child was a trial to raise.

Stephen gave his father-in-law a cautious greeting. Kate, however, ran to her grandfather, blazing red hair flying out behind her. In another moment, she was dragging him across the room, pointing at something out the window.

"You are back early, love," Isobel said as Stephen settled down on the bench beside her.

"I was worried," he said and kissed her cheek. "But I assume all went well, since I did not find your father with your blade in his heart."

She smiled at him. "Tell me about your day."

Stephen rubbed his hand over his son's head as he gave his report. "We've lost no more cattle to raiding, and the fields look good after yesterday's rain."

"Who would have thought my wild young man would make a contented farmer?" She pinched the hard muscle at his side. "I expect you'll go to fat soon."

He leaned close until she felt his warm breath in her ear. "We shall both be contented, once I have you alone."

Isobel turned at the sound of Kate's happy shrieks ringing through the hall. As she watched her father toss the giggling girl into the air, the last of the resentment she held in her heart cracked and melted away.

Forgiveness made her feel light, happy. She turned, smiling, to Stephen.

He gave her one of his slow winks, full of the devil. "As soon as your father leaves, we'll lock the wild heathens in with their poor nursemaid, and..."

Isobel threw her head back and laughed for the sheer joy of it.

Historical Note

The map of Europe might be different today if Henry V had not died in the prime of his life at the age of thirty-five. At the time of his death in 1422, he controlled all of Normandy and was well on his way to becoming the ruler of France. To make peace with Henry, the French king agreed to marry his daughter to Henry, disinherit his son the Dauphin, and name Henry as his heir.

Under this arrangement, Henry permitted the ailing King Charles to remain the nominal king during his lifetime. This would have been a politically astute move had Henry outlived his father-in-law and been crowned king of France. The long years of fighting, however, took a heavy toll on Henry's health. During the lengthy winter siege of Meaux in 1421–1422, he fell ill, probably with dysentery. By July, he was so ill he had to be carried on the campaign in a litter. He was dying when he was brought to the castle at Vincennes, outside Paris, where his French princess waited. He died August 31, 1422, predeceasing his father-in-law by two months.

Henry left a nine-month-old babe as heir to two kingdoms. The men who ruled on his son's behalf were for the most part good men who did their best to carry out Henry's vision. However, none was Henry's equal.

If Henry had lived, he might have succeeded in securing all of France. He might, on the other hand, have cut his losses and settled for Normandy when Joan of Arc came along. It seems extremely unlikely he would have lost it all, as his son eventually did.

I should mention that there is some dispute among historians as to whether there was a massacre when the English took Caen. I assumed there was one because it served my story. If a massacre did occur, it would have been contrary to the king's orders. Henry V prohibited his soldiers from committing the rape and mayhem that was common for victorious armies at the time.

Henry V was held up as the ideal to which later kings should aspire. For many years after his death, men sought to preserve his legacy and carry out his will. They continued to be The King's Men.

Acknowledgments

I will be forever grateful to Alex Logan at Grand Central Publishing for plucking *Knight of Pleasure* from the vast sea of manuscripts before her and saying, "Yes, I want this one." A special thank-you also goes to my agent and friend, Kevan Lyon, for her faith in me.

When I started my first novel, my favorite librarian (my sister) told me to join Romance Writers of America (RWA). Thanks to her sage advice, I am part of the generous community of romance writers. I am grateful to the members of my local RWA chapters, who cheer me on every step of the way; to my critique buddies, who always tell me what they really think; and to the published authors who were exceedingly kind in their support of my first book, *Knight of Desire*.

I beg forgiveness of my friends and family for neglecting them while I wrote this book. (We all know I will do it again.) My love and thanks go to all of them, especially my husband.

About the Author

Margaret Mallory, a recovering lawyer, is thrilled to be writing adventurous tales of sword-wielding heroes rather than briefs and memos. Since abandoning the law for romance, she's become a *USA Today* bestselling author and has won numerous awards. Margaret lives with her husband in the beautiful (and rainy) Pacific Northwest. Now that her children are off on their own adventures, she spends most of her time writing, but she also likes to travel and hike. She loves to hear from readers.

You can learn more at:
MargaretMallory.com
Facebook.com/MargaretMallory.Author
Twitter @MargaretMallory

Looking for more historical romances?
Get swept away by handsome rogues and clever
ladies from Forever!

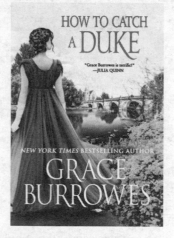

HOW TO CATCH A DUKE
by Grace Burrowes

Miss Abigail Abbott needs to disappear—permanently—and the only person she trusts to help is Lord Stephen Wentworth, heir to the Duke of Walden. Stephen is brilliant, charming, and absolutely ruthless. So ruthless that he proposes marriage to keep Abigail safe. But when she accepts his courtship of convenience, they discover intimate moments that they don't want to end. But can Stephen convince Abigail that their arrangement is more than a sham and that his love is real?

THE TRUTH ABOUT DUKES
by Grace Burrowes

Lady Constance Wentworth never has a daring thought (that she admits aloud) and never comes close to courting scandal . . . as far as anybody knows. Robert Rothmere is a scandal poised to explode. Unless he wants to end up locked away in a madhouse (again) by his enemies, he needs to marry a perfectly proper, deadly-dull duchess, immediately—but little does he know that the delightful lady he has in mind is hiding scandalous secrets of her own.

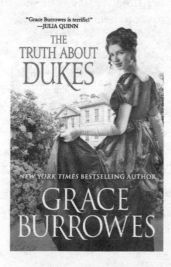

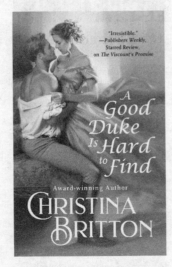

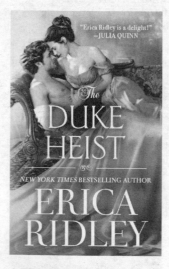

"Erica Ridley is a delight!"
—JULIA QUINN

The
DUKE
HEIST

NEW YORK TIMES BESTSELLING AUTHOR
ERICA
RIDLEY

THE DUKE HEIST
by Erica Ridley

When the only father Chloe Wynchester's ever known makes a dying wish for his adopted family to recover a missing painting, she's the one her siblings turn to for stealing it back. No one expects that in doing so, she'll also abduct a handsome duke. Lawrence Gosling, the Duke of Faircliffe, is shocked to find himself in a runaway carriage driven by a beautiful woman. But if handing over the painting means sacrificing his family's legacy, will he follow his plan—or true love?

A ROGUE TO REMEMBER
by Emily Sullivan

After five Seasons of turning down every marriage proposal, Lottie Carlisle's uncle has declared she must choose a husband, or he'll find one for her. Only Lottie has her own agenda—namely ruining herself and then posing as a widow in the countryside. But when Alec Gresham, the seasoned spy who broke Lottie's heart, appears at her doorstep to escort her home, it seems her best-laid plans appear to have been for naught...And it soon becomes clear that the feelings between them are far from buried.

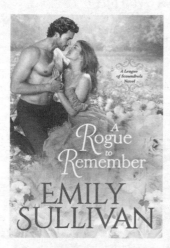

A League of Scoundrels Novel

A Rogue to Remember
EMILY SULLIVAN

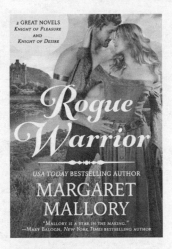

ROGUE WARRIOR
(2-IN-1-EDITION)
by Margaret Mallory

Enjoy the first two books in the steamy medieval romance series All the King's Men! In *Knight of Desire*, warrior William FitzAlan and Lady Catherine Rayburn must learn to trust each other to save their lives and the love growing between them. In *Knight of Pleasure*, the charming Sir Stephen Carleton captures the heart of expert swordswoman Lady Isobel Hume, but he must prove his love when a threat leads Isobel into mortal danger.

ANY ROGUE WILL DO
by Bethany Bennett

For exactly one Season, Lady Charlotte Wentworth played the biddable female the *ton* expected—and all it got her was Society's mockery and derision. Now she's determined to take charge of her own future. So when an unwanted suitor tries to manipulate her into an engagement, she has a plan. He can't claim to be her fiancé if she's engaged to someone else. Even if it means asking for help from the last man she would ever marry.

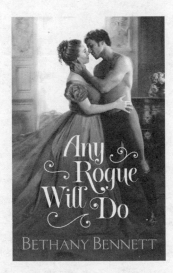